THE TESTING

I sensed the power that burned in the sword's glow, great and terrible, and I felt a wave of cold fear sweep onto me. My death could come here if I had not the strength to lift the sword. I took a deep breath, reached out, and began to draw it forth. It was hot, hot as flame, and my hands were burning. The light in the ruby leaped, rose, fierce and red, red as blood, and I was certain my hands were being burned off. . . . I drew the sword farther, and suddenly it was clear of the sheath, and I screamed because the light and fire of it suddenly ran along my very soul. It was slaying me, for I was impaled by its light, and it was not a sword for mortals at all. . . .

HAWK OF MAY

"A welcome new light on the horizon of popular Arthurian legend . . . delightful . . . a strong sense of lore and mysticism . . . a ripping adventure tale"
—*Booklist*

"A nice blend of fantasy and historical detail, plenty of action and a good solid feel for the era and Welsh legend . . . will appeal to anyone who has enjoyed Mary Stewart's *Crystal Cave*, T. H. White, Victor Canning, or even Thomas Berger's *Arthur Rex*"
—*School Library Journal*

Winner of the Hopwood Major Fiction Award

Great Reading from SIGNET

HAWK
OF
MAY

*Gillian
Bradshaw*

Ø
A SIGNET BOOK
NEW AMERICAN LIBRARY
TIMES MIRROR

SIGNET TRADEMARK REG. U.S. PAT. OFF. AND FOREIGN COUNTRIES
REGISTERED TRADEMARK—MARCA REGISTRADA
HECHO EN CHICAGO, U.S.A.

SIGNET, SIGNET CLASSICS, MENTOR, PLUME, MERIDIAN AND NAL
Books are published by The New American Library, Inc.,
1633 Broadway, New York, New York 10019

First Signet Printing, May, 1981

1 2 3 4 5 6 7 8 9

PRINTED IN THE UNITED STATES OF AMERICA

DEDICATION:
Parentibus Optimis
"Siquid adhuc ego sum, muneris omne tui est."

NOTES

The historical background of this novel is partially but by no means entirely accurate: I have used some anachronisms and made some complete departures from what little is known about Britain between the Roman withdrawal and the Saxon conquest. My worst offense is in the Orkneys, where I have antedated the Irish conquest, invented places as well as persons, and described a situation completely unlike anything that actually existed there. But it is barely possible, if improbable, that some of the Britons whom the Emperor Honorius instructed to organize their own defenses viewed these organizations as continuing the late third–early fourth century "Empire of the Britains," and could have maintained an increasingly Celtic Roman empire into the sixth century.

For the legendary background I have drawn first on various Celtic sources, second on everything Arthurian written up to the present. Some of the poems are loosely based, anachronistically, on Celtic originals: the one on pages 51–52 on a fifteenth-century Deirdre poem; on page 66, an earlier Irish poem; on page 72 on the eighth-century "Voyage of Bran." The song on pages 195–196 is, in fact, the sixth-century (or earlier) hymn known as "Patrick's Breastplate" or "Deer's Cry." A version of it beginning "I bind unto myself today" is still sung, at least in the Anglican church, and has a lovely tune. The poem on page 245 is also Irish, but later. The others are my own, but represent the sort of poetry current in Old Welsh and Irish—except, of course, for the *Aeneid* passage, which is book VI. 125–9.

On pronunciation, Welsh looks more intimidating than it is (Irish is best left unmentioned). "w" is usually a long "u," except in a few cases such as after "g" and before a vowel, when it is the familiar consonant. "y" is usually a short "u" sound: "Bedwyr" is thus three syllables, and comes into later legend as "Bedivere." "ff" is as in "off," but "f" a "v" sound as in "of." "dd" is the soft "th," as in "bathe"; "ll" something like the sound in "little." "si" is a "sh" sound—"Sion" is the equivalent of Irish "Sean" and English "John," and has nothing to do with mountains. The other letters are not too different from their traditional values. "ch" is as in Scottish, German, or Greek; "r" is trilled, and the vowels in general are pure, as in Latin. Accent is usually on the penultimate syllable.

I have used modern Welsh forms, on the whole, as I was uncertain of the old Welsh ones. Place names are in complete confusion, but I imagine they were at the time as well: I have used Celtic forms when these are recorded. Sorviodunum/Searisbyrig is modern Salisbury (or rather, Old Sarum); Ynys Witrin is Glastonbury; Camlann, South Cadbury where the excavations are. Caer Segeint is Carnarvon; Ebrauc is York; Din Eidyn, Edinburgh; and Yrechwydd a name from poems which might be several places but which I have relocated to suit myself. This should be enough to give the reader some orientation, but, since the novel is only partially historical, geography is not that important.

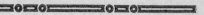

ONE

Wʜᴇɴ ᴍʏ ꜰᴀᴛʜᴇʀ ʀᴇᴄᴇɪᴠᴇᴅ ᴛʜᴇ news of the Pendragon's death, I was playing boats by the sea.

I was then eleven years old, and as poor a warrior as any boy in my father's realm of the Innsi Erc, the Orcades Islands. Since I also was a very poor hunter, I had little in common with the others I lived and trained with in the Boys' House; and I had still less in common with my elder brother, Agravain, who led the others in making my life difficult, almost as difficult as my father's plans for me did. To escape from the insistent world of warriors and warriors-to-be, I went sometimes to my younger brother, but more often to a secret place I had by the sea.

It is about an hour's ride south of my father's fortress of Dun Fionn. A small stream falls down the cliff that edges our island on the west, carving a gully into the rock. At the bottom, trapped by a ledge of harder stone, the stream forms a deep pool behind a gravelly beach before it escapes into the ocean. Overhanging cliff walls make it invisible from the cliff-top, so no one but myself ever knew of its existence. As it was also very beautiful, this made it mine. I gave the place a name—Llyn Gwalch, "Hawk's Stream," in British—and considered it to be a world apart from and better than the Orcades and Dun Fionn. Sometimes I took my harp there, and sang to the waves that came pounding at the beach, flowing into the pool at high tide and hissing in the gravel at low tide.

1

Sometimes I would build fortresses of gravel and mud, and plan battles by the stream as though it were a great river, the boundary between mighty kingdoms. I would picture myself as a great warrior, good at every art of war and sung of in every king's hall in the Western world, admired by Agravain and my father. But my favorite game was to build boats and to set them sailing out of the dark pool into the wild gray sea that pounded at every shore of the world at once. I sent my boats west: to Erin, from which my father had sailed years before; and beyond Erin, to that strange island or islands which druids and poets say lie west of the sunset, invisible to all but a few mortals, where the Sidhe live in eternal happiness.

I loved my Llyn Gwalch dearly, and jealously guarded it against any intruders from the outside world. I told only my younger brother Medraut of its existence, and then only after swearing him to secrecy. So, when I heard the clatter of a stone from the path above my head, I drew back hurriedly from the curragh I was building and began to clamber up the gully. I had left my pony tethered at the top, and I did not want anyone to come down looking for me.

"Gwalchmai?" The voice from the cliff-top was Agravain's.

"I'm coming!" I called, and scrambled faster.

"You'd better hurry," said Agravain. He sounded angry. "Father's waiting for us. He sent me to find you."

I reached the top of the cliff, shook my hair out of my eyes, stared at Agravain. "What does he want?" I didn't like the sound of it. My father hated to wait, and he would certainly be angry by the time I got back to Dun Fionn.

"It's no business of yours what he wants." Agravain was, indeed, angry, tired of looking for me, and probably afraid that some of our father's anger would spill over onto him. "By the sun and the wind, can't you hurry?"

"I am hurrying." I was untying my pony as I spoke.

"Don't answer back to me! You're going to be in trouble enough as it is. We're late, and Father won't like you appearing in front of the guest like that. You're a mess."

"Guest?" About to mount, I paused. "Is he a bard or a warrior? Where's he from?"

"Britain. I don't know what kingdom. Father sent me out to look for you as soon as he'd spoken with the man, and it's a good thing Diuran saw you riding south, or I'd still be looking." Agravain kicked his horse and set off across the cliff-top at a gallop. "Come on, you little coward!"

I swung onto my pony and followed him, ignoring the over-familiar insult. I must be a coward, anyway. If I wasn't, I wouldn't ignore the insult. I'd fight with Agravain, even if I did always lose, and we'd be friends afterward. He was always friendly after a fight. —A guest, from Britain, and an urgent summons. The Briton must have brought some important message. My father had many spies in Britain who reported to him regularly—but they sent their messages by indirect means, never coming to Dun Fionn themselves. A messenger from Britain meant some important event, a major victory over or defeat by the Saxons, the death of some important king: anything that my father could use to further his influence in the south. The Saxons had suffered a major defeat at the hands of the Pendragon's young warleader only a year before, so it couldn't be that. Some king dead, then, and my father about to make a bargain with his successor? A bargain with some part in it that Agravain and I could fulfill? I urged my pony faster and passed Agravain at a gallop, anxious and miserable now. My father always made plans for me, but I fulfilled very few of them. The sea wind and the wind of my speed dried the salt in my hair, and my pony's hooves echoed the beat of the surf; better to think about these than about my father. It would be good to get the confrontation over quickly, as quickly as possible. At least, I thought, looking for some good, Agravain hasn't asked me what I was doing at Llyn Gwalch.

The thought of my father made me look back in alarm. He was a good hundred paces behind me, struggling with his horse on the rough path and scowling furiously. There were two things I could do better than he: riding and harp playing. He liked to forget this, and, as he was infinitely the better at fighting, I tried not to remind him.

Now I had done so. I cringed, knowing that he would pick a quarrel with me on a pretext later in the day, and slowed my pony to a trot.

He passed me without saying anything and rode in front of me, also at a trot. That was Agravain. He wanted to be first, and nearly always was. Firstborn, first choice to succeed my father as king, first among the boys of the island who trained to be warriors. My father was immensely proud of him, and never stayed angry at him for long. I stared at my brother's back and wished that I could be like him.

We rode on to Dun Fionn in silence.

The fortress is built from a very light stone, from which it takes its name, "White Fortress." It is a new stronghold, completed in the year of Agravain's birth, three years before my own, but already it was as famous and powerful as any of the other, older forts, Temair or Emhain Macha in Erin, or Camlann and Din Eidyn in Britain. It stands at the highest point of the cliff, overlooking the sea, ringed by a bank and ditch and its thick, high walls. Two gate towers, copied from old Roman forts, flank the single westward-facing gate. The fortress was designed by my father, and the power and fame were the result of a myriad of schemes and maneuvers, political and military, carried out with unvaried success. If it was my mother who was the ultimate source of the schemes, it was my father, King Lot mac Cormac of the Innsi Erc, who had carried them out in such a way as to make himself one of the most powerful kings in either Britain or Erin. As Agravain and I rode in the gates, I wondered nervously what he wanted me to do.

We left our horses in the stable and hurried to our father's room behind the feast hall. The room was small and plain, and the dusty sunlight filtered in through the space left between wall and roof for the smoke. My father had evidently been waiting for some time: The messenger must have left the room long before, and the air had the tense, still feeling of a conversation interrupted. My mother sat on the bed, studying a map, a goblet of imported wine on the lamp table beside her. Another goblet on its side—Lot's—lay near it, abandoned. When we entered, my father turned from pacing the floor to

4

face us. My mother glanced up, then fell to studying the map again. The air tingled with expectation: My father was angry.

He was not a tall man, yet unmistakably, he was king, radiating arrogance and command. His thick yellow hair and beard seemed almost to stand out from his head, unable to contain the energy of his lean body, and his hot blue eyes could scorch anyone who crossed him. My ancestors come from Ulster, and they say that Lugh of the Long Hand, the sun god, had many sons in my father's line. All who spoke with Lot for any length of time came away at least half convinced of it.

He ignored Agravain and glared at me. "Where have you been, these two hours?"

When I fumbled for words, Agravain answered, "He was down by the sea, collecting oysters or some such thing. I found him a good hour's ride from here."

Lot glared harder. "Why didn't you stay here and practice your spear throwing? You need the practice badly enough."

As always happened in my father's presence, all my words were dried in my throat, and I stared unhappily at the floor.

Lot snorted. "You'll never make a warrior. But you could try, at least, to learn enough to not disgrace your clan."

When I still found nothing to say and would not meet his eyes, he clenched his fists angrily; then, giving a liquid shrug, turned and began to pace again. "Enough of that. Can either of you reason out why I called you?"

"You got a message from Britain," Agravain answered quickly, eagerly. "What's happened there? Did the Saxons defeat someone, and do the kings want your aid now?"

My mother Morgawse looked up from her map and smiled, and her eyes rested for a moment on me. My heart leaped. "Have you nothing to say, Gwalchmai?" Her voice was low, soft, and beautiful. She was herself beautiful: very tall, dark where Lot was fair; her eyes were darker than the sea at midnight. She left breathless anyone who only looked at her, and drew eyes as a whirlpool draws water. The legitimate daughter of the

High King Uther, she had been given in marriage to Lot when she was thirteen, the seal of an alliance she had since worked constantly against. She hated her father Uther with all her soul. I worshipped her.

Lot paused, glanced toward her, realizing that she had decided something about the map. He nodded to himself, then glanced back to me.

"There . . . there's an important king dead, isn't there?" I asked, taking my courage in both hands. "Is it Vortipor?"

My father gave me a surprised look, then smiled fiercely. "Indeed. There is a king dead. But not Vortipor of Dyfed." He walked over to the bed and stood, looking at the map, tracing Dyfed with his finger, then following the line of the Saefern River up through Powys, then tracing the sea coast of Elmet and Ebrauc up to Rheged, down again along the east border of Britain. Morgawse's eyes were glowing with a deep, dark fire, with triumph and silent joy. I knew then who was dead, and what my parents were planning. There was only one king whose death would bring such joy to my mother.

"Uther, Pendragon of Britain, lies dead at Camlann," said Morgawse, very softly. "The high king is dead, and of sickness." Her smile was softer than snowflakes falling from a black winter night.

Agravain stood in silence a moment, then gasped, "Uther!" in wonder.

Lot laughed, throwing back his head and clapping his hands together. "Uther, dead. I had thought the old mare's son had more years left in him than that!"

I looked at Morgawse. She was rumored a sorceress through all of Britain. I wondered if Uther had suffered, how long the sickness had lasted. If she had done the thing . . . no, how could anyone in the Orcades kill a man in Dumnonia . . . and I was glad that the man she hated was dead.

". . . that is not all," my father was saying. "There is a debate over who is to succeed him."

Of course there was a debate. I had heard it debated often enough even in the Orcades. *Uther had no male heir, only many bastards.* There would be civil war in Britain, as there had been thirty years before at the death of Vortigern. My father, who had made three of the kings then reigning in Britain, would have a chance to try his hand at making a high king.

Lot went on, talking out his own plans now, back and forth across the floor, the dust swirling in the sunbeam. ". . . Docmail of Gwynedd claimed the high kingship at the council, saying that the kings of Gwynedd ought to be high kings because they are descended from the Roman High King Maximus, but Gwlgawd of Gododdin opposed him . . . Docmail made alliances with Dyfed and Powys, and he has sent messages to Gwlgawd telling him to renounce his claim to the Pendragonship. Gwlgawd is afraid and seeks to form an alliance of his own. He has sent messengers to Caradoc of Ebrauc . . . and to me." Lot smiled again, triumphantly, and stopped short by the bed, looking at the map. "Caradoc may join or not, as he pleases. I will come. With my warband and supplies from Gwlgawd, we can sweep Docmail into the sea! And Gwlgawd . . . he will be easy to control." He snapped away from the map and again began pacing, his eyes blazing, fists clenched as he reckoned kings and kingdoms, loyalties and enmities. "If we arrive in the north in force to join Gwlgawd, Strathclyde will probably join Docmail, and Urien of Rheged may claim the Pendragonship for himself—a force to be feared, Urien—still, he is my brother-in-law, and must try negotiations before he declares war; we can spin out negotiations . . ."

"Be careful," snapped Morgawse. "The alliances will be unsettled, and one can never rely on any alliance in Britain. There will be other claimants to the title before this war is ended, and too many kingdoms have not yet declared themselves."

Lot nodded, without breaking his step. "Of course. And we must separate the kings as much as possible, and see that we divide the spoils evenly with our allies—Diuran can help with that, and Aidan. And then there must be time and a blind eye to blood feuds, at intervals, but we cannot let the Ui Niaill begin fighting or there'll be no stopping it." He fell silent, considering how to control blood feuds. In the end, he would ask Morgawse, and she would tell him what she had long before thought out, and it would work.

Feeling very nervous, I managed to stammer, "W-what about Arthur?"

Lot scarcely glanced at me, though Morgawse gave me a sharp look. Arthur had been Uther's warleader, and, if half the stories told were true, the high king's warband would follow him, Uther or no Uther. Because of this Arthur had power, although he was only one of Uther's bastards and a clanless man. He could have no claim to the Pendragonship himself, but he was certainly in a position to make a high king.

"Arthur?" Lot shrugged, still thinking of blood feuds. "He will support no one. He will continue to fight the Saxons, with the royal warband—or as much of it as he can support."

"Be careful," Morgawse warned again, even more sharply. "The lord Arthur is dangerous. He is the finest warleader in Britain, and he will not remain neutral if he is provoked."

"Oh, have no fear." Lot was still casual. "I will be very careful of your precious half-brother. I've seen him command."

"So have I." Her voice was soft, but Lot stopped, meeting her eyes for a moment. He was silent, looking at her. It seemed for a moment as though the sunlight paled, and the dust hung frozen in the air, and some chasm opened behind the world. I shivered. I recognized that dark light in her eyes. Hate, the black tide that had drowned Uther, turning his friends to enemies, stirring up foreign invasion and civil dissension, until at last that chasm had swallowed him, perhaps . . . and now Morgawse's hatred turned toward Arthur. I wondered again how Uther died.

Agravain shifted slightly. He had stood silently during the talk, his eyes glowing with excitement. He knew that, with his fifteenth birthday in another month, he was old enough to be taken along on the campaign. Now, in the stillness, he burst in with, "Am I coming?"

My father remembered us, spun about, grinning again. He crossed the room to my brother and slapped him on the shoulder. "Of course. Why do you think I called you? We leave next month, in March. I am giving Diuran charge of half the warband and the auxiliaries from the

Hebrides, and I will give him charge of you as well. Pay attention, and he will show you how a warband is run."

Agravain ignored the question of how to run warbands and plunged into what excited him. "Can I fight in the battles?"

Lot grinned even more, resting his hand on Agravain's shoulder. "So eager? You are not to fight until I am certain you know how—but no one learns to fight by casting spears at targets. You will go into the battles."

Agravain seized Lot's hand, kissed it, ablaze with delight. "Thank you, Father!"

Lot threw his arms about his firstborn son, gave him a rough hug, shook him, laughing. "It is well. You will receive arms tomorrow, early, you and the others who are of age. Go and tell Orlamh that he is to prepare you for the ceremony."

Agravain left the room to tell Orlamh, my father's chief druid, and was nearly jumping with delight at each step. I turned to follow him, but my father said, "Gwalchmai. Wait."

The room seemed to shrink into a trap. I turned back and waited.

When Agravain was gone, Lot went to the lamp table and picked up his goblet, poured some wine into it. The sunlight struck it, bringing out a deep red fire as he poured it. He sat down on the bed and stared at me, weighing me up. I had felt that stare often enough before, but still I shifted uneasily and avoided his eyes. My father sighed.

"Well?" he asked.

"What?" I looked at the bedspread.

My father's voice went on: "Your brother is very excited about this war, and eager to prove himself and win honor for himself and for our clan. What of you?"

"I'm not old enough for the war," I said nervously. "I still have at least two more years in the Boys' House. And everyone knows that I'm a poor warrior." I glanced up at Lot.

The corners of his mouth drew down. "Yes, everyone knows that." He drank some more of the wine. The sunlight caught on his gold collar and brooch, glittered on his hair, making him look more like Lugh the sun god than ever. He looked over to my mother. "I don't understand it."

I became angry. Another thing that everyone knew was that my younger brother Medraut was not Lot's son, though no one knew whose he was, and Lot suspected something similar of me. I certainly do not look like my father, as Agravain does. I resemble my mother enough to disguise any other inheritance. Though I sometimes doubted myself whether I was Lot's son, I didn't like Lot to do it.

He caught my anger. "Oh? What is it now?"

Afraid again, I forced myself to relax. "Nothing."

Lot sighed deeply and rubbed his forehead. "I am going away next month. It is to a war, which means I may not come back. I do not think that I shall die this time, but one must be prepared. So, since I will have other things to think of until I leave, I want to know, now"—he dropped his hand and stared at me fiercely, his hot eyes full of energy and arrogance and harsh brightness—"I wish to know, Gwalchmai, what you are going to become."

Paralyzed, I fumbled for an answer, finally replied, "I don't know," simply, and met his eyes. I held them for an instant.

He slammed his fist against the lamp table and swore softly, "By the wind, by the hounds of Hell, you don't know! I will tell you: I don't know either. But I wonder. You are a member of a kingly clan, son of a king and a high king's daughter. I am a warleader, your mother a planner of wars. And what can you do but ride horses and play songs on the harp? Oh, to be sure, to be a bard is an honorable profession—but not for the sons of kings. And now we go off to war, Agravain and the clan and I. If Agravain is killed, or should our ally Gwlgawd prove a traitor, do you know what will become of you?"

"I could not be king!" I said, shocked. "You can choose anyone in our clan as your successor, Diuran or Aidan or anyone, and all of them better suited than I."

"But they are not my sons. I want one of my sons to be king after me." Lot stared a little while longer. "But I would not choose you."

"You could not," I said.

"And it does not even make you angry?" asked my father, bitterly.

"Why should it? I don't want to be king."

"Then what do you want to be?"

I dropped my eyes again. "I don't know."

Lot stood, violently. "You must! I want to know what you will become while I am away at war!"

I shook my head. Desperation loosened my tongue. "I'm sorry, Father. I don't know. Only . . . not a king, or a bard, or . . . I don't know. I want something, something else. I don't know what it is. I can't be a proper warrior, I've no talent for it. But one day . . . nothing is important enough now, but sometimes I have dreams and . . . and there is something in songs. And once I dreamed about a sword, burning, with a lot of red around it, and the sun and the sea . . ." I lost myself in my thoughts, trying to name what it was that moved within me. "I can't understand it yet. But it is important that I wait for it, because it is more important to fight for this than for anything—only I don't understand what it is. . . ." I trailed off weakly, met my father's eyes again, and again looked away.

Lot waited for more, realized there was none, and shook his head. "I do not understand you. You speak like a druid, pretending to prophesy. Do you want to be a druid? I thought not. What, then?"

"I don't know," I said wretchedly, and stared at the floor. I could feel his eyes still on me, but I did not look up again. After a bit the rushes sounded as he walked back to the bed.

"Well, I expected as much." His voice was cold and brisk. "You don't even know what you are speaking of, and you can't fight. When a quarrel begins, instead of standing up you run off. Agravain and your teachers say that you are afraid. Afraid. A coward. That's what they call you in the Boys' House, I hear. One without honor."

I bit my lip to hold back the angry shout. I cared something for my honor, but I didn't look on it as others looked on theirs. Perhaps, I thought, it is not the same thing.

"Stay here at Dun Fionn, then," said Lot. "Go and play your harp and ride your horses. Now get out of here."

I turned to leave, but just as I reached the door I felt my mother's eyes on me and looked back. I realized suddenly that she had been watching me ever since I had spoken of my dreams. Her eyes were darker than night and more beautiful than stars. When they met mine she smiled, a slow, secret, wonderful smile that was mine alone.

As I left the room, my misery lightened by her notice, I felt her eyes following me into the open air. And, even though I worshipped her, even though I could set her smile in the balance with my father's anger and be contented, still I wondered again how her father Uther had died, and was uneasy.

TWO

M Y FATHER SENT OUT THE call to the kings of the Orcades, telling them to gather their warbands, the rest of their men and their ships and supplies and come to Dun Fionn. Slowly they began arriving, tall men in brightly colored cloaks, warriors glittering with jewelry, their sharp, long-bladed thrusting spears glinting, short throwing spears in quivers and swords on baldrics flashing by their sides. Their whitewashed shields were flung over their shoulders, and often painted or enameled with bright colors. The kings and finest warriors wore chain mail, imported from northern Britain or from Gaul, shining like fish scales. Lesser men had leather jerkins sewn with metal. The warriors brought their war hounds, great gray beasts whose collars shone with silver, and hawks sat on the shoulders of the kings, ruffling sharp-edged feathers and glaring with brilliant eyes. They came and encamped about Dun Fionn, a camp from each island that was subject to my father, and more from the Picts and Dalriada to the south as well as the men from our own tribe. All told, there were more than a thousand professional warriors, and some three thousand other men. Going southeast of Dun Fionn one could see their ships, row upon row of great twenty-oared curraghs, sails furled against their masts. There was a constant coming and going of these ships: going to fetch more supplies or to send messages from Dun Fionn to our allies in Gododdin; coming in with the supplies and messages and more men. About and within Dun Fionn itself was a great hustle and bustle as my father organized and planned and prepared, my mother always beside him. Not only did he have to feed his great host, but he also had to mediate the quarrels between his various under-kings, prevent blood feuds between rival clans, and arrange details of the alliance with Gwlgawd, king of Gododdin. I saw little of either him or Morgawse.

I hung about the fringe of things, staring and wondering. It was the first time I had seen my father marshal his power, and I was astounded at the strength displayed before me. I understood, even then, that it could not be supported long in one place without a war. The cost was tremendous. But the bright colors, the splendor, the glitter of arms, the loud, laughing confidence of the warriors and their ready fellowship—these all impressed me immensely and filled me with vague yearnings I did my best to smother. I was no warrior whom any great lord would wish to have in his warband. And yet, and yet, and yet . . .

It was glorious. I sometimes wished fiercely, like any other boy on the island, that I was going too, to win honor and fame for myself, my clan, and my lord.

Agravain had no doubts that he would do well in the war. He received his weapons with the other fourteen- and fifteen-year-olds, and strutted and boasted more and louder than any of them. He picked fights with me even more frequently than usual, being so stiff with tension and eagerness that his temper snapped, as they say, at a footfall.

In mid-March the army sailed for Gododdin. They would make their way about the coast of southern Pictland by sail or oar, as the wind held, then follow the estuary which halves Manau Gododdin, and beach their ships near Gododdin's royal fortress, Din Eidyn, and fortify a camp there. My father had been sending letters to various of the kings, including those in alliance with Docmail of Gwynedd, the rival of our ally Gwlgawd in the contest for the high kingship. As a result, one member of that alliance, Vortipor of Dyfed, was now wavering in his allegiance and likely to desert Docmail at any moment. But it was uncertain whether Vortipor would join my father or claim the Pendragonship for himself.

Vortipor was more crafty than a fox, and could not be trusted any more than a viper. He was almost more trouble as an ally than as an enemy. Almost: Dyfed is a strong, rich land, and the men there learned their way of fighting from the Romans. Vortipor himself kept the title of Protector, to remind Britain of the days when his province had sheltered the whole island from Irish raiders. Vortipor was himself of Irish descent, but his ways were as Roman as his fighting, and he had support, too much to be ignored. My father and mother had debated for hours over what course he would take and what to do when he took it. From the Boys' House I could see the light in my father's room late at night. It was strange to see it dark when the army sailed and Dun Fionn was left with only a token guard. All the lights seemed to have gone with the army, leaving only some torn and yellow patches in the grass, and the black spots where the campfires had burned.

Still, from my point of view, the time became a pleasant one. Without Agravain or my father around, I had more freedom than at any time in my life. In the Boys' House, the training and competition became less rigorous and intense. There were no older boys to bully us, and no more late feasts for the men who trained us to ache from or quarrel about the next day. Most of the boys used the free time to play hurley. I occasionally joined them, but as I am a bad player, spent more of my time at Llyn Gwalch, or in riding about the island.

The Orcades are very beautiful islands, and gentle ones, despite their British name of Ynysoedd Erch, "Frightful Islands." The climate is mild, varying only a little throughout the year: In winter it is warmer at Dun Fionn than at Camlann far to the south. The land rolls in low, stony hills covered with short grass and heather which provide pasture for sheep and cattle and a good living for farmers. The wide gray sea, full of fish, pounds eternally at the shore, which is rocky and steep, especially at the west coast of my home island, and sea birds of all kinds nest in the cliffs. The sound of the sea is always present at Dun Fionn, so much so that it becomes a sound like the beating of one's heart, too continual to notice. The puffins clamor on the cliffsides, and the gulls wail over the gray green of the waves, calling to each other across their flashing white wings. The sound of their voices seems almost as beautiful, sometimes, as the voices of the skylarks inland, who on sunny days seem to drip music from the sky like honey from a comb. They say that the land one lives in when young becomes a part of one. I believe this, for even today, the sea and the mourning of the seagulls bring back to me Llyn Gwalch in the mist, with the mist wetness dripping from the heather.

That spring the islands were particularly beautiful.

I sometimes rode out with my younger brother, Medraut, beside me, sharing with him all my thoughts and telling him stories. He thought me a better storyteller than my father's bard Orlamh, and, though this was only because he was unused to the bardic style, it delighted me.

Medraut was seven at the time, a beautiful child. Whoever his father was, I was sure he must be noble. Medraut had fair hair of a paler shade than Lot's, and wide gray eyes. His complexion was our mother's, his features his unknown father's. But his spirit was closer to Lot's. He wanted to be a warrior, and had no doubts that he would be. His favorite tales were those of CuChulainn, the hero of Ulster. He was very brave, being altogether unafraid of tall horses and weapons and bulls and other such things most children fear. Once, when we were climbing down the cliff to look for gulls' eggs, he slipped and hung by his hands from a narrow ledge until I could come and help him. When I asked him if he had not been afraid (and I was shaking with fear) he stared at me in surprise and answered, no, why should he have been? He had known, he said, that I would save him. Not only was he brave (and generous as a high king and fierce as a wildcat: qualities of a great warrior) but he also loved and admired me. I could not understand both of these existing together, but I accepted them joyfully and gave to him all I had, save what would bewilder him. Though precocious, he was only seven, and that is too young to care for dreams properly.

At times, though, instead of playing at Llyn Gwalch or with Medraut or riding about the island, I practiced with my weapons. The sight of the great host had moved something in me, and I strove to improve myself in the arts of war. To my surprise, I discovered that I was doing better, and not only because I was practicing more. Without Agravain at my elbow with every spear I threw, without his friends and our cousins taunting me when I practiced with spear or sword, I could throw or thrust straighter and more strongly.

But the most important thing that happened to me after the army left was unconnected with any of these. Morgawse taught me to read.

She came up one afternoon as I was throwing spears at a straw target, in the yard back of the Boys' House. One moment I was staring at the target, spear in hand, and the next I felt her eyes on my back and turned.

She stood by the corner of the house, dark and pale in the gold of the afternoon sun. She wore a dress of dark red wool, caught tightly with a golden belt at the waist, low cut to reveal the line of her white neck. She wore a brooch of gold set with garnets, golden arm rings, and gold in the black hair that seemed to drink the light. I dropped the spear and stared at her. In that instant she did not seem like a mortal woman, but like one of the Sidhe, the people from the hollow hills.

Then she was crossing the yard, smiling, and the spell was broken.

"Gwalchmai!" she said. "I have seen little of you, my hawk, these past few months, so busy have I been with this planning for your father's war."

I started when she called me "hawk," although my name, in her native tongue of British, means Hawk of May. The name is such a warriorlike one—"hawk" being a common poetic name for a warrior—that I always tried to forget its meaning. But when my mother used the name for me, I loved it and her.

"M-mother," I stammered. "I . . ."

"You are sorry for the loss?" she asked. "So am I, my hawk."

This could not be true, I knew. My mother had given me to a nursemaid immediately after giving me birth, and had shown no great interest in me since. But I believed her, because she said it and I wanted to believe her.

"Yes, I am sorry," I told her.

She smiled again, her deep, secret smile. "Well, we shall
have to talk a bit, shall we not? I see that you are doing
as your father wished and practicing with your weapons."
She eyed the pile of throwing spears beside me—I had just
withdrawn them from the target, or the ground around
the target, and there was nothing to show the quality of
my aim. "Will you show me how well you throw them?"

I picked up the spear I had dropped, looking at her,
then turned to the target, determined to hit it. Perhaps
because of this determination, the spear went in well,
slightly to the left of the center, plowing completely
through the straw. Morgawse raised her eyebrows in surprised pleasure. I picked up another spear and sent it
through the target, this time a little raggedly, then threw
the other five in succession. Only one missed the target,
and one hit the center. I turned back to my mother,
beaming.

She smiled at me again. "So, it seems that you are not
so poor a warrior as Lot thinks, if not so fine a one as
Agravain. Well done, my falcon."

I wanted to sing. I glanced down and murmured, "You
bring me luck. I have to do everything well when you
are here, Mother."

She laughed. "My! So you have a way with words
too, then? I think we should spend more time together,
Gwalchmai."

I swallowed and nodded. My mother was the wisest
and most beautiful woman in all the islands of Britain and
Erin. To be allowed to spend time near her was a gift
from the gods.

"Listen, then," she said. "I have been talking to Orlamh.
He says that you are a fine harper, as good as many
bardic students, but more interested in the stories and
sweet tunes than in the knowledge involved. It seems to
me that it would be a fine thing if you could learn the
histories and genealogies without having to know the
chants by heart. Would you like to learn to read?"

My jaw dropped. Reading was the rarest of all skills in
the Orcades. The druids had their ogham script, but they
taught it to no one but their initiates, and forbade its use
for any purpose but memorial inscriptions, saying that
what a man memorizes he has forever, but what he writes

down he may easily lose. To learn to read meant to learn Latin, which was spoken in parts of southern Britain, but used as a written language from Erin to Constantinople. In all the Orcades, I believe only my mother could read. The skill is common enough in Britain, and, now, in Erin in the monasteries there, but in the Orcades it was regarded as a kind of magic. And now my mother was offering to share her power with me!

"Well?" asked Morgawse.

"I . . . Yes, yes, very much!" I choked out.

Morgawse gave a smile of satisfaction, almost, I thought for a moment, of triumph, and nodded. "When you are finished with weapons practice, then, I will give you your first lesson. Come to my room."

"I'll come right n—"

She shook her head. "Come after you have finished with these. Hit the target fifty times for me. The Latin will wait."

I hurried with the spears until I realized that hasty throwing would not help me hit the target, and finally got my fifty hits. I raced to the Boys' House, dropped the spears in their corner—I would have been whipped for leaving them in the yard where they could rust—and ran to my mother's room.

The first lesson was a simple one, though it seemed hard to me. She explained to me what an alphabet was, told me the letters and their sounds several times, and told me to memorize the letter forms and come back after weapons practice the next day.

I ran to Medraut and told him about it, showed him the letter forms, told him what Morgawse had said about my skill with weapons, and jumped for joy all over the stables.

The rest of the summer was wonderful. I continued my lessons in Latin, learning the language and the reading and writing of it simultaneously. I improved with my weapons to a point where I could hold my own with the other boys and was no longer the butt of every joke. My twelfth birthday came in late May, and I began to dream of when I would be fourteen and able to take up arms, a dream that now I hoped to fulfill. I could become a warrior in my father's warband, and he would be pleased.

The war, though, seemed incredibly remote from the slowly passing summer days, with their long, green twilights and the short nights when the stars were like silver shield rivets in the soft sky. But my mother listened to the reports from Britain tensely, and sent messages to Lot, advising him.

It was not as easy as my father had planned. At the very beginning, my father and our ally were surprised by a sudden attack from Urien, king of Rheged. Lot had counted on the marriage tie holding Urien back for another month or so, and, even though the British king was defeated and forced to withdraw, my father and Gwlgawd were forced to cancel their plans for raiding Gwynedd immediately. Urien's defeat confused the situation in other ways as well, for Vortipor of Dyfed was sufficiently impressed by it to declare himself the ally of Gododdin and the Orcades, and commence raiding Powys, his neighbor, while March ap Meirchiawn of Strathclyde managed to win Urien's support for his own claims to the high kingship. Vortipor then changed his mind, wanted the high kingship for himself, found allies, and attacked Gwynedd. He was defeated; my father and his allies took advantage of the situation to attack Gwynedd themselves, and won a victory and a great deal of plunder, but, returning from this expedition, met with Urien and March and their allies. There was a great battle.

It was nearly two weeks later before we heard, even with good winds and fast ships. Gwlgawd our ally was dead, though his son Mynyddog had succeeded him and renewed the alliance. But our enemies had prevailed, and the army had fled across Britain to Din Eidyn, leaving its supplies and the plunder from Gwynedd. My father was sending back as many ships as he could find men to man, and he asked for supplies. My mother found them, ruthlessly and hurriedly, and sent them south with some advice. I thought at the time that she was troubled for Lot and Agravain and the rest; but I believe she was angry, angry with Lot for losing the battle, and angry even more at the delay in her plans.

But the rest of the summer was passed in fruitless quarreling and recrimination among the kings of Britain. March and Urien Rheged, recently allied, returned to their more usual dislike for each other, and Urien claimed the high kingship for himself, which led to still more quarrels and scheming. Then it was harvest time, and the large armies that the kings had raised dissolved as the men went home to their farms, leaving only the kings and the royal warbands; and still nothing happened, while every king was afraid to raid, not knowing who his enemies were. In the south and east the Saxons were becoming very restless and beginning to raid their neighbors. Only the old royal warband, still led by my mother's half-brother Arthur, prevented a large-scale invasion.

Toward the end of October Lot finally despaired of the war beginning again in earnest, and the army came home for the winter.

Every king took his own warband home to his own island. They settled like tired hawks in their hilltop fortresses and sighed with relief that it was over for the year and they had time to recover their strength and heal their wounds.

When Lot returned with his warband it was not a shining, stirring sight as before. It had been a bad war, an uncertain, nerve-straining war, and they were tired. Their shields were hacked, the bright colors chipped, their spears notched and dull, colorful cloaks tattered. Many bore wounds. Come spring, though, they'd be thrusting up those hacked shields as proof of how bravely they had fought, flaunting their scars in one another's faces, polishing their spears, and eager to go again. But as they came into Dun Fionn, tramping stolidly through the pouring rain, it did not seem possible that they would ever boast.

Morgawse, Medraut, and I stood at the gate, watching the warband come up. Morgawse wore a dark, striped dress, a silver brooch on her dark cloak. She wore the rain in her hair like jewels. Lot, riding at the head of the warband, straightened to see her, and urged his horse to a canter. He dismounted before her in a rush and swept her into his arms, burying his face in her neck, saying her name in a hoarse whisper. I saw her face over his shoulder, the still, cold disgust in her eyes mixed with a strange pride in her power.

"Welcome home, My Lord," she murmured, disengaging herself. "We are glad to see you home unharmed."

Lot nodded, muttered, and looked toward the hall and his chambers there.

"And where is Agravain, my son?" she asked, softly.

Lot recollected himself, took one arm from about her and turned to the warband, which was now pouring through the gate, talking and laughing with the gladness of coming home. "Agravain!" he shouted.

A blond head jerked up, and Agravain rode across to Lot. He was a little older, a little taller, much dirtier, and looked more like Lot, but I recognized at once that he was not much changed. He slid off his horse, smiling widely, delighted to be back.

"Greetings, Mother," he said.

"A thousand welcomes," said Morgawse. "There is a feast tonight for the both of you . . . but you will want to rest now. To sleep, My Lord." She smiled at Lot.

My father grinned, took her arm, and hurried off.

Agravain watched them go, then turned to Medraut and me. "Well," he said, then grinned hugely, "by the sun and the wind, it's good to see you again!" and he hugged both of us hard. "What a summer!"

"I can get you some ale if you want to come into the hall and talk," I suggested, glad, in spite of everything, very glad to have him home.

"A marvelous idea!" said Agravain. "Especially the ale." He looked at Medraut, rumpled his hair. "Gwalchmai, I swear our brother's grown inches since last I saw him. Even you've grown."

"You too."

"Have I?" he asked delightedly. "That's wonderful! When I'm tall enough Father will give me a mail coat. He promised."

We walked over to the feast hall, where I got him some ale and asked him about the war. He was near to bursting from eagerness to tell someone, and told us for an hour and a half.

He had not, it seemed, actually fought as a warrior, but he had ridden in the middle of the warband, and in the great battle had thrown spears at the enemy.

"I think one of them may have hit someone," he said hopefully. "But, of course, we couldn't go back to see whether it had. We barely escaped alive at all."

His manner was a little different from what it had been when he left. His energy, always overflowing, had found a channel. He enjoyed being a warrior. He had copied the speech and mannerisms of the older warriors so as to fit into their society. But underneath it I could tell he was exactly the same.

He was overjoyed to be back. The last months of the war had been especially unpleasant. A major blood feud had almost begun between two of Lot's under-kings, and at one point there had been a threat of war with Gododdin as the warbands tried to ease their tension by sneering at foreigners. The peace and familiarity of home seemed, after this, marvelously attractive.

After talking himself out, Agravain yawned and decided to go to sleep. He stayed in the hall to rest since he was officially a warrior, and I didn't see him till late the next day.

Lot, after settling himself and the warband back into Dun Fionn, began to work toward the next season's war. It plainly would be a war lasting several years, and such enterprises are costly. The plunder taken that summer would not pay for even the fighting that had acquired it, let alone buy new weapons, and the harvest had been a bad one. My father increased the tribute as much as he dared, and the people grumbled. There had not been a war on this scale for nineteen years, and they were unused to it.

For a little while Agravain tried to help our father, but then he found statecraft boring and turned once more to his weapons, riding or sailing off on hunting trips. I was not surprised. Agravain needed action, quick and preferably violent, simply to keep himself occupied. Statecraft offers exercise for cunning, organization, eloquence, and subtlety, rarely for direct action. My father was more cunning than a fox, and enjoyed the complicated processes by which he kept his subject kings obedient, kept them paying the tribute, prevented their wars and blood feuds while at the same time holding their favor and thus his own position. Agravain did not understand the delicate nature of Lot's "game," tired quickly, and ran off to seek entertainment. He went a-hunting, but he did not forget me.

A few weeks after the warband returned, toward the end of November, he came to the yard of the Boys' House while I was at weapons practice. I was working with the throwing spears again. It is harder to throw a spear straight while running than it is to master a thrusting spear or a sword, but important to be able to do so. Thus, I spent most of my practice time hurling spears at a straw target, sometimes running toward it, sometimes standing still. I was standing this time.

Agravain walked up behind me and stood watching as I made three casts at the target. All of them hit, one in the center. Agravain frowned. "You've been working at these, this summer, haven't you?"

I turned to him, flushing a little with pride. I had not yet shown off my new skill before my father and brother, and I was eager to. I nodded. "Yes, an hour a day with the throwing spears, and an hour with the thrusting spear or sword and shield, beyond the training time. I'm better than I used to be."

He nodded, then scowled. "You're better, and that's good. But if you try to throw like that in a battle you'll be run through. . . ."

"Durrough says there's no harm in standing like this, and he's the trainer. . . ."

"He doesn't expect much from you. Put your left foot farther back and your left arm closer to your body. You have to hold a shield, you know!"

"But . . ."

"Oh, by the sun, why are you arguing? I'm trying to help you." He grinned.

Was he? The grin faded as I continued to stare at him, and he scowled again, fists clenching and unclenching restlessly. I took the stance he suggested and hurled the spear, nervously. I missed.

He shook his head. "By the sun and the wind, not like that! Hold the spear straight, may the Morrigan take you—not that a war goddess would want someone who throws like that!"

I cringed, threw another spear. It, too, missed.

Agravain snorted. "You can't see what I mean. Here, let me show you." He stooped over, picked up my other spears and hurled them. All three hit the target squarely and cleanly. "That's the way. Now you try."

We went and fetched the spears. I stood, and Agravain corrected my stance. "Try again now," he told me.

I looked at the spear in my hand, heavy, shafted with wood from the dark hills of Pictland, headed with dull iron. The weight of it in my hand was suddenly very great.

"Go on, Gwalchmai," Agravain said impatiently. "You said that you were better. Show me! Or are you afraid of your own spear again. Not much of a hawk if you are."

Morgawse still called me "my falcon." Hawk of May. It was such a fine, warriorlike name. It was what I wanted for myself.

I threw the spear, and it flew crooked. Agravain snorted and slapped his thigh. "You may have learned to throw better when you stand like a farmer plowing, but you had better learn to throw standing like a warrior if you want to be one. Or do you want to be a bard? A druid? A horse tamer?"

"No," I whispered. "Agravain . . ."

"I'd wager you still spend most of your day on horseback," he continued, oblivious. "But that's no use. Horses are a luxury, and no more than that: The real fighting is always done on foot. Horses are like gold brooches and fine clothes, excellent for a warrior to own to show others that he is rich and important, but dispensable to the real business. For that you have to throw spears properly. Try again."

"Agravain . . ." I repeated, gathering my courage.

"What's the matter now? Are you afraid to throw? Stop being foolish."

I felt foolish. I clutched the spear desperately. I would throw it standing my way. It was not the usual stance, but it did not leave me vulnerable, either. I put my left leg forward, dropped my left arm. I really am good, I told myself. I can hit the target this way. I have to now. I must.

I threw and missed.

Agravain nodded reasonably. "Now will you do it my way? If you want to be a man and a warrior you must listen to . . ."

"Stop it!" I shouted, furious.

Agravain stopped, astounded.

"You are not helping me. You aren't trying to help, though you may think you are. . . ."

"I *am* trying to help you. Are you calling me a liar?"

"No! But I don't want your help. If I'm no warrior, let me fail in my own way, and don't bother me with right ways and wrong ways. If I'm not a warrior, perhaps I will be a bard or a druid. Mother is teaching me to read so . . ."

"She is doing what?" demanded Agravain, completely aghast.

"Teaching me to read. She's been doing it all summer, while you were gone. . . ."

"Do you want to be a sorcerer?" Agravain's eyes blazed and his bright hair glittered like the sun.

"No . . . I just want to read. . . ." I was confused.

He slapped me across the face, so hard that I fell backward. His face had gone red with anger. "You want to be better than us! Morgawse is a witch, everyone knows that, and you want to learn from her because you're such a poor warrior. A word in the dark instead of a sword in the sunlight, that's what you want. Power, the sort of power fit only for cowards, for traitors and kin-wrecked men and women and clan murderers. . . ."

"Agravain! I don't! I only . . ."

"Stop lying to me!"

I scrambled to my feet, facing my brother. I felt a blind fury descend on me, cold as ice, cold as Morgawse's eyes. "I am not a liar," I said, hearing my voice cold and quiet, like someone else's. "I do not dishonor my clan."

He laughed at me. "You are always dishonoring our clan. Do you call it no dishonor that the king's own son can't throw a spear straight? That he can't kill as much as a sparrow when hunting? That all he *can* do is ride horses and play the harp—play the harp! That you want to learn sorcery and the casting of curses so that you won't have to fight. . . ."

"It's not true!" I screamed.

"Now you want to make me a liar!" yelled Agravain, and struck out at me.

It is good that I was not right by the spears: If I had

been, I believe I would have used one. I jumped on my brother with a fury that surprised him, and struck as hard as I could. I felt cold, deathly cold, filled with a black sea. My fist hit Agravain's face, contacted again. He grunted with pain, and I felt a thrill of exultation. I wanted to hurt him, to hurt everyone who hurt me, who hurt Morgawse, who hurt Medraut, who belonged to a world I could not enter, and hurt, and hurt, and kept on hurting.

Agravain flung me off and fought back, coolly, calmly, not even very excited any more. I realized that he had not really believed his own accusations, had only been angry at my doing something he could not. . . . I tripped and sprawled on the grass. Agravain kicked me, jumped on top of me, and told me to yield.

I thought of Morgawse's eyes; of Medraut's, admiring. I thought of my father smiling and imagined praise, of warriors, bright weapons and swift war hounds. I tried to fight some more. Agravain became angry and hit harder. I scratched him. He cursed.

"Call you a hawk, but you fight like a woman! Like a witch! Yield, you little bastard—you're no true brother of mine. . . ."

I tried, still, to fight, and was hurt worse. The black wave ebbed a little, taking with it the insane strength it had lent me. I was no warrior, I knew. Not really. I couldn't fight Agravain. I was no true brother of his anyway, and had no real claim to the honor of our clan, so he and Lot, at least, must believe . . . I went limp.

"Yield?" asked Agravain. He was panting.

I felt sick. I had no choice. If I didn't yield, he would only hit me some more, and call me names, and laugh at me.

"I yield."

Agravain rose, dusted himself off. Two bruises were beginning to blotch his face, but he was otherwise unmarked. I rolled over, got on my hands and knees, stared at the packed earth under the grass on the practice yard, damp from winter rains. I was smeared with it and with blood.

"Remember this, little brother," said Agravain, "and forget about reading. Try to learn how to throw a spear straight, the right way, and maybe you'll someday make a warrior. I'm willing to forget about this and come and help you some more tomorrow."

I heard his footsteps going, striding, confident. A warrior, my brother, a sun-bright prince, firstborn of a golden warrior king. But I remembered Morgawse, dark and more beautiful than anything on earth, who held Lot's fate in her slim white hands. Morgawse, who hated. Hate. I realized that the black tide had not left me, but was coiled down within my being, waiting. It was hate, strong hate. I was my mother's son.

Morgawse knew when she saw me. I had cleaned up somewhat before coming to her, but I had clearly been in a fight and it needed no guessing with whom. She saw when I came into her room that I was ready, and she smiled, a slow, triumphant smile.

She said nothing of it at first. She poured me some of the imported wine from a private store, told me to sit on the bed, and spoke to me gently, compassionately, asking what had happened, and I told her of the quarrel with Agravain.

"He said that you were a witch," I told her. "He accused me of wanting to fight my enemies with curses and magic in the dark of the moon, rather than with honest steel."

"And you wanted no such thing," she said.

"That is so. I wanted only . . . to be a warrior. To bring honor to our clan, to please Father . . . and even Agravain. Diuran, the warband, everyone. I wanted them not to think that I was worthless. I wanted . . ." I found my throat constricted, and it hurt with a sudden intensity that all my wants were vain. I sipped the wine, rolled it about my mouth, swallowed. The taste was dry and rich. It was red wine. In the shadows of Morgawse's room it was dark as blood, not the ruby fire it had been that day with Lot when I heard that the Pendragon was dead.

"I don't want those things anymore," I said. "I'm not a warrior."

"Not of their sort," said Morgawse. She sat beside me, close. She and the room both smelled of musk, of deep secrets. The pupils of her eyes had expanded, drinking all the light of the room into her sweet darkness.

I sipped the wine again. It was stronger than the ale I was used to. It was good.

"But I want to fight them," I said. "With knowledge. With things they don't understand because they are afraid to look at them. I want to show them who I am and make them know I am real."

"Ah?"

"Is it true that you are a witch?"

"And if it were?" Her voice was soft, softer than an owl's feathers in the darkness.

"If it were, I'd ask you to teach me . . . things."

She smiled again, a secret smile just between the two of us. "There are many sorts of power in the world, Gwalchmai," she said. "Many powers. They can be used by those who know how to use them, but each sort has its own dangers. Yes, the dangers of some are so great, my hawk, that you could not understand them. Yet the rewards, also, are great; the greater the power, the greater the reward." She clutched my hand suddenly. Her grip was cold as winter, strong as hard steel. "Great rewards, my spring-tide falcon. I have paid certain prices . . ." She laughed. "There will be more to come. But mine is the greatest sort of power. I will gain . . . immortality. There are none living who can match me in magic now. I have power, my son! I have very great power. I have spoken to the leaders of the wild hunt, to the lord of Yffern, to the kelpies of the deep sea and the demons who dwell in the far keeps of the underworld. I am greater than they. I am a queen, Gwalchmai, a queen of a realm that Lot only suspects and is afraid of.

"And I have watched you, my hawk. There is power in you, and strength. Now, at last you have come and asked for teaching. You will receive it."

I felt fear, but remembered Agravain's contempt and ignored it. Morgawse spoke of serving Darkness, but what of that? She also spoke of ruling it.

"Then show me," I said, my voice as low as hers.

"Not so quickly! You forget, I also spoke of dangers. I will teach you, Gwalchmai, but it will be long before you can control the power you seek. But you will learn to. Oh, learn it you will, my hawk, my son. . . ." Taking a knife from a hidden sheath she made a cut at her wrist, then held her arm so that the blood flowed into the cup of wine. She handed the knife to me, and, without being told to, I did the same.

Morgawse took the cup and drank from it, lowered it, the red wine and red blood dark about her mouth. She handed it to me.

It was heavy in my hands, fine copper overlaid with gold, rich, cold, fine and beautiful. I thought of the winter sunlight outside, of Agravain, of the scorn of warriors. For a second the thought returned to me of Llyn Gwalch and the wide purity of the gray sea. No, I thought. That is a lie. I raised the cup slowly and drained it. It was thick, sweet, and dark—darker than the deep heart of midnight.

THREE

THINGS WERE, SOMEHOW DIFFERENT AFTER that. My
mother taught me nothing but more Latin, Agravain
"helped" me in weapons practice, and I grimly accepted
his help, laboring with the rough wood and heavy metal
that was so light and flashing in his hands; I rode about
the island, practiced my own style of fighting, sometimes
on horseback. Agravain quarreled with me over this, saying that I was ruining myself as a warrior, and that I
ought to listen to him—life seemed to have settled into its
usual pattern. But there was a difference, a shadow that
made all the familiar things seem strange. I had made a
pact and was bound to it. A seed had been planted, and I
waited sometimes, awake in my bed at night with the soft
sleeping breath of the other boys about me in the dark,
waited for the plant to grow and blossom with some fan-
tastic black flower.

Agravain noticed nothing. He beat me less hard when
we fought, but this was only because I did not fight as
hard. I no longer wished to defend an honor I could not
understand. Honor belonged to Lot's world, Agravain's
world. My world had no room for such things.

Medraut, however, noticed almost immediately. I began
to catch him staring at me with confused eyes in the
middle of some talk or game. He would ask the question
plainly sometime, I guessed. I wondered how I would answer.

On Medraut's eighth birthday Lot gave him his choice

of any pony in the royal stables. I went with my brother to help him choose one. When Lot named the gift Medraut had been very excited, but on the walk to the stables he sobered up. Together we looked at the ponies—they were all the small shaggy breed common to the northern islands—and discussed the merits of each of them. Medraut listened to my horse talk in his grave, intent way, then, quite suddenly, as I was checking one of the animals' legs asked, "Is there something wrong, Gwalchmai?"

I started and looked up from the pony, twisting about on my knees to face him. "No. Not with his legs, but he has no withers at all. . . ."

"No, no, not with the pony. Is there something wrong for you?"

"For me? No. What makes you think so?"

He stood facing me in the cold, dusty sunlight of the stable, drably dressed, his gray eyes wide and anxious. The light glinted palely on his hair, the only touch of brightness in the place. He looked vulnerable, and very innocent.

"You've been so strange," my brother said nervously. "You go away . . ."

I smiled. "Well, I've always liked to go riding. Now that you have your own horse you can come with me more often."

"That's not what I mean." Medraut's voice was sharp. "All summer, you've been here. You were here, with everyone. You used to go away with Agravain and Lot, but you were here this summer. But now . . ." Medraut bit his lip and looked away from me. "Now you're gone. I can't talk to you anymore. You even go away from me."

"I don't understand," I said, though, in truth, I had a very good idea of what he meant.

"You had a big fight with Agravain," said Medraut unhappily.

I looked away, shrugged.

"After that, something happened. You went away from everyone after that."

I had felt, on some of those days, that I watched the world from a great distance behind the mask that had been my face. Went away . . .

"And you haven't gone to Llyn Gwalch."

I thought of Llyn Gwalch, the seaweed gleaming on the rocks, the drops of mist and sea spray on the mossy boulders. Such places have no bearing on the world, I told myself. One must live in the world that is real. "That was a childish game," I said. "I'm too old for it now."

"But what happened?" Medraut crossed the space between us and caught my arm. "You must tell me!"

"Why?" I glared at him, aloof as the hawk of my name.

He stared at me for a long moment, then put his arms around me and buried his face in my shoulder. It hurt. I did not deserve it from him.

"I went to Morgawse and asked her to teach me sorcery," I whispered.

He lifted his head from my shoulder, eyes wide, and went still. I put my arm round his shoulder and we were quiet.

"Why?" he asked at last.

"Because I can never be a warrior."

He thought for a while. "I wonder . . . do you think I could learn sorcery?" he asked, finally.

I felt the shock as physically as if someone had kicked me in the belly. Not Medraut. Not the young warrior, the child of light, who was everything I wished I could be: proud without being arrogant, fierce without cruelty, sunlight without the searing heat of Lot or Agravain. He could not follow me into failure and darkness. He must not become too close to Morgawse. I thought of her light-drinking eyes.

"No!" I said.

"Why not?"

"It is wrong for you. Very wrong, 'mo chroidh,' my heart."

"But Mother is a sorcerer, and you will be. Why shouldn't I know something about it too?"

"Morgawse is Morgawse. I am only myself. You are Medraut."

"Why couldn't I learn it? I am clever enough. . . ."

"That isn't the point! It is wrong."

"Is Mother wrong, then? Are you?"

I stopped in the middle of my reply. Medraut had always trusted and admired me. Still . . .

"It is wrong for you. You can be a warrior and fight in the sunlight. I can't, and Mother can't, and that is why we use this path."

He argued further, but I argued against him, hard and fast. Eventually he abandoned the subject, cheered up, and chose for his pony a gray with a white mane and tail. He called it Liath Macha, "Gray of Battle," after CuChulainn's horse, and was happy.

Spring came slowly, barely noticeable after the mild winter of the Orcades. But the days grew slowly warmer, the sky was occasionally blue, and the great cold gray sea fogs rolled less frequently up from the west.

Agravain and I had yet another quarrel over my habit of practicing with my weapons on horseback. Lot, however, who happened to be nearby and to inquire into the reason for the difference, looked thoughtful.

"Perhaps you are doing ill to punish Gwalchmai for this," he told Agravain. "True, we do most of our fighting on foot, and to be able to 'jump about a horse's back like a juggler at a fair,' as you were pleased to put it, is no great use to a warrior now. But Arthur the warleader has taught all his men to fight from horseback, and they say that his victories over the Saxons spring from the strength of his cavalry. Let Gwalchmai be."

Agravain frowned uncomfortably. He had no liking for the idea of the styles of warfare changing, and less for being told that he was wrong. He found a pretext for another quarrel later that day. But he left me more, though not entirely, alone afterward, and sometimes watched me with a frown. I think that even he was beginning to notice the change in me, and it puzzled him.

By that time Morgawse was beginning to teach me, as she had promised. Not the important things, the summonings and dark spells, but the basic things: the characteristics of that universe that exists alongside of and within our own. I do not know all the law that governs it; neither did Morgawse. But some of it I learned, and many things that before I had not seen became apparent to me.

Once Medraut adjusted to the change in me, we were as close as ever, perhaps closer, though he gave me occasional measuring looks I did not like. But I took him with me on my rides about the island, told him more and more stories, and played the harp for him. I was becoming very good at singing. Any bard, of course, did far better, but I have some small gift for it. I no longer cared that my father considered it shameful for me to spend time harping. I no longer cared what anyone found shameful.

April arrived, a bright month, and my father still had not left for Britain. The war was late in starting. All the labored-over alliances of the winter fell apart again with the spring, and the British kings scurried to build new ones. Several blood feuds had started, and some old ones reopened, and a war had begun between two of our enemies who had formerly been staunch allies, springing from a quarrel over some plundered cattle. This catastrophe disrupted all the old alliances and added a new faction to the civil war.

All that summer the war wore on without anything becoming clearer, and Lot made ready to invade, fumed, and waited for an invitation. Agravain, sixteen years old and considering himself a man, polished his weapons and hoped.

In early August, Gwynedd's old enemy Dyfed and our one constant ally Gododdin decided to attack Gwynedd. It was a sensible idea, but ill timed, and our allies finally made the long-awaited step of calling for my father to join them. It was nearing harvest time, and my father knew he could not raise his army, but he summoned his subject kings and their warbands, and sailed by night past Dalriada to attack Strathclyde, and to proceed from there to join his allies.

Morgawse rejoiced in her husband's departure. She ruled the Orcades absolutely while he was gone, and she loved the power. She spent very little time with me. There were two reasons for this. The first was simply that, unlike the summer before, there was a great deal for her to do. Most of the men remained in the Orcades to bring in the harvest, and from the harvest she must see that the king's tribute was exacted and collected and stored. But the more forceful reason probably was that she no longer needed to draw me to her. I had come, and been trapped. She did not think that I could escape.

Knowledge of sorcery had not brought me happiness, as I had thought it would. It gave me a secret place, and a secret cause for pride, yes, but I was never entirely certain whether what I felt was pride or whether it was shame. The burdens were heavy. I would see things that no other saw, and they frightened me. Sometimes I heard the baying of the hounds of Yffern overhead, which hunt the souls of the damned to Hell, and the clear silver sound of the huntsman's horn. I puzzled at the meaning of this, and it always meant death. I came to realize that I would die, and I feared this. Morgawse, my mother, also feared it, but she had done something to keep the hunter from her back, something she would not explain, and this gave her security. I envied her. I tried to learn more, to cure my fear, to lighten the burden, but I only succeeded in deepening the fear and loading my heart until it sank into the black sea which sometimes possessed me. And I did not think I could escape, either. Nor did I truly want to. There was nowhere else to go.

It was a hard winter. It does not usually snow in the Orcades, but it snowed that winter. In northern Britain, where the war had by then settled, the cold clasped the mountains with a brutal hand, casting great drifts and barriers before the path of any warband hardy enough to plow through them. Usually, most kings allow their warbands to rest in the winter, and most of the warriors scatter to their own households, to gather again when the leaves first begin to bud. That winter was different.

In the east, the Saxons were restless. They had by no means been altogether neutral in the war, but had enthusiastically taken part in the plotting and politicking, and taken what advantage they could from the fighting. They made small border raids which grew into larger ones, driving farther and farther across the boundaries that had been established in blood in the last major war against them. Arthur, the warleader of the old Pendragon, tried to fight them. But he was a clanless man, and relied on Constantius, the king of Dumnonia, for his support. Constantius had his own warband as well as Arthur's to pay for, and could not spare tribute enough to keep the whole royal warband, which the whole of Britain had paid taxes for when there was a high king. Many warriors followed

Arthur by preference, giving up much of the wealth a good warrior expects, but still there were not enough to protect even a part of the border.

The Saxons are a fierce people—young, vigorous, wholly barbarian, overflowing with brutal energy. They seem, however, to have an ability to keep peace among themselves which British kings have never learned. Some of the Saxon kingdoms were officially tributary to the British high king, since they were founded as colonies by the Romans under the last emperors, and sworn to protect the empire. But they are always land hungry, for their numbers increase more and more as other Saxons come over the sea, and the newer kingdoms acknowledged no ancient oaths. Only the strength of the high king and his warband keeps them from overrunning Britain altogether. Like wolves about a sick stag, they watched the British kings at war.

We did not fear the Saxons in the Orcades, nor did we have to worry about the other menace to Britain, the Scotti, who came from Erin in their long war curraghs to plunder all the western shores of Britain. There was no peace between the Scotti and the Orcades—my father had left Erin because of a quarrel with the kings who led them—but the raiders would not brave the long journey to our islands, where they would be met with the cliffs and walls of Dun Fionn.

There were no raiding ships so foolhardy as to brave the Irish Sea in winter, but the Saxons and, most of all, the winter itself, made the British kings cautious, highly unwilling to leave their fortresses. Only my father, faced with no domestic enemies, felt free to travel. Our warband went the length and breadth of Britain, winning rich plunder and supplying themselves from the goods of their enemies.

Medraut was always full of talk of the war, though even more full of talk of how Morgawse was governing. She controlled the realm in a way which made my father's grip seem light. Medraut, like myself, was full of adoration and fear of her.

She worked magic, too, that winter, in her room. Usually she was alone, but sometimes she let me watch. Whatever she was doing, it strengthened her. Every day she seemed more beautiful. She went bare armed in the cold, her long dark cloak flapping from her shoulders, fastened with a brooch set with stones as red as blood. No blood, though, showed in her white skin, and the gaze of her eyes was softer than darkness. Any room she entered seemed to dim, and others, beside her, seemed faint and unreal.

Medraut still said nothing more about learning sorcery, but I could tell that he often thought of it. There were pauses in our closeness when he watched me, thinking, perhaps envying, or wondering what it was I saw which made me swerve about the empty air. But such times were of short duration, and he would come back near to me, asking me about the day's depression or telling me his thoughts. We often rode out together on our ponies, thundering along at full gallop in the low hills, scattering the sheep and trailing plumes of steam, or stopping to throw snowballs. I was most nearly happy when I was with Medraut.

He had his ninth birthday that winter, and entered the Boys' House to begin learning the proper use of weapons. He excelled among the boys of his age, as I had expected. He was quick, nimble, intelligent, and he learned rapidly. He was so much better than the others at riding that he had nothing to learn from his teachers. He was deficient only in skill in composing on the harp, but he made up for this with his speed in learning a song, and his enthusiasm for the music. Being together in the Boys' House we were with each other most of the day, but we shared everything and never quarreled,

When Morgawse asked me about Medraut, I found myself evading her questions. She was beautiful. she seemed to me perfect, she ruled the Darkness—but I did not want Medraut to follow her.

In March Lot and the warband returned, but only briefly.

I saw Agravain, and was shocked at the change in him. He had now completed his growing spurt—he was nearly eighteen—and seemed entirely a young warrior, and more like Lot than ever. He was tall, and his gold hair, which he wore long, to his shoulders, glowed in the sun. The whole warband was in fine condition. Though the winter fighting had been difficult, the plunder had been rich, and there had been plenty of time to rest—but my brother stood out among them. He had a fine bright cloak, jewelry won from the men of Gwynedd and Strathclyde, Elmet and Rheged, where he had fought; he had his mail coat, and his weapons gleamed. He rode up to the gates of Dun Fionn behind our father on a high-stepping horse, carrying the standard. The people of Dun Fionn, and the clansmen from the surrounding countryside who had come to watch, cheered to see their king and his son together, so splendid were they. Agravain grinned and raised the standard, the warband laughed and shouted the war cry as one, and the people cheered even louder.

Agravain was pleased to be home, to see Medraut and me again. He told us about the war, about the long series of carefully planned and successful raids, about how he had killed his first man in a border clash in Strathclyde, how he had traveled over all Britain, and once even fought with a Saxon raiding party in Gododdin. He had become what he had been destined to be: a warrior-prince, a some-day king of the Orcades. He no longer resented my few small talents, but accepted my gains in skill with a good-humored laugh and some praise, glad to see me, eager to be friendly. He was confident, and had no more need of pettiness. Medraut was very impressed, and held Agravain's great spear while Agravain talked, stroking the worn shaft. I listened, but mainly I watched Agravain. Splendid sun-descended hero, knowing nothing of Morgawse's "greatest power," of the strength that lies in Darkness. I envied him.

He did not stay for long. After checking the state of the islands and collecting more warriors, Lot sailed off again. The war was going well. The young men were anxious to return to it.

By May, when I had my fourteenth birthday and left the Boys' House, the situation in Britain seemed to have taken a definite shape at last. My father stood firmly in our old alliance with Gododdin and Dyfed; Powys and Brycheiniog opposed him uncertainly and Ebrauc squarely—the middle kingdoms of Britain, all anxious to have a Romanized, anti-Saxon king—and finally Gwynedd, the first claimant to the high kingship, in a shaky alliance with Rheged and Strathclyde—the anti-Irish, anti-Roman party. In the balance was the kingdom of the East Angles, a Saxon kingdom which had sent envoys to both Dyfed and Gwynedd during the winter, and Dumnonia, the most Romanized British kingdom, resolutely neutral. It appeared as though a few pitched battles would decide the war.

But, in June, all plans were swept away together.

The Saxons, as I have said, were restless. Those who had been settled longest raided the most widely, killing, looting, carrying off men, women, and children as thralls, but chiefly seizing lands. They needed it. Since the borders were last determined more Saxons had come to Britain: relations, fellow clansmen, fellow tribesmen, new families drawn by the promise of better land, families ousted from old lands by new invaders, and single men drawn by the desire for war and adventure. They all wanted land to farm, to own, to build their squat, smoky villages on. They had much of the best already. The old land of the Cantii, the gentle hills and woodland about the old heart and capital of Britain; the fenlands that had belonged to the ancient tribe of the Icenii, and formed another province; the oldest Saxon kingdoms, Deira and Bernicia, given by the Roman high kings to their Saxon mercenaries—all these were theirs, and it was not enough. They were officially subject to the British high king, successor of the Roman high kings, and they had sworn him the same oath the British kings swore, but they never thought of keeping it. They resented the British who kept them back, when Rome itself had fallen before their kind. They needed only a small excuse to start them on a full-scale invasion of Britain.

And, in June, a great force of Saxons landed on the southwest coast, the Saxon shore, taking the Roman fort of Anderida, allying themselves with the South Saxons and sweeping into eastern Dumnonia, crushing all before them. Their leader was a man named Cerdic, and they said that he was a king such as men would follow to the gates of Hell. They certainly followed him into Dumnonia. And what Cerdic and his tribe began was continued by the other Saxon tribes. First the South Saxons, then the East Saxons, then the tribes of the Angles, the

Jutes, the Franks, the Frisians, and Swabians all swept into their neighboring British kingdoms, not just to raid but to settle there.

Despite this, the British did not turn their attention to fighting the Saxons. The civil war had gained momentum now. There were blood feuds involved in it, and honor, and many ancient hatreds. A man will not suddenly drop so old an enmity for a new one. The Saxons had been defeated before and could be defeated again. So the civil war continued, and the Saxons were allowed to seize portions of the eastern marches, while Cerdic began forging a kingdom. The western lands, such as Gwynedd, who did not have a border with the Saxons, were pleased that their British enemies were in difficulties; and everyone agreed that Dumnonia had been too large before, nearly the whole of an old province; and that it was well that the principal sufferer from the invasion was the one neutral kingdom. My father was annoyed at the Saxons and with this Cerdic, but he was confident that, when the war was over, he could see that the Saxons got some of the land they wanted and that Cerdic, after acquiring honor and a kingdom, was conveniently assassinated (it is not safe to allow great leaders to live among the enemy). Then a Britain slightly reduced in size would be ruled from Dun Fionn.

So, after some dislocation, the war might have continued, had the invasion not elicited another claim to the high kingship.

Uther's warleader had been the lord Arthur, from the time that Arthur was twenty-one, and Uther could have chosen many others for the position than this one of his many illegitimate sons. Arthur was twenty-five when Cerdic invaded, and had been fighting the Saxons throughout the civil war, supported only by Dumnonia, of all the British kingdoms. All acknowledged that he was a brilliant warleader, the most innovative and successful since Ambrosius Aurelianus, who was the first high king after the legions left. And yet, no one had expected that Arthur would take sides in the struggle, or, indeed, that he would do anything but fight the Saxons. But when he saw the Saxons invading on a large scale and realized that the British were not going to drop the civil war to fight their common enemy (he thought half like a Roman, when it came to such matters) he was apparently "provoked," the circumstance my mother had warned against.

He rode with the royal warband to Camlann, the royal fortress of Britain, abandoning his lonely and massively outnumbered position against the Saxons. There he met Constantius, king of Dumnonia, and there he declared himself high king, Augustus, and Pendragon of Britain.

This produced more effect on the kings of Britain than Cerdic's invasion had. But Arthur ab Uther did not leave them any length of time for their shrieks of protest at usurping bastards. He raised the largest army he could and attacked first Brycheiniog and then Dyfed. He took the royal fortresses of each land after subduing and dispersing the warbands, each time defeating forces larger than his own. The kings of both countries were forced to swear him the Threefold Oath of Allegiance, and to provide supplies for Arthur's forces. This accomplished, he proceeded to conquer Gwynedd.

Docmail king of Gwynedd never swore allegiance to Arthur, but proudly took poison in his own fortress of Caer Segeint, cursing Uther's bastard son, three hours before Arthur arrived there on the tail of Docmail's defeated warband. Docmail's son, Maelgwn, who was only a year or so older than myself, had been designated by Docmail as his successor. He swore fealty to Arthur without protest.

It was not yet July, and no other king had even had a chance to prepare to fight the man who claimed the Pendragonship. Arthur moved very fast. By the time Docmail died, however, the new claimant to the title found all the nations in Britain allied against him, foremost among them Urien of Rheged, and, with our allies, my father. The simple reason for this sudden concord was this: It looked as though Arthur could win.

Arthur was not caught unprepared by this new alliance. It was discovered that, before claiming the title, he had made an alliance of his own with a king in Less Britain. Less Britain is in Gaul, a rich and powerful land. It was first begun as a colony by the High King Maximus when Rome still stood, and it increased in size as the legions withdrew, and men made landless by the Saxons went there for lack of a better place. When Arthur made his alliance Less Britain was not defending itself against the Saxons or the Goths or the Huns, and there was a civil struggle brewing between the two sons of the old king over who would succeed. The dispute had not reached the point of war, but this was inevitable once the old king died. Bran, the younger brother, had once fought beside Arthur, and had leaped at the chance of an alliance. He sailed from Gaul with his warband and a large army besides, landed at Caer Uisc in Dumnonia, and joined Arthur in Caer Segeint a few days after it fell. From there he was immediately rushed to Dinas Powys, which Arthur wanted to take before the other kings could unite their forces against him. There was a brief, fierce struggle in Powys, and Arthur was again victorious. He rode into the fortress in triumph, accepted the fealty of Rhydderch Hael of Powys, and dispersed Rhydderch's warband.

The other British kings finally managed to unite. They were by no means one army, and by no means ready to fight in unison, but their strength was very great. There were Gwlgawd king of Gododdin, and the king of Elmet, and Caradoc king of Ebrauc, and March ship owner of Strathclyde, and Urien of Rheged, called the Lion of Britain—and my father, Lot of Orcade, the strongest king of Caledon, the sun's descendent.

Arthur had the royal warband of Uther, which had followed him faithfully during the preceding two years of civil war, and he had his allies Constantius, king of Dumnonia and Bran of Less Britain, together with sworn and enforced neutrality from Gwynedd, Dyfed, Brycheiniog and Powys.

The story of the battle between these two forces is one often told, and more often sung, in the halls of all the kings of Britain, Erin, and the Saxon lands. In the Orcades we heard of it two weeks before Lot himself returned with the warband.

It was late in July, a hot day, with the air heavy enough to cut with a knife. The messenger came riding up from the harbor on the east coast at a trot, too hot and tired to go faster. Morgawse received the man in her chambers, gave him the obligatory cup of wine, and impatiently asked his news. I sat on the bed, watching.

The messenger drank the wine eagerly, mixing it with about half water. His clothes were stained and dusty and soaked with sweat. He was one of my father's warband, though not a kinsman of mine, as half the warband was, but a Dalriad attracted to us by my father's fame and generosity. His name was Connall.

He began by telling us what the last messenger had said: Arthur, impatient for battle, had ridden north and west with his men, and the armies of the kings of Britain had drifted from various directions to encounter him. Morgawse nodded impatiently, and the messenger hurried to continue. The armies had met east of the upper part of the river Saefern, by one of its tributaries, the Dubhglas. It is hilly country there, and Arthur had had time to place his forces carefully.

Morgawse frowned. From the condition of the messenger it was already obvious that there had been some kind of defeat, and she began to suspect that it had been a severe one. Arthur was famed as a warleader.

"It was about three weeks ago," continued Connall. "We stood about and they stood about, waiting to fight. It was hot—stinking hot. We stood there in our leather jerkins and mail and sweated and waited for Arthur to make up his mind what to do. We could see the standards of Bran and Constantius down the valley from us, but not Arthur's. We cursed the lazy bastard for making us wait, but he was the great enemy, and we had no choice.

"About midmorning, someone came up carrying the red dragon standard, and the enemy all cheered. We became very angry. It seemed a piece of impudence for him to declare himself high king and use the Pendragon standard, and he without a clan. Lot commanded us to charge, and we were ready enough. We raised the war cry splendidly and ran at them. All the other kings in the valley—for we were all in the valley, the hills being too steep to fight on properly . . ."

"Fool!" snapped Morgawse. Connall stared at her uncomfortably. "What idiocy, to allow himself to be trapped by such a . . . Continue."

Realizing that she had been addressing Lot, not himself, Connall went on, "At all events, we attacked. They put up a good fight. They are strong men in the shield wall, those men of Less Britain. But there were more of us, and we are no weaklings ourselves. Your son and your husband, Lady, fought gloriously, side by side, thrusting with their spears almost as one, their shields locked together, laughing. They carried everyone before them. And that Urien of Rheged is a fine war hound, a lion indeed. The men of Rheged . . ."

"I said, continue!" said Morgawse intensely. Her dark eyes narrowed on the messenger. Connall swallowed, looked away from her, and continued.

"Arthur's forces retreated, slowly. We pressed after them down the valley. It was a hard struggle. About noon, though, they began to falter—at least they seemed to—and we redoubled our attack. They broke. Their shield wall collapsed inward, and they started running as fast as they could.

"We cheered as loudly as we had the breath for—which wasn't very loud, for we were wearied by such fighting in that miserable heat—and ran after them." Connall's face lit a little as he recalled the elation of the moment, then shadowed suddenly. "And then Arthur brought out his horsemen."

Morgawse groaned, threw away her wineglass. "From the hills."

"From the hills. They came down, so fast . . . on horses. One does not ride horses into battle, not against spearmen. They can be spitted so fast that . . . well, no matter. They rode the horses down, hurling their throwing spears, breaking the shield wall before they reached it—it was breached along the flanks anyway because of our haste after the rest of the army. And then they were among us on those horses, riding us down, stabbing with spears, and striking with swords. We had spent all our throwing spears long before, and we did not know how to fight them. We could not re-form our shield wall, because they were inside it. Arthur was with them—he had only sent someone else to the others with his standard—and he was laughing and shouting the war cry of the high kings. The men of Less Britain and Dumnonia, who had been fleeing from us, picked up the cry and rushed back at us. We couldn't hold them, for the horsemen broke our shield wall and the horses were trampling us underfoot. We broke. Lot kept shouting at us to hold, to regroup about him, but we couldn't. We couldn't. We went running away. Our shield wall was broken, and we threw away our shields to run faster. Lot stood, Lady, weeping for rage, and your son with him. Some of us remembered our vows to him, and the mead he gave us in this hall, and we returned to preserve our honor. We tried to retreat slowly, and some others joined us, or came back—but we couldn't hold, even for a little while. Our shields were hacked to pieces, and we were retreating across the bodies of our comrades who were killed while they fled. Lot said—I was by him—'I will die, then, fighting with my warband.'"

Morgawse laughed harshly. "Die! Would that you had. But Arthur had no desire for your death, Lot of Orcade. He wished no more war with the Orcades."

Connall nodded miserably. "Constantius came up with his warband and asked us to surrender. I . . . I . . ."

"And you surrendered!" shouted Morgawse. Her face was flushed with anger. "You surrendered and swore the Threefold Oath never to fight Arthur or any whom Arthur supported, ever again!"

Connall dropped his head. "It is so. We had no choice. It was surrender or die. And Arthur was not, after all, to be our king."

Morgawse moaned as in pain and covered her face with her hands.

Connall hesitated, then went on. "The rest of the warband had fled with the armies of the kings of Britain, and were caught with them. They were driven like cattle up the valley into the Dubhglas. There had been rains, and the river was high. It is swift there, too, and there was no crossing it, not in that press. They surrendered, they all surrendered—Arthur had given orders that no one was to kill the kings—and they swore the Threefold Oath of Allegiance to Arthur. The next day he gave himself some Roman title and said there would be a council at Camlann. But he told Lot to take us and go home, or he would burn our ships and have us killed. But he is keeping your son, Lady, for a hostage. He saw that Lot loved Agravain.

"So we went back to Gododdin at great speed. I went ahead, Lady, to bring you this news. . . ."

"Arthur Pendragon," whispered Morgawse, without moving. Her eyes were fixed on something infinitely far away. I shivered, for I knew that the hate she had borne for Uther had been conferred in double measure on Uther's son. "Artorius, Insularis Draco, Augustus, Imperator Britanniarum. That is his Roman title, man. Arthur, Pendragon, High King of Britain. Arthur . . ." Morgawse dropped her hands, glared at Connall and beyond him. Her face was twisted with a fury and hatred beyond human comprehension. Hate was a black fire in her eyes, deep as the inner black ocean which I knew had swallowed her. "Arthur!" she screamed, "Arthur! Oh, this battle is yours, brother, but the war is not over, I swear, I, Morgawse, rightful and legitimate daughter of a high king! Death, death upon you, death upon your seed, that it will rise against you, for all your new gods and empire and sorceries. Death and eternal agony! Be secure now in your new power and glory, you whom Uther loved, but my curse will find you out and give you to damnation forever. I swear the oath of my people, and may the earth swallow me, may the sky fall on me, may the sea overwhelm me if you do not die by your son's hand!"

Morgawse had risen and lifted her hands. To my eyes, darkness blazed in a corona about her, and she was more beautiful than ever any mortal woman was, and I was blinded by her darkness and beauty and worshipped her in terror with all my heart. Connall, as terrified as I, cringed, unable to mutter a prayer, staring at her with wide eyes. As the final syllables of the binding Threefold Oath fell on the shocked air, she remembered him, and turned on him. She was angry that he had seen her rage, angry as a goddess. But she laughed, and her control was back, veiling but not hiding the splendor beneath it.

"So, you believe that I am terrible," she said. "You do not know how terrible, man, Connall of the Dalriada. Shall I show you?"

He collapsed away from her, cringed toward the door. Morgawse's hands rose and she wove a spell. My eyes saw it as the black strength came together like threads on a loom, into a strange pattern.

"My power makes no great show of warriors, as Lot's does, or Arthur's," she whispered. "It is subtle, working in the dark, in the places beyond your sight, hidden in fear in your own mind. No man is free from me. No man, not even Arthur. Certainly not you, Dalriad . . . shall I show you, Connall?"

He shook his head, licking his lips. His back was flat against the door, his fingers spread against it. The leather bolt was not fastened, but he was as incapable of opening it as if it had been locked with chains of steel. Morgawse approached him, and, beside her, he seemed as pale and unreal as a ghost.

"Do not, Mor Ríga, Great Queen," he muttered.

"You do not wish to know your queen's power?"

He shook his head, shuddering.

Morgawse stepped back, relaxed her hands. The darkness that had nestled there dissipated into the air. The coldness of the room suddenly vanished. I became aware that it was still July.

"Mention nothing of what I have said to anyone," said Morgawse, "and you never will see that power. Leave here."

Connall fumbled, found the door bolt, and fled. Just as he left the room, his eyes touched me and widened only a little.

As the door closed and Morgawse sank once more onto the bed and began to laugh, I realised that I, too, was gaining a reputation for witchcraft.

FOUR

T HE ARMY CAME HOME, EACH king returning to his own island, and Lot and the warband returned to Dun Fionn.

We rode down to the port when they arrived, and found them still at work beaching the war curraghs, dragging the long round ships up on the beach and securing them. We had brought horses, and, when he had finished with the ships, Lot rode back with us and the warband to the fortress.

He was very tired, that was plain. His bright energy was dimmed, and his hair had a few early strands of gray to dull its brightness. His eyes were bloodshot and had dark circles beneath them, and lines of bitterness curled about his mouth. He was very quiet.

I was quiet too, riding in back and watching my father. It seemed incredible, unreal, that he had been defeated. It seemed wholly unbelievable that Agravain was a hostage. I wondered how it was for him, all alone in the court of Arthur. Hostages are never badly treated—my father had a hostage from each of his subject kings, and they all fought in the warband and had many of the rights of the other warriors—but the mere fact of being a hostage would be crushing to Agravain. I could see him, striking out at the foreigners who ringed him in and mocked him for his father and his defeat; see him struggling desperately to improve his poor British, miserable, alone in a strange land . . .

I was no compensation for the loss of Agravain, that too was plain. Lot looked at me, at Morgawse, back to his own hands again and again, and always his mouth curled in pain. I wanted, for a while, to help: to try again as I had tried before to be what Lot wanted me to be. But I argued myself out of it, along with my pity for Agravain. I was my mother's son. I had left the Boys' House now, and had not become a warrior, and I was certainly no descendent of Light. And Lot and Agravain had wronged me.

Morgawse, too, was silent, but her silence was that of scorn. She was furious with Lot for being defeated, and she showed him her contempt without words, showed him what she thought of his strength and valor and virility. I watched Lot's hands tighten and loosen on his horse's reins as he stared at her stiff back.

The warband was in poor shape. There were not too many lost or maimed, for their fighting had been largely successful, until they met Arthur. But they had lost all their plunder and fine things to Arthur's men, and returned to Gododdin by forced marches with inadequate supplies. It seemed that the new Pendragon was hungry for wealth and provisions. He would need them to support a large warband, and he would certainly need a large warband if he wished to protect Britain against the Saxons. But now we in the Orcades would pay for Arthur's war, and rely on the next harvest alone for our lives.

When we reached Dun Fionn, we stabled the horses in silence, and in silence the men went to rest. There was a gloomy feast that night, in which the warriors brooded over their mead and Lot sat grim as death at the high table, glaring off to the door that led from the hall to Morgawse's room. Orlamh, my father's chief bard, sang uncertainly, the songs falling flat on the stale air.

The men were drinking very heavily. I knew, for I was pouring the mead. My father, too, drank heavily. With the drink glinting in his eyes he looked about the hall. He saw me, and his eyes fastened on me. He slammed his goblet down.

"Gwalchmai!" It was the first time he had addressed me directly since his return, and it was a rare enough occurrence at any time.

I set down the jug of mead. "Yes, Father?"

"Yes, Father," Lot repeated bitterly. "Agravain . . . well, Agravain is a hostage. You know that?"

"Yes, Father."

"You would. You know how to read, write, and speak Latin, to play the harp, sing like a bard, make songs, ride horses—damn horses!—and spear men from them, and you know other things. What other things?"

He had never mentioned even the Latin before. I shifted my weight uneasily. All the warriors were watching me, measuring me.

"Nothing else, Father."

Lot stared at me. The warriors stared at me. I saw that my reputation had indeed reached them. I stared back, determined not to back down.

"You certainly are no warrior," my father said finally. "Oh well. Go take that harp from Orlamh and play something, something pleasant. I'm tired of his weary plunking."

Orlamh sighed and gave me the harp. I took it, sat down, and stared at the strings. I was angry, I realized, but not filled with hatred. I felt sorry for Lot. I became more angry, but I still felt sorry for him.

What could I sing? Something to take him away from Dun Fionn and his defeat.

I touched the strings carefully, drew the melody out as gently as if it were a web of glass, and sang the lament of Deirdre on leaving Caledon to go to Erin and her death.

> *Beloved the land, this eastern land,*
> *Alba rich in wonders,*
> *And to depart I had never planned,*
> *Did I not leave with Noise.*
> *I have loved Dun Fidhga, loved Dun Finn,*
> *Beloved is the stronghold above them;*
> *Inis Draighen, its seas within,*
> *Dún Suibhne: I loved them.*

The hall was very still, and the warriors sat quietly, not touching the mead horns by their hands. Was it possible, I wondered in surprise, that I was doing it? Well, the song was very famous and familiar. I sang on, trying to catch the bright irregular rhythms and complex yearning.

> *Cuan's wood, where Ainnle would go—*
> *Alas! the time was short,*
> *Brief the time, as we both know*
> *Spent on the shores of Alba . . .*

> *Glen Etive, where first I raised my*
> *home,*
> *Lovely the wood is there,*
> *The fold for the rays of sun when they*
> *roam*
> *At the dawn of day, Glen Etive.*

And so through the verses. The final stanza came, addressed to the beach Deirdre embarked from:

> *And now beloved is Draighen's beach,*
> *Beloved now the waves, the sand—*
> *Never would I go from the east*
> *Did I not go holding Noíse's hand*

I swept the notes upward and brought them down slowly to silence, making them weep, thinking of Deirdre, a beautiful woman five hundred years dead, stepping into the boat and going to her doom.

When I finished, the hall was very silent, but with a different kind of silence. Lot looked at me strangely for a moment—then laughed. He was pleased.

I sat and stared at the harp and did not believe it.

"That was good," said Lot. "By the sun! Maybe you'll become something after all. Play something else."

"I . . . I . . ." I said, "I'm tired. Please. I want to rest."

His smile vanished again, but he nodded. "Go and rest, then."

I set the harp down and left. His eyes followed me, puzzled, all the way out of the hall.

I did not rest. I lay on my pallet and turned about, and stared at a patch of moonlight crawling across the floor all night. I had pleased my father. To be a bard was a very honorable trade, lower only than that of a king, if one was good enough. I had pleased my father more than Orlamh, who was good. I watched the moonlight and thought: "I have come too far down the path of Darkness to forsake it."

And I stared too at the cold black place within me, and wept, within myself, alone in the darkness.

I found the next morning that Lot and Morgawse had not slept that night either. My father had become drunk and made his way to my mother's room to claim his rights. She had tried to throw him out, but he had decided that he was her husband and she must be obedient. For the next few days she wore a high-necked gown to hide the bruises. Lot, though, was the one who looked sick and worn, while Morgawse smiled quietly with complacent satisfaction. I suddenly realized that, if my father used her beauty for his pleasure, she fed upon him like a shadow upon a strong light, and drained his power slowly away. I shoved the thought aside as soon as it occurred to me, for it made me uncomfortable.

August wore away slowly, and September after it. I did all that I had done before—still practiced with my weapons, had lessons with Morgawse, went out riding and playing with Medraut—but there was a difference now. Lot ordered that everyone learn some of the new ways of fighting from horseback, which Arthur had used against the spearmen, and suddenly I was first instead of last, not only among those my age, but even among most of the older men. I was fourteen, beginning to grow, and I knew all the tricks which no one had bothered to study: how to move about on horseback, how to take a spearman on the ground without being thrown from the horse, and make the horse rear and back when the place was too narrow or the press too great to manage—things that called for agility and speed instead of strength and order, and so had been neglected in the usual methods of fighting. The tricks I had practiced on my own.

We received news, too, from my father's spies in Britain. My father was hoping that Arthur would be killed in battle, though he was unwilling to arrange such an event himself, for the sake of Agravain and for his oath. But there was no such good fortune. Arthur took tribute from every king in Britain, and even from the Church they have there. I had never really understood this Church. All of Britain, except, of course, the Saxon lands, was of the Christian faith, since the Roman high kings had decreed that they should be, and this faith had been explained to me as a strange worship centered on a god who was really a man, who had pretended to die but really hadn't, or some such thing. At any rate, the Church was very rich from the donations of its followers and from the lands held by priests and monks. It was powerful, as well, but this seemed natural to me. Even fifty years ago the Ard Filidh, the chief druid, had been as powerful as any king. Now, of course, Erin too is Christian, and perhaps the rest of the West will be Christianized as well, though I do not see such a thing being done by the British Church. The British Church was and is interested largely in increasing its own wealth and prestige in Britain. It disapproves of foreigners.

In spite of this, one was supposed to give money to the Church, not to take it away. Arthur, especially, had been expected to be generous. He was famous as a sincere Christian. He had been raised at the monastery at Tintagel by the learned and peaceable monks, who, out of charity, cared for the bastards of the neighboring districts when these were orphaned or unwanted. He had taken to this upbringing, it was said, and was rumored to pray before fighting his battles, and by this means win divine assistance. As they said, this could account for all the victories. The Church had been eager to recognize him as Pendragon, despite his uncertain claim to power.

Once established, however, instead of delightedly showering gifts upon the Church, Arthur immediately demanded from it a tithe on all its possessions. When the priests and abbots angrily refused and reviled him, the new high king declared for all Britain to hear that, if they cared to fight over possessions rightfully owed him, he would be happy to oblige. The abbots and bishops considered this, decided that he was in earnest, and provided the supplies. But they were very angry, and began to work against him.

My father listened to all the news and hoped. When

Arthur gave some of his new wealth to Bran of Less Britain and sent him home, Lot stayed up all night dictating messages. He also came every day to see how the men were doing at the new methods of fighting, and himself practiced them until he was dripping with sweat. He also began scheming for control over the northern Hebrides, renewing an old enmity with Aengus Mac Erc of Dalriada. But something of the brightness had gone from these endeavors. My father was not going to control Britain by means of any puppet kings. Arthur controlled Britain.

My mother also laid plans. In September, in the dark of the moon, we killed a black lamb at midnight. I held its head while she cut it open with a stone knife, examining the entrails while it still struggled and bled over us. She was angry with what she saw, but did not explain it to me. Eventually, the next day, I asked her why she could not simply destroy Arthur, as she had destroyed his father

"It is not so simple," she told me. "There is some Christian counter-spell he has made against me, and I do not understand the nature of it. Did you not see, in the lamb last night, how the entrails were woven into knots?"

I had not wanted to look. These things still sickened me.

"Do not mind that, though," she said, beginning to smile. "I have cursed him, and the curse lives, and has lived. In the end the Darkness will take him, too."

I watched that Darkness in her eyes as she gloated, and was awed by it. I knew that she was planning some other action, though, and that she had killed the lamb to see how it might turn out. She was filled with tension, waiting. But when I asked, she would not tell me what she waited for, only smiling a soft, secret smile.

As October wore slowly away and the great sea fogs blanketed the islands I began to guess when she would act, if not what she meant to do. At the end of October there is a night called Samhain. It is a festival, one of four great festivals—the others are Midsummer, Lammas and Beltene—which are sacred to the powers of the earth and sky. Samhain is the night when the gates between the worlds lie open. On that night, the dead can come creeping back to the world they left, and places are laid for them at table among the living. Other, yet darker things come across the worlds on Samhain, and they are not usually spoken of, and still other things can be summoned then, by wish or by rite, and these are mentioned least of all. As the end of October approached, I knew what my mother was waiting for.

On the day of Samhain I went to her room for the usual lesson. But most of the day we did nothing but read. Morgawse had bought a Roman poem called the *Aeneid* from a traveling merchant for the value of ten cows in gold. She had seventeen books, which were worth a frightening amount, and I had read all of them. I was enjoying the *Aeneid* more than any of the others, though it was full of strange names and I understood very little of it. I regretted that we had only the first six books, the first half of the poem, and that we had nearly finished these.

> ... *sic orsa loqui vates: 'sate sanguine divum,*
> *Tros Anchisiade, facilis decensus Averni:*
> *Noctes atque dies patet atri ianua Ditis;*
> *sed revocare gradum superasque evadere ad auras,*
> *hoc opus, hic labor est.*

I smoothed the page and began translating again: "Thus the ... prophet?"

"Or poet," Morgawse murmured. "Like an ollamh."

"Thus the prophet began to speak: 'You who are sprung from the blood of gods, Trojan, son of Anchises, easy is the descent of Avernus: night and day the gate of black Dis is open; but to recall your step and to come out to the upper air, this is toil, this is labor ...'" I stopped, swallowing suddenly. "Avernus. That is Iffern, isn't it? The Dark Otherworld?"

She nodded, her eyes cold and amused. "Does that frighten you, my hawk?"

I put my hand over the page, shaking my head, but the catch was still in my throat. Easy is the descent, but to recall your steps ... She was still looking at me.

"Very well, enough for today," she said. "And what do you think of Aeneas now, my hawk?"

"He still . . . He relies upon his mother, the goddess, for everything. I don't really like him. Not as much as CuChulainn, or Connall Cearnach, or Noíse Mac Usliu. And yet . . ."

"Och, it is an ill thing to rely upon one's mother, then?" she said, laughing, and I looked at her and felt my face grow hot.

"She was less of a goddess than you," I said.

"Prettily said! Aeneas is weak, and so is his mother Venus. And yet, the Romans consider this their greatest poem. They were not artists. They could not understand the depths of a thing, the passions of the soul. They built a strong empire on the blood of men, and made good roads. Other than that . . . Arthur is half a Roman."

"He is? But I thought all the Romans left a long time ago."

"The legions left. 'Defend yourselves,' Honorius told the provinces of the Britains, 'for we cannot defend you any longer.' But they left their memory, men willing to try to set up a fallen empire. In the south, many still think like Romans. Arthur does. That is why he leads the Britons against the Saxons: He wishes to preserve the last stronghold of the empire against the barbarians, one nation defending itself against another. He does not see that Britain is no more one nation than the Saxons are. His is a peculiar way of viewing things, and has many weaknesses. I know them. I have seen and known Arthur."

She fell silent, thinking, smiling.

"Come here tonight," she said in a low voice after a long time. "I have planned that tonight you will have your initiation into real Power. It is a good night for it. I will have you accepted by the Darkness, my son, and you will see why I am strong. After tonight, you will have Power as I do."

I heard, nodded, bowed, and left the room without saying anything. I saddled my horse and went for a long ride out by the sea. I could not stay in Dun Fionn. But with each step my horse made I became more afraid, anticipating something I did not know. I had seen deeply into the Darkness by then, and it frightened me. I desired to be like my mother, to have Power and escape from the fear, but I found the Power still more fearful. I did not know what I wanted, now, but I would go that night.

I realised that the path was familiar, and found that I was going to Llyn Gwalch. Well, why not?

I reached the place where the stream fell over the cliff's edge, combing the gravel with clear fingers. There was a light mist that day, which turned all the low hills so soft a shade of green that it seemed they would dissolve into the gentle sky. The sea beat-beat at the cliff, a sound as constant as my heart. It seemed to me that I had never heard it before.

I dismounted and hobbled my horse, then climbed carefully down the path.

When I reached the beach with its little pond, everything seemed smaller than I remembered it, and I realized how long it had been, and how much I must have grown. But it was still beautiful. My old dreams hung about it yet, glowing faintly in my mind with colors brighter than those of earth. The pond was infinitely deep, still, and clear, dark in shade because of the multi-hued gravel lying rounded in its bottom. The sea clutched at the beach, hissed on the stones, and sighed out. Its smell was salt and strong, wild, infinite, and sad. A seagull flew over my head, flapping and gliding. It wailed, once, and some more sea birds hidden in the mist cried back.

I went over to the pool and knelt by it, drank from it, then studied my reflection. A boy, looking fourteen or older, stared back. Thick black hair, held back with a bit of worn leather. Smooth skin still dark from summer, a face slightly resembling Morgawse's in the shape of the bones. A thoughtful face whose dark eyes met mine openly, trying to look into the confused mind that lurked behind them. It was so very dark in there.

Who is this Gwalchmai? I wondered. A name, but what beyond that? Something beyond my understanding.

I leaned back on my heels and looked up at the gray sky. I remembered those dreams I had had of myself as a great warrior, and the dreams that had come at night, the sword burning with light, tattered shreds of glowing color, and, above them all, the song rising from nowhere, like the sound of a harp played elsewhere on an empty day, but sweet enough for a man to leave his life behind to hear it better. I remembered playing with boats in that very place, sending them out, so far out, into the open sea, dreaming of the Land of the Ever Young, Lugh's hall, with its walls woven of gold and white bronze and its roof thatched with the wing feathers of birds. The sea pounded and sighed on the shore, and the birds keened. I wondered what had happened, and where the Darkness had begun. I felt like a man looking back on his childhood, and I wondered if one could truly be a man at fourteen, and what it was that I had lost. I sat and listened to the gulls, drawing my cloak around me. Tonight it would end. Tonight, truly, it would end.

The night was one of wind and broken moonlight which poured raggedly through the clouds driven over the moon, only to be whipped away again. Crossing the yard from the hall, where I slept most of the time now, to the room of Morgawse the queen, I looked up at that moon's worn face and thought of the old prayers to it. Gem of the night, breast jewel of heaven . . . How many, I wondered, had looked up at her face through the years? Warriors planning raids by her light, lovers laughing to her, druids and magicians praying to her, poets making songs to her, all these she must have seen countless times. But surely, it was all chance whether she shone or no, and I could expect no help from her. And perhaps, when I returned this way, I would no longer want any.

The very air seemed to be vibrating when I reached my mother's room, as if with the aftermath of a scream. The door bolt shivered in my hand like a living thing. There was power in the air, so much dark power that it was hard to breathe.

My mother had already prepared the room. The floor had been laid bare, and the wall hanging raised so that no light could enter. She had dug a trench across the middle of the floor, and made designs about it with white barley and water, and set candles around it. She stood now in the middle of the room in a gown of red so dark that it appeared almost black, her bare arms pale and strong and cold looking in the eerie light. Her hair fell about her, a river of gleaming darkness down to her waist; she was barefoot and ungirdled, since it was a time to loosen knots and not to bind them. She was drawing a design in the air about the final candle.

I felt a weakness rise in me, gripping my stomach with icy hands, unstringing my knees. Darkness lay in the air, thick, smothering. I wanted to cry out, beat at it with my hands, run, not looking back to what might follow from the corners of my mind.

I closed the door softly and stood silent, waiting until Morgawse was finished.

She set the final candle down and straightened. She was very tall, and the Darkness hung about her like a cloak, so that all the candle flames bent toward her like seaweed toward a whirlpool. She seemed more than ever to be not of the Earth, but a queen in some other realm. Terrified, I loved her. She smiled when she saw me, a smile blurred by the flickering of the flames and by the Darkness she wore around her, but her smile still, secret and triumphant.

"Good," she said. Her voice seemed to come from a deep void, colder than January ice. "Go over there. Stand, be still, wait, and watch what I do."

I obeyed her.

She took a jug of something red, wine or blood, I was not sure which. If it was not blood, there would be blood before the night was ended. She poured it over the design she had already traced, muttering strange words which I had heard separately before. Then she broke the jug and put half of it at each end of the trench. She turned to me again.

"Could you follow that?"

I nodded, not trusting my voice.

She smiled again and turned to one of the wall hangings. Just then, the door opened.

I whirled in guilt and terror, expecting Lot to burst in with angry demands or with armed men. I was ready to fight him, and my hand was at the dagger in my belt.

In the doorway stood Medraut.

"Close the door," Morgawse ordered calmly. "Stand there, opposite Gwalchmai."

"What . . . ?" I asked. How could Medraut have

stumbled onto this? I had been careful to tell him nothing. "Medraut, leave. Now. This is not for you."

He looked at me in surprise, and then his wide innocent eyes fixed themselves on the pattern again with a fierce eagerness. "But Mother said I should come."

I suddenly remembered how Medraut had stopped speaking about magic, about unexplained absences of his from training, about a thousand other little things I had never accounted for before, and the realization hit me so that I cried out, "No!"

He stared at me. "What do you mean? Morgawse has been teaching me Latin and witchcraft too. We can all learn together now. Oh, I know that you don't want me to, but it will be much better this way. You can't begrudge me the Power that much."

"No!" I repeated. "You cannot. You will destroy yourself, Medraut. The Darkness will crawl inside your mind and devour your soul until it has eaten all that is you and leaves only a shell. Go, while you can!"

He flushed. Morgawse stood, the rope for the hangings in one hand, watching. Her eyes were on me.

"Why?" asked my brother, growing angry. "You never give a true reason. If this is so wrong, why are you here too? It is just that you don't want me to learn. You want to keep me a little boy forever, while you become wise and powerful."

"Medraut, that is false. It is wrong, but I am all wrong, and you are not, so you must not. Please, for your own sake."

"So this is wrong, and Mother is wrong, too? That is impossible. Mother is . . ." His eyes sought and found her, and his anger melted into adoration.

"Medraut, get out of here," I said again, desperately, though he was not listening now. "Tonight we will do a very strong and dreadful magic."

"I came for it," he said. "I've been learning too, Gwalchmai." And then he spoke in the language of sorcery. The ancient syllables spurted from his mouth like the yammering of some strange animal, incongruous, hideous beyond belief. I could not bear to listen and clapped my hands over my ears, staring at him, feeling the tears start to my eyes.

"It is enough," said Morgawse. "Medraut will stay."

I looked at her, ready to cry out in protest, but could not speak. The room became cold, achingly cold and dark. The candle flames swam before my eyes, as if from miles away. I sobbed for breath in the black tide that drowned me.

Morgawse jerked back the wall hanging.

One of my father's warriors lay there, bound hand and foot. I had known there would be blood. The man's eyes above the gag were wild with fear, running about the room without fixing on anything. I recognized Connall of Dalriada.

"Oh," I said. There was a sick taste in my mouth.

"He went to Lot and told him of my oath," said Morgawse. "I fulfill a promise. We will do to him as we did to the lamb last month, but a man is better for these things." She smiled again, looking at Connall. "Pull him to the center."

Medraut stepped forward. I stood, staring, sick. Connall's eyes met mine. His held the knowledge of horrible death.

I looked at Medraut and thought of what he had said, "So this is wrong, and Mother is wrong . . ."

Lastly, I looked at Morgawse, and for the first time saw her without illusion: a Power wrapped in human flesh, long ago consuming the mind that had invoked it. A dark Power, a queen of Darkness. She had summoned it as a servant for her hate, had welcomed its control when she controlled it, and every day became more it and less herself. A Power that drank life and hope and love like wine. Ancient beyond words, evil beyond thought, hideous despite its beauty, the creature stood there and gazed on me with a black, insatiable hunger.

I screamed and my hand rose to ward it off, and I saw that I held my dagger.

Her face changed, became as a woman's again, turning to fury. She lifted her arms, and power surrounded her leaping up like fire.

"Gwalchmai!" Medraut was shouting. "What are you doing?"

"Get out," I said, finding my voice steady. "This has not been Morgawse daughter of Uther for years. You must get out, while there is still time. If you love me, if you love your life, get out of here!"

He looked at me, then at the queen of Darkness. His face twisted desperately—and then he stepped toward Morgawse, stepped again, past me, to stand beside her. "You are mad," he said. "Mother is perfect. It is Father who is wrong. Put down that knife and come help us."

I began to weep. "She will sacrifice Connall."

He looked uncomfortable for a moment, but she touched his shoulder and the unease faded from his face. "She is perfect. He insulted her. He deserves to die."

"She will kill Father one day."

Medraut actually laughed. "Good. Maybe then . . . I will be the successor to the kingship. Mother has promised me. And, after all, Arthur is a bastard too."

I stared at him where he stood under her upraised hand, his eyes again wild with misery, and with a pain I had only suspected. I had been wrong about him. I should have realized that his ambition was not just to be a fine warrior, but rather to be something beyond his reach. It was too late to help, even if I could have. Too late.

I looked again at the creature who had once been Morgawse, daughter of Uther, and knew that my knife could not harm her. I was only alive because she hoped that I would come. And I could come, could drown in the black tide, forgetting confusion and loneliness and guilt and, yes, gain a kind of immortality. Easy is the descent of Avernus, I thought.

I lowered my hand slowly. Medraut smiled with joy, and my mother smiled again also, at me.

And then I threw the dagger straight into Connall's throat, saw the thanks in his dying eyes, and dragged open the door, fleeing the Darkness that rose up behind me.

I heard Medraut run to the door after me, his shout ringing across the yard, "Traitor. Traitor, traitor, traitor . . ." There was almost a sob in it.

Then I was in the stables and my horse stood waiting in his stall, ready for me to mount and go flying away from Dun Fionn and from the Darkness that ran behind me, thick with the fury of its queen and heavy with her desire for my death; and I was mounting and riding off through the moonlight and cloud shadows, riding away from Dun Fionn, riding . . .

My horse's hooves kicked up stones on the path, and the fortress was limned for a moment against the wracked sky, and then I rounded a hillside and it was gone. . . .

Gone.

FIVE

THERE WAS SAND AND GRAVEL under me, and somewhere very near the sea was pounding.

I lifted my head and looked out over the western sea which beat-hissed on the narrow beach and flooded up toward the deep pool of fresh water by the cliff's base. Llyn Gwalch.

The memory of the night before returned to me, and I lay still for a while and considered it. I felt tired, too tired to feel anything, and the memory was heavy and hard. After a while, though, I realized that I was very thirsty, so I crawled up to the pond and drank from it. The water was very cold, clear and fresh, delicious. I splashed it over my head when I had quenched my thirst, then went over and sat down against the cliff to look out at the sea.

I thought about the wild ride, down along the cliff path, with the demon of Darkness chasing me, catching at the edges of my mind. I remembered reaching Llyn Gwalch, dismounting, and sending my horse on with a slap, then scrambling down the cliff to lie, exhausted, in my only refuge. And apparently it was indeed a refuge, for I was still alive and sane. I wondered how long it would last, then wondered again because it did not seem to matter much. I felt weak and empty but not sick. In fact, I felt better than I had for a long, long time. I was free. Even if I lost my life, I was free.

The sun had risen behind the cliff, and its rays crept

closer across the ocean. I smiled at the light and spoke an old poem of greeting to it:

> *Welcome to you, seasons' sun*
> *Traveling the skies from afar*
> *Winged with glad strides the heights you run*
> *Joyful mother of evening stars.*
>
> *With night you sink on the perilous sea*
> *But arise from the waves' bower*
> *Leaping from harm and darkness free*
> *As a young queen in flower.*

And in a moment of dizzy triumph I thought, I have followed the sun, the young queen. I have recalled my step from Avernus. And then, close behind the triumph came the pain. My mother was trying to kill me. As vividly as if I relived it I saw her fury when I threw the knife at Connall—poor Connall!—and saw the Darkness leaping from the shadows behind her.

I shuddered. I could not return to Dun Fionn. I pressed my hands together until it hurt, trying not to realize what that meant. I would never ride into those light walls again, nor listen to old Orlamh's dryly courteous explanations of meter and genealogies, or Diuran's coarse jokes. In one blow I had separated myself from my kinsmen and home forever. Even if somehow, at some later time, I returned, I would never regain what I had just lost. I had lost the world of warriors before, and now had lost the other world I had desired, and if I were free, it was with the freedom of the outcast, clanless, nameless, placeless. I could not return to Dun Fionn—and for that matter, whyever was I safe at Llyn Gwalch?

Perhaps, I thought, distracted from the pain by surprise, perhaps there is some force here that thwarts the queen.

I remembered Arthur.

Certainly my mother would have destroyed him long before, if she had been able to. She hated him enough. But she was unable to, because of his new gods and his counter-spell that she didn't understand.

I reminded myself sternly that Arthur had defeated my

father, and that he kept my brother as his hostage. He ought to be my sworn enemy. And I reminded myself of the constant wars that racked Britain, and the invasions. But the sternness was no use. I began to think of all the places that I had heard of: Camlann with its triple banks, new heart of Britain; Caer Ebrauc, a great city, massively walled, Sorviodunum, Caer Gwent, Caer Legion, splendid fortresses. Monasteries filled with books and learning, great roads from one end of the island to the other, triumphal arches tall as trees, mosaics in the courtyards of rich villas, fountains and statues, theaters and arenas, things I had read of but never seen. Britain, the last remnant of the empire of the Romans—except for the east; but Constantinople was farther away than the Otherworld and more unreachable. Britain, surrounded by men who desired her, unconquered in the midst of defeat. There, in that fabulous land, the High King Arthur Augustus had raised the dragon standard, and he was protected by a magic Morgawse could not overcome. And I remembered that, although by his acts I might be counted his enemy, by blood he was my uncle, and that might win me a place. I was no warrior to join his warband, but there might be something I could do if I joined him.

Yes. I would try to journey to Camlann, or to the High King Arthur wherever he was, and I would offer him my service.

This decided, I stared out to sea again and wondered how to go about it.

For some reason, Llyn Gwalch was safe, if only for a little while. But Morgawse had raised the Darkness against me, and I knew that if I climbed back up the cliff I would be destroyed long before I could reach the port in the east of the island. And even if I did reach the port, what would I do for a boat? If I stole a small boat, how could I, a fairly inexperienced sailor, hope to travel the treacherous northern waters to Pictland with the winter coming on? And I had nothing to pay for passage on a larger vessel.

For a moment I thought of going to my father with the story, but dismissed the idea at once. Morgawse would not possibly allow me to tell my father that she had accomplished the death of one of his warriors. I wondered what she would tell him as it was. That I had killed Connall? Probably not. That would require too much explaining. No, she would pretend to know nothing of either Connall's disappearance or mine, and find some way to dispose of Connall's body. My horse would return to the stable riderless, or perhaps be found wandering about the cliff, and my clan would conclude that I had gone mad, and ridden along the cliffs on Samhain. And Medraut—he might weep. I felt sick again. Poor Medraut. If only I could have . . . or have understood. But it was too late. Perhaps it had been too late for a long time. It was best that he thought me dead. If he knew that I was alive, he would hate me.

I stared at the sea and pondered all these things, twisting them about in my mind and running off on tangents. But the answer—or rather, the absence of an answer—remained the same. I was trapped at Llyn Gwalch.

By noon I felt quite hungry, though stronger than I had been when I awoke. I looked hopefully in the pool for fish and found none. There were some oysters clinging to the rocks along the cliff foot, though, and plenty of sea birds nesting in the face of the cliff, if it came to that. I stripped and swam out, then along the foot of the cliff, collecting oysters in my tunic. I had a good amount when I felt a sudden chill, colder even than the water. I looked up. The sun shone on the cliff face, hazed by a light mist. Halfway down the cliff lay a patch of shadow. I looked upward, then looked at the shadow again, and realized that there was nothing on the cliff to cast it. Hurriedly, I turned and swam back to the beach, and the cold became merely the usual cold of the North Sea in November. So. The creature Morgawse had summoned was waiting for me.

I laid my tunic in the sun, wrapped myself in my cloak, shivering, and ate the oysters. They tasted very good, but I knew that they would not support me forever. I could not stay at Llyn Gwalch; I could not leave it.

Well, sooner or later I must leave, but I would rest first. I looked up at the sun. It was already dropping toward the horizon, and the mist was thickening imperceptibly. Winter was coming on, and the days were shortening. I dropped my eyes to the beach, the clear stream running out into the ocean over the wave-smoothed stones, the seaweed and driftwood. I smiled, and decided to make a toy boat.

I had not forgotten how. The curragh I made from driftwood and seaweed floated perfectly on the pond. It was a pity I couldn't build one large enough to hold me, but the thing was beautiful enough as it was. I watched it float down the stream, anxious whether it would overturn in the surf. It jerked when it reached the waves, rolled, then, caught by the current, began to glide out to sea. I watched it drift away and thought again of the Isles of the Blessed. Suddenly I wondered what they were. The forces of Darkness were real and powerful enough. What about those of Light? Arthur's magic was strong enough to baffle Morgawse: If he could claim the Light's protection, perhaps I could as well.

I had been in a great Darkness, near to drowning in it, and the thought of a Light opposed to it was sweet. So, as I watched the curragh bobbing on the waves, I spoke silently within my heart: "Light, whatever your name is ... I have broken with the Darkness and it seeks my life. But I would follow you, as a warrior does his lord. I swear the oath of my people, I will serve you before any other for as long as I live. Protect me, as a lord does his warrior, and bring me to Britain. Or let my kinsman, Lugh of the Long Hand, if he exists and is indeed my kinsman, help me from the islands to which my boat travels. I beg you, help."

The curragh slipped on over the waves as though it bore a message. I watched it until it vanished from sight.

The sun sank slowly down into the west, bursting free of the mist at its setting, and splashing red-gold on the face of the sea. There were heavy clouds beneath it, looking like an island. There was one of the great winter fogs coming. It would arrive before morning, and would be cold. I watched until the sun was quite gone, and, after that, watched the twilight deepening its shade from the first soft green into blue, while the sea became first silver, then gray, then silver and black as the moon rose over the cliff, cloaked with pale gold in the mist. I sat drenched with its light and half-drunk with it and the Earth's beauty. I sang songs to it, and the rise and fall of the sea seemed to answer me. When I lay down at the cliff's base, the driest part of the beach, I had scarcely wrapped my cloak about me when I fell asleep.

I woke around midnight, opened my eyes to stare, rigid with terror, into the blank darkness. Some dream which had swept black wings through my brain departed, leaving a foul memory. There had been a sound. The demon! It had broken into my refuge and must be creeping upon me; best to whimper and dig into the earth.

I sat up and flung back my cloak. I reached for my dagger, remembered that I had left it in Connall's throat. You must go out as a warrior, I told myself.

But there was no shadow on the beach, nor any hint of the Darkness. The moonlight was dim with mist, but I could see clearly enough that I was alone on Llyn Gwalch. There was only a boat, resting, prow first, on the beach.

It was a strange boat, a lovely one. It had a high prow and stern, unlike a curragh, though otherwise it resembled one. But it had neither oars nor mast nor rudder, and the color was like no wood or hide I had ever seen, but gray-white in the luminous mist. It was no derelict, either, I saw. Cushions and coverings were heaped in it. And yet no one sat in it. The prow lay on the stones, and the waves, grown very quiet, lapped and sighed out into the mist. There was no other sound.

I stood slowly, staring. No boat should have landed so at Llyn Gwalch. The current of the stream, combined with an undertow which was often fierce, pushed any floating things onto the rocks at the side. I took a few steps toward the boat. It rested there, half on land, half on water, like a pale flower. I noticed now that it was not a trick of the moonlight in the mist, that the boat really was shimmering softly in the dark. I sensed the magic woven into its fabric, an awareness of it stirring my hair like a faint breeze, and I stopped and watched it.

And yet . . .

It did not feel like a dark magic. It was light and swift and clean, like a seagull swooping over the waves. And though things could be other than they seemed, I had spoken words that afternoon as I watched my curragh sail off, and the silence in my heart had listened.

And even if this were a trick, a trap made by the demon lurking on the cliff, what would it mean except that I would die now instead of later? I decided, and walked forward to place my hand on the boat's prow. It was soft, warm, like a living thing, a trained hawk which rustles its feathers in the eagerness to fly. I took my shoes off, threw them into the boat, and pushed it off the stones, clambering in when it was a few feet from the beach.

While the boat hung there, bobbing in the calm sea and I searched for an oar, I sensed a stirring above and looked up. The shadow lay on the cliff-top again, like the shadow of a cloud now. My fists clenched, and again I longed for my dagger. Then I started, for the boat began to stir of itself, very slowly, turning from Llyn Gwalch till its prow faced westward. It began to move forward over the waves which shivered with the moonlight.

The shadows on the cliff grew smaller, darker. It raced down the cliffside, swinging about Llyn Gwalch. A cold Darkness seemed to brush past me, like an unseen bird, and the sick, suffocating feeling of the night before touched me again. But the boat was picking up speed, gliding over the waves, and I suddenly remembered what is said of evil and open water, how some spirits may not cross the wide sea. I laughed. The black tendrils fell away from me, overextended and worn out.

I watched over the stern as Llyn Gwalch shrank behind me, becoming a pale place in the cliff wall, then a soft spot in the frothing of the light surf in the moonlight, with the waterfall of the stream a chain of silver hung down the cliff—then the mist grew thicker as the boat ran into it, and Llyn Gwalch and the island I had lived on all my life faded from my sight. I could not think to give it any farewell, and looked westward over the boat's prow. We were still increasing in speed. I laughed again, feeling the same exultant triumph and liberty I had felt that morning, and sang a song of triumph in war. The boat leaped forward like a willing horse and glided on, swift as a gull or a falcon, through the fog into the moonlight again, and the foam glittered at its prow as it ran along the path of light cast by the sinking moon.

I yawned, realized that I was still very tired. The cushions I had noticed were soft, the coverlets of silk and ermine much warmer than my worn cloak. It was cold in that rush of speed across the open sea. I lay down and drew the coverings over me, whispering thanks to the boat and to whatever force had sent it.

I do not remember falling asleep, but the next thing I saw was the light of the sunrise pouring onto me, brighter than any dawn I could remember. I lay on my back in the bottom of the boat and stared up at the streamers of color that covered the sky from the east to the zenith. Such radiance promised a destination of equal loveliness.

I sat up. The boat was still moving, but a little more slowly now. Its prow and sides glowed with reflected fire on the water. Even the sea was like no water I had ever seen before. It was clear, but tinted with emerald and azure, colors brighter than any on Earth, jewel toned in their brilliance, and they glittered in the dawn light. The sun cast my shadow before the prow of the boat, and we ran down it as down a road. As I watched, birds flew out of the west, white and gold wings flashing. I looked eagerly onward, hoping to see the land they came from.

Soon we approached it. It rose green-gold from the ocean. The sun struck some bright surface, and a pure clear light flashed up like a shout of joy. Truly, this had to be the Plain of Joy which so many songs spoke of. The Light had heard me. I lifted my arms to the morning and sang one of the songs about the islands I was fast approaching:

> *... there one sees the Silver Land*
> *Where dragonstones and diamonds*
> *rain,*
> *And the sea breaks upon the sand*
> *the crystal tresses from its mane.*
>
> *Throughout earth's ages still it sings*
> *To its own hosts its melody;*
> *Its hundred-chorused music rings*
> *Undecaying, deathless, free ...*

I hardly had time to finish before the boat swept up to a white dock which jutted from the land into the sea, and there stopped itself, its journey over.

I stood and stepped out onto the dock. I glanced back into the boat, a little afraid to leave it. But then I looked at the land, the green grass, the gold-sanded path leading up from the dock, the tall trees—trees! Things rarely seen in the Orcades—swaying like dancers; and I began to walk up the path, slowly and wondering. I did not feel the stunned disbelief one would expect. Though wonderful, all seemed perfectly natural, as things do in a bright dream. Later, I realized, the astonishment must come. But now it was impossible. This Isle of the Blessed felt more real than the Orcades. It was what I had just left that seemed a dream.

I went up the path, savoring the beauty around me. Everywhere there were flowers, no two alike. Their smell blended with the song of the birds, the music of the breeze in the trees. I walked faster, then ran for the sheer joy of motion, until I rounded a bend and stopped, for I had found the hall that was the center of the place.

It was much like its descriptions. The walls were of white bronze and gold filaments woven together, polished and brilliant. The roof was of the wing feathers of every sort of bird that had ever lived, of every color, and none clashed. It glowed almost as brightly as the sun.

I walked slowly toward it, half-afraid, although I knew that I would not be there if it were not intended for me to come. I approached the great silver doors and tapped on them softly. They opened of themselves, revealing their inner hall, which is beyond description. Yet it was enough like any earthly feast hall that I knew where to raise my eyes to the man who sat at the high table, above the others who crowded the place. They were all beautiful enough to bring tears to my eyes, and I felt my humanity and filthy clothing as though they weighed the whole world on me. But the man who sat at the high seat, the lord of the hall, smiled at me—a bright, fierce smile—and gestured me nearer.

I walked the length of that hall in silence, with the eyes of the company upon me; and I cannot describe or explain what I saw there. Slowly I climbed onto the dais and stopped, facing the lord across the high table, not knowing what to do or say.

He rose and smiled again, and it flashed across my mind that Lot and Agravain really did look much as he would if the blazing radiance of him were dimmed.

"Welcome, kinsman," said Lugh the sun lord. "Be seated. You have traveled far and must be hungry."

So I sat at the high table in the hall of the Sidhe, and ate with them and drank the sweet, bright wine that is like an essence of light, and I talked with Lugh of the Long Hand.

He asked me of Lot and I told him of Arthur. He listened to me, then nodded. "It is fated. One day rises when another is fallen."

"Does Arthur of Britain, then, serve the Light?" I asked.

"He serves it." Lugh shrugged. "This is a greater matter and much is woven into it, and the end is not clear to me. My day, too, is over."

I stared at him in astonishment. "You, My Lord? But you are ruler here!"

"Yet on Earth, where once I had power, I have little strength. Once all the West turned to me. Now they turn elsewhere. In time what little I have left will cease, and I will become only a memory, and my hall and my people but a story told to children. In time, not even that." He spoke calmly, as of certainties, and without regret.

"Is this light to be quenched, then?" I asked, looking about that radiant hall.

Lugh shook his head, smiling at my question. "This light? Not so. We shall feast here till the Earth's end and beyond. Time does not touch this place, nor death, nor any sorrow. It is better than the Earth where we once dwelt."

"Then you did live on the Earth, as the songs say?"

"Long ago." Lugh sipped the wine, and his blue eyes were hot and bright as the sky. "In what might have been Erin. Men were but a dream in the East, far from my domain. I came into being here in the West, not born as men are born, and here my people lived and made music. My mother was Balor's daughter, my father, Cian, son of

Diancecht the Healer. Like yourself, Hawk of May, I am created of both Light and Darkness. And once it was offered to me as well to serve either, and I chose the Light. I reigned in it, for a time, though I knew my reign would be hard and not endure forever."

"You know of my mother, Morgawse."

"I know of one who is called the queen of air and Darkness, who is become Morgawse. She is an old enemy, once of my people. She seeks the destruction of the world she can no longer possess."

"But you possessed it once."

Again he smiled. "Once I drove my chariot along the wind from Temair of the Kings, though it was not the same Temair where the lord Ui Niaill now sits. Once my kind ruled over the earth, commanding fire and water and air as a king commands men. But that time is long past, so that even the land forgets it. Which is as it should be."

"I have heard a story," I said, "which said that the sons of Mil came to Erin, the first humans to reach its shores, long ago; and they found the Sidhe there, who were then called by another name. And it is said that the sons of Mil fought with the Sidhe, or that they were judged between by Avairgain the poet of the sons of Mil, and that Erin was given to men."

"The second story is closer to the truth," said Lugh, "though the issue was not decided by Avairgain."

"Who decided it, then?"

"The high king, the Light who shines forever. He gave me my kingdom, and he took it away again and bestowed it on the sons of Mil, and Avairgain the poet told the first men that this was what had been done. But the queen of Darkness would not heed me, nor the Light, nor Avairgain, but desired to keep the land for herself."

"The Light, this Light," I said. "I do not know what is meant by it."

He looked on me gently, amused. "And how should you? None do, when first they encounter it, and you are newly come from a great Darkness. Darkness blinds the eyes. But have you not sworn to follow and serve it?"

"I have."

"Then you will come to know it better soon enough.

The Light is a strong lord, a great king, and often a demanding master, though a kind one. The Light is eager for servants and friends, and will show you more things to do than you had thought could be done by any. So, at least, I have found it."

"You found it . . . but I thought . . ."

"That I was the Light? Not so, indeed. Many have thought that, and once, in Erin, I was worshipped as the Light. But it is sought differently now, better. There have been many changes on Earth. I too am only a servant."

So we spoke, and drank the wine. I was not aware of time. I do not think one can be aware of time in that place. Perhaps those in the hall go out, sometimes, into the island—there are songs of the horses of the Sidhe, and chariots of gold racing across fields of flowers, and dancing, and also of wars—but I think all these must happen without time, not at the same time, nor at earlier or later times, but with a sequence set by the spirit and not by the passage of the sun. I cannot make it clear even to myself, but so it was. But when I had spoken to Lugh for a while—I cannot say, "for some time"—the feasting ended and a man of the Sidhe who had been sitting to my right at the high table rose and went to a great harp in the corner and played upon it. That song was everything all men have dreamed of and sought for, which they only grasp for a few moments before it dissolves into the human world. It was light, fire, the pure ecstasy of immortal joy, totally unmingled with sorrow which always accompanies it on Earth. I listened and felt as though my spirit would break from my body and go soaring off on that golden wind to the very pinnacle of heaven. I listened, wholly lost in the mazes of the music, feeling nothing but the sequence of each note. I would have sat so forever, if Lugh had not touched my arm.

At this, I realized that I was weeping. I sat bemused and wondered why, and the harper played on. Lugh rose and gestured for me to come with him. I followed, tearing myself free from the music as painfully as a man might tear his own flesh from a deep wound. We left the hall, and when the music had grown faint behind the walls it struck me fully, and I sat down on the floor and wept for sorrow. Lugh stood patiently over me in silence.

When my grief had run its course he dropped to one knee beside me and laid his hand on my shoulder. "You should not have stayed and listened for so long," he said gently. "The songs of the Sidhe are not for men. For you there is too much pain in ecstasy, and the fire burns too fiercely to be endured. Nonetheless, it is good that you have heard Taliesin sing here. Now you know something of the Light. You must remember it, and when the Darkness surrounds you, think upon it. It will aid you, along with that which I will give you now, if you can accept it."

At this I looked up at him, and he nodded and again gestured for me to follow him. We rose.

He led me through some passageways behind the hall, going down, until I judged that we were underneath the feast hall. It was very quiet there, and the passages were dark but for the faint light that seemed to glow in the walls, and the brighter, quicker fire that surrounded Lugh, master of all arts. It was beautiful there, but there was a feeling of great power, like a banked fire. I was not exhausted by the song in the hall, as I would have been on Earth, and so was sensitive to the strength that beat in the place like the heart's blood.

Lugh stopped before a door of a deep gold-colored wood latched with red bronze and rested his hand on the latch. He turned to me.

"You have wondered why you were brought here, Hawk of May," he said. His voice was almost a whisper, but it held the same note as the silent beat of the power burning beyond that door.

"I have, Lord."

"It is well that you thought to wonder. You were not brought simply to see this island and rejoice, though it was necessary that you see light after so much darkness. Nor were you brought to my hall merely that you might escape the demon that pursued you, though that, too, was necessary. But you were brought for this: to take up arms to fight against the Darkness which you above others now can recognize. You are nearly seventeen now, and this is an age to take up arms."

"Lord," I said, "I still lack half a year before I am fifteen."

He shook his head. "While you sat in my hall, winter passed on Earth, and spring and summer, and another year after them. It is now March in Britain. By the time you return, May will have begun."

I felt cold then and looked away. I knew the stories of how a man may go to the lands of the Sidhe for what seems a single night, and find on returning that a hundred years have passed, but I had never considered that it might happen to me. Nearly three years. Well, perhaps it was good. I would have grown, and have more strength of arm. But still . . .

Lugh smiled, very gently. "It will be no longer than that, spring falcon. I give you my word. But, you see, you are past age to take up arms. And if you return to Earth you will need a weapon to protect yourself from the powers of Darkness, which will seek your death. As well as this, you have sworn in your heart to accept the High King of Light for your lord. Do not forget that a warrior must fight for his lord."

I nodded.

"You must have a weapon," said Lugh, "and here I will give you one."

He opened the door, stood holding it, and I walked slowly into the room.

It was a plain room, altogether dark except for where, at the opposite wall, a sword stood with light glowing deeply in the great ruby set into the pommel. Its shadow fell behind it on the wall in a cross shape. I sensed the power that burned in it, great and terrible, and I felt a wave of cold fear sweep onto me.

"Lord," I said to Lugh, who stood behind me in the doorway, "Lord, this is too great for me. This is not a weapon for men. I am honored that you should think of it for me, but I could not bear such a sword."

"But it is a sword for men," Lugh said gently. "True, its power is great enough to destroy many, and the bearing of it often brings the bearer sorrow. But it is a weapon such as only men need; my kind use other weapons."

I knew that he was right, but still I stared at the sword where it slumbered against the wall, awaiting the hand

78

that would draw it in fire. And what fire that would be, what consuming Light.

"If you truly do not wish to accept this sword," said Lugh, "you may refuse it. I tell you, you can still serve the Light if you reject this."

For an instant I wanted to accept this offer. But it was impossible. I could not disobey the Light immediately after it had saved me. If my new lord desired that I draw the sword, I must try to draw it. Surely, I comforted myself, the Light would not wish this unless I was able to do it without being destroyed. And whatever else is true, a warrior must obey his rightful lord. So I shook my head. "I will try to accept this gift." My mouth was dry and my hands damp.

I did not see but sensed Lugh's smile. "Go then, and draw it."

I walked over to it, each step heavy. My death could come here if I had not the strength to lift the sword. . . . I was standing before it, and the light, warm, deep red, spilled over me. I dropped to my knees.

"Light," I said, "My Lord High King, the sea is around me and the sky over me and the earth under me, and if I break faith with you, may the sea rise up and drown me and the sky break and fall on me, and the earth open and swallow me; so be it." The Threefold Oath was, I knew, unnecessary, but it was always sworn when one's lord gave one arms. I took a deep breath, reached out both hands, closed them on the hilt of the sword, and began to draw it.

It was hot, hot as flame, and my hands were burning. The light in the ruby leaped, rose, fierce and red, red as blood, as the blood which beat in my ears and shook my whole body with its pulse. I pulled at the sword, and light slid along the exposed part of the blade, still red. I was aware of my hands only as centers of pain, was certain that they were being burned off; could almost smell the stink of them. . . . I drew the sword farther, and suddenly it was clear of the sheath, and I screamed because the light and fire of it suddenly ran along my very soul, and I was burning in it, and saw myself, all of myself, revealed in the light. All the Darkness I had known lay there, and all the Darkness that was a part of me shrieked at me to drop the sword before it slew me. And it was slaying me, for I was impaled by its light, and it was not a sword for mortals at all . . . but the Light wished me to draw it (oh, Ard Rígh Mor, Great High King!) so I held on, feeling the air rush white hot into my lungs, searing every part of me, heart, mind consumed in a light that was no longer red but burning white as the heart of the sun. My strength failed me, and I retreated back into myself, seeking some power that would hold the sword in that agony. For an instant it seemed that I had none, that I would be annihilated, for it was too late to drop the sword. . . .

And then I felt a sudden power within me rush into my limbs, clear and white hot, the core of my being, which had long before dreamed of this, and which before this I had barely suspected. I lifted the sword high above my head, the point raised to the sky, dimly aware how it now burned pure and brilliant as a star. I cried out in triumph not knowing what I said, for I had conquered, and it was mine.

And then, suddenly, the pain was gone, and I was kneeling before the blank wall and the sword was dimming slowly in my hands.

"It is done." said Lugh, very softly. "I am glad."

I looked at the sword, then at my hands. They were not burned at all. I looked at the sword again. Its light had dimmed to a glimmer along the blade. I turned toward Lugh who stood, still, in the doorway, surrounded by a bright clear light, smiling. "The name of the sword is Caledvwlch, 'Hard One,'" he said. "It had a different name before, but now it is yours, and a new name is given it for a new day."

"It is mine," I said, still bewildered. A wave of great joy flooded me. "My lord gave me arms."

Lugh nodded. "You are the Light's warrior now. Do not forget that, Hawk of May. Now"—Lugh crossed the room and helped me to my feet—"our lord is engaged in a war, and you must use that weapon of yours."

"Where is the battle?" I asked, "and what warband shall I join?"

"The battle will be all about you. And take warning: It

is not always to be fought with the sword, even with a sword like yours."

"I understand, Lord. I have conquered my own Darkness, but cannot destroy it."

He nodded, smiling. "And if you remember that, you will be wise. The Darkness can use your own will, and you can use others when they are themselves ignorant of it. You have walked in the Darkness and chosen Light, and will be hard to deceive. But it will not be impossible. There is much sorrow on Earth, and the Darkness is very strong—" He stopped abruptly, and turned his eyes from the future to the present and me. "For warband, you will be able to recognize those who serve the Light. Arthur you already know of. Go to him, and accept him as your lord on Earth, if he will have you. But you will need to convince him that you have abandoned the Darkness, first: Do not expect that it will be easy. Whatever happens, I am certain that great things will be done on the Earth in these days, for there is a great struggle taking place. What the end will be I do not know and cannot see, except that it will be strange, and different from what is expected. But I think you will fight honorably. Now, come."

I followed him from the room, carrying my sword, and he led me through a maze of passageways out, somehow, onto a kind of platform just below the roof of the feast hall, of the kind men use for trimming the thatch. We stood just beneath the roof of feathers and looked out to the west. The sun was going down, covering all the world with light, and it seemed closer and brighter than on Earth. Lugh pointed westward, and I followed the direction he indicated. I could see the whole of his island, right to the sea which circled it, and beyond that still into the sun itself. Just for a moment, it seemed to me that a light like a new star burned behind the sea, beyond the horizon; and in that instant, I felt that I understood the song in the hall, and to what I had pledged my sword. I fell to my knees and raised the sword before me, whether in homage or in defense I am unsure. Lugh threw his arms up as in acclamation, and the light within him seemed to leap up. Then the sun touched the horizon, covering that other light, and he turned to me again.

"It is time that you go," he said gently. "Perhaps you will return one day, when the Earth has passed, and then you can hear the end of that song. But till then, I fear, we will not meet, nor will you ever again come to my realm. So, kinsman, I give you my blessing." And he rested his hands on my shoulders as I still knelt. "Carry it well in whatever battles are before you." He helped me to my feet, then embraced me, more tenderly than my father ever had. "Go in Light, mo chroidh, my heart, and do not wonder at what happens."

Stepping back, he lifted his hands and spoke a word which the wind caught and repeated about me. The gold and bronze wall of the hall, the setting sun on the feathers of the roof, dissolved into that sound; and the plains and woods and ocean of the Isles of the Blessed faded slowly with the wind. Last of all, Lugh himself, now standing afire with light, faded into a luminous mist, still smiling, and the last echoes of the magic word carried me back softly, ever so softly, to Earth and sleep.

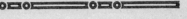

SIX

A HAWK WAS FLYING IN SLOW circles through the air above me. I watched him tilt his wings, balancing on the wind, then drift up sideways into it. I let my mind drift with him, swinging slowly along the blue sky and not really watching the blur of memories that lay below. I felt light, strong, purposeful: That was enough.

Presently, however, it occurred to me to wonder what had happened, and why I had this strange feeling of confidence, and I looked into my memories.

Llyn Gwalch. I had ridden there, with a demon riding after me through the night. I had stayed there for a day, and afterward . . . no, a long blaze of color and light, pain and glory and ecstasy. A song overwhelming everything, and a sorrow too deep for words. And an oath, a commitment. The Isles of the Blessed. Tir Tairngaire, Land of Promise, the Silver Land, the Land of the Living: a crowd of names for it rushed to me. Lugh of the Long Hand—no, it had to be a dream. Indeed, it had the strange enchanted feeling of a dream, in which colors are too bright and time and distance changed, alien and meaningless. Llyn Gwalch, then. I had certainly been there, so presumably I still was, here. Later in the day I would have time to consider the feeling of being changed, but for the moment I had better try to find something to eat.

I sat up, yawning, and looked about me; went rigid.

I was on a hilltop, seated in the low grass and heather

that covered it. To one side the hill swept down, up into another range of hills, then clothed in an incredible shadowing of forest bright green with the spring. On the other side, the hill continued into a range of taller hills. The sky was an unimaginably clear blue, and seemed to rise forever.

"No," I said out loud. "It is impossible." There were no hills this tall in all the Orcades, and no forests. It was not spring, but autumn.

But the earth and sky were indisputably real. I clutched my head, terrified. Where was I? This could not be a dream, but if it were not, then . . . the other couldn't have been a dream either.

"Do not wonder at what happens," Lugh had said before he sent me back to Earth. I remembered the words clearly, and remembered his face as he said them, and the west spread out below the roof of his hall. I remembered the room beneath the hall, and the agony of drawing the sword; the joy and power when I had drawn it. The sword . . . My hand fell to my side.

It was there.

I closed my hand about the hilt, and it seemed to flow into and become a part of me. I lifted it, looked at it. It was real. The whole voyage had been real, and the magic of Light was no less real than the power of Darkness. I had sworn fealty to the Light, and it, he, had given me arms. I held in my hand a weapon not forged on Earth.

I laughed, gripping the hilt with both hands, doubt and terror departing without leaving a trace behind them. I sprang to my feet and lifted Caledvwlch to the sun.

"My Lord, Great King!" I shouted. "I thank you for this, and for delivering me from my enemies, and taking my oath!" As I spoke, the sword blazed again with light, but this time it did not burn me; rather, it seemed to radiate my own joy. I lowered it slowly, looking at it. "And I thank you, too, kinsman, Lord Lugh," I added, "for your hospitality." The light burned a little while longer, then dimmed until it seemed as though I held an ordinary, if very fine, sword in my hands.

I had not really noticed the fashion of it before. It was a two-edged slashing sword such as a man could use from horseback. It was somewhat longer and thinner than most

HAWK OF MAY

such swords, and perfectly balanced. The hilt was very beautiful: the crosspiece far longer than usual, each branch coiled with gold which then intertwined up the grip to the pommel, which was set with a ruby. The blade, as the inner light died from it, caught the sunlight with the true "snake" pattern of well-forged steel. It was sharp, too: I drew the edge along my arm, and it cut every hair without pulling. It would be a fine weapon to use in an ordinary battle, without the addition of unknown powers against the Darkness.

Looking down, I saw that it had a sheath. This was very plain, of simple wood and leather, and fastened to a plain leather baldric. I set the sword down and put this on, then sheathed the sword and adjusted it. It was an easy weight to carry, since I felt lighter with it than without it.

The question now was, which way to walk? I had no idea where I might be. Lugh had said that I should go to Arthur, and Arthur was presumably fighting the Saxons somewhere in Britain, so I was probably in Britain, rather than in Erin or Caledon—or Rome or Constantinople, for that matter. Britain, though, is a large land, and there were few in any of her many kingdoms who would welcome strangers from the Orcades. Well, if Arthur was fighting the Saxons, presumably I had been sent to somewhere near him. That might mean I was near the border of one of the Saxon lands, but, again, it might not. A well-planned raid may strike a region over a hundred miles from the raiders. And most of the British kingdoms bordered Saxon lands on the east. Well then, at least I should not walk east. I checked my directions by the sun.

The chain of hills lay directly to my west. These looked to be hard walking, and I was unused to traveling long distances on foot. I looked for easier country.

I looked again at the sky. The hawk I had seen earlier was still visible, circling slowly southward. That seemed as good a direction as any. I started off.

After three steps I had to stop again. My boots pinched dreadfully. Sitting down to check them, I saw that they were far too small. So, for that matter, was everything else I was wearing. I remembered then that Lugh had said

85

that two and a half years had passed during my single day on the Isle of the Blessed.

I stared at the boots. Everyone must think me dead, would even have forgotten me. It was late spring. I must be fully seventeen.

Almost against my will, I recalled tales that are told of those who visit the Sidhe. Sometimes, returning only to look again at their homeland, such travelers crumble into dust when they touch mortal earth and their age returns to them. Or sometimes they themselves were left unchanged, but the world had known centuries since they left, and they wandered about earthly lands for years, asking for persons long dead and forgotten. I felt sick. Suppose that this had happened to me. Suppose that it was not just two and a half years, but ten, twelve, a hundred years? Suppose I went to the nearest farmstead and asked about Arthur the Pendragon, and the people said "Who?" and looked at me with strange eyes?

No, I told myself firmly. Lugh said two and a half years, and he would not deceive me. This is spring, and two and a half years from the time I left Llyn Gwalch. And if it is not so, then it is because the Light wills it not to be, and the Light is your sworn lord and you must accept and have faith in his judgments.

I unlaced the boots and took them off. I had been warned, after all, I told myself. And the advantages were great. I had grown some before I left Dun Fionn, but now I was fully adult, and could swear service to any lord in Britain—any that would have me, that is. Doubtless I was still a poor fighter.

This thought made me smile, albeit shakily, and I remembered Agravain and Lot and all those who had tried to train me at Dun Fionn, when I had still wanted to be a warrior. It had been hard then, bitterly hard. Now, at least, I knew what my road was and knew that it was good, even if it might be difficult. The ascent from Avernus apparently was not to be made in one step. I remembered suddenly the light I had seen at sunset in the Isles of the Blessed, and struggled to recall what it meant. I could not. But the song in the hall I could remember, still sharp and brilliantly clear. Too clear: The sorrow flooded over me in a great wave, mingled with homesickness, and I crouched a moment, staring at the heather. Best not to think of that for a while.

I tossed the boots aside—I could easily go barefoot on that grass—and started down the hill.

It was a fine day for walking. It was warm, about as warm as it ever becomes in the Orcades (though it is often much hotter in Britain) and I first loosened, then took off my stained cloak. The sky was very clear and blue, and there was only the slightest of breezes to ripple the grasses. Skylarks dropped music from overhead, rabbits jumped off on all sides, and once, as I walked by the edge of the forest, a herd of deer leaped up and ran off before me in great startled bounds. Flowers abounded, in types I had never seen in the Orcades. The woods were a marvel to me, who had seen none before, and the play of sunlight through the leaves seemed too wonderful for words.

After noon, when I was becoming thirsty, I found a stream running from the hills into the forest. The water was sweet and clear. After drinking, I rested by it for a bit, soaking my feet, which were already sore; then set off again, still southward.

As the day wore on, the hills became lower, finally blending into the surrounding countryside. The forest grew thicker, and marvelous as it was, I became uneasy with the trees so tall about me, and began to wish for the open hills of the Orcades and for the sea. My feet were cut and sore, and I was also growing tired and stopping to rest more frequently. I had seen no sign of human habitation all day, and I wondered where in this great land Arthur could be. When it was growing late in the afternoon, however, I found a road.

It astounded me. Never had I seen such a thing. It was paved with great stones, slightly arched in the middle, and the forest had been cleared for some distance about it—although loose scrub had grown since that clearing. It was a road wide enough for the largest cart and firm enough to withstand the fiercest rains and coldest winters. I had heard of the Roman roads, but had always thought their virtues exaggerated. Well, I now knew them to be real.

This road ran east-west, straight as a spear shaft. I

walked cautiously from the forest onto it, then began walking west. It was easy walking after the forest, and I made good time.

When twilight was only an hour or so away I saw people coming down the road toward me. The setting sun was behind them, and I could not see them clearly. Nonetheless, I ran forward eagerly to meet them. They were the first humans I had seen since awakening—in fact, the first in two and a half years—and I felt the need of company after the strange forest and stranger things preceding it. Besides that, men meant houses, fire, food. And even more than the hunger, I felt a peculiar turning of my mind toward other men, an eagerness for them, almost as though all humanity was my clan, and I wanted their shared warmth against the vastness and awe of the powers of Light and Darkness. It is a strange feeling, but whenever I have been nearest the Light, and thus, farthest from common humanity, I feel so.

The party emerged as eleven men leading three pack-laden horses and driving a cow. The men were warriors. The sun glinted off the tips of their spears, limned the oval shields slung over their shoulders, and shone warmly on their steel-topped helmets. I stopped, frowning. The warriors of the Orcades do not wear helmets, and none of the British warriors who had been attracted to my father's warband had done so either. Most warriors consider it cowardly to wear one, and, besides, unless it is very well made a helmet merely blocks one's vision without providing much protection.

As I stood, stupidly staring and thinking this, one of the warriors hailed me, shouting in a language I did not know. Then I realized that I should have fled. I knew Irish, British, Latin, and some Pictish, all but one of the languages spoken in Britain. The one I did not know was the Saxon tongue—and Saxons also wore helmets. But I had hesitated too long, and now it was too late to flee. The warriors were almost upon me. I would have to try to bluff, and hope that the Saxon reputation for unthinking violence was mistaken, and that their reputation for lack of imagination and stupidity was correct.

The Saxon who had called before repeated his greeting.

I nodded in what I hoped was a half-witted fashion and stood aside to let them pass.

They were all tall men, I saw now, and most had the oddly pale fair hair that is also a part of the Saxons' reputation, though three were dark. They were well armed with swords, throwing and thrusting spears, and the long knives, the *seaxes*, which give them their name. The horses were laden with food: three pigs, grain, and some plain sacks containing either fruit or vegetables. The party walked toward me, more slowly now, and the leader suddenly stopped and frowned. He said something ending on a questioning note, I shook my head.

He took another step toward me, hesitated again, staring intently. He made a gesture with his left hand. One of his comrades made some comment in their odd guttural language, and the leader shook his head dubiously and asked another question. There was a strange note in his voice, of uncertainty, almost of fear, and his comrades had dropped the points of their spears. I shook my head again.

The leader glanced back at his friends, then spoke British. He had an accent, but I understood him well enough. "Ich said, greatinges to you, whoever you may be." He hesitated again, watching me, the whites of his eyes showing oddly, then continued belligerently, "Who are you, ant why do you treavell this road, so close to nightfalle?"

"I . . . am traveling because I must," I said. "Come nightfall, I will stop."

One of the other Saxons stepped forward angrily, leveling his spear. "Theat is no answer, Briton! What do you in the domain of the West Seaxons? If you be a thrall, where is your master? If you be no thrall, what do you?"

"Eduin!" said the leader in an alarmed tone; and in the abrupt and tense silence that followed he studied me again, as though he did not like what he saw. I stood quietly, thinking hard.

The second Saxon, Eduin, argued something quickly with the leader, gesturing eastward. The leader looked uncertain, chewing his moustache, then became angry, and turned back from his companion to me. "Where is your master, Briton?" he demanded.

They thought I was a thrall, then, and they had called this the domain of the West Saxons. I struggled to remember what I knew of the Saxon kingdoms. It was so easy to say "the Saxons" and think of one nation covering all the east of Britain, and ignore the real divisions between them, the different tribes of Saxons, Angles, Jutes, Franks . . . but the West Saxons had attracted attention enough to register on any memory. Cerdic was the king of the West Saxons, and had claimed one of the old Roman provinces, the eastern half of Dumnonia. In such an area, newly conquered or perhaps actively resisting the invaders, any Briton would be either a thrall or an enemy. It was safer to be a thrall, especially when the odds were eleven to one, and that one a poor fighter.

"Weall, answer me, Briton!" said the Saxon leader. Again there was a tone in his voice that I could not understand, a note almost of desperation.

"I . . ." What could I say? "I have none."

The leader too leveled his spear, the point only a foot from me. "You are not a thrall, then?" he asked, in a very low voice. "What, then? Do you fight? I fear no . . ." and he added a word in Saxon. The other warriors drew closer, spears lowered, one or two slinging the shields from their backs, though they plainly did not understand their leader's British.

I realized that my hand had dropped toward Caledvwlch's hilt, and, astonished at myself, stopped it, tried to relax and look cowed and bewildered. I could not fight them with the sword. I would have to see if I had inherited any of my father's famed cunning.

"But I am a thrall, Noble Lord!" I said, forcing a note of terror into my voice. It was not difficult to do. "I—Arglwydd Mawr, Great Lord, my master's dead, and I don't know . . ."

At my first words the Saxon had relaxed with a shudder. Now he spoke with an arrogant and aggressive self-assurance. "You try to flee to your British high kyning, no? Just because Arthur the Bastard is within a hundred miles you run from your master and try to join him."

"No, My Lord!" I cried. "I only . . . I am running, yes. My master is dead, I told you! And my elder brother with him. I fear, My Lord, that they will kill me, too. I need your protection. If I were running to the high king, would I have hailed you, My Lord?"

"He would have hid himself, when that we came," Eduin said to the other. "He is a thrall brat, Wulf, liken to any."

Wulf frowned, though. "How did your master die? Who are 'they'? Aenswer me quickly."

"There was a duel, My Lord," I replied at once, remembering the stories told by one of my father's spies. "My master killed a man, about a month back; and the man's kin accepted the blood price, because of the war, and because the king wished it. But still in their hearts they were angry, and when we were going across the hills to take possession of some lands the king had given him, they sprang on him from an ambush and killed him, and all with him. My brother, another of his thralls, was there, and him they killed as well. I hid beneath a bush until they were gone, and then I ran. I am afraid, My Lord, for I know they will kill me too, to stop me from saying that they broke their oaths concerning the blood price."

Wulf nodded. My story was apparently plausible. "What was your master's name, then? Ant who are these oath breakers?"

I dropped my eyes and fidgeted. "My Lord," I whispered, "I dare not tell you. I am only a thrall. They would kill me."

He studied me for another moment, then noticed the hilt of my sword for the first time—I had put my cloak back on with the evening cool. He frowned at it unhappily.

"What is that sword? Your master's?"

"Yes."

He hesitated, began to ask for it, then stopped, shook his head. I looked at my feet.

"Ant you think we can protect you?" Eduin asked sardonically.

I fidgeted more, praying desperately to the Light that they would ask no more about Caledvwlch.

Eduin laughed harshly. "It haeppens we have no need for British brats underfoot, unless they are useful. What can you do?"

I allowed myself to relax a little. Be careful, I warned myself. Fortunately, with my bare feet and outgrown clothing I must look like a thrall, and biddable slaves were rare enough to be potentially valuable. If I made myself appear valuable enough they would let me live, either to keep themselves or to sell, but if I made myself appear too valuable it would be the more difficult to escape, and I might draw questions I could not answer. But if I appeared worthless they would probably kill me out of hand. Light, I thought briefly, why did you let me come here?—well, do not wonder at what happens.

"D-do, My Lord? I'm good with horses. I cared for my master's stable. And I can play the harp a little, and serve a table."

Wulf chewed his lip, said something to Eduin. He still looked anxious. Eduin replied sharply, and Wulf seemed to argue with him. Eduin shrugged and said something that angered Wulf, who turned back to me.

"Very weall, Briton, we keep you. If you try to run away, you will be whipped. Care for our heorses, and later we will sell you to someone who will use you properly, if we cannot find your master's kinsmen."

"Thank you, My Lord." I bowed to him, thinking, Later? When? When they reached the army from which they must have set out as a raiding party? They had mentioned that the Pendragon was near. It would seem that I was in the midst of the war. I wondered what had happened to Britain while I was in the Land of Promise.

Wulf explained me to his followers, and the Saxons gave me their horses' leads and commenced walking east without further comment. As I watched them, I became the more certain that they were a foraging party sent to fetch supplies. I cursed my bad luck in finding them. Had I encountered a lone warrior or farmer first I would have had some warning of my location, and could have abandoned the road (assuming that I survived such an encounter) and continued west safely. As it was, I was trapped and in danger. The Saxons would certainly not allow me to keep the sword. I could not understand why they had not asked for it already. And I did not like to think what would happen when they tried to draw it; it would give me away altogether. Moreover, I would have to come up with a name for my imaginary master—if I did not immediately give myself away by some piece of ignorance any thrall would have been free of.

Well, I consoled myself, there must be some way out. Surely the Light would not throw my life away and let my sword fall into the enemies' hands so soon after saving me and giving me arms. The Light had delivered me from Morgawse; surely it could save me from the Saxons. But I was afraid. The Light had saved me from the Darkness, yes, but that was magic working against sorcery, and the Saxons were physical power, flesh, blood, and steel. It had happened so quickly that I had had no time to feel anything. But now I wanted to drop the Saxon horses' leads and run. It was as though I had stepped from Morgawse's world into Lot's, where Morgawse could work only indirectly. And the Light?

The Light is high king, I told myself. He has brought you here; he can bring you out.

But the doubt persisted, and the fear. The Saxons had an evil reputation.

At least, I told myself, the High King Arthur is somewhere nearby, making war against these Saxons. Arthur, Arthur, Pendragon of Britain. Arthur who fights the Darkness. When Lugh had told me that, I had not questioned him, but now I began to wonder. Arthur, as far as I knew, fought the Saxons. He had done so, and seemed to be doing it still. But the Saxons could not be the same as the Darkness. I could sense no deep evil in the warriors I walked beside, and, had it been there, I would have known. They acted much like any warriors. They could be atypical, but I doubted it. The Saxons had a reputation for being violent, brutal, slave drivers and maltreaters of women; for being also dull, gullible, naive, and stupid. There were many jokes about these supposed latter qualities of theirs—though, watching Eduin's cool wariness, I began to think that this part, at least, of the Saxon reputation might be mistaken. But as to the rest, all warriors are violent and most are brutal, if need be, and all nations are, at times, cruel to slaves and women. Deliberate evil was never ascribed to the Saxons. They seemed, indeed, less given over to torturing, poisoning, and black magic than the Romanized Britons, and were certainly better at keeping their oaths to one another. If the Saxons kept more slaves, it was because British and Irish clan holdings couldn't afford or didn't need to keep as many slaves as the Saxon villages could; and the British and Irish women weren't abused as greatly simply because they wouldn't permit it, as the Saxon women apparently did. I could not see that the Saxons were uniquely servants of Darkness. Yet Arthur gave all his strength to the war against the Saxons. If he indeed served the Light, there must be some reason for that.

I remembered, suddenly, how my mother had used my father, and was chilled by it. If some force were using the Saxons that way, and if that force recognized me for what I was when I reached the Saxon camp, this journey could easily mean my death.

Of course, to attempt to escape meant death, and whatever way I came to the Saxon camp would be hazardous. And even if I could survive, and escape from the Saxons, what use would I be to Arthur? He needed warriors, not ... whatever I was.

Lugh had said, "Do not wonder at what happens." Again I fixed upon that. The Light had heard me and delivered me when I spoke to it without words at Llyn Gwalch. It, he, had fashioned the fire of Caledvwlch and given it to me. He had brought me to the kingdom of the West Saxons from a world beyond the Earth. He was unimaginably powerful, and I could not assume that he was ignorant. There had to be some reason for this. I had only to wait, to watch and be strong.

I sighed and turned my attention to leading the horses.

The Saxons did not stop at sunset, but kept on walking stolidly. My feet had gone numb by that time, which was fortunate, for they were blistered and bleeding. My legs ached and felt like stone after the unaccustomed walking. I was ravenously hungry and very thirsty, but I said nothing and struggled to keep up, and the Saxons did not offer to help or wait. I judged that they would not burden themselves with a slave who was useless, so I steeled myself go as not to fall behind and perhaps be disposed of. The camp must needs be close if the Saxons continued walking by night without even stopping for a meal. We should not have to go much farther.

The stars were out when we reached the camp. It was a large one, for the whole of the army of the West Saxons, and built accordingly. The site was plainly an old hill fort, but had been fortified by the Romans as a military base and a town. The Saxons had moved into some of the old Roman buildings, and added some new Saxon houses of their own, and the wide area of cleared fields about the town had been newly sown with seed. I was impressed by the place, even through my exhaustion. I had never seen a village before, much less an almost-Roman town. The hill was steep, and the bank and ditch about it were clean cut—the fort was obviously a good one—and nearly all the space enclosed by those banks was filled by the houses of the townsmen, or the tents of the summoned warbands and armies. As it was early summer, and the planting was over, the farming men had been summoned to join the warbands—the fyrd, the Saxons call it—and the numbers were very great. But all the camp was orderly and closely guarded. Sentries were posted on the walls, and one of these stopped us before allowing us to enter the fortress, checking carefully that no spy should enter.

My band of Saxons went directly to one area of camp, where they unloaded their supplies. Others crowded around them, asking questions and congratulating and backslapping in a manner that made it plain that they were the kinsmen of the foraging party. Wulf answered the questions, waved toward me, and I caught the word "thrall." Eduin made what sounded like a joke, and laughed. The Saxons glanced at me casually, then gave me a second look, and stared at Caledvwlch. There was another moment of uncomfortable silence before they shrugged and went back to their fire, over which a sheep was roasting. It was nearly done, and filled the air with a scent which made my mouth water. I drifted toward the fire myself, but Wulf stopped me.

"First, caêre for the heorses," he ordered. "They are theare, tied up. Caere for them all, not just these new ones."

I nodded, though I wanted to either strike him or weep. Only the knowledge that disobedience would mean a beating at the least restrained me. "Yes, My Lord. Where is the food?"

Wulf pointed to a pile of hay of rather poor quality and went over to the fire.

I tended the horses. There were eighteen of them, all in bad condition, and it took me quite a while to finish with them. The poor creatures had obviously had no grain and much hard work for months, and that without the most ordinary care. By the time I was done with them, the sheep had been devoured to the bones and the Saxons were sitting about, drinking mead and boasting. (I knew they were boasting by the tone of their voices. Irish, British, Saxon, or Breton, all men boast alike. They even tell the same stories.) I crept up to the fire very quietly and managed to gain one of the sheep bones and a cup of water without being noticed. I was retreating to eat when Wulf noticed me again.

"Here!" he called. "Are you finished with the heorses?"

"Yes, My Lord."

"Heorses is sick," said one of the other Saxons, his accent so heavy I could barely understand him.

"Not sick, My Lord," I replied, trying to sound respectful. "But they need proper care, or they will become very sick. And they need shoeing."

"Whu-hut?"

Wulf translated for me. The others nodded wisely, commented on horses and drank some more mead, curiosity satisfied. I guessed that they knew very little about horses, and felt a bit less afraid. I had wondered whether they treated their thralls the same way.

I gnawed my sheep bone, trying to think of a way to slip off into the night while the Saxons drank. The thing seemed impossible. The camp was too well ordered and well guarded, and the sentries would certainly be alert to British thralls trying to leave the camp by night. Besides that, I knew I could not go far before collapsing. Perhaps tomorrow, I thought. They will have to give me some shoes, and when I am rested . . .

"You! Briton!"

I looked up; the voice was Eduin's. "My Lord?"

"You can play the harp?"

"I have said so, My Lord."

"Then take the harp over there by the supplies ant play somethinge."

On the her hand, perhaps they did treat their thralls as they treated their horses. I set the sheep bone down, hobbled over to the harp. The Saxons, pleased to have someone to play for them, leaned back expectantly.

"What kind of song do you wish, My Lord?" I asked Wulf.

"A battle song. A good one."

I let my fingers wander slowly over the harp strings, tuning a couple of them and considering. A British battle song, full of the deaths of Saxons, would hardly please them. I did not wish to arouse their suspicions by singing in Irish and showing myself to be from so distant a place as the Orcades. I settled for a song from Less Britain about a sword dance (Fire! Steel and fire! Oak tree, night; earth and stone and firelight . . .). They liked it, beating time with their palms against their thighs, eyes gleaming out of the darkness. When I finished they actually gave me a hornful of mead.

"Play an othaer," said the one with the strong accent.

"Of what kind, My Lord?" I asked, savoring the mead.

"A lament for the fallen, harper," commanded a voice from the dark behind me, in clear and accentless British. The Saxons leapt up as one.

"Se Cyning!" exclaimed Eduin. I had heard that title before, affixed to the names of all the important Saxons in Britain. It means "king."

"Cerdic!" said Wulf, and added some formal greeting.

The king of the West Saxons returned it, coming forward into the firelight. Another stood behind him, still only a shadow.

Cerdic was not a tall man, and did not even look like a Saxon. He was slight and wiry, with fox-red hair and green eyes. His beard had a tendency to straggle, and he was not remarkably good-looking. But he wore his power with the same casual ease with which he wore his cloak, tossed back over one shoulder and showing the purple as if by accident. He smiled at my Saxons and waved his hand, bidding them to be seated again, then sat himself,

managing somehow to be familiar and lordly at once. I
could well believe that he was a great leader. But as the
firelight caught his eyes, I saw with one of those sudden
brief moments of clarity that there was Darkness in him
as well, and a ravening hunger that made all his powers,
his talents, and his followers alike no more than spears
cast at his goal. And from the one who stood behind him
I sensed Darkness like a black fire, burning the very
shadows about him. This other stepped forward after
Cerdic, and brushed off the ground before folding himself
down onto it. He was very tall, with the pale blond hair
and pale blue eyes one thinks of as natural to the Saxons,
and he was very good-looking. He was in his mid-thirties,
and dressed like a great nobleman. He felt my eyes on
him and glanced in my direction; for an instant our eyes
met, and his gaze sharpened suddenly and tore at me, demanding something. I looked away.

Wulf gave the two newcomers some mead, speaking
respectfully as he offered it. Cerdic sipped his and raised
his eyebrows.

"Fine mead, Wulf Aedmundson," he said, still in
British. "From your new holding? I told you the Downs
were good country for honey. Have you tried growing
grapes there yet?—Well, Briton, play as you were bid."

"Yes, My Lord," I whispered, not looking at him. "A
lament for the fallen."

His eyes had merely passed over me before; when I
spoke he saw me. He glanced at his companion. The
other's mouth tightened, and he drummed his fingers on
his knees. Cerdic frowned.

I swept the strings with my hand, played a complicated
prelude without really thinking. They were important,
these two. Cerdic, Cyning thara West Seaxa, as his own
people would put it, and the other . . . who? He was
strong in Darkness, Cerdic, I thought, does not compre-
hend the Darkness, but, from ambition, wishes to use it;
but this other one is like Morgawse.

A lament for the fallen. There are plenty of laments,
more than there are battle songs. Laments for those fallen
by the hands of the Saxons, men such as I sat among. I
sang a famous lament, a slow, fierce, proud thing that was

made when the province of southeast Britain was overwhelmed by the Saxons, an old song which called the province by its still older name, the land of the tribe of the Cantii.

> *Though they made the Saxon hosts to sleep*
> *By the sea's white cliffs, and made women weep;*
> *The fullness of glory was not complete,*
> *The host rides to Yffern in defeat*
> *And in their fields the eagles feast.*
> *Bitter the harvest now to reap:*
> *They fought the Saxons, fought and fell,*
> *We shall gather corpses, make tears our well,*
> *And the host of Cantii will not return . . .*

Cerdic listened intently. When I struck the final note, he nodded. "A very fine song. And very well sung. You have had more than a little training in harping."

"Thank you, Great King," I said in a flattered tone. I could not give him reason to suspect that I was anything more than a common thrall. I drew my cloak closer about my shoulders, as though I found the night cold, and hoped that it would cover my sword.

"Play another," ordered Cerdic, and I complied.

The king began to talk with Wulf, drinking his mead and paying no more attention to me. But his companion, the other nobleman, watched me still, lids half drawn over those pale but oddly dark eyes.

I played on, realizing that I was better than I had been at any time before. Perhaps it was from hearing the song in Lugh's hall, perhaps it was simply freedom from the Darkness, but I could tell that I was making the music live upon the strings and in the heart, a thing many professional bards cannot do. I became uneasy, and wished that I had had the sense to play badly at the beginning of the evening.

Cerdic eventually finished whatever business he had come to speak with Wulf about, and rose to leave. I began to relax again.

But when the companion rose, he nodded to me. "You play well, Briton," he said. His voice was cool, and he spoke slowly, drawing out his words in a mocking tone. "Well enough to make yourself valuable. But not so valuable that you should be allowed to bear a sword, which is against all law and custom. Give it here."

I stared at him for a long moment, horrified, though I should have expected it. Close on the horror followed an unexpected rage, anger at this arrogant Saxon sorcerer treating me as a piece of merchandise, at his demanding my dearest possession; anger at the casual callousness of the other Saxons; and most of all, anger at myself for accepting slavery and abuse instead of laying down my life for my honor as I should have done. I raised my eyes and met the sorcerer's gaze directly, my hand dropping to Caledvwlch. "I cannot give you the sword."

"You defy me?" he asked, still drawling and amused. "A slave defying the king of Bernicia?"

So that was who he was, had to be: Aldwulf of Bernicia, reputed the cruelest of the Saxon kings. I stopped, struggling to control myself. His eyes were again questioning, demanding something. His lips moved, and I recognized the unspoken words, and my grip tightened on the sword as I recalled how Morgawse had taught them to me.

"I am sorry, Great Lord," I said, my voice sounding, even to myself, too soft, "the sword is my master's. I cannot give it to any other"—I tried desperately to force myself back into the role I had chosen, reminding myself that I was no warrior—"to no one but my master, or his heir."

But the Saxon smiled as though he were satisfied at something. I saw that I had made some mistake, that now he knew what he had been demanding of me, and I felt cold.

"So, you are loyal, too," Aldwulf said, still smiling. "Keep the sword, then, for your master's heir." He glanced over to Cerdic and said something in Saxon. Cerdic directed a sharp question to him, and I caught the words, "ne thrall," at which some of the other Saxons grunted. Aldwulf replied languidly and shrugged. Cerdic looked thoughtful, turned to Wulf, and asked him some question, to which Wulf replied at some length. When he had finished, Cerdic turned to me.

"Wulf has said that you can take care of horses as well as harp, and that your master, by your report, died today in some blood feud about which you fear to give information. I am considering whether to buy you, Briton. What is your name?"

I stared at my hands on the harp, feeling sick. If the king bought me, how could I escape? And, since Aldwulf was clearly the driving force in this inclination to buy me, what would happen to me if I did not escape?

"Gwalchmai." I answered Cerdic's question with the truth.

"A warrior's name, not a thrall's."

"I was born a free man, Chieftain. My master did not care to change my name, seeing that I was used to it."

"And you are loyal to this murdered master, but not so loyal as to give information about the feud. How long have you been a thrall?"

"Three years, Chieftain." A good enough length of time.

He looked me up and down carefully, and I cursed my stupidity in singing so well and acting like a free man instead of a thrall. Be no one, I told myself. Make them doubt that you are anything. Here in the seat of his power this man can destroy you with a word.

"He sings well," Cerdic said to Wulf. "I will buy him from you, if the price is appropriate."

Aldwulf smiled again, looking at me steadily while Cerdic bargained with Wulf and Eduin. After only a little of the bargaining, Cerdic stripped two heavy gold armlets from his right arm, then added a third. A good price. Most slaves, in these days when men were cheap, brought scarcely more than half of that. Cerdic would not pay it because he liked my singing—but that was obvious.

"Well, boy, now I am your master," Cerdic told me. "Come."

"Yes, Lord. Did you buy the harp as well?"

"Thaet I give you, dryhten, Lord," said Wulf. "A token of honor from my clan for their cyning." He sounded sincere. I wondered what he and Cerdic had said to each other.

Cerdic nodded thanks and set off. I stumbled after him,

my feet doubly sore after the short rest, carrying the harp.

The king stopped at one or two other camps and a house within the fortress, I guessed to discuss with the leaders of influential clans. He required me to sing something to amuse the various warriors, perhaps to show off his new purchase. But Aldwulf abandoned us at the first stop, and I felt much better for his absence.

It was after midnight when the Saxon king finally decided that it was time to rest. We went to a fine Roman government building at the center of the fortress. I was staggering with exhaustion by then, and didn't even pause to notice the mosaics or the pond in the atrium. Cerdic turned me over to his servants with a brief word of explanation in the courtyard, then went off to his own apartments to sleep.

I stood, facing Cerdic's thralls. They looked back with a stranger blend of suspicion and fear—the same look that Wulf had given me when I met his party on the road. I was too tired to puzzle at it, though, and said only, "I am Gwalchmai. Your master has, I imagine, just told you that he bought me tonight because I harp well and can tend horses. I have been walking or working all day and I am tired. Where can I sleep?"

The thralls hesitated, still unsure of me, then finally showed me through the house to the servants' quarters by the stables, and there I collapsed and fell instantly asleep.

I woke again in less than three hours. I lay still for a little while, dizzy with weariness and stiff, wondering why I had woken. Some dream slid through my mind like a silver fish and vanished. I sighed and sat up, reaching for Caledvwlch.

As my head closed about the sword hilt, the ruby began to glow. I sat, staring at it.

"Is there something more I must do tonight, Lord?" I asked, aloud.

There was only silence, and the warm glow which answered a deep, almost buried fire within me.

I stood, adjusted the baldric I had forgotten to take off, and walked from the room.

The black bulk of the house loomed above the stable against the starlit sky. The town was dark, except for the distant watchfires at the walls. I shivered in the night air, though, despite the spring coolness, it was not really cold. No, there was a sensation I recognized in the air, a sensation that radiated from the house. I turned back into the house, found my way to the atrium, then, after hesitating, made my way into the mosaiced living quarters of the nobles. All the thralls slept.

It was dark in the house, a deep silence and a black heat, different from but still similar to Morgawse's icy cold. It was difficult to breathe. I stood for a minute, allowing my eyes to adjust, then, with my hand on the hilt of my sword and a prayer to the Light in my mind, I walked forward to the closed door at the end of the corridor, and opened it a bare inch to look beyond it.

The first thing I saw was a shadow that swung backward and forward against the wall, and only after that did I see the body that cast it. The man was dead by then, head wrenched grotesquely sideways by the rope he had been hanged from. He looked to be British, but in that light one could not really tell. I recognized the pattern that was drawn on the floor beneath him, drawn in his blood, and the pattern around the single thick candle near the door. Aldwulf of Bernicia knelt before the first pattern, casting a handful of rune-sticks upon it and reading off the words they formed. Cerdic, who stood to one side, his eyes bright from the hunger in them, gave no sign of understanding what the runes meant. I, may the Light protect me, understood.

A shadow seemed to gather about the hanged man's head, and the body swung back and forth more rapidly, sending the shadows spinning across the wall. Aldwulf cast the runes. He had summoned no great power, I saw, but merely a messenger. "A bargain," Aldwulf said aloud, speaking in the language of the runes as he cast them—the ancient, cold language of sorcery. His voice was no longer drawling and soft, but harsh and deadly. He arranged the sticks for his own message. "Give a message. To your master. I wish a bargain."

The body swung more slowly. Aldwulf cast the runes, read the reply silently, scarcely moving his lips, then arranged the sticks again. "Death," he read out, "for . . .

Arthur, the high king. For his death, death. An offering. Acceptable."

The body ceased to swing, but the shadow remained crouched upon it. Again Aldwulf cast the runes, this time reading the reply aloud. "Not acceptable. Mortal life little. Impossible. Release." Just below the threshold of hearing a faint keening began, thin as a knife blade, venomous, terrible to hear. Aldwulf placed his hand over the runes and spoke aloud, still in the old language; "It is no ordinary mortal life. We hold one who must be of the race of the Sidhe, at least in part, a servant of the Light, whose name is Gwalchmai. He carries a sword that is powerful for Light, of use to you."

I closed my eyes, leaning against the door frame, sickness on me like a great cold hand.

The keening stopped. The body began to swing again, this time in a circle which grew more and more violent. Aldwulf cast the runes. "Possible," he read, "With sword, possible. Kill . . . offering first. . . ."

"No" he added, covering the runes and looking up again. "First kill the Pendragon, and you will have your offering."

The keening began again, and the body jerked on the rope, as though it were trying to come to life again. Aldwulf tossed down the rune sticks. "Impossible. Need sword. For sword, need killing. Kill."

"Very well," said Aldwulf. "But tell your master that, if he does not kill the High King Arthur after I have given him his offering and the sword, I, the Flamebearer, will seek out as many of his kind as I may and destroy them until he will regret that he cheated me; and I will destroy you first. Do you doubt me, demon?"

The runes themselves jerked into a new pattern. "The bargain . . . will be fulfilled."

"In two weeks, then," said Aldwulf, and rising abruptly, snuffed out the candle. At once the shadow vanished. The body swung slowly to a halt. Aldwulf walked over to one wall, out of my sight, and I heard him striking a flint. Presently a torch flared up, and Aldwulf walked across the room with it to light another torch on the other wall. He surveyed the body and the pattern on the floor, then looked up at Cerdic and smiled.

"You see, King of the West Saxons?" he asked, his voice again pleasant and drawling.

"Your power is real, Aldwulf," replied Cerdic, "but you had proved that to me already. You have arranged with Woden for Arthur to die?"

"Arthur will die when we have made the offering."

"Woden seems to have a great taste for dead men," Cerdic commented, eyeing the corpse.

Aldwulf shrugged, scuffing out the pattern with his foot. "If you think the price too great, say so. But this time it is not just any death, my friend, that Woden desires, but that young fool who is not quite human and is asleep in your stables. They want his sword, and he must be dead, I think, to get it away from him. We were very lucky in finding him."

Cerdic grunted. "So you say. When Arthur is dead, then I will believe."

"What? All that I have done, and still you disbelieve me? What of the flood? What of the horse I gave you? And speaking of that horse . . ."

"He is not yet broken," Cerdic said harshly. "Very well, I believe in your powers well enough. I admitted as much. But it is said that Arthur has some Christian or druidical magics to protect him. When he is dead, and only when he is dead, will I believe that your god is stronger."

"He is strong," said Aldwulf confidently. "He is very strong."

Yes, the Darkness is very strong, I thought as I walked back to my place by the stables. Oh, Light, protect me. I am afraid.

Not, I thought, as I lay down in the stable again, that Aldwulf's demon was likely to succeed in killing Arthur where Morgawse had failed. I did not see how they could use the sword for that. Aldwulf might be powerful, but was still weaker than the queen of Darkness. Aldwulf was still mortal, and Morgawse was not.

But knowing that Aldwulf's bargain would not be fulfilled would do me little good if Cerdic and Aldwulf offered me to their demon.

I held my lower lip with my teeth, stifling a desire to jump up and run screaming away from the place. Offer me. Put the rope around my neck and set my body swinging back and forth by the candlelight, possessed by demons. I could almost feel the cord around my neck, see the terrible darkness. Sacrifice me. Why? Because I served the Light, owned a sword and . . .

And was not fully human.

So Aldwulf thought. And suddenly I realized what the expression on Wulf's face and on the faces of his kinsmen had been, the same look with which Cerdic's servants had greeted me. It was the great fear, the fear of the unknown thing from the dark, the unnatural, the supernatural.

I sat up in the darkness, clutching Caledvwlch's hilt.

"I am human," I said out loud. My blood beat in my ears, I was sick with weariness and fear, my legs ached, my feet were sore and blistered, and my clothes itched and were too tight. I was human, I thought, clinging to these things. How could they believe differently?

But they did. They all had, at the first meeting at least. I looked at the ruby in Caledvwlch's hilt, dark in the night as my own fear.

Who am I? I asked myself desperately, Gwalchmai. Gwalchmai ap Lot, a warrior of the Light, yes. But human! What has happened to me?

My King, I said in my heart, My King, I am afraid. The Darkness is very strong, and I who am to fight it do not even know who I am, and fear even myself. How can I escape? Even if I can match Aldwulf, Cerdic has an army, hundreds of warriors, thousands of soldiers, ranks of steel and set minds all afraid of the supernatural: solid, worldly power, unarguable blood and iron. And they do not think that I am human, and my mother is queen of Darkness and desires my death.

My mother. I thought of her again, and of all that she had taught me. How deeply had it marked me? Deeply enough for Aldwulf to suspect me, deeply enough to unnerve anyone who so much as looked at me. Or perhaps that one day or three years in the Islands of the Blessed had changed me without my noticing it into something completely different, something unalterably alien from my fellow men.

And what land is this? I asked myself. Far, far from

home. Far from my kinsmen and my clan, people who knew me and laughed at me and would protect me, and who must all of them think me dead. And I would be better dead than alone as a thrall in a strange kingdom, fated to be hanged as a sacrifice to an alien god, as Connall almost was. . . .

Connall of Dalriada, my knife bringing him a quick death. Morgawse's demon, and the escape. Lugh's hall, the song in it, the fire of Caledvwlch, and the light behind the sunset . . .

I cried, shaking silently in the dark stable. I am sorry, My Lord High King, for doubting you. You would not abandon your warriors to die, and I have no right to flee from the battle after you rescued me once.

The light rose slowly into Caledvwlch, glowed, burned, blazed. I held the crosspieces, leaning my forehead against the pommel and feeling the light move within me, rising upward like a flood of music. Have faith. Do not wonder at what happens.

SEVEN

IT WAS LATE WHEN I awoke the next day, past mid-morning. Cerdic's thralls were pleased when I finally woke, for I was in their way, but strangely had been unwilling to wake me. When I was up, though, I was told to go to the well to wash, and, after I had done so, the chief thrall brought me some clothes. They were worn, but clean, and they fitted well, as did the new pair of boots and the cloak. I felt slightly more human when I had put these on, and I slung Caledvwlch over my shoulder.

At this, the chief thrall frowned. "What are you doing with that?" he sked. "You've no right to bear weapons. You must know that."

I shrugged. "No one's taken it from me yet, and until they do, I'll keep it."

He shook his head. "You can be beaten for that, even killed. Are you new to thralldom?"

I nodded.

"Well then, take my word for it, you had better not keep that sword. Give it to the master."

"I think that I will keep it, nonetheless," I said quietly. "It means something to me."

The old man looked distressed, then shrugged. "Well, it is your back risking the whip, not mine. Would you like something to eat?"

"Very much."

He gave me oatcakes with honey and milk, which I devoured in a very short time. The thrall grinned at me.

"You've had little to eat recently, haven't you? Those warriors the master bought you from must have traveled a fair ways. Tell me"—a glint came into his eyes—"were you with the Pendragon? How goes the war?"

With the coming of daylight and my appetite, he seemed to have forgotten whatever he had felt about me the night before. I smiled, but regretfully shook my head in answer to his question. "I don't know. I have come from over the sea. I hoped that you could tell me."

He shook his head. "They tell us nothing. We have ways of knowing: We hear from farmers, or overhear—but we're never sure whether what we hear is true or only a rumor. Sometimes we never do know." He stood and began clearing the dishes. "My name is Llemyndd ap Llwch, from what used to be eastern Ebrauc. I am the chief thrall here, the steward of Cerdic's house. It was my father who was captured from Ebrauc: I was born Cerdic's thrall. And you? You said that your name is Gwalchmai, but what of your kinsmen and country?"

I was about to answer truthfully, when I felt a sudden uncertainty. This Llemyndd might be other than he seemed. "How strange," I said. "My father's name is Llwch, too"—which it was, if one put it into British—"but I am from Gododdin." I was willing to wager that there would be no thralls from such a distant kingdom in Cerdic's house who could give me the lie, and I had heard something of that country in Dun Fionn.

Llemyndd whistled. "That is a long way distant."

I nodded. "I came south with my elder brother three years ago, by sea. We went to Gaul to buy some of those Gaulish war-horses for breeding. My clan deals in horses, and, as you must know, the Gaulish breed is the best. All the warriors were wanting horses like those the Pendragon has, and my clan thought that there should be a fine profit in it. And there would have been, too, if our ship had not been found by a Saxon longship off the coast of East Anglia."

"Anglia? That's a long way north. How did you come down here among the Franks and Saxons?"

"Ach, we were not bested by that pirate," I improvised

quickly. "Mine is a noble clan, and we fought back. But our ship was badly damaged, and we decided to go about to Dumnonia, down the Saxon shore, and travel to Gododdin by land. But our bad luck turned worse: A storm arose, and we foundered against the cliffs of the Cantii. My brother and I found the keel of the ship and clung to it, praying. The next morning, when the waves stilled, we managed to swim ashore, but we were taken by a Saxon of the land thereabouts."

Llemyndd nodded wisely and drew the rest of my story from me with great care. I told him what I had told Wulf and Eduin the day before, adding details of how kind my "master" had been to us, and how I had come to like him, despite resenting the slavery, and how treacherously his enemies had killed him. It was a good story, and a few of the other thralls came in to listen while I was telling it. All were sympathetic, though all looked at me with a searching hesitancy, questioning what they had seen the night before.

My suspicions of Llemyndd proved justified. He tried to trap me, subtly, testing my story with unexpected questions. It is fortunate that he knew less of Gododdin than I did, or I would have been caught at once. But, finally satisfied, he went off, and I suspected that he went to tell Cerdic what I had told him. I doubted, remembering Cerdic's sharp green eyes, that the Saxon would believe the tale.

One of the other household thralls watched Llemyndd leave with a half-concealed bitterness that confirmed what I had suspected: Llemyndd was Cerdic's, mind, spirit, and body.

"Now the master will know everything," said the thrall.

"So that is the way of it, then," I replied.

"It is indeed."

The other thralls looked uneasy. "Hush," said one "You talk too much, Gwawl."

Gwawl hushed. A few more questions revealed to me that the thralls hated and feared Llemyndd, and most of them disliked their master Cerdic as well; though a few had some good to say of him. "The master is fair," I was told. "Do your job, and he will not punish you." I nodded and settled down to trying to discover what my own situation actually was.

It took time. The thralls would not talk to me freely the first day, or the second either. They might never have done so but for the music. They were sick for familiar songs. The British are the most civilized people in the West, and they love music as only civilized men can. They sing to themselves constantly, as the men of the Orcades or the Irish do, and any wandering bard is assured of a welcome among them. In Erin or the Orcades it is easy to see why bards and druids are so important, for in those lands it is the trained bards who memorize the laws and recite them to the kings, and who can chant the genealogies and histories and say when it is time for planting corn and such. But the British bards have no other job but to sing songs, while the rest of the work is done by books, and yet they are no less honored than the Irish fillidh. These thralls of Cerdic's could sing as they worked, and a few knew harping, but proper bardic music they had missed for years. The first time I played for them they wept for joy. For a song they would tell me anything I wanted to know of their master's secrets, and not reckon the punishment for telling.

Aldwulf's name was familiar to them. Aldwulf Fflamddwyn, Aldwulf Flame Bearer, they called him. Somehow his private sorcerous name had become the property of all Britain. He was feared by his own men, while Cerdic was loved and admired. Because of this, beyond his own clan he had few warriors in his warband, and when he raised an army from the farmers of his kingdom, more than the ordinary number of men never showed up. Nonetheless, Aldwulf was wealthy and powerful, and, allied with Cerdic, he was much to be feared. The alliance between the West Saxons and distant Bernicia, a thing surprising on the face of it, had in fact begun nearly two years before. Cerdic had been bested by Arthur in a series of engagements, and had responded by forming treaties with all the other Saxon kingdoms. It was not a proper military alliance, however, merely an agreement between the Saxon kings to lay aside private differences, and to render aid and sanctuary to any other Saxon who happened to be in difficulties with the British in their territory—"Saxon territory" being defined as more than half of Britain. A few of the Saxon kings had entered into armed alliance as well, mainly in the south. Aldwulf was not of this number, but had come south, with most of his warband, to give aid and cousel to Cerdic. He wished to prevent the British high king from coming north. He had arrived at the beginning of April and had wormed his way into Cerdic's confidence with gifts and—so the thralls added in whispers—by magic. They were extremely unwilling to speak of the magic to me, but they were sure he was a witch, and one or two of them—including one of Cerdic's few Saxon thralls—told me various tales about his witchcraft, some of which were certainly false. None of the thralls liked Aldwulf, and those that liked Cerdic bewailed the day their master had met with the Bernician king.

Cerdic had been fighting the High King Arthur for nearly three years now, and the war had become more difficult for him with each month. He had had great success when first he invaded, but Arthur's first move after establishing himself in power had been to outflank Cerdic's invasion force and plunder his base, the old Saxon shore fort of Anderida. Cerdic had kept most of his supplies and all his plunder there, and the loss had been great. The Saxon was forced to retreat to Anderida, and Arthur had gone on to win victories against some other Saxon kings, one on a surprise raid as far north as Deira. Cerdic had heard of the last and moved against his British enemies while he thought the high king was staying in the north, only to be caught by Arthur's over-rapid return. It was at this point that Cerdic had arranged his treaties with the other Saxons.

Cerdic's problem was that Arthur had no regular army. He could command the allegiance of any British kingdom, and hence was able to request the king of whatever land he wished to visit to raise the farmers and clansmen of his territory, and most of the kings would comply. Arthur's strength lay in his warband, the largest and finest of any king in Britain. Half of this warband consisted of the infamous cavalry which had caused such grief to my father, but all of the warband owned several horses apiece and could borrow more when Arthur needed to hurry across Britain. This gave the Pendragon a kind of speed and mobility that Cerdic could not hope to equal: Cerdic had no cavalry at all, and, although he could raise a very large army, most of the men in it were clansmen and farmers who could not fight in the harvest or sowing seasons and who were ill trained and ill equipped and, worst of all, ill disciplined. Movement of such a force took a long time. Cerdic also had his own warband, of course, those professional warriors who depended upon him alone for their support, but this alone, or even this in alliance with the warbands of several other kings, was no match for the High King Arthur.

Cerdic's thralls had a great deal to say about Arthur. The British thralls, even those who had been born to slavery, admired the high king with great passion and delighted in recounting the ways and occasions on which he had bested the Saxons, in spite of the fact that Cerdic had forbidden anyone to mention Arthur's name within his house without his permission. It seemed to me as I listened that Arthur's warband must be increasing in power, even allowing for the accumulation of legends and the exaggeration of the thralls. It was reasonable to suppose it: If a king is victorious in battle and generous in his hall, warriors will flock to him from all over the Western world. Even some notable Saxon warriors had joined the high king's warband. Two and a half years after beginning his war against the Saxons, Arthur must have a band of men unequaled in the West—probably unequaled in the world. They could and regularly did, it seemed, defeat four times their number.

"But the past two years," one thrall complained to me, "there's been little to do. The master raises the fyrd and gathers his warband, then sits here in Sorviodunum—your pardon, Searisbyrig—sending out raiding parties and spies; and the emperor just sends raiding parties and spies back."

It was a sensible move, on Cerdic's part, I thought. A large warband, like Arthur's, is expensive to keep. Since he had no kingdom of his own, Arthur relied on tribute from all the kings of Britain. But he had gained the purple by defeating those very kings he exacted the tribute from, and they had not forgotten it. He needed their support and their armies against the Saxons; he could not antagonize them further by demanding vast amounts of tribute. While he fought and defeated the Saxons, he could support himself from plunder and sweeten his subjects' tempers by sharing the booty, but when the Saxons retreated and sat firm in a strong fortified position, content with guarding their borders, Arthur had to rely upon his subjects. They would be the less inclined to support him when they could see no tangible tokens of victory. Cerdic was hoping to provoke the British kingdoms into another civil war, and I learned from one thrall that there were kings in Britain who were willing to try to overthrow "the usurping bastard," and that messages had been sent to and from some of these men into this fortress, Sorviodunum, or Searisbyrig. Cerdic understood statecraft. Unfortunately, most of his followers did not, and many, to whom he had promised land, felt cheated and muttered angrily that Cerdic was afraid. The war had become a race between Cerdic and Arthur over who would first be forced to raise the full armies and offer a pitched battle. At the moment it seemed that Arthur might win the race, and Cerdic was desperately angry.

I came to admire the Pendragon in those weeks. He sounded, more than ever, to be a lord worth following. At the same time, though, my worries increased. Arthur would have no use for unskilled warriors like myself, who would do nothing but drain his already strained resources.

On the other hand, I told myself whenever I considered this, I might die by Aldwulf's hand at the dark of the moon, and the matter would not concern me at all. And I would throw myself into some other task so as not to think of it.

Cerdic did not set me any tasks in the house, which was fortunate, for I soon realized I did not know how to work as a thrall. I had not noticed how much I took it for granted that I was a king's son, even a younger and despised king's son, and that there were certain things those of a royal clan do not do. I found that I expected others to open doors, fetch things, pick things up. I had no notion of how to go about cleaning a floor or mending the thatch, and was, at first, angry when told to do some menial task. Continually I had to correct myself, and tell myself that these servants were fellow servants. I did not fool them. Coming into the stable one day I heard one of the grooms saying to a house servant, "If he's a thrall, I'm the Emperor Theodosius. Do you know . . ." —and he stopped abruptly when he saw me. No; there were few tasks for me as a thrall. But Cerdic expected me to be ready to play the harp at any time of day or night, and I had my own inquiries to make. Besides that, I was attempting to learn the basics of the Saxon tongue . . . and then, there was Ceincaled.

Leaving the stables on my first day as Cerdic's thrall, I saw a crowd of men gathered in a circle on a hillside just beyond the Roman part of the town, and I went to investigate. Aldwulf had mentioned that he gave a horse to Cerdic to prove his power at sorcery, and Cerdic had accepted it as proof, although unable to break the horse. As I came through the circle and saw the stallion that reared in the center of the ring. I understood why.

No earthly mare had borne that horse. The steeds of the Sidhe, praised in a hundred songs, show their immortality in every line; and that horse was a lord among even such horses as those.

He stood three hands taller at the shoulder than the largest horse I had seen before, and that had been a giant of a plow horse. He was lovely: pure white, splendid and powerful as a storm on the sea. The white neck curved like the sea's waves before they break, the mane was like foam flung up from the rocks. No seagull skims the water as lightly as those hooves skimmed the earth, and no sea eagle struck at the ground with such fierceness or such freedom. The horse's nostrils were flared wide and red, defiant in anger, his eyes dark and savage with pride. I held my breath at the sight of him.

The Saxon who had just been thrown scrambled out of the way, and some grooms from Cerdic's stable drove the horse back to the center of the ring with whips and flapping cloaks, cursing him.

"That beast is a man killer," said one of the thralls, who was standing a few feet from me. "Cerdic cannot believe that he will ever tame it."

"He is beautiful, that horse," I said. The man looked at me, surprised and suspicious. He recognized me, shrugged uncomfortably.

"Of course," he said, "and strong and swift. He could out-run and out-stay any horse in Britain, that one. But what is the use of all of it, since he can't be ridden? You are new here and wouldn't know, but we have tried for a month now to break him, with kindness and with blows, with riding and with starving, and we are no nearer to taming him than we were when Cerdic first acquired him. I know horses, and I say that this one will die before he obeys a man. And before he dies he will probably take some of us with him. . . . Watch out, there! Hai, you! . . . Cerdic won't name him till he's ridden him, but we of his house call the beast Ceincaled, Harsh Beauty, for that, surely, is what he is."

It took little time for me to see the truth of the man's words. The horse tried to kill every human near him. There was no viciousness in these attempts, no hatred of humanity such as one finds in an animal that has been badly mistreated, but instead a wild, pure, elemental power which could bear no subjection. He was proud, Ceincaled, not with a pride such as men have, but as a falcon or eagle is proud. He was like the music in Lugh's hall: splendid, but not for men. I wondered what dark spell of Aldwulf's had captured the stallion and brought him from the Plain of Joy to captivity and eventual death in the lands of men.

There were times during the next two weeks when I felt a strong sense of kinship with the stallion. I was not immortal, but my problem was similar. I was trapped, and all my efforts to escape only wasted my time and brought nearer the time set down for my death.

Cerdic had all of his large warband with him in Sorvio-dunum (to use the Roman name), three hundred and twelve picked warriors, who guarded the fort. He had also an army of some five thousand—as always, the exact number was uncertain. The camp was continually prepared for war, and raiding parties left or returned nearly every day, if only from short forays. I thought of trying to slip from the camp· when one of these arrived, and hung about the gate and a low spot in the walls for a while, until I was warned off by the guards, who, besides being exceedingly vigilant, were suspicious. I considered the forest I had walked through, and looked out over it from the hilltop center of the fortress. I thought it must be easy to disappear into the trees. Unfortunately, though, the forest only extended toward the northeast. There were miles of open plain adjoining the town on the west, where lay the nearest British kingdom. And I was watched, even if there had been some way to cross the walls and the plains. No one forbade me to roam about the town, but some thrall or some warrior always seemed to be about. Cerdic did not wish his semihuman sacrifice to escape. It disturbed me nearly as much as the fear of death and my still unresolved fears about myself. I had always wanted solitude, and to be denied it grated on my nerves.

I prayed to the Light, but he did not respond. I began to want, and want badly, to simply draw Caledvwlch and try to slash my way out of the fort. I knew that it would be certain death to do so, but at least it would be a clean death, and a warrior's death. I was tired of being a thrall. I was trapped, and that word seemed to resound continually through my mind, all of each day. At night I dreamed of it, and I thought of it before anything else each morning when I woke. I felt trapped, like a hawk that has flown by mistake into a fisherman's net, who, when he beats his wings only discovers how truly entangled he is, and exhausts his strength against the ropes.

I became aware of time with a terrifying intensity, of how the sun rising in the morning splashed the sky with colors whose softness I had never noticed so clearly before; of how the shadows shortened and lengthened as the hours passed during the day. At night I watched the moon, sliding from full down into its fourth quarter, growing thinner with every night that passed. The moon was my friend, my ally. While she still shone I would not die. But she was leaving the sky, and when she had gone, all would be darkness.

Sometimes I felt that the Light had withdrawn in the same way. After alerting me to Cerdic's plan, it had become as silent as the moon. Two weeks is not a long time, but those two weeks, full of the tension of waiting

night of my own shadow, when the sun was behind me. How, I asked myself, beginning to find it very funny, how could I ever have been so stupid?

And was my other problem so simple as this? I asked myself as I edged around to Cerdic. All my questioning of my identity, would it too come clear in a burst of light when I looked in the right direction? My High King, Lord . . .

"My Lord King," I said to Cerdic, who had noticed my approach and was eyeing me without enthusiasm. "Could I try to ride the horse?"

Cerdic gave me a furious glare, then hit me hard enough to make me stagger for balance. "You insolent dog! You slave, do you think to succeed where a king failed? I should have you whipped!" I saw that I had misjudged the degree of his anger about the horse and bowed my head, trying to think and rubbing my jaw.

"Cerdic," Aldwulf interrupted suddenly. "You might let him try."

"What!"

"They may be from the same land. Who knows? The boy has been caring for the horse." Aldwulf's thought was plain. I would use magic on the horse, tame it, be killed, and the king would have both my sword and the horse. Aldwulf was smiling in a very satisfied fashion. It had been a sore point with him, I think, that his fine horse was unridable.

Cerdic looked at me, remembering what Aldwulf said I was. "Very well," he said at last. "Try, then."

"Thank you, Cyning Cerdic," I said softly. "I will do my best."

Cerdic nodded to Aldwulf. I turned back toward Ceincaled.

He had been caught by the grooms again, and waited patiently while they held him, conserving his strength for his rider. I walked over, thanked the man who held him, and took the bridle. As I held it, I suddenly doubted my ability to ride him, which a minute before had seemed so clear. I had always been good with horses, and the stallion knew me now, but that might well be no use at all. He objected not so much to the Darkness in his riders as to being ridden at all. It would take a spirit equal to his own to hold him, and even then he might die rather than accept defeat. But I had to ride him, or die that evening.

I stroked the white neck, whispering to the horse. He jerked away from me, then quieted, waiting, preparing for the battle. He was more intelligent than an ordinary horse. I had watched him fight Cerdic and knew this.

I ran my hand over his back and withers, tightened the girth of the saddle, speaking in a singsong, in Irish, no longer caring who heard. In my heart I asked the Light to rein in that proud spirit for me, and grant me the victory. Then I placed my left hand on the stallion's shoulder and vaulted to his back.

The only way to describe what happened next is to say that he exploded. The world dissolved into a white cloud of mane, and Ceincaled fought with all his terrible strength and limitless pride. I held his mane and the reins both, gripping hard with my knees and bending down onto his neck, and barely managed to stay on.

He circled the ring, rearing and plunging, and the onlookers were a blur of flesh, bright colors, steel, and distorted shouts. I felt that I tried to ride the storm, or hold the north wind with a bridle. It was beyond the power of any human, and now that I tried my strength against an immortal I knew that I was no more than human. Ceincaled was pure, fierce, wild beyond belief. He had no master and could accept none. . . .

And he was glorious.

I stopped caring about past and future, about thought and feeling. Aldwulf might hang me or I might fall from Ceincaled and be trampled, broken by the wildness of the power I had tried to master. But even as I saw these things they became as distant and unimportant as an abandoned game. There was a sweet taste at the back of my mouth, like mint in the middle of a rainy night. Ceincaled was leaping again, clothed in thunder, and death and life were both unreal. All that mattered was the sweet madness that possessed both the horse and me, madness that had swept onto me from within and changed the world to something I could no longer recognize, or care to. When I had drawn Caledvwlch there had been something of the sensation of light, but this was more a lightness, a blazing sweetness in my mind. I loved

Ceincaled totally, and in mid-leap he felt it and returned the love, and we were no longer fighting each other but flying, dazzled with delight, filled with the same and equal fierceness.

Ceincaled reared one last time and neighed, a challenge to all the world, then dropped onto all four legs in the circle and stood tensely still.

Through the battle madness that made the world seem sharp edged, almost frozen, I saw the onlookers staring at me in wonder, Aldwulf frowning in a sudden unease, and Cerdic, eyes alight with greed.

"Good," said the king of the West Saxons. His voice sounded far away. "Now give me my horse."

I laughed, and he started, flushing with anger. Aldwulf, realizing now what was happening, grabbed Cerdic's arm. Cerdic began to turn to him, an angry question forming on his tongue. . . .

I had Caledvwlch out, and its light leaped up, pure and brilliant as a star. Ceincaled rushed Cerdic. Someone was screaming in terror.

Cerdic flung himself aside, rolled, Ceincaled's hooves missing him by inches. Aldwulf, pressing back into the crowd, was less quick and less fortunate. He cried out before my sword touched him, blinded by its light, shrieking some curse—then screamed as the blade struck him. But Ceincaled struck the rope that bounded the makeshift ring, breaking it, and my hand was jerked back. Aldwulf was not killed, though he would miss his left eye, I wanted to go back and finish him, for he deserved destruction; but Ceincaled was stretching into a run and I forgot Aldwulf with the taste of the wind.

The Roman streets swept past, blurred with speed, and behind us someone was shouting to stop me, kill me. A warrior on the street ran into my path, dropped to one knee, his long thrusting spear braced against me. Everything narrowed to him as I approached. I saw his face, grinning in fear and excitement, sweat gleaming on it. I saw the sun flash off the top of his spear, and loved the leap of it, loved him as well, knew that Ceincaled was only three paces away. I touched the horse with my knee, forcing him to swerve the barest fraction, and the spear tip, flashing forward, missed us. With my left hand I caught the shaft and with my right swung down Caledvwlch. My mind was still dazzled with madness as the sword struck, blazing, and the warrior's neck spurted red as it was cut through. Then I was past. There were others, at the gate. I killed the nearest with the spear I had taken from the first, and cut through the spear shaft of the second and let Ceincaled run over him. I found that I was singing, laughed again. How could they hope to stop me? The Saxons were fleeing now. One threw a spear, but I swerved Ceincaled and it missed. My horse leaned into the race, and there were no others before me, only the open gate and the Roman road stretching into the west. We flew down it like a gull, like the hawk of my name. The Saxons were far behind. Even when they mounted a party to follow us, they were far behind. Too far to catch up again, I thought, remotely; too far to ever catch us again. We were free.

EIGHT

THE REST OF THAT RACE is not clear in my mind. It was a
sweet rhythm of flying hooves and wind, and the empty
hills of the plain before and about me after we abandoned
the road. I sang for pure joy, laughing, loving the world
and all men in it, even Cerdic, whom I would gladly have
killed had he been there. Oh, the Light was a strong lord,
a great high king. Any warrior would be proud to serve
him.

It was late afternoon, and Ceincaled began to tire a
little. I reined him in to a canter. We still had a long way
before us, I reminded myself.

How long a way? I could not guess. I was totally uncertain of distances in Britain, and had no idea of how far
we had come. A great distance, surely, at such a speed.
Some of the blindingly bright light died down within my
mind, and I looked about myself.

I was nearing the western edge of the plain. And land
to either side of me looked something like the Orcades in
that it was open and hilly, but these hills were wider and
greener. Checking by the sun I discovered that I was going north as well as west, and realized that I must have
been doing so for some time. I had a vague recollection
of the Roman road following the curve of a hill and
Ceincaled galloping off it onto the plain, northwest. It was
good, I decided, that we had turned west on the Roman
road. If we had not—and in that madness we could easily
not have—Ceincaled and I would have gone tearing off

east, into the heart of the Saxon kingdoms. The thought made me smile, and the rest of the ecstasy departed. I slowed Ceincaled to a trot and turned him due west again.

Westward the hills became steeper, and soon there was a dark line of forest before us. Before we reached this, however, we came upon a river. It was a small, sleepy river, still dark with spring mud, and it calmly reflected the oak trees on its farther bank. I rode northward along the bank for a way, until I found a place where the river was low enough for Ceincaled to cross it easily.

When he approached the water, the horse snuffled interestedly. I dismounted and let him drink, talking to him softly while he did. He was thirsty and wet with sweat, but, incredibly, not hot to steaming, as any other horse would have been after anything resembling our race.

Watching the horse drink made me thirsty. As I knelt by the water, I saw that I was still holding Caledvwlch. I smiled and began to sheath the sword—then realized that there was blood on it.

I remembered, with an almost physical shock, the Saxons who had gotten in my way. I remembered Aldwulf falling back unconscious into the circle of Saxons, the left side of his face cut open, and the others dying, and how I had laughed. I dropped the sword on the grass and leaned back on my heels, staring at it, as though the killing had been its responsibility and not mine. Then I saw the horse was drinking too much, and stood to pull him away from the water and walk him about to cool him down. I had killed. I had just killed three men, and horribly wounded a fourth, and I had not even been aware of it until now. No, killed four men, if one counted Connall. But that had been mercy, and this was . . . it was war, a battle.

I let the horse go back to the water and drink some more, Lugh had given me his blessing, to carry into whatever battles lay before me. Could that madness that had possessed me be such a blessing? CuChulainn, they say, went mad in battle, and he was the son of Lugh. There are kinds of madness that are said to be divine or scared. Mine had felt so. But it frightened me, that I could kill and not care. But could I say that I had been wrong to escape as I did?

I cleaned the sword on the grass, rubbed it on my cloak, and sheathed it again. Then I knelt and drank from the river. The water tasted like its source's appearance: slow and rich, peaceful. It was calming, so I sat on the bank and watched it. Ceincaled had finished his drink, and now waded in the stream, enjoying the feel of it. I went to him and unfastened the saddle, quickly, then rubbed him down with a handful of grass and allowed him to splash into the stream again, and again myself sat down.

I looked at my reflection, which trembled with Ceincaled's disturbance of the water. I had changed since I last studied my face, back at the pond at Llyn Gwalch. It was a strange face now, marked by strange things. The eyes, though, floating reflected on the dark water, were the same, and just as puzzled by what they saw as before. But now there was a kind of intensity to the face, the look of a warrior and something uncanny as well. I shook my head and looked at Ceincaled again. I, a warrior. I had killed three trained Saxon warriors and wounded a Saxon king. But how could I, Gwalchmai Mac Lot, the worst warrior in all the Orcades, an utter failure in arms, do such a thing as that? The warriors had been frightened and off-balance because of the size and speed of Ceincaled and because of the fire that blazed in my sword. Otherwise I would have been killed at once. Certainly, it sounded like a dashing exploit such as a famous warrior might boast of in a feast hall, but I knew better.

Knew what better? I thought of the fierce being I had been only an hour before and wondered. I remembered what I had seen in myself when I first drew Caledvwlch, that Darkness, and afterward the power and certainty as I held the sword; and I remembered Lugh's warning. How, in that mingling of human passion and divine madness, to distinguish between Light and Darkness? The disturbing idea that I was something other than human returned to me. I knew now, though, that whatever had happened I remained as human as any, even if I could ride Ceincaled. The horse had shown me that. I had not mastered him, but he had consented to obey me, out of love. It would take an immortal to break that stallion, and I was only human; I could only persuade him. This was comforting to me. It is human to be in ignorance, to be uncertain, and assuredly I was that. I was only a man who had seen things greater than those most men have seen, and the essence of those things had touched me, as a warrior is touched by his work, and a king by his. (Morgawse, Mother, I wondered, how deeply have you touched me?) But that was all, that was the whole of the explanation.

I laughed at my reflection. "You truly are a proper fool, do you know that?" I asked it. "The answer was directly in front of you, and you turned your back on it. You worry too much."

Ceincaled pricked his ears forward, listening, then tossed his head. I laughed again, stood, and went and caught his bridle. He snorted, then pushed his nose into my hair and nibbled at it, as horses do.

"Hush, brave one, bright one," I told him. "That is not grass. It is not even the proper color."

Ceincaled nickered, and I ran my hand down his neck. It was a shock to recall where he had come from. Poor Ceincaled. Torn from the marvels of those islands beyond the sunset, subjected to Cerdic's greed and Aldwulf's spells, to whips and starvation, the bit and the spur, to Darkness and to death, when all that he should have known were the fields of golden flowers, the endless spring for all eternity. I picked another handful of grass and brushed him down again. He was beautiful, this horse, too beautiful for Earth. With him I had won my freedom. Now, I felt certain, the Saxons could never find me again (barring accidents), and I no longer needed Ceincaled. In fact, he could easily become a hindrance, since such a horse is noticed and remarked upon. Had there been a choice, I would have kept the horse and given him up to no one: I loved him, his beauty and his splendid spirit. But I had no right to repay the gift of freedom he had brought with the death which would result from my keeping him.

Slowly, I took off the bridle. Ceincaled stood very still, and his image in the dark water trembled only slightly. "Go, friend," I told him. "You have won your freedom. Go home. Perhaps Lugh, Master of All Arts, will ride you, but you are suited to no lesser being. You fought well and bravely, and I give you my thanks."

Ceincaled hesitated, as though listening and understanding, then tossed his head, snorted at the bridle, and plunged into the river. When he had crossed it he galloped off westward. I watched him vanish among the trees, then sighed, crossed the river myself, and headed west.

The forest was not so thick as the one near which I had woken. Still, it was thick enough to confuse the Saxons if they were still following me. I doubted, though, that they were. Cerdic must have sent men after me, but I suspected that they would not notice where I left the road. And I had crossed the plain which the thralls had said lay between Dumnonia and the Saxon lands, so I was certainly in British domains by now. There could be a raiding party in the area . . . no, the last raid the king had ordered had been to the north, into Powys. I should be too far south to meet with it. I was probably safe; if I traveled a little farther west I should certainly be secure.

I walked until nightfall—no long time—then stopped where I was and slept under a tree root, wrapped in my cloak. The following day I journeyed on, feeling worn and dirty.

I had not gone far when I reached a road. It was no Roman road but a plain dirt track which wound along the hilltops. It was easier to walk on the verge or through the surrounding wood than on the road itself, so deep and thick was the mud. Nonetheless, I followed the track, turning south on it. There was some risk, but not much, and I wished to find someone who could tell me where to find Arthur. The land was inhabited, I knew, for I had seen the smoke of hearth fires the evening before, but I judged it safer to meet someone on the road, and, I hoped, someone traveling alone.

The risk paid off. I had walked for only half an hour when I found a cart stuck in the mud. The man who strained to push it out was stocky, red haired, and swore in British.

"Ach! Yffern's hounds run you down, horse, can't you pull any harder than that?" he shouted at his mare. She gave a few halfhearted jerks, without success. The man cursed some more and kicked one of the wheels of the cart. He did not notice me as I came up behind him.

"Greetings," I said, after watching his performance. "Can I help you?"

He stopped pushing and whirled about, afraid. His eyes widened when he saw me, and his right hand flashed through a peculiar motion. "Who are you?" he demanded, and his hand had now dropped to his belt knife. "What do you want?"

"I do not want anything from you, certainly not your life, so you can take your hand off your knife. I was offering to help you with your cart."

The man gave me another long, uncomfortable stare, then shrugged, ran a heavy hand through his hair, and rolled his eyes in exasperation. "Ach! Well, you're no Saxon. . . . Can you help me? No, indeed not. I drag my carts here for the sheer pleasure of pushing them out of the mud."

I decided that I liked this man. I smiled. "In that case, I am sorry that I have interfered with so enjoyable a pastime, and leave you to the pleasure of it."

He frowned, puzzled, then grinned. "There; but I was angry, and it is a most generous offer. If you can help me get this demon-plagued thing out from this thrice-damned hole, I can give you a ride. I am going south and east, to Camlann."

Camlann!

"I wish to go there myself," I said. "Here, let me see this cart. How is it stuck?"

It was badly stuck, in a deep hole which had been disguised by a thin crust of drier mud. It took an hour of shoving and massed wood from the forest under the wheels before the cart finally lurched from the hole. The carter gave a crow of delight when it slipped free at last.

"It is lucky that you came along," he said. "I'd never have gotten it free alone. I'd've had to go back to my holding and ask my clan to help, and it's no safe thing, leaving a loaded cart on the road these days, what with the bandits and the thieves, and the Saxons in Dim Sarum." (Another name for Sorviodunum/Searisbyrig, I remembered.) "And there's more work at the holding than we've men to do it, and we could ill spare the hands to drag loose a cart." He climbed into his cart, untying the reins from the post he had fastened them to, and beckoned me to come up beside him. We started down the road, half on—half off the verge. "My name is Sion, by the way," the man said, "Sion ap Rhys, a farmer. My clan's holding is up north of here, near Mor Hafren."

Mor Hafren, mouth of the Saefern River? Had I come so far north?

"I am Gwalchmai," I said, without adding my father's name. I should give little information, I decided, until I knew how the sons of King Lot of Orcade would be received in Dumnonia.

"A fine name," said Sion, after a short, uneasy pause. "A warrior's name. And you wish to go to Camlann?"

"Indeed. How far away is it? I have never been to Dumnonia before."

He shrugged. "We should be in Ynys Witrin tonight. It's not far, but I won't push the horse, and we'll need to spend more time digging this accursed Hell-axled cart out of the mud before we reached the west road. There are times when I think that no amount of profit is worth traveling for in the spring."

"What profit do you expect, then?"

He grinned. "Considerable. That is wheat flour in the back there. My clan found we had more than we needed when the winter ended, so we decided to sell it. And what better man to sell to than the emperor? With his warband he always needs supplies badly. If I find the right man to bargain with I should get twice the price I'd find at Baddon."

We rode together for the rest of the day, and I enjoyed it. Sion was a talkative man and a cheerful one, which last was fortunate, for the cart became stuck three times more before we reached the "west road," the old Roman road. Sion must have consigned every inch of that track to Yffern a dozen times over, together with the cart and the horse, but he swore with great equanimity, and the horse merely flicked its ears back as though he were consoling it.

Long before we reached Ynys Witrin the forest vanished, and then the hills, until we were crossing a low marsh on a road that was elevated on an earthen bank. Narrow rivers of deeper water wound through the sodden marsh grasses. We saw the town of Ynys Witrin long before we reached it. The great hill on which it is built stood above the land like a fortress. Ynys Witrin is a holy city. It was sacred before the Romans came and it is still sacred, though now to a different god. They say the first church in Britain was built there, and the monastery has been there a long time.

I was very impressed by the road into the town, and tried to imagine the amount of work needed to build it. Sion noticed this, and asked if I were a foreigner, hesitating a little before the final word. I told him that I was from the Orcades. He was confused.

"The Orcades? Where is that?"

"The Orcades, the Innsi Erc, the islands north of Pictland," I said, surprised.

"Oh, the Ynysoedd Erch! Where Lot is king, with the witch-queen. A frightful place, they say, and terribly far away."

"Very far away," I said, "but not at all frightful."

"We-ell . . . did you ever see King Lot ap Cormac, then? Or the Queen Morgawse, daughter of Uther? They tell stories of those two that make the blood run cold. I wouldn't care to meet either of them, not at all, at any time. My son, of course . . ."

I smiled. He had told me all about his twelve-year-old son, who was a fanatic admirer of Arthur and who wanted to be a hero, told it in the middle of telling about the difficulties of farming and about a blood feud his clan had been involved in twenty years before. He was, as I said, a talkative man.

"Not that I believe the stories," Sion added. "Men will tell tales about anything, and the more marvelous it is, the more interesting they find it. There are tales they tell now about the Pendragon in every marketplace which would have been laughed at ten years ago, but because he is emperor now and has taxed the Church, the fools all pull their beards and believe them. But I am a Christian, a good churchman, and I don't hold with such tales. . . ." he trailed off, gave me a sideways glance, fell silent a moment, then continued, "But I was wondering what the king and queen of the Ynysoedd Erch look like."

"I have seen them," I admitted reluctantly.

"Indeed? Then tell me of the witch-queen, the Pendragon's sister. She was born here in Dumnonia, but I have never seen her. Is she beautiful?"

I thought of Morgawse. Morgawse, with her black hair and her eyes like pools of night, queen of Darkness, no longer human. I looked down at my hands, forgetting the road, the man beside me, Camlann and all Britain with the horror of the memory. The cart rim creaked beneath my fingers as I gripped it. Light, can I never be free of her?

Sion muttered something under his breath and made the same hand gesture he had used when he first saw me.

"What?" I asked, waking from my reflections.

"Nothing," said Sion, but he reined in his mare and looked at me. "What do you . . ." He stopped again. "There is something strange about you, Gwalchmai."

"What do you mean?" I asked, meeting his eyes evenly.

Sion shook his head abruptly and shook the reins so that the mare started forward again. "It's just the light," he muttered. "This late afternoon sun makes things look . . . well, I am sorry."

I smiled, my fingers curling about Caledvwlch's hilt. It was something, at least, that he was sorry for thinking I was not human.

"Look there!" said Sion, cheerful again. "There is Ynys Witrin."

We had turned directly west again, since the road was built from the main road to the east of the town, and the long rays of the afternoon sun made the buildings of mud and wood look fragile, as though they floated above the marshes. The steep tor should have looked peaceful: Instead, it made me catch my breath. It was certainly a place of power, and that power was of more than one kind.

Sion's little mare picked her way eagerly toward the promised shelter. It was for her sake that Sion wished to stop at Ynys Witrin, instead of traveling all the way to Camlann. The cart, loaded, was heavy for her to pull all day, and the farmer could not afford to wear her out. I considered with a pang that Ceincaled could have traveled the whole distance we had compassed that day in a few hours. But Ceincaled had the right to immortality. I could not have kept him.

We crossed a bridge—the river was called the Briw, Sion said—and entered the Island of Glass, Ynys Witrin. The great hill loomed over us, the fortress at its top keeping watch over the marshland. The fortress belonged to a minor lord, a subject of Constantius of Dumnonia. Sion did not intend to ask his hospitality, since the lord followed the usual custom of offering guest rights to none but warriors and craftsmen. It was to the monastery that common travelers went. This lay on the flank of the hill, to the east of the fortress, at the center of an old, largely abandoned Roman town.

Sion drove up to the gateway and, getting down from the cart, rang an iron bell that hung beside it. After a few minutes, a monk came and viewed us through a slit in the door.

"Who are you and what do you want?" he asked in an irritated tone.

"Sion ap Rhys, a farmer. Hospitality for the night."

"A farmer?" The monk opened the door. "You are welcome then. The hospitality of Ynys Witrin will cost you . . . What is in the cart?"

"Cost me!" exclaimed Sion. "What kind of hospitality is that?"

"The hospitality of monks taxed beyond their means by a tyrant!" snapped the monk. "What's in the cart?"

"Wheat flour," replied Sion sullenly.

"It will cost you a sack of wheat flour."

"A sack. A whole sack. Man, I could buy two chickens for a whole sack of flour, this time of year!" said Sion.

"Are you seeking to plunder the Church, the holy Church, your mother? Do you not think that it pleases God to be generous to his servants?"

"I think it pleases God when his servants are generous. Ten pounds of flour is more than I can afford, but I'll offer that."

"Three-quarters of a sack . . ." began the monk.

After a time, it was agreed that for half a sack of flour Sion could have a place for himself and his mare for the night.

"Now, who is that in the cart?" demanded the monk. "You can't say that he is your son; he's nothing like you."

"No," I answered. "I am merely a fellow traveler."

"You pay separately, then," said the monk, with satisfaction. "Is some of the flour yours?"

"No . . ."

"Then what do you travel for?"

"I seek service with the Pendragon."

The monk gaped at me, then snarled. "The Pendragon! Arthur the Bastard has too many men serving him already. Far too many. And who supports them?"

"The Saxons have recently, by being plundered," I said. "All Britain, when there is no war. But have you ever met the Saxons?"

"Why would I have met the Saxons?" asked the monk, forgetting, in his surprise to be angry.

"Never mind. What will you charge me? I have no goods."

"None?" He looked at me carefully, decided that I must be telling the truth. "Your sword then."

"No."

"Your cloak."

Sion was outraged. "What sort of hospitality is this, even for Ynys Witrin? To take the very cloak of a man who comes to you without a penny, and knows no more of bargaining than a three-year-old child? I will pay for him."

"A sack of flour," said the monk quickly.

"Half a sack, as for myself," answered Sion firmly, "and no more, you thief from a thieves' den."

The monk complained some more, saying that he was being asked to support the plunder of the Church by giving hospitality "to a godless lover of tyrants," but he wanted the flour and eventually let us in.

"I am sorry," I said to Sion, as the cart rolled through the gate. "It is true that I know nothing of bargaining. You should have let him take my cloak; I am sure to get a new one at Camlann. As it is, I have nothing else with which to repay your generosity."

Sion shrugged, but he was pleased. "Keep it. You'd've been a fool to give a new cloak for a night's lodging; it's worth at least a week's. And that man was a fool to even mention the sword, for I, who know nothing of weapons, can see that that sword could buy a holding, herds and all." He gave me a shrewd look, and I felt foolish indeed, for I'd not thought of this at all. "It is only one sack of flour," he added. "And"—he lowered his voice—"the sacks aren't whole-measure sacks. They're smaller. That fool didn't even notice, and gave us a generous rate without knowing. Well and good, for monks ought to be poor in the world's goods, and, with God's help, I'll do what I can to make them so."

We settled Sion's mare in the abbey stables and saw that the cart was safe in the barn, then gave the gatekeeper his sack of flour. We then went to the chapel, since it seemed that the monastery was crowded and the monks had set their guests to sleeping in the chapel porch. Sion threw down a pack in the porch, whistling, then stomped on into the chapel itself. After a moment's hesitation, I followed him. I had never before seen a church, and I found it confusing. I stopped just inside the door, staring at the columned basilica and the carvings along the lintel. Sion, however, went immediately to the far end and knelt before the altar there. He made the same hand gesture I had seem him use twice before, and now I recognized it as the sign of the cross. I walked up to the altar, silently, and stood looking at it.

It was a plain altar, with a cross of carved wood standing against the whitewashed inner wall. The cloth over the altar, however, was richly embroidered, covered with interlocked and interlacing designs, frozen and moving at the same time, like the designs I had seen on bowls and mirrors and jewelry all my life. This also had animal designs, though, strange winged beasts prancing through the interlace, seeming to dance in the light of the two candles on the table. Something about the place reminded me of the room where I had drawn Caledvwlch. There was something of the same feeling of banked power, rigid and vibrant as the designs on the altar cloth. There was a feeling of centrality, of being near the heart of something, and an intense stillness.

I drew a deep breath, shuddering with excitement like a nervous horse, and forced myself to calm down. On an impulse I knelt behind Sion, who was muttering some prayer in Latin. I drew Caledvwlch and held it before me with its tip resting on the ground, so that the cross of the hilt echoed the cross on the wall. Light stirred within the ruby, rose to a steady flame, and I willed it to quiet, knowing that I would be unable to explain the sword to Sion or to the monks. It stilled, and I tried to follow Sion's example, and pray. Pieces of various songs floated through my mind, and the old druidical invocations of the sun and the wind, the earth and the sea. Then I brushed these aside, deciding that I wished, after all, to speak to my lord the Light, not to any mysterious and unknown god who was new to me; and I spoke to him silently.

Ard Righ Mor, My King . . . I would keep my oath to you. I have killed since I pledged you fealty. Let that . . . oh, I am lost and cannot understand it. Let there be forgiveness of it. My Lord . . ." I wanted to sing, suddenly, but did not know what to sing. "My Lord, I am your warrior. Command me. Aid me. Let me find Arthur and find service with him. Let me . . ." What? I thought of Morgawse, of Lugh, of Ceincaled. "Let me know your will in this, since it is yours to rule. God of this place, if you are my lord the Light, hear me."

There was a moment of stillness, a silent, deep listening quite different from the exaltation I had known before. It was as though the troubled water of a deep pool had stilled, and one could look down into it through limitless depths, as if into a lake of glass. At the heart of that stillness was a light, quiet as the candle flames, and a sense like the first notes of a song. I felt only this, and only for an instant. But I knew that my prayer had been heard, and I could go to Camlann with a quiet mind. I stood and sheathed the sword.

Sion turned, looked at me, frowned, then grinned. "Consecrating the sword?"

"In a fashion."

"A good thing to have done, a very good thing. Come, let us see if they have anything to eat in this thieves' den."

In the porch of the chapel there were three other farmers and a trader, all bound for Camlann, who greeted us cheerfully and began to complain of the monks. Sion joined them in this pastime with great enthusiasm, and outdid them all in eloquence. None of the men did more than glance at me, for which I was grateful.

Presently a young monk brought us our evening meal in a basket, together with some fine yellow mead that did much to mollify the anger of the guests. After the meal we unrolled the straw pallets which were kept there for travelers, and we spread our cloaks on these, wished each other a good night, and curled up to sleep.

I woke up in the darkness, sometime near midnight, and lay very still. There was something in the chapel porch, something which had no right to be there.

It was very dark, too dark. Beside me Sion's breathing had taken on a labored, drugged sound, and seemed to come from a distance. It had become cold with a soul-chilling empty cold, and the air tasted thin and flat.

Stealthily I put my hand to the hilt of the sword I had placed by my head. Caledvwlch was warm, and as welcome to my hand as a hearth fire after a winter drizzle. I rolled over, got my knees beneath me, ready to move.

Whatever had entered the chapel was definitely there. I could see nothing, but I sensed its presence. It was prowling, creeping along the line of sleeping men, searching . . . it was at the opposite end of the porch from me, a pulsating core of darkness, cold, and desolation. And it was strong, frighteningly strong.

I waited for it, my pulse thudding dully in my ears and shaking me with the force of my life. I felt divided: I wished to run from the horror of it; I wished to leap up and destroy it.

The shadow had crept halfway along the line of men, still looking. Looking for me. It was not the one Aldwulf had summoned in Sorviodunum; it seemed, even, to be too strong for him to have sent, though I knew he must have sent it. He would want vengeance for what my sword had done to him.

I could see the creature now, a darker patch in the blackness, lying across the floor like the shadow of a tree, only there was no tree to cast it. I swallowed, and tasted again the sweetness that had been there when I rode Ceincaled, and I was glad that this demon had come.

. . . it had moved to Sion . . .

I cast aside my cloak and stood, drawing my sword.

It stopped, drawing in on itself, and for a long moment there was a thunderous silence.

Then it attacked, as Morgawse's demon had attacked: I was smothered in a cold darkness, falling, unable to see, unable to breathe. I staggered, sickened and chilled to the marrow—by the Light, it was strong! And sweet Light, I was glad, and raised my sword between us; here was an enemy worthy of destruction! The fire of the sword flared into the blade, heating it in my hands, and the coldness in my mind blinked from existence. The shadow flew across onto the wall, trembling like the shadow of a tree in a storm. It radiated confusion, anger . . . and fear. It had not expected this. Steel does not hurt such creatures, and they have no fear of helpless men. This was different.

I smiled and advanced. "Come," I said, my voice strange in the darkness and the unearthly silence which lay so close. "Come, my enemy. You are bound to this, and cannot return to your place until you have performed that which you were sent for."

It made a high, thin, keening sound and leaped.

I was ready. I brought Caledvwlch down, and the creature gave a voiceless scream, screamed again, twisting on the floor, but now with rage; and before I could recover the sword it had slid across the floor and touched me. I fell backward. There was a deadly cold and intense pain which clawed inside my skull, and a flood of hatred, a black tide like the hatred I had once felt for my brother Agravain, or the hatred Morgawse felt for the world. I was drowning in it; I could not tell what were my own feelings and what the desires of my attacker. I did not know who I was, or where; all time and all clarity were swallowed in one gulf of Darkness. In the confusion I seemed to remember something: my mother, clothed in terror, commanding; then Aldwulf, his face covered with a blood-stained bandage, kneeling before the runes and screaming, "Come! Any power that will destroy Gwalchmai, the Light's servant! Come, take your price!"—and I heard, who had been wandering, trapped in the hated light of the world, and came, saying, "Where is Gwalchmai, son of Lot, son of the queen of Darkness? I seek him."—No. It was not my memory, it was the demon's. This was the power Morgawse had summoned that night on Samhain after I had fled, which had pursued me to

Llyn Gwalch to destroy me. For nearly three years it had wandered the world, seeking me, unable to depart until it had carried out her command, and then Aldwulf had called, and it had found me again. The thought, the realization brought me to myself, as a man and apart from the dark power, and I brought the sword up, pressing the hilt against my forehead.

The demon released me, screaming, and fell across the floor. I got to my knees and slashed at it again, and it writhed madly, speaking to me now, pleading inside my mind without words and saying that it would obey me in everything if I would spare it. I laughed and brought the sword down.

The demon's death cry shook the air, seeming to penetrate the very fabric of the world; then it faded slowly with the cold and the silence into nothingness.

I raised the sword again, panting, and looked for something else to fight.

Silence. The soft breathing of sleeping men, now without the drugged, labored sound of earlier. A night bird called outside, and the wind rustled in the eaves. I lowered the sword. The fire faded, both from the blade and from my mind, leaving peace and a great weariness.

My King, I thought. You are the greatest of lords, the most splendid of warleaders. My thanks for the sword, and for the victory.

Then I went back to my pallet, sheathed Caledvwlch and lay down, too tired to stand.

As I settled, Sion stirred, woke, raised his head. He looked about the chapel porch for something, paused, then looked toward me uncertainly.

"Gwalchmai?" he whispered.

I was already half-asleep, and did not want to talk, so I pretended to be wholly asleep. After a minute, Sion shrugged and lay down again. I closed my eyes. Sleep was like a boat, drifting lazily across a vast and peaceful ocean.

NINE

Wʜᴇɴ ɪ ᴡᴏᴋᴇ ᴛʜᴇ ɴᴇxᴛ morning the feeling of peace remained. Sion, however, seemed anxious. He picked at the bread that the monks had provided and brooded. The other farmers discussed land and crops and the weather, laying plans, but Sion did not join them. Halfway through the meal he stopped eating, a piece of bread raised in one hand, and looked at me evenly. "I had a strange dream last night," he announced.

"Oh?" I asked, amused. "What was it?"

Sion looked back at his bread, shoved it into his mouth and chewed moodily before replying, "A dark thing came into the chapel porch."

My amusement vanished and I stared at him. He went on without looking at me, or at anyone else, though the others were now listening with some interest. "I felt it come in through the door and stand there a moment. At first it looked like a shadow, and then I blinked and saw that it was . . . well, a little like a man. Like a corpse, blackened and half-rotted. It started to come forward, shambling a little, like a trained bear, and I tried to wake up, because I was in a cold sweat at the sight of the thrice-damned thing, but I could not wake."

"Ah," said one of the farmers. "I knew a man who had a dream like that, and when he woke up in the morning he found that his daughter had died. They are strange things, dreams."

"They are indeed," said Sion, "but that was not the end of it." He began addressing me again, refusing to be side-tracked. "You did wake up. You stood and drew your sword, and the sword lit up like a pine torch catching light. You held it between yourself and the thing of per-dition, looking like you'd just been given your heart's desire, and then the two of you began fighting." Sion shrugged uneasily, eyed Caledvwlch, continued, "And then it was as though you were frozen, just beginning the fight, and I looked up at the wall behind the black thing, and there was a woman standing there."

I found that my hand was somehow about the hilt of my sword.

"A dark woman, she was, with a white, starved face and terrible eyes, more beautiful than any woman I ever saw, but with something sick about her. I've seen such a look as that in a town beggar starving in a gutter and cursing the passersby, but never in some proud beauty like that woman. She saw you about to fight the spirit of Yffern, and reached out to touch it; as she did, the darkness tripled. But then she looked up, and grew angry, and I looked behind me and saw there was a man there, a yellow-haired man cloaked in light, and he raised his hand, forbidding the woman to interfere."

I saw and stared at Sion. I started to speak, could think of nothing to say. I had considered this man a simple farmer. A farmer he was, but not simple. Men are not simple, and I had forgotten that others, besides myself, might serve the Light. "And that was the end of the dream?" I asked. Even to myself, my voice sounded strained.

Sion shook his head. The other farmers looked con-fusedly from one to the other of us, but Sion ignored them.

"No. But the dream changed after that. Suddenly I was not standing in the chapel porch, but on a great, level plain full of people. The sky was very dark in the east, as though a thunderstorm were about to break. In the west I saw the emperor with his warband, and suddenly the dragon broke from his standard and rose into the air, glowing like hot gold, and then it seemed that I was standing in the middle of a battle, for all the people on the plain had begun to fight. Near me there was a tall man, a Saxon, from his looks; the left side of his face was scarred, and he held a black flame in his left hand. The dragon passed over, and I shut my eyes for a moment, and when I opened them, the Saxon was dead, and over him stood a young man with pale hair, wearing a brooch in the shape of a lion. There were other struggles going on all about me, but I don't remember them now. Everything was in confusion."

The trader snorted suddenly and shook his head. "Indeed it is. Confused nonsense. Anyone who expects more from dreams is a fool."

"I've not finished," snapped Sion. "Let me tell this tale to the end, and if you do not wish to listen, don't. —It kept growing darker, and the shouting and clash of arms grew louder, and the dragon kept flying back and forth along the lines trailing fire; then there came a flash of lightning from heaven and I saw the ground behind me scattered with bodies, and one I noticed especially, a man in a red cloak, lying dead. There came a burst of thunder, and darkness full of fires, and I turned away, because I was afraid. When I turned I saw a man standing there, and he caught my arm. He was the emperor's chief poet, Taliesin—when the emperor took the purple, I fought with the army, so I recognized the man from then. But in the dream he was wearing a star upon his forehead, and he was the only one, in all that dream, who saw me. He said, 'Remember these things, Sion ap Rhys, and do not be afraid. Though they are terrible, no harm will come to you by them. Have faith.' So I bowed my head and all became dark. And then"—Sion took a deep breath—"then I woke up." He shrugged. "But all was quiet, and you were asleep."

The trader laughed at this, and Sion scowled.

"Dreams are strange things, to be sure," said the farmer who had spoken earlier. "But I cannot make head or tail of that one, I never heard of anyone fighting devils in dreams. But a dream about the Pendragon, that is plain enough. The thunderstorm would be the Saxons. Only I could not tell what they did, in your dream."

"It is nonsense," the trader repeated. "Though to be sure, you had us listening. But a man cannot heed dreams. I knew an old fool once who . . ."

Sion stood abruptly. "I think I will go into the chapel and pray."

"Indeed," said one of the other farmers. "Light a candle, and perhaps have the monks say a Mass. That may avert it."

"Avert what?" asked the first farmer. The second shrugged.

"I will join you," I said to Sion.

He gave me another of his steady looks, then nodded in satisfaction. The others looked at me uneasily, shook their heads. One crossed himself. As we left the farmers began talking in whispers, while the trader tried to resume his story.

There was a monk in the chapel, replacing the burned-out candles. Sion ignored him and knelt before the altar, crossing himself and beginning to mutter a prayer in Latin. I knelt slightly behind him, wondering. It was indeed a strange dream. Like the farmers, I could not guess at what most of it meant, but some of it was frighteningly plain. Sion was an unlikely prophet, but I wished I could better understand the dream.

"Gloria in excelsis Deo," said Sion, as though reciting something. "Glory to God in the heights, and in Earth peace to men of good will . . ." He went on in this vein for a bit, then stopped, and stared silently at the crucifix. I wished I understood his religion better. It seemed to worship the Light, and I did not know how to do that on my own. I knew just enough to disbelieve the rumors and strange tales about that faith, the stories of cannibalism and unnatural orgies which had been discussed at great length in the Boys' House. It would be comforting to have some fine words like Sion's to say to my lord now, after the victory of the night before and now this dream.

Not knowing what to say, I drew my sword again and rested it before me, one hand on each of the crosspieces. I felt again, suddenly stronger than before, that deep silent regard, and again wished to sing, but all I could remember was a song to the sun, in Irish.

Hail to you, bright morning,
Shattering the sky of night,
Blazing fair, victoriously dawning,
Ever-young, the new-born light!

Welcome is this morning,
Golden-handed, sunlight lender:
Welcome is the day's high king,
Light's liege lord, morning's sender.

It seemed appropriate enough. The monk finished with the candles and left, his feet making soft padding sounds on the wooden floor. The door closed behind him, and we remained, staring at the altar.

The ruby in the hilt of Caledvwlch began to glow, burned brighter; the light steadied and became more intense, casting a clear rose-colored light brighter than the candles. Sion saw it cast his shadow before him and turned. He stared for a moment, then let out a long sigh.

"It is true, then," he said. "I was not certain."

"I know that some of it is true," I replied. "The rest, though, is beyond my understanding. I am only human, Sion ap Rhys."

Sion blew out his cheeks. "I know."

I was surprised, and showed it.

"Oh, I know," Sion explained. "Indeed, I did think differently yesterday. You came from the forest out of nowhere, and I looked once and said to myself, 'It is one of the People of the Hills.' But you were obliging with the cart, and got yourself covered in mud pushing it loose on that Yffern-bent track, and I thought, 'Perhaps not.' All the way to Ynys Witrin I was uncertain. I have dreams, you see, and sometimes one has a sense of things. It runs in the family. Usually I ignore it—the supernatural is best left alone—but I know enough to pay heed when something strange is happening; and even those farmers can sense that there is something strange about you, and they knowing no more than a Saxon's sheep does. Yesterday, when I mentioned that witch, just before we came to Ynys Witrin, I was nearly certain that you were of the Fair Ones, and you had taken a human form for some purpose of your own. But when we arrived, and you tried

143

to give me your cloak in return for half a sack of flour, and afterward followed me into the chapel here and prayed, I knew that you had to be human. The People of the Hills don't pray. And besides, it made no sense that one of the Fair Ones would get covered with mud about a cart of wheat flour. Only you have had dealings with the Otherworld, haven't you? There is still something strange about you, though today it is less strong."

"I . . . have. But what of your dream? You have had other such dreams?"

He shrugged. "On occasion. Before my clan finished our blood feud, twenty years back, I had a dream. And I had another one before Arthur claimed the purple, and one or two others about smaller things. Nothing as long and accursedly frightening as the one last night, though. Tell me, Gwalchmai, how much of that dream was true?"

I looked down at the hilt of my sword, where the light had died now. "I did fight a demon last night, and I did kill it, though to me it looked like nothing more than a shadow. And I know the man and the woman you saw watching, as well, though they were not here. The Saxon in the confused part, the one with the scarred face and the black flame—that was Aldwulf, King of Bernicia. But I don't know who the man that fought him was. I know nothing of the rest."

"Aldwulf?" asked Sion. "I have heard of him, but never that he had a scar. In fact, it is always said that he is handsome as the devil, and proud of it."

"He has a scar now," I said. "I put it there. It was for that that he called the demon to send after me."

Sion's eyes widened. "How? Aldwulf of Bernicia is said to be in Din Sarum, with Cerdic and the whole Saxon army."

"He was, but—I had been captured by the Saxons, and was pretending to be a thrall. Aldwulf had captured a horse as a gift for Cerdic, one of the horses of the . . . People of the Hills, as you call them. I tamed the horse and rode out over Aldwulf before anyone could stop me."

Sion shook his head in wonder. "Dear God. As plainly as that, 'I rode out over Aldwulf.' So; and who were the man and the woman I saw watching you, then?"

I hesitated. "The man was Lugh of the Long Hand. I think you call him Llwch in British."

He stared, off-balance. "A pagan god?"

"Not a god. Not a human, either. Beyond that, I do not know, except that he serves the Light. It was he who gave me this sword."

"And the Light, I take it, is God. Very well, I can make no sense of it. What of the woman? I could see that she was a ruler of Darkness, but what connection has she with you?"

"She is my mother," I said unhappily. "Morgawse of Orcade."

Sion went very still. "The witch herself," he said at last. "Your father, then, is King Lot of the Ynysoedd Erch?"

I nodded.

"Well," said Sion, after another long pause. "It is not only dreams that are very strange, these days. You are not what I pictured for the son of a king and an emperor's daughter, especially not when both of them have such a reputation, and when I had heard that the younger sons of the Queen Morgawse were . . ." He broke off. He had heard, plainly enough, that the younger sons of the Queen Morgawse were likewise witches. Poor Medraut, if he had acquired that reputation now.

"And you are not what I pictured for a prophet," I returned.

"I? A prophet? Do not talk foolishness!"

"What else was that dream but prophetic? I think that many of the things you saw must be still to come."

"It is only a dream, not to . . . damn," said Sion. He had not thought of the light it cast on himself. I laughed. He glared at me for a moment, then grinned. "I am a plain farmer," he said, "and I do not think that any such thing will happen to me again. I have no part in any of these great and terrible battles, nor want any part: It is trouble enough, more than trouble enough, to run a holding in these days, and see that there is peace and good order in my own house. Still, I am glad that this has happened, for how can one not wish, in times such as these, to preserve civilization and the empire and the light of Britain." He frowned again, then said, in a very low voice, "Remember me, Gwalchmai. —Lord Gwalchmai, I suppose it is. I know that I have not done anything in deed, only told you a dream. But it would make me glad to know, ten or twenty years from now, that one of those in the center of the battle might remember me if I went and spoke to him."

"It is not likely that I will forget you or your dream," I said. "But I doubt that I'll have any great part in the things that are to come."

Sion gave me a look of flat disbelief. "You have. Someday, I will tell my grandchildren how I met you on your way to Camlann and gave you a ride in my cart, and they will not believe a word of it." He stood, dusting off his knees. "They will say, 'There is Grandfather, pretending that once he knew all the kings in Britain and making himself foolish.'"

I shook my head. What fighting I did would surely be in dark places, where there is no fame to be brought back to the sunlit world. "Why don't you wait until Arthur has accepted my sword before planning what you will tell your grandchildren?" I asked. "You might say, 'And once I met Gwalchmai mac Lot,' and they will only reply, 'Who?'"

Sion shook his head stubbornly. "That they will not say. Do you wish to leave me now for Camlann?"

We were just leaving the chapel when we heard the sound of shouting and of horses from the abbey yard. We glanced at each other and hurried out into the sunlight and found the other travelers, most of the monks, and a group of warriors standing about within the gate and shouting. There were about a dozen of the warriors; they were British, mounted on tall war-horses, and their arms gleamed.

One of the monks was doing most of the shouting. He was the abbot, I guessed from the quality of his clothing and the jewels on the gold pectoral cross he wore. "What more?" he was demanding. "We have had to ask more from our flock to cover what you have taken already, and we've barely enough to last us until the harvest even so. . . ."

"Do you think you can put us off with plain lies?" answered one of the warriors. He was a very big man, so

big that his war-horse looked small. His red hair bristled
in all directions, and his light blue eyes glittered danger-
ously; he wore more jewelry than I had seen on one man
before, and brighter colors. "You have enough and more
than enough to grow fat on, without taking double tithes
of your miserable 'sheep' and gouging every traveler who
comes by expecting hospitality. If the Saxons came here,
they would take all you have, down to the last rush and
candlestick. Aren't you grateful to us for keeping them
away?"

"The Saxons are only an excuse, a pretext put forward
by a tyrant!" said the monk fiercely.

The warriors laughed. "Perhaps now you prefer the
Saxons to the emperor," said another, a lean, dark, one-
handed man in plain clothing, "but you would think otherwise if the Pendragon ceased to fight them."

The abbot snarled. "It is the duty of Christian kings to
protect their people; it is not their duty to rob them. We
cannot give . . ."

"Oh? Hear him, brothers!" said the redhead. "He cannot give. But we can take."

"Robbers!" cried the abbot.

"Be careful, Cei," warned the dark warrior. "Arthur
said we must not push them to breaking."

Cei shrugged. "But if we bend them a little? Perhaps
with a little fire? Just a small one, on top of the gate-
house?"

The abbot looked at him furiously, decided not to risk
seeing whether he was serious. "You godless killers," he
said. "We keep some supplies over there, only a few, but
all we have."

The dark warrior gave his comrade, Cei, a meaningful
look. "Yes, perhaps you keep the tenth part of your
goods there. Truly, Theodorus, it does you no good to
lie to us. Last time you said you had no gold, and then
came to us wanting us to recover what you'd sent to Sorviodunum for safekeeping. Very well, I suppose that will
have to do for now." He turned from the abbot to Sion
and the other travelers and announced, "The Pendragon
has won another victory, for he came across a large
Saxon raiding party in Powys, and destroyed it. Praise to
God."

The farmers cheered. The Saxon raids would probably be eased slightly now, and their lands and herds were safer.

"It is good that you are pleased," said Cei. "In token of it, you can lend us any carts and horses you have. You can claim them in Camlann, and you'll be paid for any goods you've brought."

The farmers fell abruptly silent.

"By my name saint!" said Sion angrily. "I've a fine load of wheat flour in my cart, and my best horse harnessed to it. I'll not lend it to any before you pay me."

The other farmers muttered angry agreement. The dark warrior shrugged. "You will be repaid. The emperor will not cheat you."

"You misheard me," said Sion. "I said, I will not lend you my cart and cargo without payment."

"Yes you will," said Cei. "You will lend it for payment later, or lose it altogether."

"That is not just," I said, becoming angry with the farmers. "I do not think that your lord could approve of it."

The dark warrior lifted an eyebrow. "We need supplies," he said, very calm and reasonable. "We need carts and horses to move the supplies, and all of ours are damaged or being used for the wounded. My lord Arthur approves. You will be paid, never fear." I continued to stare angrily, and suddenly he frowned and gave me a sharper look.

The other spokesman for the warriors, Cei, ignored the whole exchange and simply asked the farmers. "Where are your carts?"

Sion spat and crossed his arms. "First pay me." The other farmers followed his example and remained stubborn.

"Give them some token now," I suggested to the dark warrior, "or at least mark down the value of the goods, so that they can be sure of their full payment when they reach the high king."

Cei glared at me. "Who, by God, are you? You're no farmer. What's your business here?"

"My name is Gwalchmai, and I was going to Camlann to seek service with the Pendragon."

Cei laughed. "Arthur has no need of swineheads. You

had better go back to wherever you came from and leave warriors' matters to warriors." He said it as a challenge, speaking as Agravian often had.

The dark one shifted uneasily, "Cei, stop."

"What? Bedwyr, you cannot want to defend this base-born meddler?"

Bedwyr shook his head dubiously. "Let him be. If he speaks the truth, he may be our comrade soon."

"Him? A warrior? Look at how he's dressed! He doesn't even have a horse!"

"Nonetheless," said Bedwyr, "let us take what we need and go, without fighting. We must reach Camlann quickly."

"Bedwyr, my brother, do not turn moralist on me again. I swear the oath of my people, you Bretons are worse than Northerners, and almost as bad as the Irish."

Bedwyr smiled. "So, it is 'bad as the Irish' again? There speaks a true Dumnonian. But I seem to recall that . . ."

"*Per onmes sanctos!* There are exceptions; I admitted that I was wrong about him. God in heaven, how you revel in my mistakes. Why am I cursed with such disloyal friends?"

At this the warriors began to laugh and Bedwyr smiled again.

"Truly, Cei," he continued, "you are over-fond of fighting; and it will hurt us here."

Cei sighed. "Very well." He looked back to me. "I will overlook it, you. Now, men, where are your carts?"

"Where is your justice?" replied Sion, but uncertainly now.

"Be quiet, Farmer!" snapped Cei. "Or I will teach you when to hold your tongue."

My hand dropped to Caledvwlch's hilt. Cei saw the movement and drew his own sword with a ring of metal, his eyes lighting. The warriors fell silent.

"What do you mean to do with that, my friend?" asked Cei, soft voiced now, and courteous.

"Cei . . ." Bedwyr began again, then stopped, seeing that it was useless.

"I do not mean to do anything with this," I said, my voice also soft, "but I will not have you threatening my friends as well as stealing their goods."

Cei dismounted and came closer, grinning fiercely. Abruptly I realized what I had done and wondered what could have come over me. How could I fight a professional warrior, one of Arthur's men? The most I could hope for was not to be hurt too badly.

But I could not withdraw now, and something of the same lightness fell on me. I drew Caledvwlch. Cei grinned still more widely and took another step forward.

"Cei! Who is it now?" came a voice from the back of the group. The warriors glanced around.

Another of their number had ridden up, carrying some of the monks' supplies, and Cei's band made room for him. He was a tall man of about twenty-one, with long gold hair and a neat beard and mustache. He wore a purple-bordered cloak fastened with gold, and radiated energy and strength. His hot blue eyes skipped lightly over me to rest on Cei. "If this man is all, he's not worth it."

"He began it," said Cei in an injured tone.

"The day someone else begins a fight with you, rivers will run backward," said the newcomer. "By the sun and the wind, for once let us obey Arthur and simply take the supplies and go."

Cei paused, glanced back at me. I sheathed Caledvwlch.

Cei sighed a little, then sheathed his own sword. "Well enough. It is not worth it; and it is too soon after a battle besides." He swung up onto his horse. The blond man grinned and turned his own horse. The tension was gone: The foraging party would take what it wanted and go.

"Wait!" I called. The warriors stopped, turned, looking inquisitive. I smiled, feeling a strange emotion, half joy, half an old envy and bitterness—bitterness that dissolved away, leaving only the joy.

"A thousand welcomes, Agravain," I said to the blond warrior.

TEN

My brother sat motionless for a moment, staring at me with his old hot stare. Then he dismounted hurriedly, ran a few steps toward me, stopped, walked on slowly.

"It is impossible," he said, his face growing red. "You ... you are dead."

"Truly, I am not," I replied.

"Gwalchmai?" he asked, "Gwalchmai?"

"You know him?" demanded Cei in astonishment. Agravain did not even look around.

"I had not thought to see you so soon," I said. "I am very glad."

He smiled hesitantly, then beamed, caught my shoulders, looked at me, and crushed me in a hug. "Gwalchmai! By the sun and the wind, I thought that you were dead, three years dead! Och, God, God, it is good to see you!"

I returned the embrace wholeheartedly, laughing, and it seemed that finally all the dark years of our childhood were blotted out for me. We had both endured too many things to feel anything but gladness on meeting each other again.

"What is happening?" asked Cei, in complete confusion. "Why are you jabbering in Irish?"

"Cei!" shouted Agravain, releasing me and whirling about to his comrades, "This is my brother, Gwalchmai, the one who died—the one I thought had died! I swear

151

the oath of my people, I do not know how, but this is he."

The warriors reacted by staring in astonishment, except for Cei, who gave me a look of, first, embarrassment, then apology. But the farmers around me drew away a little, and the monks stared with increased suspicion.

"So he is the famous Agravain ap Lot," said Sion, looking at my brother—the only one in the crowd who was.

"Is he famous?" I asked, remembering my old worries for Agravain's case as a hostage. Clearly, they had been wasted. "Och, well, it might have been expected." Agravain grinned at that.

"Where have you been when you were considered dead, that you heard nothing of your brother's fame?" asked Bedwyr quietly. I looked up, met his eyes, and felt respect for him.

"I have been to a distant place," I said, "and through strange things, too many to tell quickly."

"Indeed," said Bedwyr, not questioning at all, and shook himself.

"These are strange matters enough," said another of the warriors. "Come, let's finish our business here and go to Camlann. Arthur and the rest will be there soon, and there's nothing to eat there but pork rinds and cabbage."

Most of the foraging party set about loading the monks' goods into the already loaded carts, and, at my insistence, taking down the amount and kind of the farmers' goods. Agravain and I stood looking at each other and trying to decide how to begin. Then the carts rolled out into the yard, and Sion, who had been harnessing his mare, reluctantly jumped from the seat. "You will see that my horse is well treated?" he asked me.

I nodded, then, realizing that it was intended that he was to continue to Camlann on foot and that I might not see him again, I caught his hand. "And I will remember you, Sion ap Rhys, if the thought of that gives you pleasure. If I do not see you at Camlann, remember that. And if ever you need any help, and I can give it, my sword is yours."

"I thank you," he replied, quietly. "And . . . may God grant you favor with the emperor."

"And may you walk in Light." I climbed into his cart

and took the reins. "I will drive this one," I told Agravain. He nodded, and I shook the reins. The little mare started off, trotting down the hill toward the causeway. Those warriors who had taken the other carts followed, and Agravain rode his horse beside me. We left Ynys Witrin and turned east for the main road and Camlann.

"Why don't you let the farmers drive their own carts?" I asked Agravain.

"They would go too slowly, and when they arrived in Camlann, drive the prices up by their bargaining. As it is we can have the standard price ready for them when they reach the gate, and send them off at once. You seemed friendly with that man; where did you meet him?"

"On the road, yesterday."

Agravain checked his horse. "Yesterday? What did he do for you, that you let him take liberties?"

"He gave me a ride in his cart, and paid for my night's stay at Ynys Witrin. I had nothing to pay with."

Agravain scowled. "And for that you take his hand? You should merely have repaid him doubly, and not demeaned yourself. Why in God's name had you nothing to pay with?"

"In God's name," I said. "Have you become a Christian, Agravain?"

"God forbid!" he said, grinning, then frowned again. "You should not let commoners become so familiar. They are always wanting favors then."

I sighed. "Sion is a good man. I was lucky to have met him."

Agravain's frown deepened, but he shrugged. "Well, you can choose your own friends."

"I think he is capable of that," said a quiet voice on the other side. Bedwyr drew his horse in beside us. "Come. We must hurry. I do not want Arthur to have to wait for his victory feast at Camlann."

Agravain spurred his horse and I urged Sion's mare obediently, though she did not like the brisk trot with the heavy cart. We fell silent again, and Cei came up and rode beside Bedwyr, giving me interested looks.

"You destroyed Cerdic's raiding party, then?" I asked, finally thinking of something to say. "That is good, but surprising. I would have thought his parties move too quickly for even the Pendragon to reach them before they returned to Sorviodunum."

"It was more chance than foresight," said Bedwyr. "We were returning from fighting the East Saxons when we heard news of this raiding party from Sorviodunum, and we caught them only just in time."

"That was a thing Cerdic hadn't planned for," said Cei with satisfaction. "They say that the sorceror of his, Aldwulf Fflamddwyn, had been telling him where Arthur is. But even Aldwulf cannot predict where Arthur will be."

"Nor can we," said Agravain, "even when we are with him. He is a great king. Gwalchmai. It shames me that ever Father fought him. We should have made alliance with him, and not with those Northern cattle."

"Now, that is true," said Cei, "and it would have saved you time, as well."

"But your brother must believe this, too, Agravain," Bedwyr added, "otherwise he would not be seeking to serve Arthur."

Agravain frowned again. "What were you expecting to do, Gwalchmai? Arthur takes only warriors and a few doctors with the warband. You could stay in Camlann, I suppose, if you are not planning to go home."

"I cannot go back to the islands," I said. "—But you, Agravain, how is it that you are fighting alongside Arthur's own warband? And gaining fame in it, as well? I have not heard any news of you, not since you were taken hostage."

"Och, that," said Agravain. "That came of itself. The high king was kind to me, after Father and our kinsmen had gone; and I had some admiration for him already, because of his skill of war, though I hated him for an enemy."

"But he let you fight beside his men?"

"Not at once." Agravain suddenly grinned at Cei. "This hard-handed lout of a Dumnonian decided to give me the sharp edge of his tongue, and that is a sharp edge indeed. I understood little enough of it at the time, for my British was still not good, but I understood enough. And so one day, when he and the Family, returned from a raid, were at Camlann, and he began to say, 'The only worse men than the Saxons are the Irish,' I up and hit him. So he hit back, and we were at it like hammer and anvil. Only, as you see, he is bigger than I, and got the better of me."

"Only you would not stop fighting for all that," Cei put in. "*Gloria Deo!* I was certain I was fighting with a madman."

"And when he knocked me down for the fifth time, and I tried to get up again, and had to hold on to a table to do it, he said, 'You mad Irishman, don't you know enough to stop fighting when you are beaten?' and I said, 'I do not, and I wish my father had not either.' And he said, 'You're a wild barbarian, but by God, you've heart enough. I take back my words,' and helped me up. And when the high king next wanted him to lead a raid, Cei said, 'Let me take Agravain, then. It is the only way to keep him out of trouble.' "

"Not," added Bedwyr, "that Cei wanted to keep out of trouble. On the contrary, there is nothing he likes better, and he was the more pleased that he had a friend to make it with him."

"So I have fought for the high king," Agravain concluded, "and it is well and good. Father has sent messages, from time to time, saying that he is pleased to hear that I fight well. But what of yourself, Gwalchmai? For three years I have heard nothing of you, not from the Islands, nor from Britain nor from anywhere else. Where have you been?"

I looked away, unsure. I owed it to my brother to tell him the truth, but what he would do with that truth I could not guess. Probably, refuse to believe it. Still, I would tell him. But how could I speak of Morgawse before Bedwyr and Cei? Agravain would have to believe what I said of her—he knew her just well enough for that—but it was not for the ears of others.

"Perhaps you should begin at the beginning." suggested Agravain when the silence became awkward.

"There is time enough for you to tell the tale." Bedwyr added. "It is miles yet to Camlann."

I studied Bedwyr. Here, I realized, was another man who served the Light, but one completely different from

Sion. He had seen at the first that I had had dealings with the Otherworld, too, and his eyes were still doubtful. Now Cei too was giving me a peculiar look. Only Agravain noticed nothing.

"Agravain," I said, "I can tell you. But not now."

"By the sun and the wind!" exclaimed Agravain, using his old oath, which touched me hard with memories, "You have just returned from the dead, as far as I know, and you wish me to wait patiently and make light conversation?"

"That might be best," I said. "It is a family matter."

"I have another family now," replied Agravain, waving his hand toward the warriors around him. "And what concerns me concerns them."

"If you wish to join us," Bedwyr commented, "you will have to tell us as well. There is no vengeance taken for past blood feuds or such once a man has joined the Family."

"Gwalchmai join the Family?" asked Agravain. "That is as unlikely as his engaging in a blood feud. He is not a skilled warrior."

Bedwyr looked thoughtful. "Perhaps."

"I am not," I said. "I hope to serve the Pendragon in some other way."

"Arthur does not take many men with us," said Cei, "But he might make an exception, if you can ride well."

"He was the best rider in the islands," said Agravain. "He can join us in some fashion, then, if not as a warrior?"

"That is up to our lord Arthur," Bedwyr said.

"But if you wish to, we have a right to know what you have done," Cei told me. "Shortly after Agravain joined us, he had a message from the Ynysoedd Erch saying that his brother had ridden off a cliff, and he went into mourning for weeks. Anything that affects him thus is my concern too. So, tell us now."

I looked from him to Bedwyr to Agravain, then shrugged. "As you wish. But it is a strange story, and I do not know whether you will believe me. And there are things Agravain and I can understand that you may not. I am not a skilled fighter, to be involved in duels and blood feuds, but this is a matter of Darkness. . . ."

The doubt in Bedwyr's eyes flamed into suspicion. Agravain gave a start, like a frightened horse shying. "Then it does have something to do with Mother," he whispered.

"It does," I agreed. "Would you prefer that I wait, Brother?"

He began to nod, stopped again. "I had heard that you went riding at night, on Samhain. By the cliffs. It was a mad thing to do, but like you, and I had heard also that . . ." He trailed off, and I saw that he too was familiar with my old reputation for sorcery. Cei and Bedwyr glanced at each other, the same thought in their minds.

Then Cei snorted. "Your mother, the famous witch, and an old pagan festival, and this is a reason for disappearing? I do not believe in such things. I did not think you believed either, Agravain."

"I don't," said Agravain. But he did not look at Cei. He believed, well enough. It was impossible to know Morgawse and not believe in her power.

"Shall I go on?" I asked.

"Yes," said Agravain. "Cei and Bedwyr are also my brothers now; they have the right to hear."

Well, if that was how it was to be, I would tell the tale to the three of them. But I didn't want to. It would be painful enough to tell to kinsmen, let alone strangers. "Agravain," I said, "what did you hear of my death?"

"Only what I said, that you went riding at night on Samhain, and your horse was found by the cliff next day, riderless. No one could expect you to turn up two and a half years later, eighteen miles from Camlann, dressed like a servant and picking fights with Cei— Couldn't you have chosen someone else? He's the best foot fighter in the Family."

Cei grinned and nodded his agreement with this.

"And you have grown! It has been so long since I saw you—you are seventeen now, and the last time was, what?—more than three years ago. Come, explain how it happened."

I drove the cart in silence for a while, trying to decide where to begin, and praying that my brother would accept the story. "You recall a certain summer, years ago, when I first began learning Latin?" I asked finally.

He thought back. "Yes. A wise thing to do; they speak a good deal of it here, and I still cannot understand a word of it."

"That is where it began. We had a quarrel over my learning such a thing, and you called me a bastard and said that I was trying to learn sorcery."

Agravain looked surprised. "I did? I don't remember that."

"I suppose you wouldn't. It didn't mean much to you. But I was foolish, and it meant a good deal to me. I determined to truly learn sorcery." I lifted my eyes from the road and met Agravain's hot stare. "And I am certain that you did hear of those matters."

He shifted uneasily, flushing, and looked away from me. He nodded. I looked back at the road.

"So I went to our mother, and she taught me many things, all terrible."

Agravain's hands had tightened on the reins, and now his horse snorted, trying to stop and shying at the unsteady jerk. He quickly relaxed his grip and edged the horse back to the cart.

"She is very powerful, Agravain," I said urgently. "She is much stronger, probably, than any other on earth, so much that she is scarcely human now. At first she hated her father, and her half-brother Arthur, and then all Britain, and I think now she hates all the universe, and wishes to drown the world in Darkness."

Agravain's horse started again, laying its ears back, catching fear from its rider. Bedwyr dropped behind the cart, then drove his horse up beside Agravain's, to steady it. Agravain closed his eyes for a moment, his face strained and white. "No," he whispered. "She can't truly want that."

"She does," I said, wanting to reach out to him, but not quite daring. "You know her. Think."

He turned his face away, shoulders shaking a little. For a long time we rode in silence, the hooves of the horses clattering on the causeway, the cart jolting in the sunlight. The marsh reeds shook in the wind. Cei was puzzled, Bedwyr withdrawn.

After a long time, shortly before we reached the main road, Agravain's hands slowly relaxed and he nodded. "It is true," he said in a choked tone. "I would rather not think of her. Gwalchmai. But it is true. By the sun, why?"

I shook my head. He expected no answer.

"Go on," said Agravain, after another stretch of silence, when we had turned south on the main road. I noted that he controlled himself better. Three years before he would either have started a quarrel with me or driven his horse ahead at its fastest gallop.

"I said that our mother hated Arthur. She has cursed him many times, but her magic does not seem to work on him. Two and a half years ago, on Samhain, she wanted to try some other spell to kill him."

"God," said Agravain in a strangled tone. "What affair is it of hers? What harm has he done her?"

"She hates him. You know that. And I think every black sorcerer in the West is seeking the death of Arthur. Aldwulf Fflamddwyn certainly is."

"What? —Och, I know she hates the high king. But can she? . . ."

"I do not think she can," I said.

He stared at me earnestly for a moment, wanting reassurance, then nodded, relaxing. "*Laus Deo*, as they say here in Britain. But, by the sun, she should be destroyed. Someone should kill her; though she is my own mother, still I say that she should die."

"Perhaps she should," I replied, "but who could kill her?— She wanted me, and Medraut, to be there that night. . . ."

"I had heard that Medraut . . . but I was sure that was false. No one was altogether certain that Medraut was . . . and it is unlike him."

"It is true, though," I said, "though I did not know it till that night." Again I thought of Medraut with pain. She must have devoured him by now, sucking out all his innocence and love for life, replacing it with hatred and bitterness and more ambition. And there was nothing I could do.

Agravain looked at me miserably. He had been trying for years, I think, to forget Morgawse, as he had tried for years to ignore her. But he accepted this now.

"Do you remember Connall?" I asked. "The Dalriad, the one in our father's warband."

"Of course. A brave man, and loyal, and a good fighter, as I well know from campaigning with him in Britain. The first time I ever went whoring he took me, back in Din Eidyn."

"Morgawse was going to kill him," I said, "and, Agravain, I could not endure it. Not him and Medraut also. I killed him quickly and fled, and she tried to kill me."

He looked sick. "This is madness. Why can't people fight with swords, simply, instead . . ."

"People never fight simply with swords," Bedwyr broke in. "Even you and Cei do not do that."

Agravain paused, blinking at Bedwyr. "What does that mean?"

"No one takes up the sword without a reason. Even love of battle is a kind of reason. In the end, the reasons are never simple, and they are as important as the sword itself."

"Philosophy," said Cei. "You read too much of it, Bedwyr."

"The reasons remain important," said Bedwyr imperturbably. "Go on, Gwalchmai."

"Our mother set a curse on me, and I fled from it, without thinking where I was going, until I came to Llyn Gwalch—that is the place on the cliff where I spent so much time, when we were children, Agravain—and let the horse go. The demon couldn't follow me there. I don't know why, except that I once believed in the place, and the Light . . ." I stopped. How could I tell Agravain about that? He could not possibly understand. I did not understand it myself.

"Our mother could not kill the Pendragon," I began, because Arthur fights against the Darkness, with the force that is also against the Darkness. When I was trapped there, I called on that force, because I was very wearied with the Darkness and hated it. And an ancestor of ours, who serves the Light, sent aid."

"An ancestor?" asked Agravain in confusion. "This becomes more difficult as you go on. What ancestor?"

"Lugh of the Long Hand."

He shook his head again. I saw that I was beginning to

lose him. "I do not know what to think of this, Gwalchmai. If anyone else came to me with a story like this, I
would laugh at him. But you . . ."

"I think that you must believe him," Bedwyr interrupted softly. "I do not know that I have ever seen a man so
deeply touched by the Otherworld."

Agravain glared at his friend. "There is nothing wrong
with my brother. True, he is a poor warrior, but that
gives you no right to insult him."

"I am not insulting him." Bedwyr seemed mildly
amused. "And I think he can look after his own honor.
Gwalchmai, go on."

"Lugh sent a boat from Tir Tairngaire, at the urging of
the Light. . . ."

"What is this 'Light' you keep talking about?" asked
Agravain irritably. "The sun?"

"I think I understand," Bedwyr said slowly. "In a sense,
the sun. As the sun is a type of Light, since all other
lights are ultimately derived from it, by reflection or by
dependence with the rest of the world, so the Light
which your brother speaks of is the source of good and
of illumination, and other goods are known only in it.
—Yes, Cei. I did read it in a book of philosophy. But am I
right?"

"I . . . I think so," I said, astonished. "Yes, if I understand you. I do not know any philosophy. I know only
that the Light sent a boat, and I embarked, and it took
me to the Islands of the Blessed."

"Oh God!" said Cei, at last releasing his growing anger.
"How many have made that claim? And how many have
been to those islands? None, because those islands do not
exist outside the songs of poets! Agravain, you are my
brother, but this brother of yours is another matter. He
has been spinning gossamer from clouds of lies this whole
while, and you've been taking it for a true yarn. But I
can't. When you have had enough, I will be riding up
ahead."

"He is not lying, Cei," said Bedwyr.

But Cei only gave me a look of disgust. "No, indeed.
He is merely giving a poetic form to the concepts of philosophers, and discoursing upon the *summum bonum* or
whatever you call it. This is a fine enough tale for Breton

mystics and philosophers, Bedwyr, but I am a Dumnonian and a Roman, and I want no more of this." He
spurred his horse to a gallop and left us, reining in beside
some other warrior.

"Go on," said Agravain. "I will listen."

But he was beginning to agree with Cei. "I am not lying," I said.

"I do not say that you would, deliberately," said Agravain, apparently deciding to be very honest. "But after
what had passed, you could easily have had some kind of
dream."

"I thought it was a dream, when I woke up and found
myself in Britain," I said. "But I still had this." I touched
Caledvwlch's hilt.

Agravain looked at it, his brows knitting. "A sword. I
noticed it earlier. It looks to be worth a good amount.
You think it was given to you in the Land of Promise?"

"It was, by Lugh, from the Light. When I woke up
southeast of here, returning from Tir Tairngaire, I knew
that I had not been dreaming or gone mad, because it lay
beside me. Its name is Caledvwlch."

Agravain glared at it. He was becoming angry now,
and I dreaded the results of his anger. "A sword. A fine
sword, as far as I can tell. Let me see the rest of it."

I drew Caledvwlch. His eyebrows went up and he
whistled. "Och, fine indeed; I should like such a sword.
But it is not supernatural."

Bedwyr stared at the bright steel for a moment, then
looked away. He apparently did see something supernatural in it.

I considered making the fire burn in the blade, to show
Agravain the power as well, but decided not to. It was
too violent and obvious, and abuse of the power. Besides,
I had no desire to be thought a witch, and I did not
know the warriors. So, "Lugh gave it to me," I reiterated.

Agravain snorted. He was rejecting the story now. Perhaps he could simply not accept it of me, of Gwalchmai,
his weak, ineffectual little brother. "Go on," he said, however. "You woke up with the sword, east of here, after
spending—how long?—in the Isles of the Blessed."

"It was nearly three years. It seemed only a day. But
time was strange there. I woke in the hills in the border-

land between the kingdom of Dumnonia and the land Cerdic claims, and when I was walking west I walked directly into a Saxon raiding party on its way back to Sorviodunum."

Agravain calmed at this; this he could believe. "Couldn't you tell a Saxon from a Roman?" he asked.

"I did not know where I was. For all I knew, I might be going to Constantinople, though I thought it unlikely. So I told them that I was a thrall, and my master had died in a blood feud, and they brought me back to Sorviodunum and sold me to Cerdic."

"Why should he buy you? Did he suspect that you were a king's son?"

"I don't think so. Aldwulf of Bernicia told him to, and Aldwulf, like Bedwyr, or Sion, or most people these days, was not sure I was quite human when first he saw me."

"That is ridiculous," said Agravain. "Why should they think that? You did not, did you, Bedwyr?"

"Your brother is right," said Bedwyr. "I think you underestimate him."

"I know him better than you," snapped Agravain. "—Go on."

"Aldwulf wanted to kill Arthur, as I said, and thought that if he killed me and used the sword, he could manage it, by sorcery. But he had conjured up a horse of the Sidhe for Cerdic, to prove his power in sorcery, a horse that could out-run and out-stay any horse on earth. Cerdic was trying to break it, but could not. I could—you must remember that I was good with horses, though this one was different—and I did, and I rode it out of Sorviodunum as fast as possible."

"Then where is it now?"

"I let him go. He was of the Sidhe; I had no right to keep him. That was the day before yesterday; and yesterday I met with that farmer you disliked and came to Ynys Witrin, where you came this morning."

"A fine story," said Agravain scornfully. "Very fine, indeed. But you forgot a few details, Gwalchmai. What about the hill fort full of armed Saxons? But doubtless you slew them by the scores as you rode off on the king's horse."

"They did try to stop me, they just weren't quick

enough. —No, I am not claiming any skill at arms. We both know better. But the Saxons were afraid. They did not think that I was human, and I had the sword."

"Your sword! Why should they fear that?"

"It . . . I imagine it can be frightening."

"Gwalchmai," said Agravain, his voice level and controlled, but plainly very angry, "Cerdic's warriors are not children to run away from a reputed magic sword. And what of the king, and Aldwulf of Bernicia? You say that Fflamddwyn is a sorcerer, and so his name and fame are in all Britain; couldn't he have ruined that famous sword for you?"

"I do not think his power is that great," I said. "I do not think anything could quench Caledvwlch, except its bearer. If I turned against the Light, since it is by Light that the sword burns . . . whatever. Aldwulf was unconscious when I left. I'd cut his face open with Caledvwlch."

Agravain reined in his horse to a complete halt. "And how many Saxons did you kill leaving the camp?" he asked quietly.

I stopped the cart. Sion's mare halted gladly, her sides heaving. "There." I knew what was coming now. "Agravain, I am not trying to claim that . . ."

"You have said enough," Agravain went on firmly. The entire foraging band was halting now, and the warriors were turning their horses back or driving their carts forward to see what was happening. "The first part of your story I believe, the second is a dream or some confusion honestly and easily made, but this . . . this can be nothing other than an outright lie. You, striking down a Saxon king, and killing three of Cerdic's warriors single-handedly? You can't even throw a spear straight."

"Agravain, I said it was not from skill but . . ."

"Was it by magic, then? You said you'd rejected that, and rightly so."

"No, it was not, but . . ."

"Then your tale is a tissue of lies," Agravain proclaimed fiercely, "nonsense you made up to give yourself some honor which you are afraid to win honestly in battle. You are hopeless as a warrior."

"I've never said otherwise."

"And I will show you how hopeless." My brother ruthlessly thrust aside my attempts to fend off what was coming. "Get out of that cart and I will teach you not to lie. . . ."

"I will lend you my horse," Bedwyr said to me, quite suddenly, "and my spear and shield as well, so that you can fight as a warrior should."

There was an instant of startled silence. "Thank you," I said at last, slowly, "but I fear I will disgrace your weapons."

"Perhaps," said Bedwyr, "and perhaps not."

"I wager he will," said Cei cheerfully. "I stake a gold armlet that Agravain downs him. You are right, Agravain, to do this; no one could believe that tale but a Breton."

"I would accept your stake," said Bedwyr, "only I do not share your taste for jewelry. I have my reasons for believing the tale, Cei."

Agravain scowled. He had wanted to fight me in the way he was best accustomed to, with his fists. But he decided that this would do. "Very well. Hurry. We must teach Camlann before too long."

I climbed down from the cart, tying the reins to the corner post, and Bedwyr dismounted. He gave me his spear and shield, tying a rag around the point of the spear and telling me to use the butt end, then gave me the reins of his horse, which was a long-boned dappled Gaulish war steed. I thanked him, feeling resigned to my inevitable defeat. It would be only another fall, I told myself. It could not hurt me.

I mounted Bedwyr's horse and rode it in a tight circle, seeing how it responded and trying to get an idea of its temper. It was a good horse, though, of course, nothing like Ceincaled.

We moved off the road to the cleared land about it. Now that we had left the marshes behind, the road wound through steep hills, covered with plowed land and pasture. The pastureland by the roadside was soft, so a fall would not be very painful. The warriors of the band formed a circle, not really understanding what was happening, but interested. No one accepted Cei's wager.

Agravain rode to the far side of the circle, leveled the

blunt end of his spear, and nodded briskly. "I won't hurt you," he warned me, "but you must learn."

I nodded, sighed, and raised my shield. He would be cheerful again once he had downed me, and it was a small enough price to pay for that. Still, I wished that he would believe me. It hurt a little that he could so quickly call me a liar.

Agravain urged his horse to a trot, angling his spear and following the line of the circle. I followed his example, trying to remember what I had struggled to learn in the Boys' House. My brother saw I was ready and swung his horse toward me, touching it to a canter.

Suddenly, everything narrowed, and time itself seemed to slow as I touched Bedwyr's horse to a gallop and rode to meet him. My heart soared, and I swung my spear out of line. Agravain saw it, smiled, and confidently came on. The world narrowed farther to his spear end and right shoulder, and around these points all was blurred. He was almost upon me; I swerved my horse just half a step, caught his spear on the edge of my shield, sending it glancing off, dropped my own spear into line and thrust it against his shoulder, braced for the impact.

Time resumed its normal flow, and Agravain fell from his horse, his eyes wide with surprise, and I reined in and turned my animal quickly, dropping my spear to threaten him.

He lay still for a moment, then rose, slowly, rubbing his shoulder and scowling in bewilderment. I came to myself and stared, first at him, then over at his horse, which was now nibbling the thick grass. I could not understand what had happened.

"We will try again," said Agravain loudly. "Now."

"It was an accident," I said. "I could not do it again. I know that you're the better warrior of us, Agravain." Of course he was; it was his world.

"We'll do it again, damn you!" shouted Agravain. He went over to his horse, remounted it, jerked savagely at the bit and rode over to the opposite side of the circle.

"Cei," said one of the warriors, "is the wager still on?"

"If you want," said Cei.

"Fair enough; I've armlets too."

Agravain lowered his spear, and began trotting around

the circle again. I did the same, waiting for him when he turned his horse nearly backward and came up with a swerving course. This time I reined suddenly as we approached, bringing Bedwyr's horse rearing to a stop. Again everything contracted about us, and I felt even more clearly the wild lightness in my mind. Agravain was almost beside me, and his spear, aimed at my left thigh, was close. I beat it out of line with my shield, turning my horse and allowing his weight to join mine behind the spear as I thrust at Agravain's side. Again, he fell; again his horse ran on, this time into the circle of warriors where it was caught.

Agravain rose to his feet. He was no longer scowling, but staring in total bewilderment, like a man who has seen the sun rising in the west. The madness was still on me, and I did not wish to speak, so I sat silent and unmoving, spear ready, and waited.

Agravain went and got his horse, remounted, leveled his spear. I rode to the opposite end of the circle and nodded.

He came at me immediately this time, at a full gallop. I hurled my spear, blunt end first, as he came, and rode on drawing Caledvwlch.

The spear hit his throat and glanced off, though he would surely have a bruise to show for it; had I thrown it tip first he would be dead. He almost fell as it hit him, but recovered in time, keeping his spear straight. His thrust as we drew even would have struck me through the ribs to the right of my shield, had it touched me—but I hacked at the shaft with Caledvwlch, and it snapped. Time froze, and I lifted the sword before Agravain's horse could complete another step. The light was burning in the blade, and I was filled with a strength which seemed hardly to be my own. The world looked as though it had been etched on bright steel. I let all the force fall into my arm as I struck Agravain with the flat of the sword blade. He fell into the grass, his horse plunging slowly past me. He rolled over and lay still. There was a massive silence.

My head cleared a little and I sheathed the sword. Still Agravain lay motionless. The rest of the madness departed from me, and I dismounted hastily. "Agravain?"

He did not move. I ran over to him. By the Light, how hard had I hit him? "Agravain?"

He shook his head groggily, then climbed to his knees, holding his arm where I had struck it. He stared at me. His face was white, beaded with sweat. He climbed slowly to his feet, still staring.

"Dear God," he said, very slowly, each word falling into the ring of silence that was the watchers. "What have you become?"

"I said that you underestimated your brother," Bedwyr walked forward, still calm and unshaken. "I think that you will find a place with Arthur, Gwalchmai ap Lot."

"But the sword!" said Cei. "Didn't you see the sword? It was burning. He . . ."

"The sword?" asked another. "Didn't you see his eyes?"

Light! I thought desperately. Now they do believe that I am a witch.

"He has beaten Agravain of Orcade in fair combat, do any of you question that?" asked Bedwyr sharply.

"I question it," said Cei immediately. "That was not fair combat. No ordinary mortal being could have . . ."

"It was a fair fight," said Agravain. The warriors at once stopped glaring at me and stared at him instead. "It was a very fair fight, and long overdue. Gwalchmai is no witch, I swear the oath of my people to that. If any of you thinks otherwise, I am willing to fight again today. My brother is a warrior. God! By the sun, I have never fought anyone as good!"

"It was an accident . . ." I began, still bewildered.

"It was not. You are better than I, and we both know that now."

"One fall might have been an accident," Bedwyr stated. "Three times constitutes proof. You are very good, Gwalchmai. Perhaps better than I."

"That is absurd. You are the finest horseman in the Family," objected Cei.

Bedwyr only smiled.

Cei shook his head violently. "Nothing of this makes sense. Swords cannot burn like firebrands. His story is impossible; but if it is true, where does that leave us? He is a sorcerer. . . ."

"I said, nothing more about that!" Agravain snapped. "Whatever he was in the past, my brother is a warrior now."

"How can I be?" I broke in. "I never could fight. You know that, Agravain. You must remember how I was in the Boys' House, how I could not throw a spear straight. . . ." Agravain rubbed his throat where my spear had caught it, but I plunged on. "Everyone knew that I was no warrior. Father was disappointed in me, I was disappointed in myself, so much that I was willing to give myself up to the Darkness from sheer anger and the pain of failing. How can I be a warrior?"

"You say that you laid open Aldwulf's face with that?" Agravain began to point at Caledvwlch with the arm I had struck, then winced and clasped it again.

"I . . . yes, but . . ."

"And you killed these Saxons when you escaped from Din Sarum?"

"Yes, but Agravain . . ."

"There you are, then." He turned to the others. "He has ruined Fflamddwyn's good looks for him and fought against our enemies. Can you question that he is fighting for us?"

"We have only his account to rely on for that tale," objected Cei.

"Do you accuse my brother of lying?" asked Agravain, trying to reach for his sword and wincing again.

Cei stopped, staring at my brother. Then he sighed and shrugged. He plainly thought that I was lying somehow, but he would not fight his friend for it. "I accuse no one," he said. "But I will tell Arthur of this."

Bedwyr nodded. "And I will tell Arthur that I believe Gwalchmai." The two looked at each other for another moment, and then Bedwyr smiled gently. "You merely do not wish to lose that armlet, Cei."

Cei looked confused for a moment, then remembered his wager. He grinned shakily, pulled the armlet off, and tossed it to the man who had won it. That man sat his horse looking at it uncertainly, then put it on. Cei clasped Bedwyr's hand, remounted, and turned his horse back to the road. Slowly the others followed, and Bedwyr took his horse and shield from me and went after them.

"Agravain . . ." I began again.

"Gwalchmai." He rubbed his arm, winced again. "By the sun, I have a bruise here. Bedwyr has forgotten his spear; where is it?"

I picked it up. The rest of the foraging band had started off down the road at a walk; Sion's mare was cropping the grass by the roadside. Agravain caught his horse, gathered the reins up, awkwardly one armed. Just about to mount, he stopped, looked at me again, and caught my arm.

"Gwalchmai, I am sorry," he said.

"I am the one who is sorry. Truly, I did not mean to hit you so hard!"

"I don't mean for this." He had slipped back into Irish from the British of the warband. "Though I am sorry, and should be, that I cried liar on you. But all your life I have been calling you names to provoke you to fighting, and beating you to make myself feel better; and I have pretended to help you with the arts of war while I ruined you for them, pretending, even to myself, that it was generous of me and for your own good. —Do not say anything. I know that it is true. I began to realize it after I was a hostage here, when I was no longer the firstborn and leader in everything and when I saw it was hopeless to fight and still wished to. And when they told me that you were dead, and all Britain said, 'There is one witch the less,' then I did understand, and wished myself dead as well. I remembered how you looked at me once after a fight, and I knew it was the part of a dog and a devil from Iffern to so humiliate a brother, and I had done it, and gone hunting afterward. Listen, perhaps there is no repayment for it, but I am sorry."

I clasped his shoulders. "My heart, I have said that I was a fool then, and took things over-much to heart. If I had been able to laugh at you . . . and it is past now. Forget it."

He embraced me. I felt his chest shake, realized that he was weeping, realized that I was as well. "From this time on, Gwalchmai," he muttered, "it will be different." He released me, looking at me earnestly. "I will boast of you before I boast of myself. From now on there will be only victories."

I could say nothing, and he said again, "Only victories, Gwalchmai. Forget all that I ever said about your skill as a warrior. You will be a great warrior, a man they make songs about." He looked up the road then, and added, "They are slowing the pace for us, but we will still be left behind. Come, help me onto this horse. My arm is still numb."

When the cart was jolting and swaying down the road again, Sion's little mare trotting briskly to catch the others, Agravain fell behind. I understood very well why. He wished to be alone with his thoughts, as I did with mine, and, after such words as had just passed, we would have nothing to say to each other for a time.

I did not know what to think or to feel. I had beaten Agravain, Agravain had repented to me for the past. I had beaten Agravain, he said that I would be a great warrior. There had been a time when that was the focus of my dreams, but I had abandoned those dreams for the Darkness, and I had never thought to see them placed within my grasp. And I wanted to turn the cart about and ride away from Camlann was fast as the horse could gallop.

I looked at the worn leather of the reins, dark with the polish of use, and at my hands curled around the leather. I had sworn those hands to the service of the Light. What had Bedwyr said about the Light? Something about all other lights or goods being known only in it. And I had already come to see that the Light could do whatever he wanted, even among the Saxons. Surely he did not need my aid, and did not need to have given me Caledvwlch, or to have sent me to Britain. Agravain had asked me "Why" when I spoke of Morgawse, and I knew that he meant not only "Why does she hate?" but, "Why must she be there to hate?" And I could not see why. If the Light could protect Arthur against her strongest spells, and could save me from her, he could certainly rid the Earth of Darkness. He did not need me or anyone to run about Britain and make war. I saw with a sense of shock that I did not like the thought of war, and I saw that I believed that it was wrong to kill. I had never heard of any such idea in my life, and yet, I thought again of those three Saxons and thought that there surely should have been some other way. And if it were sometimes right to kill, as I would have killed Aldwulf, or, in a different way, as I had killed Connall—when was it right? And how could anyone be always right? The Light of its—his—own nature must be always right, if what Bedwyr had said was true, and I believed that it was. But the world of men is mixed, good and evil together, and there was no simple and clear struggle, no one decision like the one I had made at Dun Fionn.

Yet men make choices, and must make choices. I had chosen Light at Dun Fionn. Medraut had chosen Darkness. Violently, I wished that I could have stopped him, and I remembered him standing in Morgawse's room, looking at her in adoration. If I had dragged him from the room after me? But he had been calling me "traitor," the shout had echoed behind me. If I saw him again, and spoke to him, could he still change his mind? Surely, the darkness could not completely enchain his will. —And then I thought that I and the Light could not either. But who would choose Darkness, if they understood what they were choosing, understood the hunger and fear, the hatred that consumes happiness, the loss? And yet sometimes it seemed plain that we could not help but serve Darkness. And if I fought for Arthur, I would have to make choices, and it was evident that in the nature of the world I would sometimes choose wrongly. I did not want to fight in the complex world of men. It was easier to fight in the Otherworld.

I stared up at the hills before us, and found Bedwyr looking back down the road. Our eyes met for a moment; he reined in his horse and fell back till he was level with the cart again.

"Your thoughts seem heavy ones, Gwalchmai ap Lot," he told me.

"They are heavy, Lord," I replied. "Agravain says that I may be a great warrior now, and you have said as much also. And I am a hair's breadth from turning about and returning to the Orcades, a piece of foolishness such as I have never heard of."

Bedwyr's eyes glinted slightly. "And why is that?"

"You serve the Light, I think," I told him. "Is it right to kill men and to make wars?"

"Ach!" He stared at me. "I do not know."

"But you are a warrior, and when I spoke of the Light you understood it better than I did myself."

"I doubt that. I merely know the language of philosophy, and so could describe it better. You have touched on something, Gwalchmai ap Lot, which I have often questioned, I could only say what I know myself, from what I myself have experienced."

"Then tell me that, if there is time. I am sick with thinking of it."

"I think I understand that." Bedwyr's eyes glinted again with the suppressed amusement. It was very strange, I thought fleetingly, that I could speak to him so easily, and that he had so quickly taken my part against Cei. Perhaps it was that we served the same lord that created this understanding.

With his shield arm, the one with the missing hand, he brushed his hair back from his face. "Very well," he began. "As Cei has mentioned several times already, I am a Breton, and my father has estates in the southeast—no, that is not to say I have a noble clan; in most of Less Britain, clans are less important than ownership of land and civic status. My father is a *curialis*—that is his title. Officially his rank is *clarus*, but he calls himself *clarissimus*, because he likes the sound of it." Again came the glint of amusement. "We are near the border of Less Britain, and while I was young, not a summer went by without the Franks, or the Saxons, or the Swabians or Goths or Huns breaking into our fields and driving off our cattle, and demanding gold from the municipality. So I learned to fight early, as men also do here in Britain. I also learned to read, but I considered this of less importance. In Less Britain, as in parts of southern Gaul, the old municipal schools are still run for the children of the nobility, and I went there and was taught the elements of rhetoric from the *grammaticus* there; and very tedious it was. We had a textbook, though, one among the class of twelve, and it was written by a Marius Victorinus, who was a philosopher. When he wished to give an example of an exhortation, he exhorted to philosophy; of discussion, a debate about the *summum bonum*—that is, what is most excellent in human life. He thought it was philosophy. I thought he was a fool, for the Franks cared nothing for philosophy, and I enjoyed killing the Franks. Mind, I enjoyed it, not tolerated it, but took pleasure in showing off my skill. When I was seventeen, I enrolled some peasants from my father's estate, and took them off, with one or two other youths from the area, to fight for the *Comes Armoricae*—the king of Less Britain, you would say. After a few years, the Frankish king died, and the new king was busy with the Goths, and the wars seemed over for a time. Then I heard that our king's younger son, Bran, had made alliance with Arthur of Britain, and planned an expedition. I had never been to Britain, and had killed no Franks or Saxons for nearly a year, so I took my followers and went with Bran.

"You know of that campaign, I think, and how Arthur won the purple, so there is no need for me to tell you of it. But for myself, I was wounded in the battle by the Saefern." Bedwyr held up his shield arm again. "The blow was not bad in itself, but the wound took the rot, and I, who was not afraid of the Saxons, was afraid of the doctors, and did not go to them until I was sick and had to be carried. They took the hand off, but I was in a high fever from the rot, and I thought that I would die. I lay there in the monastery where they had brought us, and now I had time to wonder about how many men I had placed in this position, and the thought did not please me as it had before. All my renown was useless to me now. And I kept remembering the exhortation to philosophy from that textbook, and thinking that glory was not, after all, the *sumum bonum*.

"For three days I lay between death and life. On the third, Taliesin, the chief bard of Arthur, came to the monastery—I still do not know why. When he walked past the rows of the wounded, it looked to me as though a star burned on his forehead, and I thought that I was dead. So I called to him that I was not yet prepared.

"He stopped and came over and knelt beside me. 'For something you are prepared, Bedwyr ap Brendan,' he said, 'but not for death.' Then he turned to the doctors and said that he thought the fever would break soon. 'So you regret your life,' he said, turning back to me—I had never seen him before, and still I thought him the angel of death. 'With all my heart,' I replied. 'You live now,' he told me, 'and will for many years yet. But remember your regret when you recover, and, I warn you, things will turn out otherwise than you expect. Have faith, and do not wonder at what happens.' With that he left, and the doctors put me in a heated room with many blankets, so that the fever broke, and I began to recover."

"Who is this Taliesin?" I asked. "His last words to you were the same as Lugh's to me."

He gave me a dark, serious look. "Indeed? I do not know where Taliesin comes from or who his parents were. No one does. He is a great poet, and a healer besides. There are other stories about him, some very strange, but nothing is known for certain. I know that he is not evil, and his words then were true. I recovered from my fever, but I remembered what I had felt then, when I had thought that I would die. I asked the monks who cared for the sick if they had the textbook by the philosopher Victorinus, but they had never heard of him. They had only a few books, and those gospels. So I read one of the gospels, that of Matthew, and I came to the place where the Christ was betrayed, and led off to execution; and one of his followers drew a sword to defend him, and our lord said, 'Put your sword in its place: for those that take the sword will perish with the sword.' Then I decided that it was wrong to kill and to make wars, and I resolved to return to Less Britain as soon as I was well enough to travel, and there enter a monastery, and contemplate the Good. I anticipated that my father would be angry, but I would not have yielded for all that. So, you see, I know what it is that troubles you."

"Why did you change your mind again?"

He smiled, a quick but very warm smile. "I met Arthur. I had seen him before, but never spoken with him. He came to the monastery to visit the wounded. I was sitting in the garden: It was summer, and evening, and I was trying to read. He came up to me, calling me by name, and asked me of my wound; then asked when I would rejoin King Bran. I told him that I did not plan to continue to live as a warrior, but to enter a monastery, and he said that Bran thought highly of me, and that he did not understand.

"I explained my reasons, and, then surprisingly, he did understand. He had even heard of Victorinus—he had read of him in a book by one Aurelius Augustinus. 'But I do not agree with your Victorinus on the highest good,' he told me. 'Do you think that it is glory, then?' I asked. 'Indeed not,' he replied, 'but Augustinus says evil is not a substance, but an absence, being nothing more than the denial of good. And this my own heart teaches me as well, for I can see from it that evil begins in weakness, cowardice, and stupidity, and proceeds to hatred and desolation, while good is active. So it seems to me that the highest good cannot be a thing that sits like a picture on the wall, waiting to be admired, but must be active and substantial.' And I, 'Victorinus says that the Good, that is, the Light, subsists in all things, for if it did not, nothing would exist. But because men do not consider it, and act blindly, they create evil.' And he, 'If they do nothing but sit and consider, they are bound to create evil, for they cannot create good.' 'But they might find it and know it,' said I. And he stood and paced about the garden, then asked me, 'Is justice good? It is active. Are order, peace, harmony good? Is love? —Augustinus says that love is a property of men but not of God, but I think that, if this were so, we would be superior to God, which is unthinkable; for I am certain that these things are good, love most of all.' And I, 'The Church says that God, that is, the Good, loved and acted once, in Christ.' And he, 'I say he did then and does now, in us. Tell me, is it good that the Saxons take away the land and the cattle of their neighbors, and that men and women, and children too, are left to starve? Is it good that only a handful of nobles in Britain can read, and few of them have books? Is it good that men are reduced thus to the level of beasts, thinking of nothing but food and slaughter?' 'Why do you ask?' I said. 'These are evils, but they have come about because Rome has fallen and the empire has gone from the West. What can we do but ourselves abstain from evil in such times?' 'We can restore the empire,' he said, and stopped pacing, standing with the moonlight in his hair—for by then the moon had risen over the abbey wall. 'Before God, I will preserve civilization in this land or die defending it, because I love the

Good. And I think that to fight thus is the highest good for men, and not philosophy. What would your Victorinus say to that?' 'Victorinus had no emperor like you to follow,' I said, 'or he would have spoken differently.' And I knelt to him, and told him, 'I have only one hand to fight for you, but, in God's name, take me into your service, and all I can do, I will.' He looked at me in surprise for a moment, for he had not realized how much his words had stirred me; then he took my hand and swore the oath a liege lord swears to his follower. And I have fought for him ever since, and will do so all my life, God willing: for I now believe that to act with a desire for good, even if we may act wrongly, is better than not to act at all. But whether in the end we are justified in the eyes of God, I cannot say."

I was silent for a long time. "That is hardly comforting," I said at last.

"Life is not comfortable," he replied. "Nonetheless, I think there is more joy in struggling for the Light than in retreat."

"But the difference between us and the Saxons is not so great," I objected. "They are men too, and much like us. And I know that you are a Roman, but still, I cannot see why the empire has anything to do with the Light. No British king had some miserable slave tortured to death to see whether his master threw stones at a royal statue, or had three thousand people massacred at a theatre because they had rioted, as did Theodosius, the high king of Rome. —My mother told me of this, but still, it is true, isn't it? And I never heard of any king in Britain or in Erin having hundreds of innocent noblemen put to death, solely because their names began with 'Theod-', as Valentinianus did because of an oracle he had received, though he missed Theodosius. Moreover, the Romans took Britain by force of arms, just as the Saxons are attempting to do now, and no doubt the people here then liked the Romans as little as we now like the Saxons—why are you smiling?"

"Because you can speak Latin and read and are probably a Christian, and still, if you do not object to my saying so, you are a barbarian. —I mean no insult. It is true, the empire caused much evil and misery. But no British lordling ever created as much of good and beauty, ever gave to the world so much knowledge, art, and splendor as did the Romans. And no British king ever founded hospitals, or endowed monasteries to care for the sick, the poor, and the orphaned; or again, relieved his domains when there was famine and restored them after fire or war, which the Christian emperors did. The empire is worth fighting to preserve. That I could never question."

"Very well, I am a barbarian," I said, beginning to laugh. "You southern British—excuse it, Bretons—always say as much about the Irish. I still do not see that your empire has much to do with the Light; but, from what you have said, I think the empire Arthur desires would. And I have been given a sword, which, if it is a weapon of Light, is also a weapon of war. I do not fear perishing by it if I take it up, and if your Christ threatened nothing more than that, I would have no hesitations. Only . . . by the Light, it is too sudden. I never expected . . . I never thought that I could become a warrior, and would have to make such a choice."

"Perhaps when you meet the Emperor Arthur it will become clear. —Look, there is Camlann. We are almost home."

Camlann is ancient, older than the kingdom of Britain, in fact. It stood empty and decaying while the Romans ruled, but after Londinium fell to the Saxons, Ambrosius Aurelianus had it resettled. Arthur had it refortified with the great walls, which, when we rode up, that day, were only half-finished. As we approached, Agravain drove up his horse to ride beside me again; and Cei fell back, watching me as though he expected me to grow wings and fly off rather than enter the fortress. So I came to Camlann, driving a heavy-laden cart pulled by a spent mare, flanked by three warriors who viewed me in vastly different lights, fastening my hopes on a high king who was absent.

The gates had been thrown open for us before we reached them, and we drove up the steep hill, the warriors called greetings to the guards and shouting that they had a victory. The high king was expected back, with the rest of the warband, at any moment, and Bedwyr wanted the supplies from Ynys Witrin to be unloaded before the Pendragon returned.

"I do not wish my lord to have to trouble himself with inventories, nor to wait for his victory feast," he told one of the servants.

"Of course," said the man, eyeing the carts with some eagerness—I gathered they had been short of supplies in Camlann. "Did you bring mead from Ynys Witrin?"

"Seeing that the monks make the best mead in Dumnonia," Cei replied, "we were hardly likely to miss it."

"Good. We've only that ale we saved from last winter, and I had no wish to give that to the emperor after a victory."

The carts and horses were brought to a stable, and I cared for Sion's mare and gave her some grain. I was finishing with her when Bedwyr entered, followed by Cei and Agravain. "The emperor is almost here," he told me, "if you wish to come down to the gates."

The Family was still riding up when I went to the gates to see them. It was a long column, coming from the north, mounted men, some driving cattle; one or two wagons, spare horses on lead reins. They covered the road into the distance, glittering with weapons in the afternoon sun. At the front a rider carried the standard, a deeper glint of gold at that distance, and behind him came a man on a white horse. Arthur.

I thought of all that had happened to me up to that moment, of my mother and my father both, of Agravain, of Lugh, of the Saxons. The physical struggle and the spiritual struggle: They met here. My throat constricted and I stood, my eyes, like the eyes of all around me, fixed on the man who rode behind the standard.

The vanguard for the warband broke off from the slower-moving group which drove the cattle. Horses' manes and tails and men's cloaks streamed in the wind of their motion, and, through the dirt of hard riding, the sun glittered off weapons and mail and jewelry. The Pendragon wore the purple, gold-embroidered cloak of the Roman high kings over his coat of mail. He rode well, and held his tall spear as though he knew how to use it. As he passed the gates, the inhabitants of the fortress shouted a welcome with one voice, and they shouted, "Arthur!"

The king laughed and reined in his horse, and his followers pressed around him, catching his hands in greeting. I remained standing on the half-finished wall, staring at him and wondering that so much doubt and deep thought could come to nothing in so brief and transient a moment. I knew that somehow I had already made my choice, perhaps made it when I fled from Dun Fionn. Somehow I had known all along that I would become a warrior, and fight for Arthur.

ELEVEN

Aʀᴛʜᴜʀ ʀᴏᴅᴇ ᴏɴ ᴜᴘ ᴛʜᴇ hill at a walk, now surrounded by the inhabitants of Camlann. He was smiling, laughing at his subjects and waving off their shouted congratulations on his victories. He was then thirty, old enough to make such homecomings commonplace, but he did not treat it as commonplace, but as a thing new and surprising. He did that all his life.

On reaching the feast hall at the summit of the hill he dismounted lightly, catching his horse's bridle before anyone else could. He glanced back at the throng of welcoming servants and homecoming warriors who had followed him, then beckoned one of the servants—the steward—from the crowd and began talking to him, gesturing down the hill. Making arrangements for the cattle he had plundered from the Saxons, no doubt. The steward nodded, then gestured in reply to some other question of the king's. Arthur looked up, and for just an instant he reminded me sharply of someone else, someone with the same kind of wide gray-eyed stare, but I couldn't place the memory and was not really trying.

"Bedwyr!" called the king.

Bedwyr had been somewhere in the crowd and emerged from it as if from the air. "Here, My Lord."

Arthur gave him a different smile, one separate from the sort he had given the others, and held his hand out. Bedwyr caught it, and Arthur clasped it with his other hand as well. "Did you bring the mead from Ynys Witrin?"

"Yes. And food enough for a few days."

"*Laus Deo* for that. How much is there?"

"Gweir is making an inventory now. And I have already ordered the victory feast."

"Good man. Is there any ale here?"

"The sour leavings of last winter, nothing more."

"It will have to do. Goronwy, some ale for the Family. And Gruffydd is bringing in the wounded; send someone to see that he has what he needs for them. . . ." He went into the hall, still giving orders to various of the servants. I followed with the rest of the crowd, going up nearly to the high table, then stopped, uncertain what to do. Everyone was so busy. I could say nothing to the king yet; best to wait. I found I was in the way of some of the returning warriors and looked for a quiet corner.

Arthur dropped into a chair at the high table, caught the horn of ale offered by a servant, and took a deep drink from it.

"Welcome back," said Bedwyr.

"Welcome back yourself," returned the Pendragon. "When did you arrive here?"

"About an hour ago."

"What? For God's sake man, sit down and have some ale. Goronwy . . ." He addressed the servant with the ale in an undertone, and the man nodded. "So, Bedwyr, and how is Abbot Theodorus?"

"Dishonest as ever. But we did find the mead."

"So. And what is the matter?"

"The matter?"

"The thing that is weighing upon your mind. Were things very bad at Ynys Witrin?"

Bedwyr shook his head. Goronwy came back with some more ale and whispered to Arthur, after giving Bedwyr a horn. "Don't use all of it, then," Arthur said, apparently in reply to the servant. "Tell the men we're short and they can only have one horn each, but there's plenty of mead tonight." I had never heard of a king running short of ale before and I blinked, but no one seemed in the least surprised. "Well, Bedwyr, and did the monks throw stones and cry, 'Death to the tyrant who steals our good yellow mead! Plague upon the Dragon and his Family, since we cannot get drunk on Sunday!'?"

Bedwyr smiled. "No. There was no trouble. They were not pleased, but gave in. The matter is of a different kind."

Arthur glanced down the hall. "Your whole party looks as gloomy as men the morning after a feast. Even Cei and Agravain—especially Cei and Agravain." He leaned forward a little and lowered his voice.

Bedwyr shook his head in response. "No, no bloodshed, thank God. Where are Cei and Agravain now?"

"I sent them to help with the cattle. It concerns them, does it? Very well, we will wait. —The walls have not progressed as far as I had expected. What do you think . . ."

More of Arthur's Family trooped in and settled thirstily upon their ale, joking about it. Presently Cei and Agravain entered as well, and stood about, presumably looking for me.

"Here!" Arthur called. "Bedwyr says that there is a matter you wish me to resolve."

Neither of the two had noticed me, and Cei was frowning uneasily as they came up to the high table. I stood, uncertain whether to join them now or not. The warriors in the hall ceased to talk and listened.

"My Lord," said Cei, "we wish you to make a decision concerning Agravain's brother."

Arthur sat up straighter, setting his horn of ale down in its stand.

"Which brother?" he asked, in a very low, strained voice.

Agravain paused, looking slightly surprised. "My brother Gwalchmai, whom I thought dead. We met him at Ynys Witrin, and he came with us to Camlann. He wishes to join us.—My Lord, he is a very fine warrior. I had a match with him on the way from Ynys Witrin, and three times he downed me."

"My Lord," said Cei, "there is some reason to suspect him of sorcery."

"He is no witch!" snapped Agravain. "I swear the oath of my people to that. He is a warrior, and a very fine one. Ask Bedwyr."

Arthur looked at his friend, and the dark warrior nodded. "He is a fine warrior, and, I think, a good man. I would take oath that he is no witch."

"I have heard of Gwalchmai son of Lot." Arthur said. "And what I have heard has not been good." I closed my eyes, my hand clutching the hilt of Caledvwlch. Lugh had warned me that Arthur might be suspicious. "But you would vouch for him, Bedwyr?"

"Yes, My Lord."

"Well." Arthur looked at Cei again. "I think the matter may need consideration, but I will consider it. Where is your brother, Agravain?"

Agravain began to answer that he did not know, and I forced myself to walk out of the shadows and stand before Arthur. "Here," I said.

The gray eyes widened just slightly and fixed me. He did not move, and his face held no expression, but it was as though a shadow fell across him; and I suddenly sensed that what I had thought was a neutral tone was coldness, and that what touched him was horror.

I tried to strangle the sharp-edged misery that leaped up in me. I would not, after all, wish him to accept reputed sorcerers readily, and still I had that reputation. I did look something like my mother, and perhaps he had met her, and I had recalled her to his mind.

But within me something said that the Darkness must have touched me to the very bone, that I would never be free of it, that it blighted everything I tried to touch, and I would never outrun the shadow of my youth.

I went down on one knee to Arthur and stood again. There is still hope, I told myself. This is what you have been led to. It must come about.

"So," said Arthur at last, still in the neutral tone which was not neutral but cold. "You are Gwalchmai ap Lot?"

"Yes, Lord."

"I had not heard that you had . . . returned to the Ynysoedd Erch. Surely, if you had, your brother should have been told of it."

"I did not return to the Orcades, Lord Arthur. I have been only three weeks in Britain."

"The story came here that you fell into the sea on Samhain, more than two years ago. Now you appear suddenly at Ynys Witrin, convince the lord Cei that you are a sorcerer, and ask to join my Family. What is the truth of these matters?"

I stood silent for a long minute, trying to think of an answer that would be easier to tell, then realized that the actual truth was the only possible reply. I told my story, hesitatingly at first, and painfully aware of the listeners. I left some things out; I could not bring myself to speak of the real depth of Morgawse's evil. After a while, I found that I could ignore the watchers and concentrate on my own words, so that they said what I meant them to. No one interrupted me.

When I had finished Arthur shook himself. "A tale like the tales of poets, both in the matter and in the telling, Gwalchmai ap Lot."

"I know. Perhaps, Lord Arthur, if I wished to lie I would tell a story more easily believed."

At this, Bedwyr smiled, but Arthur's face did not move. "Perhaps. And perhaps you might expect it to be believed because of its very strangeness, which matches a strangeness in yourself. Admittedly, that is a subtle ploy, but your father also is a cunning man and your mother is . . ." The shadow across him grew darker, and I saw that he must have known her at some point, for he finished in a whisper, "very subtle."

"Lord," I began, uncertain of how he received me and afraid, "I am neither my father nor my mother. I have told you the truth. I have admitted that I did indeed once study sorcery; but I have renounced it, and never again will have anything to do with it."

"Why does Cei think that you are a sorcerer? He usually disbelieves such tales."

"It was the sword," said Cei. "When he fought Agravain he drew it and it burned. I swear by Saint Peter, it burned brighter than a torch. Ask anyone who was there, even Bedwyr; they all saw it."

"It burned with light," Bedwyr said. "But Gwalchmai has told you where he received the sword."

"Swords do not do that," returned Cei firmly. "I would have said it was impossible, but I saw it. So, it must have been some sorcerous practice of the wielder that caused it to burn, a spell he worked against his own brother."

Agravain snorted. "He needed no spells to defeat me. Even without the sword he downed me twice. And remember how Gwalchmai has fought for us already."

"According to his own account. Tell me, Gwalchmai, if you have seen Cerdic, what does he look like?"

I described the Saxon king carefully. Arthur nodded, and asked some more questions about the Saxons, and about Sorviodunum, and how many men were there. I saw what he wanted and gave all the details I could recall. Cei and Agravain fidgeted.

"What is the point of this?" Agravain asked at last. "We know this already."

"But it is not common knowledge," replied Arthur, smiling at my brother. He looked back to me and stopped smiling. "You have been among the Saxons recently, so part at least of your tale is true." He looked past me, down the hall into nothing, a wide, gray stare, remote and infinitely piercing. "And yet, that you killed Saxons proves nothing. Saxons kill Saxons. —The Queen Morgawse, your mother: Do you think she is beautiful?"

I was taken completely by surprise. "Yes."

"Why?"

I looked about in confusion. "Why? Lord, why do we think anything beautiful? She is as perfect and terrible as Death itself, and so say all who have met her."

Our eyes met for a long moment, and the thing that was common between us was a shadow, a knowledge of Darkness.

"Your story has a great deal of the Otherworld in it," Arthur said at last, "And although Bedwyr thinks highly of you, and although by blood you are my nephew, little as your mother may like the idea, I do not think that I can trust you." My heart seemed to stop, and I stood, staring back at him, swallowing. "You are free to take service with any other king in Britain, or to return to the islands. But I cannot give you a place here."

It could not be over with, not so quickly. It could not be. It was not just. I stood stupidly in the middle of the hall, still staring at the Pendragon. He looked away from me and picked up his ale horn.

"Lord, I protest!" exclaimed Agravain. "Take my oath that Gwalchmai is no sorcerer; or at least give him some chance to prove himself. Wait until we have news from the Saxons, see if his story . . ."

"My Lord, let him prove himself by fighting for you," urged Bedwyr. "I spoke with him on the way; I am certain that he is no witch. . . ."

"Do you question my judgment?" asked Arthur coldly, looking up at them.

They fell silent. Bedwyr bowed slightly. "Never, My Lord." Agravain stammered, fell silent again.

I bowed to the high king once more, turned, walked out of the hall. It was true. It was over.

"Wait!" shouted Agravain, and hurried after me.

Outside the hall, he caught my arm. "I do not know what the matter is, but this is unlike the Pendragon. He will change his mind."

"He has decided," I replied.

"He has . . . but, Iffern! It is unlike him. I do not understand it."

It is forbidden, I thought to myself, to know too much of the Darkness. How could I serve a king like Arthur, when I had such knowledge? But I had thought the Light wanted it. I had been so certain. Where was everything now? What could I do?

"Listen," Agravain said, "Cei and Bedwyr and I share a house, with two others. Come and rest there, and Bedwyr will speak to Arthur for you."

"He said that he never questioned the high king's judgments."

"And he never would, before the Family. But sometimes he disagrees with Arthur and argues the point with him, and sometimes Arthur changes his mind. The high king thinks highly of Bedwyr, he made him cavalry commander—*magister equitum*, he calls it. I told you they spoke a good deal of Latin here. Come and rest . . . and you look as though you wish to be alone."

"Yes."

So Agravain took me to his house and left me there, muttering something about seeing to his horse. I was grateful for it, and grateful that Agravain was of high enough status not to have to sleep in the crowded feast hall. I sat on his bed and stared at the rush-covered floor, gripping Caledvwlch.

But what was it for? I demanded silently of the Light. Why the sword, the power, the struggle, the voyage to the Otherworld, if, at the end of it, I can't fight? You wanted me to take service with Arthur—Lugh told me to. So why is it denied to me now?

There was no answer. I drew Caledvwlch and looked it. The sword remained dull as my own confusion.

I despaired. I was trapped, forever locked in the evil of Morgawse, damned by the road I had taken in my youth. And yet, I had refused to follow her, I had killed her demon, I had fought Light—to be sure, no Darkness is defeated forever, but I had truly conquered! That I could not doubt.

I grew angry. Sheathing the sword I stood and paced the room. Why should Arthur refuse me so quickly, so completely? It was not just.

No, the fault of necessity was in me. My tale had too much to do with the Otherworld, and I still half-worshipped Morgawse, and had told him so when I said that she was beautiful. I sat down again, and again prayed, and again found silence.

So the afternoon passed, and evening came. Agravain came back and asked if I wanted anything to eat, and I told him, no. He went off to the feast.

There was nothing I could do, I decided. Arthur had rejected me. Oh, I could not simply sit and feel sorry for myself; I must act. What had Bedwyr said that Arthur had said about action?—How could I go to another lord now, after meeting the high king?

I wanted more than ever, now that it was denied me, to serve Arthur. I wanted to have some part in his Family, the color and splendor of it, the glory mingled with the shortage of last winter's sour ale, which everyone seemed to treat as a joke. The Family was not like other warbands, and the Pendragon was not like other kings. I sat and brooded over it, locked, helpless, in despair.

Agravain returned from the feast, more than half-drunk and bad tempered. It had been a difficult day for him, as well. After a while, Bedwyr and the two others, Rhuawn and Gereint, also returned.

"I have spoken to Arthur," Bedwyr told me quietly. "He says that he does not think we can risk accepting you, not at such a time as this, and mentioned his distrust of the Queen Morgawse, your mother, who by your own testimony is plotting against him. But more than this he will not say. I do not understand it: Usually he is willing to give anyone at all a chance to prove himself."

"Gwalchmai must be a sorcerer, then," said Rhuawn, a lean, long-faced man.

"Be quiet," said Agravain harshly. "I have said that he is not." I recognized the signs: My brother wanted to fight someone. Apparently Rhuawn did as well, for he was quiet.

Finally Cei returned, quite drunk, but controlling it well. "Hah!" he exclaimed when he saw me. "Still here, are you?" He was very pleased, with himself and with his judgment. "I'd've thought you'd've gone running from here like a whipped dog by now. Or a whipped hawk?" He snorted with laughter. "But hurt hawks don't run, do they. Don't even fly. They just . . . sit. And brood. And glare. As you are. Hah!"

"Hush," said Bedwyr. "You have no cause for that."

"The practice of sorcery is cause enough for cursing," said Cei. "And I think our lord judged well!"

Bedwyr shook his head. He came over to me and said, "I am sorry, Gwalchmai. Understand, it is not Arthur's usual way, this decision. And this is Cei's way only when he is drunk."

"I'm not so drunk as all that," said Cei. He sneered again. "Well, Hawk of May, where are your spells?"

I realized that I, too, would not mind fighting someone and having some release for my anger. It was absurd, and I realized the absurdity, but still . . .

"Let him alone," snarled Agravain.

"Why?"

"Because I'll challenge you if you don't," replied Agravain quickly. He would, and would enjoy it, though I thought that Cei was not too drunk to fight.

Cei blinked at him, then shrugged and fell silent. However, a few minutes later, noticing Caledvwlch leaning against the wall where I had set it, he went over and picked it up, holding the loop of the baldric and swinging it back and forth, whistling between his teeth.

"Stop!" I called, abruptly ending my fit of brooding.

"What? You don't want me touching your precious magic sword?"

"Put it down," I said. "It is not for you."

"Are you still trying to say that it is . . ."

"It is. My story is true, even if Arthur disbelieves it."

"Liar," said Cei.

Agravain stood, clenching his fists.

I could not let my brother fight my battles for me, however much he wished to. "Stop," I said again, also standing. "Cei, put my sword down before you come to some harm."

He laughed, eagerly. "So, at last you are willing to defend yourself! *Laus Deo!* Do you want your magic sword? I will show you how magic it is. . . ."

"No!" I shouted, seeing what he planned. But he had already closed his hand about the hilt and began to draw the sword.

The dormant fire leaped, once, like summer lightning or a falling star. Cei screamed and dropped the sword, stumbled back against the wall. I was across the room to catch the weapon as he dropped it; I closed my own hand about the hilt and, without thinking, drew it. The fire blazed, pure, cool, and brilliant.

"Are you hurt?" I asked Cei. He stared, opening and closing his mouth, quite sober now. "I said, are you hurt?"

He looked at his hand. It appeared slightly burned, as though by the sun, but otherwise uninjured. "No," he whispered. "God. God."

"By all the saints," muttered Rhuawn.

I looked at my sword, then sheathed it. "It is well," I told them all. "This sword is a powerful thing, and I think that, had you drawn it, it might have killed you. Let it alone now."

"I will," said Cei. "God. I . . . I wish to sleep, now."

No one said anything as we settled down for the night: I, on Agravain's insistence, on his bed, and Agravain on the floor.

I held Caledvwlch beside me in the darkness. The power was real, real enough to burn Cei when he touched it, real enough to have killed him. The Light was real—My Lord, how could I doubt it? And the Light had led me here, and I had come, with high hopes I only fully recognized now that they were gone, and the miracle, somehow, still, had failed, and my soul ached with darkness.

I closed my eyes and ran my fingers over the sword hilt, feeling the cool smoothness of interlaced metal on the grip and the hardness of the single jewel. Simple steel and lifeless stone, yet they could fire with an unearthly light, and burn the hand that ventured to touch them. So could I, all doubts and uncertainties swept away in that white fire that three times now had burned within my mind. And yet, why should such things have happened to me? The Light needed neither men nor swords. Nothing that I did could matter. I had been delivered from the Darkness, and that ought to be enough for me.

I rolled over on the bed and looked up at the thatching of the roof, letting the sword lie on the floor where my hand could easily reach it. It is not as bad as all that, I told myself. This will not kill you. You have only to seek service elsewhere, and there is doubtless much else you can do.

Why a sword? I asked myself again. Why not a harp or a brooch or a ring, as in some tales? If I am not to be a warrior, why an instrument of war? And if I am not to serve Arthur, why be a warrior? No other king has set out to fight the Darkness. . . .

The Darkness. My mind touched it at last, and I remembered Morgawse, as clearly as if she stood there in the room, and the things I had learned from her worked in me like yeast. Morgawse's eyes found mine behind my closed lids, and she smiled and smiled. I turned my mind from the thought. Eventually, I slept.

I dreamed that night, the only such dream I have ever had.

In my dream I rose from the bed and opened the door of the house to look out at Camlann. I saw all of it at once, with the walls finished, glowing in a golden light, splendid and strong. Arthur was before the gates, sitting upon a white horse, and he held a torch in his hand, the source of the light that filled the fortress. A man I did not know held the horse's bridle, a dark-haired man on whose forehead blazed a star, and his eyes were filled with infinite knowledge. Arthur lifted his torch, and the light of it sprang across all the west of Britain. I saw the whole island, from the Orcades in the north to the southern cliffs, the forests, fields, mountains, rivers, and proud cities, lying like a child's drawing in the sea. But the east and north were covered with a profound shadow. I saw Aldwulf standing in the north, a black flame burning above his scarred face, and Cerdic in the south, lifting his arm to command an attack, though with an odd expression of puzzlement on his face. No armies answered his command, but a great white dragon, the symbol of kingship, rose into the sky on cloudlike wings. In the west, Arthur's dragon standard twisted, became a true dragon, and rose to meet the other. Yet I did not watch the combat, for a shadow fell across Arthur and he dwindled to nothing. I looked up and saw her, ruling in the north and east, queen of air and Darkness, lady of shadows. Beautiful she was in the flesh, but in the dream the flesh was gone, like a dimming veil, and she blazed in dark splendor across the universe. My heart came into my throat, and my terrible love for her returned. I wanted to fling myself before her feet and beg her forgiveness, but I reached for my sword. It was not there. She smiled, and my strength vanished, so that I could think of nothing but her.

"So, my falcon," she said, in her infinitely soft, deep voice, "the Dragon does not want you? It is most foolish of him, for you are a great warrior."

I was filled with joy at this, and wanted to run to her and . . . but I forced myself to hold back. "Arthur is free," I answered. "He may do as he wills."

"Of course," she whispered, "though he obeyed me once. But your new lord permits you also to do as you will." She leaned forward from her throne of shadows, her eyes drinking me, like wine. I remembered with night-edged clarity a word she had taught me to fend off spirits. I whispered it, and some of my strength returned.

She smiled, a very sweet, dark, secret smile meant for me alone. "My clever falcon! Yes. You see why I wished to kill you? It can be used against me and for Arthur, to establish the high king's power in Britain."

I tore my eyes from her and looked back to the island I

stood on. Arthur seemed very small after the queen, and his power only fragmentary. I felt a touch of pity for him. I saw the battle lines forming, saw myself ride up on Ceincaled, lift my hand, and speak a word of command. Cerdic clutched his throat and fell to the earth, and Aldwulf died, amazed. The Saxons were swept by plague and famine, storms destroyed their ships, and Arthur conquered all Britain. He reigned in Camlann, and I stood beside him, his most trusted counselor, honored by all. My father came from the Orcades with words of admiration and praise, and chose me to be the heir of his kingship. The Light ruled in Britain.

I looked again at the queen, and met her eyes fully. She smiled for a third time, and those eyes were full of promises. "Ah, my hawk of spring," she whispered. "You were always my favorite, and now that you are older . . . you are a strong enemy, more powerful than Arthur, and a greater sorcerer than that fool Aldwulf."

I felt deep pride and a searing black joy that she should say so. More than ever I longed to approach her. I could make Arthur accept me! I could use what she had taught me for the Light, instead of the Darkness. Then I thought of what she had taught, and remembered the look in Connall's eyes when he knew that she would kill him, and the black lamb struggling under my hands while she looked for the future in its entrails, and I felt sick again, and thought of how Medraut was lost. But I needn't use the worst, I told myself.

"Where is Medraut?" I demanded of the queen.

"That is of no consequence."

"He is your son."

"I have plans for him that are no concern of yours, my falcon. He hates you, my hawk, because you left and betrayed us."

He would hate me. I could see how she must be working on him, slowly destroying him. "And you hate me also," I whispered.

She shook her head slowly, and the black fire in her eyes was only the edge of a vast sea. "You are too powerful, Hawk of May, and too beautiful."

Dizziness swept over me, and I reached once more for my sword. Her eyes were everything in the universe, they were death itself. I could be powerful, and if I were her equal, remained her equal, she would . . .

"No!" I screamed, and flung my arm between us. She stood, terrible in her power, and smiled a final time.

"Ah, but what else can you do, my son?"

What? The Darkness was about me and within me, and I could not even find a sword with which to fight it. I fell back, thinking of Arthur, of Bedwyr, of Cei, Agravain, and then of Sion. Spinning on itself, my mind found the instant at Ynys Witrin, in the silence of the chapel, and abruptly the universe turned around again, and I saw the sun instead of the shadow. My vaguely groping hand found what it sought: my sword. I drew it and held it between myself and the Darkness.

"I will fight for Arthur," I said, my voice steady. "He cannot forbid me to follow him, even unaccepted. I will fight for him until he sees plainly that I do not fight for you. However long it takes, and however difficult it may be, this I can do, and this I will."

Her lies were gone and her plan again defeated. She lifted her arms and the Darkness leaped. But she was distant again, and I stood at Camlann. I looked up and saw Lugh standing in the west, opposite Morgawse, holding his arm above the island so that the queen could not touch it. Behind him was light too brilliant, too glorious to be seen. For a moment I saw these two confronting each other, and then my field of vision narrowed. I saw the island and the figures of armies. I saw the Family and myself in it. The armies began to move, and the sounds of battle arose. I realized that I saw things that were yet to come, and was terrified. I covered my face with my arms and cried, "No more!"

And abruptly there was silence.

Sobbing for breath, I opened my eyes and saw the thatch of Agravain's house above me. Everyone was asleep. I lay still for a long while.

TWELVE

AFTER A LONG TIME THERE came a birdcall from outside, then another. Beyond the door it was morning. I sat up and buried my face in my hands, shivering. Then I rose, dressed, picked my way across the room and opened the door.

The dew was heavy on the grass, and the earth smelled damp and sweet. The first wings of dawn were opening above the plain, over the black bulk of the hills. The birdsong ran back and forth, like water over stones. I closed the door behind me and leaned against it, watching the sun come up from the east. It was a full day before I moved again, and when I did it was to sing, a famous song, one sung over all the West, which Padraig made when he went into Erin.

I arise today,
Through the power of Heaven,
In these forces seven:
Light of the blazing sun
Radiance of the moon,
Splendor of the new flame's run,
Sweetness of the wind's tune,
Deepness of the boundless sea,
The hard earth's stability,
Stone fixed eternally;
I arise today,
Through God's strength to pilot me ...

Through the power most mighty,
Invoking the Trinity,
Confession of one, belief in three,
The Creator of Creation!

I laughed then, though I did not really understand the song, and I offered my sword to the morning light. "I thank you, My Lord!" I said aloud, then added, "And you also, for your protection, kinsman. But do not send me any more such dreams!"

I sheathed Caledvwlch and wondered if there was anything left over from the previous night's feast. I was very hungry, for I had eaten nothing since the previous morning, and had been through a great deal since then. I was considering how to find some food when I heard noises within the house. I went back inside to find that Agravain was awake.

"There you are!" he exclaimed when he saw me. He looked even more tired than he had the evening before. "How long have you been up?"

"Only a little while. I went outside to watch the sun rise."

"You would." He snorted and studied me, then grinned. "By the sun, it is good to have a kinsman here. But you cannot go about dressed like that. A king's son cannot wear the clothes of a Saxon thrall. You've left a mark on Aldwulf; that ought to entitle you to a decent cloak at the least, even if you are not in the Family. Come, we will go to the storerooms and find some gear for you."

He pulled his own clothing on and we went up the hill, past the feast hall to the storerooms on the west side of the hill. Agravain was trying very hard not to disturb me by referring to Arthur's decision or what might happen next, but instead pointed out the sights of Camlann. But I could tell that he was thinking hard.

The storerooms were a sprawling group of buildings, low roofed and dark, and mostly newly built to store the high king's plunder. They were clear testimony of Arthur's success as a warleader, for they were filled with piles of clothing, with weapons and jewelry, imported pottery, dishes of gold, silver, horn, and glass as well as wood, bronze, and earthenware. There was not much food there, but there is not much to be had by raiding in the spring. All the goods had been taken from the Saxons, either on their own lands or returning plunder laden from British kingdoms. Agravain told me that it would mostly be sold to whomever could pay for it with grain or other foodstuffs. "The high king prefers grain, though," he went on, "for the horses. The Family's war-horses devour the harvest of a kingdom, I think. Still, I have helped to win this, so I can help to dispose of it. Choose what you will. I will give you a horse, as well." He hesitated, then finally met my eyes and asked his question: "Where will you go?"

I was uncertain how to phrase it. "I will not go," I said at last, simply. "I will follow the Pendragon Arthur on my own, until he does accept me. He must see, eventually, that I am not a sorcerer and that I am a warrior worth my mead."

Agravain stared at me for a long moment, then grinned fiercely. "That is a warrior's decision, a decision worth a song! Indeed, show them all that they are wrong, and teach them not to slander you!" Then he stopped, frowning. "But it will be difficult. Arthur is a noble king, and will not refuse hospitality to you, but Cei is your enemy now. You frightened him last night, and made him look a fool and he won't stand for that. Moreover, he is the infantry commander, and has a Latin title of his own for it, and is a man to be wary of offending—though he is brave, and honest, and a good friend."

"I must try it, whether or not Cei is my enemy. It is all I can do."

Agravain was much happier as we chose some new, more "appropriate" clothing from the heaps. When I had a good woolen tunic and leggings, my brother searched through another pile of goods to find a leather jerkin with some metal plates which he had won a month and a half before and which he thought would fit me. It did, and he pressed it on me, saying that it was his to give. Such armor is not as good as chain mail, but chain mail is rare and valuable. Agravain had only one mail coat, which he would have given to me, except that it did not fit.

Besides the jerkin I found a shield, whitewashed wood
with a steel rim, plain, but good, solid work; and a long,
leaf-headed thrusting spear with a nice balance, as well as
five throwing spears.

"Now you need only a cloak," Agravain said with satisfaction. "What kind . . ."

"A red one," said a strange voice behind us.

"Taliesin," said Agravain, greeting the man who stood
in the door, watching us with mild interest. "Why a red
one?"

I stared at Arthur's chief bard, speechless. The other
memory I had associated with that name came abruptly
clear: He had sung in Lugh's hall, in the Islands of the
Blessed. And it was he who had held the bridle of Arthur's horse in my dream, and spoken to Sion in his.

But he was not wearing a star on his forehead now, and
his face was human, without that disquieting radiance the
faces of the Sidhe have—though he remained a very handsome man. His name, Radiant Brow, which is given to
the morning star, was not wasted on him.

"I know you," I said.

But he shook his head. "No, you have never seen me
before, though you may have heard some of my songs.
There are plenty of them around."

"What are you talking about?" asked Agravain.

"Your brother thought we had met before," Taliesin
stated pleasantly, sauntering into the room. "And I
corrected him. I never had the pleasure. —Your brother is
a remarkable man, Agravain."

"He is not a sorcerer," snapped Agravain quickly.

Taliesin grinned. "You are too suspicious, my friend. I
never said he was. Welcome to Camlann, Hawk of May."

I was certain that I was not mistaken. "But what . . ." I
began.

"I am sorry," he said quickly, "I cannot answer your
questions, not now. You would not understand the answers. You are thinking of a dream which you had last
night, and a dream a friend of yours had, and of what
Bedwyr told you about me. But I cannot explain. There
is something to all of them—but you know that already.
The answer would be less interesting than the mystery,
however, and I prefer things to be interesting. Also, un-

fortunately, you must discover truth for yourself. Someone tells you something: Do you listen? Indeed not; you run off your own way, and in the end, knocked flat on your back (as Bedwyr was when first I met him) you say to yourself, 'Taliesin was right'! But I am tired of being told the obvious fact that I was right."

Agravain laughed. "Oh, indeed? I wish I could understand your songs well enough to tell you that you are wrong."

"But I do not intend for them to be understood!" Taliesin protested. He hummed a snatch of music, broke off. "We poets have that privilege. —A red cloak is the best. There is one in the middle of that pile there, a very fine one."

I remembered Sion's dream, "A man in a red cloak lying dead," and I felt as though I stood on the edge of some precipice in darkness, feeling the presence of the gulf I could not see. Taliesin stopped smiling.

"I am not ill-wishing you, Hawk of May," he said gently. His expression was unreadable. "It is only that what must be, will be. Your color is red, like the dragon of Britain, or like the blood that lies upon the battlefields, and will lie there, when the night comes. When the shield wall is broken and the gate of the stronghold battered down." He shook his head. "The empire now may be compared to a tapestry, woven in many colors, by many choices; your color is red." He stopped suddenly, blinking, then recovered himself and smiled again. "Besides, red will suit you. That pile over there—And now I must find Arthur and explain to him why the walls have not progressed as far as he had expected. *Vale!*" He swept out of the room, letting the door swing shut behind him.

"By the sun," said Agravain, "what did that mean?"

"I was just about to ask you. Agravain, who is Taliesin?"

"Arthur's chief poet, one of his advisors, and occasionally a cavalryman under Bedwyr."

"Beyond that?"

"Who knows? Who can tell, with poets? Sometimes, as now, he simply says things that no one can understand, and sometimes he says that a thing will happen and it does. Before the last raid, he suddenly went up to one of

the infantrymen, Macsen ap Valens, just as we were setting out, and took his hand and said, 'Good fortune after
the end; hail and farewell.' And Macsen died on that raid.
Some say that Taliesin is a bit mad. Others tell stories. . . ."

"What stories?"

"His father or his mother was a god, or a demon—the
versions differ. He drank from the cauldron of Annwn,
and knows all things. He is a prophet, magician, devil,
saint, angel." Agravain shrugged. "Priests dislike him for
his reputation, but he goes to the Christians' Masses when
he is in Camlann. The only certain thing is that he is a
great poet. Urien of Rheged was his first patron, but Arthur persuaded him to come to Camlann. But he is not a
Northerner. You heard how he said 'farewell' in Latin—
that much I've learned. Some say he is from Gwynedd. I
know that he has the Sight, at the least. . . ." Agravain
made a druid's gesture, one meant to ward off evil, and
lowered his voice. "But all poets must be touched, else
they would not be prophets and preservers of the law.
No one can ask Taliesin questions and receive an answer
they understand, and no one wishes to insult him by
asking too many questions, for if he made a satire on you,
the only thing left would be for you to fall on your
sword. Where did you think you had seen him before?"

"In Lugh's feast hall."

Agravain looked away and made his gesture again. "He
says that it was not he."

"I suppose it could not have been." The bright echoes
of the song ran through my mind again. Taliesin's song. I
could not tell what it meant, but no one who had made it
could be evil.

"Truly," said Agravain, looking at the door again, "do
you want a red cloak?"

Sion's phrase ran through my mind again, like an ill
omen. I remembered too how often my mother wore
red—but then, it was an easy color to dye things, and
many men liked the brightness of it. And whatever
thread Taliesin saw woven for me in his tapestry, the pattern was not going to be affected by the color of a cloak.
"As much as any other color," I told Agravain.

He went to the pile Taliesin had indicated and dug into

it. "Here it is," he told me. "It is a good one. Nice thick wool."

It felt strange to wear the new things, to have the weight of the shield on one shoulder and of Caledvwlch over the other; and yet that weight was somehow right. Agravain nodded in satisfaction. "Now you look to be a warrior, and royal," he decided. "They will be more careful how they treat you, now. Are you ready for breakfast?"

The hall was full of warriors eating the remains of the previous night's feast, which were set out upon the tables. I managed to ignore the hostile or merely curious stares of the other warriors as we ate. It was not difficult, as the food was good and I was very hungry.

Agravain was more cheerful than he had been the night before, and talked about Britain and the Family over the meal. He had certainly changed in the years since I had seen him. I felt uncertain with him, as though I knew him and did not know him. But I enjoyed his company. There were times, though, when I glimpsed another thought in his face, and it was dark. I guessed that it had something to do with our mother. But she was the last thing he wished to speak of.

We had almost finished when we heard shouting outside the hall, then a cry of pain. The hall fell silent, and through the suddenly still air came a loud neigh of an angry horse.

"What on earth?" said Agravain.

But I had recognized the call. "Ceincaled!" I said, jumping up. "It is Ceincaled."

It was. He stood in the sunlight outside the hall, even more splendid and lovely than I remembered. He was angry, ears laid back and nostrils flared and red, and some of Arthur's servants surrounded him, holding ropes and lowered spears. One lay on the ground, white faced and clutching his stomach, being supported by another. Directly in front of the horse stood Arthur.

"Lord, be careful!" called one of the servants. "The beast is vicious, a man killer. Look what he did to Gwefyl!"

Arthur ignored them and took another step toward the horse. Ceincaled reared, neighed again, tossing his head.

Arthur smiled, a light kindling behind his eyes. He took another step forward and stretched out his hand, half in offering, half in command, and he spoke slowly, soothingly.

The stallion snorted, but his ears came forward. He surveyed the king with proud eyes. "Be still," said Arthur. The horse jerked his head, snorted again, impatiently. But he stood still and did not move when Arthur stepped nearer and caught his head.

"He is not vicious," said Arthur. "But he is proud, and mistrustful; and he prizes his freedom."

Ceincaled stamped and jerked his head, but his ears remained pricked forward, listening to Arthur.

I released the edge of the door which I had clutched and began to breathe again. "Ceincaled," I called.

His head came up and he tossed off Arthur's grip and cantered over to me, nudged my shoulder. I ran my hand down his neck, again awed by his beauty. "Ceincaled," I repeated, and added in Irish, "why, bright one, have you come back? This is no place for you."

"By the sun," whispered Agravain, behind me, in great admiration, "what a horse!"

"It is your horse?" asked Arthur, coming up. He had a look of disappointment, mingled with something else. "I should have realized; the horse you stole from Cerdic, no doubt."

"He is not mine. How can any mortal own such a beast? I released him, three days ago."

"I think, nonetheless, that he is yours," Arthur replied in a harsh voice. He hesitated, looking from me to the horse. He laid his hand on the stallion's shoulder, looked at me again, seemed about to shout some accusation, then stopped himself. "Well then, take him and do what you please."

"But he is not mine! I released him."

"When CuChulainn was dying," Taliesin said, appearing as if from nowhere, "the Liath Macha, which the hero had released earlier that day, returned to die beside his master, although he was one of the horses of the Sidhe and an immortal."

"That is only a tale," I said, "and that was CuChulainn. Ceincaled is real. Why should he die on Earth?"

"He came to find you," Taliesin replied calmly. "Horses are great fools when it comes to their masters, and will go where their rider is without thinking, assuming that it must be safe. Even immortal horses." He smiled and held out his hand. Ceincaled tossed his head and sniffed the hand, flicking his ears forward again.

I looked at the horse, and thought of the wonder of the Land of Ever Young, and thought of this world. I remembered the instant when I had first ridden him, and our two spirits had met, and the astounded love he had offered, and I knew that Taliesin was right. I stroked the white neck.

"You are a fool," I told my horse softly, in Irish. "Oh my bright splendid one, you are foolish. You will find nothing here, in the end, but death."

He snorted and nibbled my hair.

"As you will, then," I whispered, and bowed my head. I wanted to weep for him.

"So now you have a horse," Arthur said sharply, "and I see that your brother has found clothing and arms for you. It remains only for you to find service somewhere, and you should be able to do that easily." He looked at Ceincaled again, and his hand curled about his sword hilt, then loosened slowly. "Perhaps you will try Maelgwn Gwynedd. He wants warriors."

I twined my hand in Ceincaled's mane, staring at the king over the horse's back. Arthur stared back with a level, cold anger, and I suddenly saw that he thought I had cast a spell on the horse. I shook my head in response to the unvoiced accusation. Arthur caught the gesture.

"Another king, then? Urien might not have you: He also has no love for sorcerers. But there remain Vortipor, and Caradoc of Ebrauc . . ."

I thought that I might as well announce my plan then as at any time. "Lord Pendragon," I said, quietly and formally, "it is not my wish to take service with any lord but yourself. And it is not my wish to go out into Britain with a sorcerer's name on me."

"Your wishes are not the point. If you are a warrior, you must find a lord to support you, and I will not."

"I think, Lord, that I can support myself after a fashion, at least until the next battle, when I may win myself some goods. I will follow you and fight for you, whether you accept my oath or no."

The bystanders murmured in astonishment. Arthur gripped the hilt of his sword. For a moment I feared that he would draw the weapon, but he released it slowly. The cold anger in his stare had become white hot. "You plan well, Gwalchmai ap Lot," he said, evenly but with intensity. "You know that I cannot allow it to be said that my own nephew hangs about my court like a stray dog, and so I must give you hospitality. Very well. You may stay here, and drink my mead and have a place in my hall. But I do not, and will not—ever—accept you as mine. I require more than strength of arms, or cunning, or sorcery for that: I require a thing called honor." He glanced about and saw Cei in the circle of watchers. "Since you wish to serve me," Arthur continued quickly, "let us see how well you manage. Cei!"

"My Lord?" Cei elbowed his way through the crowd, looking a trifle confused and still heavy with sleep.

"You are to head the band that will fetch the tribute from Maelgwn Gwynedd in Degannwy. Take thirty men—you can choose them—and take Gwalchmai here. You will leave tomorrow morning."

"Yes, My Lord, but . . ."

"Very good. If you are to be ready on time, you had better begin now." The high king strode off through the crowd, his cloak flapping.

Cei gave me a surprised, then a speculative look, and whistled over Ceincaled. "So now you have a magic horse to match your magic sword, sorcerer. Well indeed, for we will have a chance to see what use they are now. You'll need both on the way to Degannwy. Especially a fast horse, for . . ."

"Come," said Agravain, "Cei is very busy." He turned and walked off toward the stables, and I followed, leading Ceincaled.

The stables were next to the feast hall on the north, and, like most of the storehouses, were new, very large, and very full. But we found one empty stall, and I gave Ceincaled water at the trough, then poured some grain in the manger and coaxed him into the stall. He did not like it at first, no doubt remembering Cerdic's stables and the trap, but settled eventually to eat the grain. I began to brush him down, and Agravain sat on the straw and fidgeted with a piece of grass.

"By the sun and the wind!" said my brother, after a time. "I have never seen Arthur so angry. Even when Vortipor of Dyfed abandoned us last summer, and left us to face the Saxons without his army, he did not speak as sharply as he did today. It is so unlike him that I cannot even be angry that he insulted you. But Degannwy! With Cei in charge of the expedition."

"What is wrong with Degannwy?" I knew of the place, a small and unimportant fortress in Gwynedd, northeast of the ancient port and royal stronghold Caer Segeint.

"Degannwy is where Maelgwn lurks for most of the year," answered Agravain, "Maelgwn, and half the Arthur-haters in Britain. You recall Docmail Gwynedd?"

"Of course. He killed himself rather than surrender to Arthur."

"Even so. Maelgwn would not have killed himself. He would have pretended to surrender and then attacked again as soon as Arthur's back was turned. He is a year younger than I am, and already he is one of the most cunning men in Britain. They say that when he is old enough he will be a match even for that fox Vortipor of Dyfed. He is too cunning to attack Arthur openly, and he will pay the tribute, but it will not be pleasant journeying. And Gwynedd, especially in the Arfon Mountains, is thick with bandits and stray warriors of Maelgwn's, who all hate anyone who has anything to do with the high king. Arthur has been planning to send a band to collect the tribute for over a year, since Maelgwn keeps promising to send it himself and never does, or says that he has and it was all lost to bandits. But Bedwyr was going to lead the expedition. Now . . . Cei will make it as difficult for you as he is able to, and he is able to make things difficult indeed, especially since he can select the other warriors for the expedition." Agravain began to beat the palm of his left hand with his fist. "Iffern take all of this! Gwalchmai . . ." He chewed his moustache for a moment, then said, "Perhaps you would do better to seek service with some other lord. Only to prove yourself, before coming back."

"If I cannot prove myself here, how can I do so anywhere else?"

"But Cei will try to provoke you, to make you either fight him or go away altogether. And you must remember how anyone could bully you."

"I will avoid trouble, if it is at all possible without losing honor. Agravain, I must go, or give up the hope of fighting for Arthur entirely." And may the Light protect me, I thought, if it is bad enough to worry Agravain in this way.

Bedwyr came into the stable hurriedly, looked around, and came over to sit down by Agravain. "I am sorry," he told me. "I spoke with Arthur again, but I cannot convince him. He believes that you have cast some spell upon the horse, which angered him, and that you then were playing the innocent, which angered him further." He looked at Ceincaled respectfully, then went on, "But now I am certain that there is some other matter weighing on his mind, something that he will not speak of. He wished to be left alone, and when I left, he was fighting with it. A thing that . . ." Bedwyr trailed off, groping for words to describe what he had sensed and finding none. "Gwalchmai. Swear to me that you have indeed given up sorcery."

"Bedwyr!" hissed Agravain, beginning to rise and reaching for his sword.

"I swear it, by the Light and as the earth is under me," I told Bedwyr.

We held each other's gaze for a moment, and then Bedwyr sighed. "Truly. I ask your forgiveness for doubting it. Arthur is my friend as well as my lord, and he is not a fool, nor usually wrong in his judgments. He has some cause which makes him wary, but it must be that it is in himself, and not in you. He will not speak of it, even to me."

I nodded, but inwardly I thought that the cause might well be in me. I had seen that I was somehow still bound to Morgawse. It was as though her shadow lay within me, inside the marrow of my bones, too deep for me to shake off.

"Perhaps," urged Bedwyr, "it would be better if you left. Find another lord—not Maelgwn. Despite what my

lord Arthur said, I believe that Urien of Rheged would
accept you. He is not a brilliant king, but is honest, and a
fine fighter. He is married to your aunt and would be
well disposed toward you. They say that his own son is
not much use in battle, and he has no other nephews with
him in Rheged, so you might do well."

"It is not a bad idea, Gwalchmai," said Agravain. "You
could advance quickly there, and, if you did, you could,
perhaps, return in a year or so."

I shook my head, tiredly. "I will stay."

Bedwyr began to speak again, but stopped himself. He
did not like the way that I angered Arthur, and clearly
felt bound to protect his friend's will and judgment, but
also felt that I was telling the truth. He sensed my determination and did not urge me again to leave.

We sat in silence for a time, wrapped in our separate
thoughts. After a time, Ceincaled finished the oats I had
given him and came over to nibble my hair and demand
attention. I caught his head.

"Why don't you put your Liath Macha out to pasture?" suggested Bedwyr, "or better yet, exercise him. It
is a fine day."

"He is not a Liath Macha; he is white, not gray," I replied.

Bedwyr stared at me blankly.

"Liath," I said, realizing that he could not understand
Irish. "It means 'gray,' like Llwydd in British. 'Gray of
Battle.' CuChulainn's horses were a gray and a black, and
both were horses of the Sidhe, though the Liath Macha
was the better of the two."

"Indeed?" asked Bedwyr. "How did he come by them,
then?"

I looked at him in surprise.

"I am only a Breton," said Bedwyr, with the same glint
of suppressed amusement I had seen the day before. "I
know little of your CuChulainn. I had not heard so much
as his name, until I met your brother. Taliesin probably
knows all the tales, but then, he knows Irish. Agravain in-
sists that he himself cannot sing the stories properly when
I ask him, though. I suppose that you will say the same?"

"He can tell them," Agravain replied immediately, "almost as well as a trained bard. No, better. He leaves out

the dull parts." His eyes grew brighter. "I have not found anyone to sing the tales for me for over a year, Gwalchmai. Do you suppose that . . ."

Eager to take their minds off the present, they searched about to find a harp and told me to sing of CuChulainn. I was glad enough of the distraction myself, and I sang the tale of CuChulainn's horses. By the time I finished, my audience had grown. Besides Agravain, Bedwyr, and Rhuawn (who owned the harp), I had the grooms and a few other servants and warriors listening. They applauded when I had done.

"You sing well," said Bedwyr, his eyes bright.

"You are better than the last time I heard you," said Agravain. "Much better. Sing how CuChulainn died."

I hesitated, for the song is a difficult one; but I began the tune on the harp, and then tried to follow what the music said with fitting words.

I had reached the point in the tale where CuChulainn's enemies succeeded in drawing the hero out into battle alone, and there I faltered, for I saw that Taliesin had entered and was listening. He nodded for me to continue, but I stopped and, on impulse, offered him the harp.

He took it silently and began where I had left off. He used the old bardic style, but in a way I had not thought it could be used, so that each word mattered. It snared the listeners in a web of sound, so that they waited impatiently for each phrase, yet wanted the present one to last. Taliesin looked at no one, nor did he watch his hands on the harp, but stared into the distance. He did not use the old tune, but a new and difficult one: a dissonant thunder for the armies, a complexity of violence and rage; and against it a clean, pure thread of music for CuChulainn, a tune now lost in the thunder, now emerging from it, until, at the end, when the hero gave his spear to the man who asked it of him, the song suddenly drowned out the armies altogether. It was a renunciation of everything, and it was triumphant, proud, totally assured. The last lingering high note came, the hero's death; and then, through the stillness, the drop of the ravens onto the field of battle. The song ended, and there was an infinite silence.

I buried my face in my hands. I had wept, as had all

the listeners. "Lord," I whispered to Taliesin, "I thank you."

He wrenched his eyes from wherever he had fixed them and looked at the harp in his hands as though surprised to find it there. "Ach, no," he replied. "There is nothing to thank me for in the mere singing of it. . . ." And then he laughed. "You have made me serious, twice in one day! Will you ruin my reputation for me? Truly, My Lord, there is nothing to thank me for. It is only a song, and I only sang it as a bard should. You yourself are able to sing well."

That anyone could be thought to sing well beside Taliesin was impossible, and I said so.

"Well, of course!" Taliesin replied, a glint in his eyes. "But do not insult me by using the same standards for others and for myself. Whose harp is this?"

Rhuawn claimed the instrument.

"You will have to sing more of the songs about this CuChulainn," said Bedwyr. "He sounds a great warrior."

"So he seems, from the songs," said Taliesin. "He killed his son, his best friend, hundreds of innocent soldiers, a few monsters, and a druid who had aided him."

"He had no choice but to kill his son and his friend!" Agravain protested indignantly.

"I did not say that he had. I said only that he did kill them. He did some other foolish things as well. There is one story . . ." he told an outrageous tale about a tryst of CuChulainn's which went awry, and strode confidently off, leaving his audience helpless with laughter. I shrugged my laughter off and ran after him. He stopped when he saw me following.

"I thought you might come. Well?"

"I . . ." I hesitated, then plunged on, "Agravain and Bedwyr believe that I should to go Rheged."

"Do they?"

"You know that they do. You knew what I had seen in a dream, and I think you know also what is to come. You must know that I am not a witch."

He sighed, nodded.

"Then help me. Why does Arthur hate me?"

He looked at me, chewing reflectively on his lower lip.

"You are very young for this," he said softly, more to himself than to me.

"I am old enough; I am seventeen."

"That is very young. I know you are expected to be men as soon as you have taken arms, and you men of royal clans are to be able to deal with anything a king can deal with, but it is not right, to set so much on those who are so young." He caught my shoulder. "Listen. I would like to give you answers to all your questions, but how can I? I do not know all things. Some things I foresee, but dimly, like things under a moving stream, and some things come to pass and others do not. Other things I foresee as clear and fixed, but fitting into no pattern, without explanation. How should I dare to trouble the waters by answering a question, and perhaps, by doing so, change the shape of what is to come? And you yourself know, in a way, why the emperor hates you, and one day you will realize it, but now you cannot. You must be patient and learn to live in uncertainty. More I cannot tell you."

"Very well," I said heavily. "But Rheged?"

"You have already made your own decision on that."

It was true, I had. "Who are you?" I asked in a whisper.

He smiled, very gently. "I am Taliesin, the emperor's chief bard. Does any other answer mean anything?"

"Are you of the Sidhe?"

But he did not answer, only turned and began to walk on.

In the afternoon I remembered Sion's mare, went to check on her, and found that the farmer had arrived and collected his cart and his money the previous afternoon. I felt, on hearing this, more uncertain of myself than ever. It was almost a relief to set out the following morning with Cei and the band of thirty for Degannwy. At least then I did not have to think about what troubles would come. There were troubles enough on the road.

The journey was indeed a rough one, especially the first part of it. Cei's thirty were hostile and suspicious of me. They used any means available to them to force me to leave, and Cei was their leader in all such attempts. If there was an unpleasant task to be done, the sort usually reserved for thralls if any are about, I was assigned to do it. I was insulted fairly blatantly, and otherwise ignored. I was not wanted there, and the warriors made it abundantly plain. But I discovered that I could use my tongue to turn the point of the insults or turn them into a joke, and this, with patience and a certain amount of pretending that I hadn't heard, prevented a duel. There was nothing I couldn't stand—though I was glad Agravain was not with us. He would have felt obliged to kill half the party.

We took the Roman road from Camlann through the hills which the British call Gwlad yr Haf, Kingdom of Summer, which they say lie close to the Otherworld, then to Baddon, which the Romans called Aquae Sulis, and northwest up another Roman road to Caer Legion, and west again into the mountains of Arfon. It was awesome country, beautiful and harsh. The road was rough there: It had taken the Romans a long time to conquer the west of Britain, and they had abandoned it quickly. Degannwy was in the midst of the roughest part of the country, a small fortress but a very strong one. Everyone in it, from King Maelgwn on, hated us almost tangibly, and gave us the bare minimum of hospitality demanded by the king's oath of fealty to Arthur. When we left, Maelgwn managed to cheat us of some of the tribute he owed, and the grain he gave us was adulterated with chaff, though we did not discover this until we reached Camlann. We were in a hurry to leave Degannwy, for we feared that if we stayed there would be bloodshed between our party and Maelgwn's men, or that perhaps Maelgwn would send his warband after us and claim to Arthur that the destruction had been the work of bandits.

The return journey was at once easier and more difficult than the trip to Degannwy. Riding up the north road with empty carts we had had no trouble with bandits. On our return journey we were attacked three times in as many days, and by large groups. The robbers attacked from ambush, using bows—a weapon no warrior will touch—and attempting to loot the tribute-laden carts before the whole party could bear up to protect them. Two warriors were killed in these attacks, and seven were wounded. We doubled the distance we had to travel by riding up and down the line of carts, wearing our shields on our arms instead of slung over our backs. I don't doubt that many of the bandits only attacked us because we were Arthur's; the whole countryside hated us. At the monasteries where we stopped to collect the tribute—they paid their taxes separately from the king—the men were full of mutterings, and of stone throwing when we left. We scarcely dared to ask for hospitality at the larger fortresses, and, when we did ask, had to guard our carts and our backs.

But the difficulties combined to make it easier for me. I fought with the others against the bandits, cared for the wounded as well as I could, and with them shared the hostility of all around us. In such conditions they would have been less than human if they had not begun to trust me. By the time we rode back into Camlann, I was accepted as a member of the Family by everyone in the band but Cei. Stubborn Cei, the songs called him. It was easy to see why. He was stubborn in battle, willing to hold a position at any cost, never afraid, never unnerved, using his sharp tongue to drive on his companions and taking no thought for himself. He was a man in every way fitted to command Arthur's infantry. But he was stubborn in his opinions as well, and that included his opinion of me. A pity, for I learned to admire him.

We arrived in Camlann again just over three weeks after we had left it. It was very sweet to me, if strangely dreamlike, to ride back through the gates at one with the band I had joined as an outsider. It was victory.

The warriors in Camlann also looked at me differently than they had when I left. Agravain, grinning, lost no time in telling me the reason for this. News of the events at Sorviodunum had arrived. The incident had become slightly distorted in the telling—I was supposed to have cut down a good dozen Saxons when I fled—but it had won me the respect of the Family.

But not of Arthur. Cei gave the high king a complete report of the journey, of Maelgwn's forces and his attitude, and of the bandits. Arthur became thoughtful over Maelgwn, gave gifts to the wounded, and praised the dead, and had a feast given in honor of the rest of the band. Both Cei and Arthur avoided mentioning me altogether.

I was not very discouraged, however. I had proved myself to Cei's band, and this was a long step toward doing the same with the rest of the Family. I was beginning to know the men, and to make friends. Bedwyr and Agravain both decided that I was doing the right thing after all—though Bedwyr was more uneasy than ever over his lord's attitude. It was my first real victory, and I exulted in it. I was certain that, with the Light's aid, I could prove myself now. I wanted only an opportunity.

Three days after the feast that opportunity opened before me. The Family was on the move.

THIRTEEN

A RTHUR AND CERDIC HAD BEEN contesting who could force the other into a pitched battle first, and Arthur had appeared to be winning, for Cerdic's followers were impatient for open war. Now came news that Aldwulf had returned to Bernicia with his followers, leaving Cerdic's men restless and still more eager to fight. The loss of his raiding party must have stung Cerdic, though he gave no sign of it, but it was expected that he would presently be pushed into raising the fyrd, the full peasant army, and marching on Camlann. Arthur had been unwilling to encounter the whole of Cerdic's army, which was much larger than the force he could muster, but, now that it seemed inevitable, decided to strike first. There was a risk involved, but the Pendragon was also concerned over the situation in the north and what might happen when Aldwulf returned and renewed his alliance with Deira, the other northern Saxon kingdom. He was willing to take the risk so as to have his hands free. The northern British kingdoms were already in difficulties: Rheged still weak from the civil war, and troubled with the Irish raids along its coasts; Ebrauc and Elmet engaged in a blood feud; March ap Meirchiawn of Strathclyde already paying tribute to the Dalriada to his north and unwilling to fight the Saxons to his south; and Gododdin, my father's old ally, still bitterly opposed to her neighbors. The northern Saxons were already beginning to raid their British neighbors heavily, and had seized some lands as well, and to stop them was a matter requiring an extended campaign, which was impossible if Cerdic remained strong and in possession of Sorviodunum.

Arthur had contacted his subject kings Constantius of Dumnonia and Eoghan of Brycheiniog and requested them to raise their armies. While they sent the spear about their domains, calling up all the townsmen and farmers, Arthur himself prepared for one of the lightning-swift raids that were so characteristic of him. With luck, Cerdic would be unaware that the Family was, in this case, backed by armies, and would lead whatever forces he had gathered into a trap.

It was a fine morning late in June when we left Camlann and rode south to take the east road to Sorviodunum. The sun was dissolving the morning mist, and the day promised to be hot. Camlann looked firm and secure, set above the heat haze on its hill, the fields were beginning to shade into gold, the sky was the palest blue imaginable, and the earth smelled rich. The Family was in a fine mood, joking and singing and boasting of the great deeds it would do. Ceincaled stepped lightly, eager to run, rejoicing in the day and in his own strength, and I felt as he did. I wondered whether it always felt so, to ride off to war, destruction, and the threat of death.

We followed the east road until we came into the Saxon lands, and then cut across the plain. We traveled by night when nearest to Sorviodunum, and, as the land was not heavily settled, managed to avoid the notice of the Saxons altogether. We pressed on, concentrating on speed, right through the land of the South Saxons and into Cantware. There we sacked the fort of Anderida, which Arthur had taken once before, seizing what goods were there and burning as much of the fortress as we could. Then we turned north and spread out over the country, pillaging it.

The purpose of raids, other than the taking of plunder, is to cause as much damage as possible to the enemy. They are thus a savage business, worse than pitched battles where warriors are fighting warriors. In raids, as often as not, one is fighting unarmed men, old men and women, and destroying their livelihoods. The only pleasant part is the freeing of British thralls, who are usually overjoyed and sometimes wild for vengeance. Set free enough, give them their masters' weapons and give them liberty to take their masters' goods and go, and they do all the damage anyone could wish. Arthur wished us to be as gentle as possible, and usually we were able to confine ourselves to firing the crops and driving off the cattle, without killing, but still, it is an unpleasant business.

We cut a wide path through Cantware and began to work westward through the kingdom of the South Saxons. Cerdic had heard of this by then, and he gathered the army he had raised and came after us. Aeduin, king of Cantware, was nearer, but had not yet raised the fyrd. He began to do so—we encountered one of his messengers—and waited for Cerdic. We regrouped, sorted out our plunder, left the heavier goods, and pressed on toward the northwest. Cerdic's army approached from the southeast, following the trail of ruin we had left. We were nearly in Cerdic's lands, now, but instead of pushing through them Arthur turned northward until we were nearly at the Tamesis River. There we again sorted out our plunder and even abandoned most of the cattle we had driven off, then turned and rode west as fast as we could. Our scouts reported that Cerdic had divided his army and left a part of it near the southern borders of his lands, but this we had avoided by traveling so far north.

The Saxon kings were enraged. We had entered their lands and done untold amounts of damage, and slipped through their hands when they tried to catch us. The three kings—Aeduin of Cantware, the king of the South Saxons, and Cerdic—now had a unified force. Cerdic was probably delighted, perhaps even thought that he had won his contest with Arthur. He would certainly have to lead his army on into Dumnonia now. He had a very great numerical advantage over our forces, even though he was unaware that we had raised the armies, but Arthur hoped our advantages of surprise and a battlefield of our choice would be enough to offset this. If his hope proved useless, then the Saxons would destroy the Family and be free to do whatever they pleased with southern Britain. But we did not like to think of that.

The Family rode as quickly as we could to the agreed-upon meeting place of the armies of Dumnonia and Brycheiniog, and found that the armies were in fact there, a thing that had been uncertain, since some of the British kings had failed in their promises before.

We had scarcely arrived, and Arthur had only just leaped from his worn horse and embraced Constantius of Dumnonia, when, on the high king's orders, fresh horses were found for the Family and the armies struck camp. I kept Ceincaled, however, for the raid had not tired him enough to warrant a new mount. And I thought I would want him if we could trap the army of Cerdic of the West Saxons.

Arthur had set men to watch the main roads, and a post arrived from one of these reporting that the Saxons were taking the east road toward Baddon. We turned directly south, marching as rapidly as we could to meet them, and Arthur fretted at the slowness of the full army's pace.

Those two weeks showed me why Arthur was so great a leader. In the whirl of speed our campaign had become he remained steady, was able to understand every detail that was reported to him, fit it into its place, and take account of it in his own plans. When everyone around him was too weary or tense or confused to think, he remained steady, certain, and in control. He fought well, without malice or hatred, and never lost sight of what he fought for, so that he never, even in the most difficult moments, commanded an action of vengeance or cruelty, nor was he ever unwilling to speak to his followers. The blood and dust and exhaustion could not hold us as could Arthur's vision; he was the kind of king who occurs once in ten generations or in ten hundred years. He demanded, simply by being, all of the best his servants could give; and we gave it gladly.

I say "we," and yet I was not able to include myself among those who served Arthur. I wished to, more so than ever, but the high king trusted me no more than he had at first. I hung about the fringes of the Family, fought when I could, and puzzled over the reason that even the sight of me seemed to anger him. I set my hopes on the battle and what it might show, half-eager and half-afraid. Perhaps, I thought, I would not like what it showed me: Nonetheless, it was the test, and I was eager for it. I prayed to the Light, grasping my sword hilt, that I would not disgrace myself or the Family.

The day before the battle we camped near the edge of the plain of Sorviodunum, in a forest by a river called the Bassas. In midmorning the following day the Saxons arrived and we were waiting for them.

Arthur had, as always, planned carefully. The road followed a curve beneath the slope of a hill to its south, and he posted the cavalry along this hill, hidden in the woods that covered it. He set the infantry of the Family, with the warbands of Constantius and Eoghan, in the center, just around the curve on the road itself; and dispersed the less skilled armies through the wood on the flanks. The Saxon forces, if all went well, would march around the curve into the foot forces, which should break their shield wall; after which, in a signal, the cavalry would charge through the Dumnonian lines to cut the Saxons off and to disrupt them.

I waited with the cavalry, beside Bedwyr and Taliesin. Agravain was fighting with the foot, near Arthur, in the manner he still preferred. The morning sun was hot, and we had already thrown off our cloaks and tied them over our saddles, and the sunlight filtered through the trees to glitter off the metal of arms and armor. In the camp behind us the camp followers were preparing for the battle in their own way, filling buckets with water and readying wagons: We could hear the called orders and the creak of yokes and wheels. We were very happy, oddly tense and relaxed at the same time, and we laughed and joked a great deal while we waited for the Saxons to arrive. I felt very light-headed, and for a time wondered if I would disgrace myself by fainting, and wondered if the heat had anything to do with it. But I did not feel so much faint as full of an exultation which mounted as the distant shadow on the road, the Saxon host, drew nearer. I looked up at the blue sky and wanted to sing. I loved the sky, the warm-smelling earth, the sunlight through the trees: all the sensations that seemed sharper and clearer than they ever had before. I loved the Saxons as well. I wondered how many of those beside me would die, and if I would be among them. Life was very sweet.

The Saxons marched up the road in good order, in a wide column which overflowed onto the verges, and the sun shone on their spears and helmets. Their scouting had been poor, for they were in a hurry to catch Arthur, and they did not know that we were waiting. They crossed the river; and then it seemed that their vanguard must have heard something or received some message from some outrider, for they began to halt. The rear ranks ran into the vanguard, questioning, and Arthur and the center began to advance.

They saw them, and, for an instant there was silence; then the neat column twisted as the army tried to spread itself out to meet the threat, the leaders shouting orders which were relayed to the rear ranks, the common soldiers milling about trying to obey, trying to avoid panic and to form a shield wall.

They had no chance to do so. The British army, which had approached slowly at first, swelled, like a wave before it breaks, gathering speed, the lines moving forward and suddenly charging, jogging along with their shields held high before them. There was a scream of war cries down the line, the glittering of weapons being raised at once, and the air flashed with throwing spears, incongruous in the morning sun. It seemed unreal. The lines were closing; some Saxons were throwing spears back, sporadically, still trying to form a shield wall, and then ...

The lines hit, with a tremendous clash of weapons that made the air tremble. The British went through the front Saxon ranks in no time, and the Saxons were swept back, leaving a line of dead like the high tide mark on a beach. The odds, which were against us, were being evened now. The shouting and screaming of the hosts were carried back to where we waited like the report of Yffern, and there was a robin singing in the trees nearby. Our line of cavalry edged forward a little down its length, longing for the battle. I felt still more dizzy. Ceincaled tossed his head, snorting.

"It will be a hard fight," said Bedwyr contemplatively, standing in the saddle to have a good view down the valley, dismounting again. "They are not as they should be; see how the rear ranks still march forward past us. They have not panicked; we had hoped for that. And it is very hot." He laughed, as though this were very funny, and we all joined him.

Arthur's dragon standard waved in the center of the battle, and the high king was now visible beneath it as the British line advanced. We caught glimpses of him now and then, recognizing him by his purple cloak. I saw Agravain at one point, too, fighting a Saxon with a gold-crested helmet. My brother thrust the other through the throat with his spear, then lunged past, and I lost sight of him. The standards of Constantius and Eoghan waved, to the right and to the left of Arthur's, but behind it. The Family fought better than the other warbands.

Now the Saxon rear ranks finally caught even with the leaders, and spread out into the wood, past us to the northwest. They engaged the armies of Dumnonia and Brycheiniog, under the trees. We could not see what was happening, but it seemed that the Saxons were unable to advance, for they did not reemerge from the wood to encircle the center.

"It is going well!" said Bedwyr, intently watching, "We have them. . . . No! Wait."

I saw Cerdic, standing in a sudden stillness in the center, standing high, on top of something, so that everyone could see him. He was shouting. I could not hear what he shouted, but I saw the Saxon ranks solidfying around him, and then attacking with fresh purpose, moving sideways off the road. Someone threw a spear at the Saxon king, but he jumped down again and vanished. The battle dissolved into chaos. I twisted my hands in Ceincaled's mane, trying to see. The center was now near the edge of the wood on the other side of the road.

"No!" hissed Bedwyr, "We have lost them . . . no, we still have them. . . . Oh Yffern! Why did Arthur have to fight with the foot today?" His horse danced nervously, and he caught the bridle more firmly. "We cannot attack now. It is far too confused, and the Saxons have their shield wall formed. But the balance . . ."

Was swinging. Despite their losses, the Saxons were rallying, forming a strong shield wall; and they had broken the momentum of the British charge. The forces had locked shields, the high-tide line of bodies moved no farther forward, but hung for what seemed an eternity, motionless. The British stumbled back a few feet, then pressed forward. The hosts swayed like a tree in the wind, like a huge, panting animal struggling to give birth. It was hot, very hot. My leather armor was stifling, and in the center the heat must be nearly unendurable. I felt even more dizzy as the pressure mounted within my skull. It is undecided, I thought. It may turn either way, and Light, let the victory be with us!

But then, just when it seemed that the outcome would become clear, I saw the south flank, the Dumnonians, whose line had been thinned by the Saxon move northward, begin to collapse. If they broke, and the Saxons came through, they could encircle the center and . . . I looked toward that center, where the dragon waved above the locked warriors. Arthur should be the one to signal us when to attack, but he was nearly in the forest now: Could he see the danger on the flank?

The center jerked forward, suddenly, and again I saw the high king. Behind him the standard wavered; Arthur turned, small with distance, and seized the standard as it fell, and swung his arm forward. The war cry rose to us, and the Family was shouting its lord's name. They thrust forward . . .

But the Saxon flank movement broke through the British line, and the British fell back, trying to lock shields again, and were forced back, falling, and then the shield wall was in pieces and the Saxons were coming through, the light making their helmets look like the heads of so many insects. I clutched my spear uselessly. We could not charge them; their line was three deep, and they could brace their thrusting spears against the ground and destroy any horsemen who managed to pass the hail of throwing spears they would throw at us. And yet, if the cavalry did not charge, the Saxons would encircle the now rapidly moving British center, destroy it, kill Arthur . . .

It was unthinkable. We all knew it. To attack against the shield wall was almost certain death, but . . . "We will charge," said Bedwyr quietly, voicing the thoughts of all of us "Mount!" He vaulted onto his horse, drew up the reins, and looped them around the cantle of the saddle; his shield was already strapped to his arm. "For

Arthur!" he called, nearly screaming it, and spurred his horse forward into a gallop.

"For Arthur!" we answered as one, and followed.

The light-headedness that had been with me all the morning suddenly transformed itself into a fire in my mind, the same blinding inward illumination, more powerful than ever before. The sun of noon was high, Ceincaled's pace flowed like music, and I felt light as air, as sunlight. I urged the horse on, no longer thinking of anything at all, past Bedwyr and out of the forest onto the Saxon lines.

They had had time enough to see us coming, and greeted us with spears. I loved them, and hurled my own throwing spears in answer, instinctively concentrating on one place in the line and hoping to break it. The world was dissolving around me, leaving only a light and an ecstasy. I threw away my spear and drew Caledvwlch. The Saxons, holding their places, leaning back and bracing their thrusting spears, wavered suddenly as they saw it, their faces distinct, pale and vivid under their helmets now. I was on them, swerving Ceincaled from the tips of two spears and striking, hard and fierce; turning the horse along the lines and striking again. I was vaguely aware of shouts and of screaming, yet the action seemed soundless and detached. The Saxons moved so slowly, recoiling, hesitating, some turning; then the rest of the cavalry also was striking into them and they shattered. We were through their lines and turning back to destroy them. I think I was singing, the same song that burned in my skull. We had the victory within our hands.

The pattern of the rest of that day is lost to me in the fire.

The Saxon army was broken in two places, I was later told, and tried to retreat back the way it had come. But the cavalry had cut off the retreat by the road, over the bridge, and the retreat increasingly became a rout, a desperate run through the forest and across the river as the soldiers dropped their shields to run and most of their arms to swim. Cerdic managed to control his warband and some of his men and retreat in order, but by then most of the British forces had crossed the bridge, and the cavalry cut him off. He surrendered to Arthur late in the afternoon, while the British cavalry still pursued the remnants of the rest of the Saxon forces.

My own memories of the battle, as of most battles, are limited, blurred by too much light, sharp-edged fragments of passion and action. It only became clear to me again when, as evening was darkening the east, Bedwyr rode up beside me and caught Ceincaled's bridle.

I knew that he had been somewhere near for most of the day, and that made me pause; but nonetheless I lifted my sword to stroke. He caught my sword hand.

"Softly," he whispered. "The battle is over, Gwalchmai." I met his eyes, which were dark and calm, and my mind cleared a little. "Softly," he repeated. I took a deep breath, lowering my sword, and he released my hand and watched me seriously. I looked around.

There were no Saxons in the immediate area, except for dead ones. I did not recognize the place; it seemed to be on the plain. A little to the west, behind Bedwyr, stood a group of Arthur's cavalry, on horses whose heads drooped with weariness. They were looking at me with a kind of awe.

I shook my head, tried to sheath my sword and couldn't fit it in the scabbard. "Where . . ." I began, and stopped. Exhaustion rolled over me in a great wave, and I caught Ceincaled's mane to stay in the saddle. My side ached, and I felt drained. Everything seemed dark, and looked different from what it had been only a few moments ago.

"We are some three miles north and east of where we were this morning," Bedwyr answered my unfinished question, steadily, "and it has been hard fighting. Cerdic has surrendered, and tomorrow he will ask Arthur for terms for a peace, and that peace he will have to keep, for a year or two. We have succeeded. Now, let us go back to the camp and rest."

It was dark by the time we reached the camp, but the place seethed with torchlight and activity. The dead and the wounded were being brought in from the battlefield by the servants and camp followers of the army, the wounded being carried to physicians and the dead guarded from looters. Men and women hurried back and forth, bringing herbs and hot water to the doctors; carrying food, for men and for horses; leading horses stumbling to the picket lines and carrying still forms on stretchers to the physicians or to the heaps awaiting burial. For many the battle had only begun. I was glad that my part in it was finished and I could go to sleep. Even Ceincaled was tired, though he held his head high; and the horses of the others stumbled, blind with exhaustion.

As we entered the camp the workers—servants, slaves, mistresses and wives and relations of the fighters—looked up, then pointed to us. Someone cheered, and some others took it up. Ceincaled tossed his head and a spring came back into his step. Some of the other warriors drew in the reins and straightened, beginning to smile back. Some of the early luster of victory surrounded us as we rode to the center of the camp, where the Family was and where we could give our horses to the grooms.

Agravain was in the central hub of the camp, seeing to some prisoners whom he abandoned when he saw me. He ran across, circling the great fire, and reached me as I reined in my horse. He caught my foot. He was unkempt and dirty, there was smear of someone's blood on his cheek, and his beard was bedraggled, but his eyes burned.

"By the sun and the wind and the sea, Gwalchmai!" he shouted in Irish, "I have never seen . . . If Father could have seen you, he would have given you half the Orcades for that charge. Iffern, he would give you all of them! By the sun, you fought like CuChulainn. I swear the oath of my people . . ."

He was drowned out by a crowd of warriors and servants who thronged about us, shouting congratulations and praise. It was too much for me. I had felt worn and bewildered before, and could only shake my head vaguely.

"I think I must indeed have fought like CuChulainn," I said to Agravain finally. "He went mad in battle. And I . . . don't remember . . ." Lugh's blessing, I thought. Yes, this sweet madness was given also to his son, CuChulainn. Again I shook my head to clear it, wishing that all the people would go away. "But I am not a divine hero like CuChulainn, Agravain. I am tired. Can you make them be quiet?"

He let go of my foot, spun on the crowd and snapped, "By Iffern, let him be now. Can't you see that he is tired? There is time and plenty for praising tomorrow."

The crowd did nothing. Agravain's face darkened and he began to shout. Bedwyr edged his horse away from the crowd a little—they still followed him—and said to Agravain, softly but clearly, "Perhaps if you spoke British they would understand you."

Agravain glared at him for a moment, then began to laugh. The other warriors began laughing as well, then the servants. The rest of the cavalry slid from their horses, and the crowd began to disperse, everyone embracing and congratulating everyone else.

I dismounted slowly from Ceincaled and caught his bridle. The horse nuzzled my shoulder, snorted in pride and contentment. I rubbed his sweaty neck, whispering some words of praise and gratitude; then a groom took the bridle from me and led the stallion off. I was about to follow, and care for the horse myself in my usual custom, but Agravain caught my arm and pulled me off to the tent we shared with Rhuawn and Gereint. I remembered what he had been doing and asked, "But your prisoners?"

"The servants will take care of them. I was really only waiting for you."

My beautiful new spears were gone, and my shield, still strapped to my arm, was hacked so badly as to be useless. I dropped it on the floor and Agravain helped me off with my jerkin. I muttered thanks and collapsed on the sleeping pallet. In the seconds before I fell asleep it struck me: I had done it. Somehow I, or the fire in my head, had become the hero of the battle and saved the Family. O My King, I said silently, you are generous to me beyond measure. The meadow grass under me smelled sweet, of sunlight and flowers under blue skies. Arthur would accept me. I had won.

FOURTEEN

I woke toward noon the following day. I would have slept longer, but I had a raging thirst. I lay still, aching all over, and trying to remember why I felt so glad in spite of this. After a little, the past day returned to me and I sat up abruptly, wondering if I could have dreamed it. But it was real, real. I sat there for a few minutes, wanting to sing and knowing no words to carry my joy. I think that that was one of the best moments of my life.

There was no one else in the tent. I rose, tried to straighten my clothes a little, and left to find some water. I noticed that I had a cut along my ribs, where a spear must have penetrated the jerkin. It did not seem to have bled much, and was a light wound for the kind of fighting I had been in; I saw that my right arm was covered with blood. Still, I decided, it would be best to have it cleaned. Even a small cut can be deadly if it takes the rot. First, though a drink; and then I would have to see that Ceincaled was properly cared for. And find Agravain, of course. I had been glad of him the previous night and he deserved thanks and attention. Besides which, I admitted to myself, I wanted to hear what he had to say about my fighting.

I found a servant carrying a double yoke of buckets from the river, and asked him if I could have some water. He looked at me suspiciously.

"And who might you be? I was bringing this to the sick tents, where it is needed."

"Oh," I said, "in that case . . ."

He gave me another look, then smiled. "Ach, it is not that badly needed. You are a warrior, plainly, and if you are just now waking after the battle—I could give you some."

"That is exactly what I am," I said. "That, and very thirsty."

He slid the yoke off his neck and handed me one of the buckets. "Drink some, and I think you had better use the rest to wash in. You are a sight. If you don't mind my asking, who are you? You look as though you were in the thick of it."

I took a long drink before answering. The water was delicious. "My name is Gwalchmai, son of Lot."

He actually gasped. "Sweet Jesu! Annwn, but you were in the thick of it indeed! My Lord, I can tell my children of this, to be sure!" The man caught my hand and clasped it eagerly. "Indeed, My Lord, you are the hero of the camp!"

"Am I? I don't remember it. I was not even sure what I was doing."

He gave me a puzzled look. "That is not the talk of a warrior."

"Well, I suppose I am not yet used to being a warrior." I felt very pleased, though. Extravagant praises are given to the finest fighters in any battle, and, though it seemed unreal, I had earned that position. My father would hear of this, and be proud. Arthur would accept me. I felt as though some inner wound had finally healed.

I took the bucket of water back to our tent, which was still empty, and there washed and put on a clean tunic. When first I saw my reflection in the water of the bucket I understood the servant's initial suspicious look. I was covered with grime and dried blood. I felt grateful to Lugh for the gift of madness that hid the memory of how that blood had gotten there. I vaguely remembered rubbing the worst of the blood off my sword the night before, but I took it out and cleaned and oiled it again now. Then, feeling still happier, I set out again to find Ceincaled.

He had been picketed in the best place in the line, well groomed and watered and fed with grain, but he was very pleased to see me. While I checked him to see if he had been at all hurt, listening to the grooms congratulating me on the way I had fought, Agravain came up.

He shouted my name when he saw me, ran over to give me one of his bear hugs, then stepped back, grinning. "I thought you would be here," he stated cheerfully. "By the sun, Gwalchmai, the thing appears no less splendid in the morning than in the night."

I shook my head. "I don't remember it. And what else could I have done? Bedwyr ordered the charge, not I."

"But the charge would have failed without you. Don't disagree with me, brother; accept the credit. You deserve it!"

I grinned back. "By the Light, it is a miracle. Arthur will accept me now."

"He'd be an idiot if he didn't, and he is certainly not that. By the sun and the wind, though! There we were at the center, slogging away, thrust and cut and push and getting nowhere, until around noon Arthur caught the standard himself and shouted for us to charge, and we thought we had them. And then we hear a sound like the sky falling, and look up, and there is the cavalry charging down. By the sun, Arthur was angry—he thought you had decided you could not wait—only then he saw what was happening. We all thought it couldn't be done, and the Saxons were even laughing, falling back a little to watch. But then you charged ahead of the rest, looking like CuChulainn, and drew that sword of yours—I swear the oath, it cast shadows all the way over to where I was—and you did it! You broke through their shield wall, and the rest came in behind you and chopped them to bits."

"That . . . yes, I remember that. But you; what happened in the center?"

"We started to yell our lungs out, and ran at the Saxons and carried them back until they were falling over themselves to get away from us. And then I and some others had to run down to the bridge, because your lot took it and left it again, and Arthur didn't want the Saxons to escape by the road. Hard fighting there, for a time. But it was the cavalry charge that won the battle, and you were the one who won the charge. There will be songs about this, brother!"

"And I am glad," I said, because to say more made the understatement even wrose.

"What did you mean, then, that you don't remember it?"

I explained, and he listened carefully. "Like CuChulainn," he said, nodding. "I wondered what you meant last night. Well indeed; there are plenty who become at least a little mad in battle."

I nodded back and asked, "Where is Arthur?"

He paused, considering. "Probably, he is talking with emissaries from Cerdic and the other Saxons. That, or asleep. He was up until dawn."

"Till dawn?" It seemed incredible, when I remembered the army's exhaustion, that anyone could have stayed on his feet until dawn. "What was he doing?"

"Och, he was trying to find out what had happened to everyone. But we can go to see if he is free." Agravain gave Ceincaled a wary pat on the neck, which the horse tolerantly accepted, and we set off. "He always tries to account for each member of the Family before resting," Agravain went on. "He meets with Cei and Bedwyr and hears who was hurt, and tries to learn whether they are dying or dead or only wounded or missing. He goes to the sick tents and talks to the wounded, especially those who are dying. And he sees that the physicians have all they need and that the wounded are being properly cared for."

"He is a great king."

"The greatest in the West," Agravain agreed, smiling widely. "Which makes him the only fit lord for a warrior such as yourself."

Arthur was indeed in consultation with emissaries from the Saxons when we arrived at his tent. We joined the crowd of men bringing matters for his decision, and waited.

Soon, I told myself, I would have a place. Morgawse would be proved wrong forever and I could stop questioning and doubting. Whatever might come next, I would have something I could rely upon. I would be a part of the Family, a servant of the greatest king in Britain, the man who was the center of the struggle raging on the Earth. In my imagination I saw it: Arthur would come out of the tent with the Saxons, see Agravain and me, and hurry over to us. He would smile, as he had not smiled at me before, and he would take my hand . . .

The tent flap opened and Arthur came out, followed by four Saxon noblemen and then by Bedwyr, who had been holding the flap of the tent open.

"It is agreed, then?" Arthur said.

"The terms are harsh," one of the Saxons said. I recognized him as one of Cerdic's men. His British was excellent.

"A matter of opinion; I think them mild. You have said this before, however. Is it agreed?"

The Saxon nodded glumly. "Tomorrow, midmorning, on the road by the bridge. We will bring the arm ring of Thunor and swear the oath on it." He paused again. "My lord will be displeased."

"Tell him that I do him great honor by giving him another form of oath than that I use for the rest of my subjects. It is plain enough that to swear the Threefold Oath in the name of Father, Son, and Holy Spirit means nothing to you."

"The terms are fair," said another of the Saxons.

"For you, perhaps," snapped the first. "You are not asked to surrender lands . . ." And he added something in Saxon.

"If your lord refuses to accept the terms," Arthur said, "he must propose others as good, or fight again. You have safe-conduct from my camp, noble lords."

The Saxons took the hint, bowed politely, and left, escorted by some British warriors. Arthur sighed, watching them leave, and began to turn to Bedwyr with some comment. Then he saw Agravain and me.

Again, his eyes widened slightly, and the shadow fell over him. Again I could feel the Darkness between us, and his horror. For a moment we both stood as though frozen, and my hopes collapsed for a second time, crumbling into dust and leaving me dazed and bitter in their ruin.

Bedwyr followed his lord's gaze, saw us, and frowned. He touched Arthur's arm, and the high king nodded and started over to us.

"Agravain," he said, clapping my brother on the shoulder. "For holding the bridge yesterday, many thanks; it was well done."

Agravain's eyes lit and he grinned. "I think we managed to set them back a bit, My Lord."

"A little," returned Arthur, smiling in return. "By Heaven, you fought like a lion, like a wolf setting a herd of deer to flight."

Agravain grinned still more widely. "Perhaps it was so, indeed. And my brother also will be praised, for he fought like a falcon, swooping upon a flock of doves, and broke the shield wall." Arthur said nothing, dropping his hand, and Agravain only then noticed that anything was wrong. "Gwalchmai, of any of us, deserves your praise," he said, more hesitantly now.

"He has my thanks," Arthur said, after a long silence, "for his part in the battle yesterday."

I bowed slightly, not trusting myself to speak. What with confusion and hurt I did not know what I might say.

"What kind of thanks is that?" asked Agravain, still confused as to what was happening. "My Lord, Gwalchmai saved the battle for us."

"And he has my thanks for it. I expect that now he will find it easy to serve any lord in Britain."

"Any but yourself," I finished for him.

The high king looked at me again, at last, and his eyes were like the North Sea in midwinter. "I would rather any man but yourself had broken the shield wall," he said, in a very quiet, level voice. "A defeat at arms I could have mended, but a victory by the wrong means is worse than a defeat. Without the dream, the war is pointless."

"I agree, Lord Pendragon," I said, "and I fought for your dream, though I do not say I understand it entirely. Do you truly believe that I broke the shield wall by the use of sorcery?"

He did not need to answer. His stare was enough.

Agravain seized his arm. "What do you mean? Didn't Gwalchmai prove anything yesterday? He has earned the thanks of every man in the Family, and of all Britain, all that fear the Saxons!"

"I have given him my thanks," Arthur said, still quietly,

but with a sharper edge to the coldness. "That alone is more than I wish; do not ask me to do more."

"You have done nothing! By the gods of my people, where is your famous justice? Gwalchmai has proved . . ."

"Nothing; except that he can kill Saxons. The which we knew already," snapped Arthur. "It is not your place to speak to me so, Agravain ap Lot."

Agravain flushed. "By the sun! I've half a mind to seek another lord, with my brother, one who will . . ."

"You cannot leave. You are a hostage, whom I keep so that your father will remain faithful to his oath."

Agravain went white, then red with anger. He seized his sword, and I caught his arm. Arthur merely looked at him, not moving, and Agravain slowly loosened his hand, dropped it from the hilt. He stared at Arthur.

"Why?" I asked.

The high king knew what I meant by it. "You already know that, son of Lot. You know it very well, too well, and would God that it were otherwise!" He turned on his heel and left, striding back into the tent; and those who had business for him stood aside, not daring to speak to him.

But I did not know, nor did Agravain. My brother stood, staring after his king, clenching and unclenching his fist.

"By the sun," he whispered at last, in a choked voice. "That he should, he . . ." He turned away abruptly. "Oh God. Why?"

"I do not know," said Bedwyr, tiredly. He had remained behind.

"Hush," I told Agravain. "He meant nothing against you. He was only angry with me."

"But why?" Agravain asked angrily. "You helped to give him this victory; you fought for him, risking your own life. What reason did he have to think that you did it by sorcery? And yet, he distrusted you from the start. Gwalchmai, he had much more reason to hate me. I bore arms against him when I fought beside Father. But when I became his hostage, he was generous to me, and never himself mentioned or allowed others to mention in his hearing that I was a prisoner and the son of his enemy. Before I joined the Family, even, he provided me with a servant to help me learn British, and treated me with all courtesy and nobility. But when you came, never having fought against him, seeking his service, and giving him a great victory, he wishes to drive you off like a stray dog. I do not understand it. I cannot understand it."

"Nor can I," said Bedwyr. "I saw him last night, when he came to ask me about my men, who was wounded and who was safe. He could not wait to praise me for commanding the charge. I have known him now for years, and think . . . No. It is not unknown, it is something that has always troubled him. Sometimes I have found him sitting silently and looking at nothing, not as he does when he plans something, but with the look he had just now; and then I do not dare to speak to him. Gwalchmai, are you certain you have not met him before?"

"Never."

"I mentioned your name to him last night, praising you, and he stopped me. 'I cannot,' he told me. 'The man is a sorcerer and the son of a sorceress. He has given me a victory, but by sorcery, madness, and darkness. I cannot take him into my Family and trust him.' He was so tired, so unhappy, and so certain. Agravain, he will apologize to you later."

Agravain nodded. "But what about Gwalchmai?"

I stood looking at the other two and thinking hard. In a way, the high king was right. I had done nothing but kill Saxons, and the madness and the fire in the sword could easily appear sorcerous—indeed, appeared that rather than anything else. No one fights with the sword alone. . . . Bedwyr had said that. In the end, the reasons are as important, and Arthur had no evidence of my reasons for fighting for him. But what could I do to show him? I thought of all I had seen of the Family, of Arthur. It was not an ordinary warband, and not only because the warriors were so skilled. There was a bond of pride among them, a common love, and a common, half-understood vision. How could I think to enter into a thing like that through strength of arms? I had been a fool to think that I could solve everything with the sword's edge.

I remembered the dream I had in Camlann, and again saw Arthur in the queen's shadow. Everywhere I turned, she always appeared, as though all shadows were her

Gillian Bradshaw

shadow. She still held a part of me, locked in bonds forged with blood, past commitment and present desire. I would not be free until I met her again, face to face, and either severed the bond or became snared in it forever. How could I say to Arthur," I am free of the Darkness"? Darkness had formed me. I had defeated it in the past, but by no strength of my own. Arthur had reasons to feel as he did; and I had no way to change his mind.

I ached with the knowledge that I had lost again, now, perhaps, forever. Perhaps I should leave. As Arthur had said, I could easily find a place with any king in Britain. If I went to Urien Rheged . . .

No. Here I had been led, here I had set my hopes. To leave would be to accept defeat and surrender. I struggled with the pain for a moment, then ignored it.

"What will you do?" asked Bedwyr, gently.

"I will go on," I told the two, looking back at them.

I might have hung about and brooded futilely for the rest of that day, but I had to visit the sick tents. I still wanted to have my cut treated.

As I approached the tents, I heard a strange sound, a kind of low drone like a hive of bees. I stopped and looked questioningly at Agravain, who was still with me. Bedwyr had left with Cei.

"The wounded," my brother answered casually. "They have settled down some now. God, but the physicians must be tired!"

"What? Do you mean that they are still working, from last night?"

"Oh, they've done the worst. They work in shifts. Now, I think, they are checking the walking wounded and getting down to work on some of the men they were unsure of last night. You know, men that come in with a bad arm and they can't decide whether or not to amputate, so they leave them awhile, or men they were uncertain would live, even if they were treated, whom the doctors left in favor of someone their skill wouldn't be wasted on." Agravain hesitated. "To tell the truth, I've no love for such places, especially at this stage of the work. Do you mind if? . . ."

"No. I will join you later."

I didn't, though.

234

There was not enough room for all the wounded inside the tents, and they had brought those who had already been treated outside. These lay on the grass, like fish on a beach after a storm. Their faces were chalk-gray, eyes glazed in resignation or abnormally bright. Some wore bandages, some did not. No one who has hunted, let alone fought, is shocked at blood, but it is different when it is a man who lies before you with his stomach open and entrails tied in, rather than a deer, and when you see him in the cool light of rationality. The badly injured lay still, moaning or mumbling every now and then—an awful sound. It was this moaning and mumbling joined together that caused the droning I had heard. Some men lay still, asleep or dead; others, less badly injured, sat apart from the others, talking in undertones. The place smelled, too, of dirt, sweat, vomit, excrement, and the beginnings of rot, a smell of pain. I picked my way through the lines of men slowly, now uncertain why I had come. One of the men saw me as I passed, and waved his hand heavily. I recognized him as one of Cei's band of thirty, and went over to him.

"Water." he muttered. "Do you have water?"

"I . . . I will try and get you some." Several of the men around him also began to ask for water. I nodded. I wanted to run from that place. When I remembered how lightly I had claimed some of their water that morning, I felt sick.

I went into the tent and stood for a while, staring. One of the doctors, finishing off an amputation, noticed me. "Well, what do you want?" he demanded harshly.

"I . . . have just a scratch. I will see to it myself."

"Thank you. Well, now that you have decided that, what are you waiting for?"

"There are some men outside who need water."

"There are lots of men outside who need water, but there are more in here who need surgery, and not enough to help with it; and the servants need sleep. The men outside will be given water as soon as we can get some more from the river."

"Would you like me to help?"

He stared at me, taking in the rich clothes and the gold-hilted sword. Then he smiled slowly. "As a matter of fact, warrior, I would—if you've any notion of how to use a knife to heal instead of to harm."

"I've never tried it, but I can learn."

Learn I did, until about midnight that night. Few warriors know of the battle that takes place in the sick tents when their fighting is done, except when their lives become a part of it. It is a hard battle, as fierce and ruthless as anything one encounters in the field, and it requires as much or more training than do the arts of war. Morgawse had taught me of various herbs, and one of her books had dealt with the properties of plants, but I had not paid much attention to the uses of medicine. I had learned to use sword and knife, but was almost unaware that they could be used to save the life of the man they are used on. It made good knowledge.

Just before midnight I pushed my hair out of my eyes and looked around to find that there was no more to do. Servants and relations of the wounded had been busy taking whomever they could off and making the rest comfortable, and that work too was nearly finished.

"You had better go rest now," said Gruffydd, the surgeon I had first spoken with. "Unless—you did have something you originally came here for?"

"Nothing—well, a scratch. I only wished to guard it against the rot."

"A wise thought. Let me see it."

He looked at the cut and shook his head. "Indeed. What made you think that was just a scratch? It goes down past the bone, here and here."

"Does it?" I was surprised. "It didn't look that deep, and scarcely hurt at all."

"Well, it doesn't seem to have bled much . . . Cadwallon, some salve and a bandage." He paused, glanced up at me. "You are not a berserker, are you?"

"A what?"

"A berserker. It is a Saxon word; it means one who goes mad in battle. Their strength is double or triple what it is normally, so they are dangerous men."

"I did go mad in the battle. How could you tell?"

He grinned. "Well, we'd heard, even in here, that you charged a Saxon shield wall"—we had exchanged names at a snatched meal—"and that is mad enough. But besides

236

that, the wound hasn't bled as much as it should have. I've seen it before, but only with men who go mad in battle." He began to clean the wound. It stung. "We've heard all sorts of rumors about you—Otherworlds and magic, wild as you please. But such nonsense is frequently attached to men who are berserkers, so that explains that." He rubbed some salve on the cut. "Though it is a damned and uncanny thing, the *berserkergang*. Those who have it normally foam at the mouth, and can't tell friend from foe, though they may be the mildest of men at other times." He looked at me shrewdly.

"No one has told me that I foam at the mouth. I do not think that it is quite the same thing."

"It is a dangerous thing, I should think. I saw a man once, who went mad in battle, and staggered in here afterward with wounds you could put your fist into. Said he hadn't even noticed when he got them. It was a wonder he could even stand; he died about an hour later. No, not a pleasant thing, this madness."

"I am glad of it. It is a gift."

Gruffydd gave me a quizzical look, but I did not wish to speak of "Otherworlds and magic," so I said nothing. He finished bandaging the wound. "Well, that is that," he said, and straightened, stretched, then paused and looked at me again. "Unless you want to come back and help another time, after a battle. No, not immediately after a battle; if you have the madness, you probably collapse afterward—but later. We would be glad of you. You have the instinct of a surgeon, and that is needed in these times."

"Thank you," I answered. "I will come."

I left feeling very happy, and more warmed by those words than by all the praises given to me by warriors. Even if Arthur had refused me, I had fought in two battles, and fought well.

Arthur fought another, private battle at midmorning the next day, on the east side of the bridge across the Bassas. It was a strange fight, against an uncertain enemy.

The high king met Cerdic and the two other Saxon kings, taking his own subject kings Constantius of Dumnonia and Eoghan of Brycheiniog and forty warriors beside. Each of the Saxon kings had brought a dozen men, which Arthur had permitted, so the group was a large one. Yet one would think there were only two men there: Arthur and Cerdic.

I went with Arthur's party, on Bedwyr's invitation, but I tried to stay out of sight near the back. Cerdic's eyes, though, swept Arthur's men until he saw me, and remained fixed on me for almost a minute before he looked at Arthur. The high king had been studying Cerdic all the while.

Cerdic bowed in the saddle of his roan steed, smiling a little. "Ave, Artorie Auguste, Insularis Draco, Imperator Britanniarum," he said, using Latin and all of Arthur's highest titles in a mocking tone.

"Greetings, Cerdic Cyning Thara West Seaxa," replied Arthur. "I am pleased to see that you recognize my status."

"I recognize your strength, *Imperator*," said Cerdic, still in Latin. "You have a victory."

"Which you think you can reverse, a few years from now?"

Cerdic smiled and changed the subject. "I do not like these terms you offer."

Arthur smiled back, a certain lightness touching his eyes. "Then offer other terms, King of the West Saxons. I will do my utmost to be just to all my subjects, even if they have been disobedient."

"That is precisely the part of the terms I dislike most," snapped Cerdic. "The West Saxons are not a nation subject to the emperor of the Britains."

"All the provinces of Britain are subject to one emperor," answered Arthur. "If you do not wish to be subject to me, you can always leave."

Cerdic spat, the red look reappearing behind his eyes. "I made a nation here, Dragon . . ."

"Which I am willing to recognize."

". . . and it is my own nation, not yours or any other Briton's or Roman's."

"I have no more desire to be king of the West Saxons than to be protector of Dyfed. But I am the emperor."

"I have heard otherwise, and from Britons."

"I have other disobedient subjects beside yourself, Cerdic." Arthur smiled again, even more lightly. "Come. You know that you will swear to my terms in the end, just as the other Saxon kings have sworn once already. Why must we stand here in the heat any longer than is necessary?"

Cerdic frowned angrily, but a faint look of puzzlement was beginning in his face. "And I must swear to recognize your claim to the *imperium*, to support no usurpers nor make war against you, to withdraw my royal forces from Searisbyrig to Winceastra and leave no more than twenty men as a guard on the border, which is to be at Wilton? And I must yield all claim to any lands west of that border, and obediently render you tribute at every year?"

"Why not? Most of the land east of Sorviodunum is thinly settled as it is. And as for obeying me and rendering tribute, you will not keep that oath any more than your fellows did, but it will give me more excuse to war on you when you break it."

Cerdic almost smiled in response to Arthur's quiet amusement, but stopped himself. "And what of my fellow kings?"

"As agreed, they will renew their oath, in a new form, and pay additional tribute for the next few years in return for their sedition."

The two Saxon kings snorted. They had paid no tribute since Uther had died, and obviously had no intention of beginning—though, should Arthur's northern campaign take less time than was expected, they might send something.

"If the Saxon nations are subject to the emperor just as the British provinces are," Cerdic began again, "they should swear the same oath."

"I have recognized that Saxons are pagans, and that to swear by the earth, sea, and sky in the name of the Father, Son, and Spirit is meaningless to them. Now if you break your oath you will be able to explain it to your own gods and not the gods of strangers. It will be easier for you."

Cerdic frowned again, and this time touched his sword. For a long moment he met and held Arthur's gaze. Then he smiled, not as he had smiled at first, nor as I had seen him smile in the two weeks I had been his thrall.

"You are everything I had heard you might be, Arthur ab Uther," he said, speaking British now. "I do not see why you bother to employ sorcerers."

"I employ none."

"Then? . . ." Cerdic looked to me again.

Arthur shook his head. "Gwalchmai ap Lot is not my warrior."

Cerdic raised his eyebrows. "Indeed. I wish I had been able to be as firm. Sorcery may be powerful, but sorcerers are unreliable—and dangerous."

I wondered how Cerdic and Aldwulf had parted. Not amicably, it seemed, for Cerdic spoke with some vehemence.

"I am glad we think alike on this," said Arthur. "Have you, then, further objections to my terms?"

Cerdic sighed and began to haggle over the wording of the oath, then stopped abruptly. "No. Why continue with this? We both know that I will swear your oath and break it when it pleases me. When next I fight you, Pendragon, you can call it sedition instead of invasion. I think you will find small difference between the two." Cerdic swung down from his horse, signaled to one of his men. The warrior rode up and dismounted, and Cerdic took from him a large wooden box carved with runes. Arthur dismounted and stood by his horse, waiting.

"This is Thunor's arm ring," said Cerdic. "We brought it from Thunor's temple, north and east of Gaul. It is very old, and sacred." He opened the box and carefully lifted out an immense ring of gold, also carved with runes, heavy, and about two hands' length in diameter. He stood looking at it for a moment, then looked up and smiled gaily. "Thunor is a warrior, if a god. He understands these matters of oaths."

"Swear the oath, then, if you are sure of his forgiveness."

Cerdic hesitated, turning the ring in his hands. Then he turned to the other kings and politely gestured them to go first.

They, too, dismounted and came forward, Aeduin of Cantware and Eosa of the South Saxons. Each in turn knelt, drew his sword, and swore on the sword and arm ring, by Thunor and Tiw and Woden, an oath that was essentially the same as the oath sworn by all kings to the high king. They were both older than Cerdic, well used to swearing oaths and breaking them, and oaths sworn to the British were particularly easily broken. It was more difficult with the new oath, but their Thunor had broken his word at least once, and they would buy new swords, in case the weapon they had sworn on betrayed them in battle. When they had finished, Cerdic drew his own sword, and stepped forward to face Arthur, who was now holding the arm ring.

The day was cloudy, but at that moment the sun broke free of the clouds, and the bare steel of Cerdic's sword gleamed brightly in its light, while the arm ring glowed with warmth. Cerdic smiled more widely, but his eyes held the dark brightness I had seen before. I became suddenly afraid, and ceased to worry over what the kings had said of me. I set my hand on Caledvwlch.

But before anyone could think, Cerdic stepped forward abruptly, lifting his sword to place its cold, gleaming tip at Arthur's throat. Constantius of Dumnonia gave a cry of horror, and Bedwyr dropped his spear into line and drove his horse a step nearer before realizing that he could do nothing and reining in, white faced. Cerdic's party pressed forward, their swords drawn. Cerdic smiled, the darkness filling him, mingled with a strange brilliance.

"I came here this morning to kill you, Pendragon," he whispered.

Arthur had flinched at first, but now he looked at Cerdic over the bright metal calmly, and the light in his gray eyes was astounding. "It would solve most of your difficulties, if I were dead," he said in a conversational tone.

"Indeed," said Cerdic. "And war is a great thing for the lowering of morals. Even Woden, king of the gods, believes this. You understand it, *Imperator?*"

I heard Bedwyr's breath hiss in the stillness, saw him alter his grip on his spear, preparing to throw it if Cerdic stirred. Cerdic did not even glance away from Arthur.

"If you still meant to kill me," Arthur said, "you would have done it by now, quickly." He stepped aside and caught Cerdic's sword hand.

"True," said Cerdic. He lowered the sword till its point

touched the earth, Arthur's hand crossing his upon the hilt. "Unfortunately, Pendragon, bastard or not you are too much of a king and too much of a man. Arthur of Britain, let us be enemies, but not fight like wolves." He dropped to one knee, reached out his left hand to take the other side of the sacred arm ring, and swore, by Thunor, Tiw, and Woden, and by the earth, sea, and sky, to fulfill all his oath to Arthur, high king of Britain, as a subject king to his lord.

Arthur smiled at the use of the Threefold Oath, and when Cerdic had finished swore the returned oath, not to infringe the rights of his subject king, and to preserve the kingdom of his tributary "secure against all foreign enemies and invaders." He ended in an oath of his own, "And I swear to make your nation part of one empire, Britain, and to hold it so, in justice and in Light, so help me God." He released the arm ring.

Cerdic took it, resheathing his sword. Cerdic's men seemed confused; Arthur's, limp with relief, and not a little confused as well.

"When next we meet, Arthur Pendragon," Cerdic said when he had mounted his horse, "I hope our positions will be reversed, and, by Thunor's hammer, I think they will be. Until then, fare well. I am glad to have met you."

"If it is till then, Cyning Cerdic, I will fare well forever. —I too am glad we have met."

All the way back to the camp Arthur kept smiling.

A few days later we brought wagons and loaded our wounded onto them, and the Family returned to Camlann, the other kings and warbands to their fortresses, and the armies to their fields. For a week and a half the Family feasted itself on plunder and ransoms from the Saxons, counted its losses, and recovered, and then we were on the move again, riding north on the main road for Rheged.

FIFTEEN

THE JOURNEY SHOULD HAVE BEEN pleasant for me. My performance in the battle had won me the wholehearted approval of most of the men in the Family. The warriors rejected, as Gruffydd the surgeon had, my stories of "Otherworlds and magic" as being a mere side effect of battle madness. They offered me their comradeship freely, with admiration and without fear. Sorcerous and supernatural events, they decided, were to be expected from the madness, but it reflected nothing unnatural on me. My wound healed cleanly and without trouble; we enjoyed fine weather and, in the luster of our victory, the friendship of the country we rode through. We set a leisurely pace, stopping at every sizable fortress along the way and being feasted there. I had money, as well. Although I was not a member of the warband and could claim no share in the considerable amount of plunder the raid had yielded, nor in the sums the Saxons had expended to ransom prisoners, both Eoghan of Brycheiniog and Constantius of Dumnonia had given me gifts, and some of the noble warriors had done the same. Eoghan in particular gave me a large gift and lavish praise, and tried to persuade me to join his warband. My refusal delighted the Family.

I had to refuse two more such offers on the way to Rheged. One was from Rhydderch of Powys, with whom we stayed for two days. The other was from Maelgwn Gwynedd. He sent a messenger to Arthur while we were at Dinas Powys, on the journey north, conveying congratulations on the victory late and in insulting terms. After delivering the message the messenger spoke to me privately, criticizing Arthur's injustice and pretending sympathy before making his offer. It pleased me to refuse that offer, as it did not to refuse Rhydderch's.

But these offers in themselves were one reason I did not enjoy the journey. Arthur, still, simply did not want me, and I could not follow him like a stray dog looking for a master forever. I had become a warrior and I had fought for him, but a warrior must have a lord. That it was so easy to find any lord but Arthur depressed me. All the kings in Britain were hungry for warriors, especially warriors who could rival the Family. Rhydderch of Powys deserved his nickname, "Hael," "the Generous," and was, as far as I could tell, a fine king and a good lord. He fought the Saxons even as Arthur did, though less spectacularly. I did not really want to refuse his offer, which was worthy of his name.

Besides this, I felt lonely. I belonged and did not belong. I wanted someone who could understand, who believed what I said to him. Before I had had Medraut, for whom I now mourned secretly, more so when I tried to explain to Agravain something or other, and he firmly and resolutely did not understand. I wished to speak with Bedwyr about his philosophy and books, but he was forever with either Arthur or Cei, and both of these avoided me as much as possible. Taliesin I could speak to for hours, but we seldom said much, apart from what he said about songs. So I lived, as Taliesin had said, in uncertainties, and brooded over my own thoughts, wondering about the men I had killed and Arthur's anger, and Morgawse, and the Darkness. It was not a pleasant journey for me.

Toward the end I enjoyed it more, however, when we crossed Hadrian's Wall at Caer Lugualid and entered Rheged. The road was much worse and the area was heavily forested, making travel difficult, but I liked the land more than I liked southern Britain. Northern Britain was never conquered by the Romans, and southern Britons call Northerners barbarian, ignoring the fact that the northern poets are generally better than southern poets, and northern and Irish metalwork is sought throughout southern Britain whenever Gaulish goods are unavailable.

Rheged is probably the strongest nation in Britain. For centuries it has suffered attacks of greater or less intensity by raids from Erin, which lies only a short distance away across the Irish Sea. This continual warfare long ago forced the kings of Rheged to build strong fortresses, and a strong warband; and the clansmen and farmers are hard, slow-spoken men always willing to join with the army and fight. Now, besides the Irish, Rheged defends herself from Saxons, and from the Irish-speaking Dalriada to the north, who gave the land many goods and ways which were familiar to me from my own home. I liked the land. Despite its heavy forests it seemed familiar, and for all their hardness the people were openhanded and openhearted, and never stopped singing.

We rode up to Urien's royal fortress, Yrechwydd, on a cold gray day in August in a heavy rain. The bare wood and stone of the walls were sharp against the sky, and the gulls called over the feast hall, for Yrechwydd overlooks the Irish Sea as Dun Fionn does the North. I listened to the beat of the waves and remembered my father's fortress, and my kinsmen, and Llyn Gwalch, and my heart leapt as though I were returning home. I looked at Agravain, and he too was grinning. We laughed and began to sing a sea song in Irish:

> *A tempest is on the ocean's plain:*
> *Boldly the winds awaken it,*
> *Winter sweeps the fierce sea again,*
> *By wind and winter are we slain:*
> *Winter's spear has overtaken it.*
>
> *When from the east the wind sets*
> *The spirit of the waves is free,*
> *They desire to sweep over all the west*
> *To reach the land where the sun sets,*
> *To the wild, broad green sea.*
>
> *The deeds of the plain, the ocean's rush*
> *Have driven alarm upon me,*
> *But what, of all, is as tremendous,*
> *Wonderful and as momentous*
> *As its incomparable story? . . .*

"Crazy Irishmen," muttered Rhuawn, drawing his cloak higher about his ears. We laughed, and sang louder.

Arthur had, of course, sent messengers ahead. We were expected. Servants waiting just inside the gates took our horses and a fire roared in the hall. Urien himself was waiting by the gates, a great brown-haired bear of a man with a loud laugh. He welcomed us warmly, congratulated Arthur on the victory, and thanked him for coming to the aid of Rheged, then hurried us into the hall, declaring loudly that no one should stay out in such weather. The warriors hung their sodden cloaks by the fire and sat down at the tables while Urien's servants brought them mead. The hall was crowded, although Urien had sent some of his own men out to make room for us—but after a taste of the mead everyone forgot this. After the welcoming cups there was a feast and a great deal more mead. The harp was passed around, and the warriors sang boastful songs of their prowess and made loud talk of how they would destroy the northern Saxons. Taliesin sang a song about the battle of Bassas River, and was loudly cheered. I felt lighthearted for the first time in weeks.

After the song, Urien called for me and gave me a place at the high table on his left, on the grounds that I was his nephew. I thanked him, but pointed out that Agravain was also his nephew.

"Of course!" said Urien, snapping his fingers. "That is the other one's name: I kept thinking 'Avairgain,' and knowing it was wrong." Urien called Agravain up to the high table as well. "Your Irish kings seem to have all the same names: It's either Niall or Eoghan or Laeghaire for all the royal clan." Urien took a deep drink of mead and shook his head sadly. "At least you have a British name, Gwalchmai ap Lot. And a name well suited to you, if Taliesin's song is true—and it always was before, so there is no reason to doubt it now. It must have been your mother's idea." Urien ignored the way Arthur, Agravain, and I went quiet at the mention of Morgawse, and poured me some more mead. "Sensible father you have, to marry a British woman, and my Morgan's sister.— How did this battle appear to you?"

"I do not remember most of it." I answered, hesitated, and added, "I go mad in battle, Lord Urien."

Urien looked momentarily puzzled, then shrugged the subject off. "Indeed? I wish some of my warriors would go mad in battle, then. I think, Dragon," he said turning to Arthur, "that you have stolen the finest fighters in Britain, and left the other kings with the dross—and that besides stealing my chief poet, alas for that! I will never find a bard to replace Taliesin—and I am fast becoming a toothless lion. No, don't laugh. When you meet my war-leader you will see it is no laughing matter, and my son . . ." The king paused. All Britain had heard of Urien's son Owain, who, it was said, could not tell the hilt of a sword from the point. "Now, if I had had better warriors or a proper warleader a month ago when I fought the Scotti at Aber yr Haf . . ." Urien launched into a description of this fight.

I sighed inwardly and only half listened. Urien sounded as though he wished to offer me a position in his war-band. He was certainly no toothless lion, but he needed more warriors. From what I had seen of him, moreover, I liked him; and I liked Rheged. If I took service with Urien I could win some honor and still fight the Saxons: I could fight Aldwulf, a truly dangerous man and one much more my enemy than was Cerdic. And yet, it was Arthur who was fighting to make real a dream, and, as he himself had said, without the dream the war was point-less. I watched the high king as he began to discuss with Urien what should have been done at Aber yr Haf, using knives and serving dishes to show the land and the forces. The shifting torchlight gleamed on his hair and glittered on the gold of his collar. His face, intent on the rough plan of the battle, seemed to hold steady in the moving shadows of the hall. Beside him, Urien looked as dull and dense as the oak table. I took a long, hard drink of mead and set the empty horn down, still watching Arthur.

We stayed at Yrechwydd for a day only before setting out southeastward, to raid the Saxon kingdom of Deira. Urien came with us, bringing twenty of his men. These were only an honor guard: He came to see how the Family fought. Most of his warband was left to guard the coasts.

We moved swiftly, as always. The Saxons were not aware of us in the north of their land until we were gone, taking with us a few hundred head of cattle and sheep, a good deal of plunder, and leaving one of their chieftain's fortresses and part of the countryside in ruins. When the news of our raid reached the king of Deira, Ossa Big Knife, he was angry enough to attempt to retaliate immediately. We were in Ebrauc when he marched on us with his warband and the few hundred men he had mustered by the fyrd in the short space of time since he had heard of us.

We gave Caradoc of Ebrauc the sheep we had driven off, and in exchange received the support of Caradoc's warband. Arthur did not think we needed Caradoc, but the British king would have been insulted if we had won a victory on his land without him.

The encounter—it could not really be called a battle—was brief and fierce. The infantry engaged the Saxons first, as usual—it was a good downhill charge, led by Cei, and left the enemy reeling—and, as usual, the cavalry made a flank attack. The fyrd panicked and the shield wall was gone, as quickly as that. Ossa and his warband, more skilled, managed to regroup and retreat, though with heavy losses, and we pursued them to the borders of Deira but no further. I cut down a Saxon chieftain and won a very fine mail coat from him, with which I was pleased. The rest of the plunder, including what we had taken on the raid, we sent to Yrechwydd.

Both Caradoc and Urien were surprised at the speed and completeness of the victory. There was a great deal of congratulating and gift giving, and Caradoc gave a feast. It was an especially splendid one, and used a large amount of the Saxon mutton we had given Caradoc, as well as great quantities of mead and wine. Taliesin sang of the recent encounter, singing the praises of the living and of the dead. He gave a stanza to me, "I will sing the praise of Gwalchmai/Whose sword was as lightning, a flash to the Saxon/Shining in the red tide, the pride of battle . . ." and so on. Urien beat the table at that stanza, and Arthur frowned. Agravain, seeing the frown, tensed angrily, and Cei grinned at him sardonically. The two glared at each other for the rest of the night.

The following morning Caradoc sent a messenger to me, and, when I had come to his rooms, offered me a position in his warband. I refused.

He frowned. "I have heard stories which led me to expect this," he told me in his dry, quiet voice. "Still, I had not thought . . . What do you hope to gain?"

I leaned against the wall, fingering a gold brooch I had won in the fight. "A place in the Family."

Caradoc shook his head. He was a small, calculating man who looked more like a monk than a king. "I do not think you will get that. Arthur has something that he holds against you. I discussed it with him last night."

I dropped my hand and stood up straighter. "Did he say what it was?"

"You do not know? No, he said only that he suspected you of witchcraft. For my own part, I think it absurd to suspect a warrior who has proved himself in battle of so weak and womanish a pursuit as that. I would be willing to give you second place under my warleader, and the rank of tribune. . . ."

"Thank you, Lord; it is a noble offer and more generous than I deserve, but I will wait for Arthur. He may yet change his mind." I bowed to Caradoc.

He steepled his fingers, stared at me for a moment, then smiled drily and nodded. "You can afford to wait, I suppose. Tell me, is it only the desire for battle and fame that makes men follow Arthur ab Uther?—I ask this as a king, and one who needs more men and is uncertain how to get them."

I shook my head. "It is not only the battle and fame. Bran of Less Britain was willing to risk his life and his followers for Arthur before he was high king, when he was still a usurping bastard. It is because Arthur is Arthur. . . . He says that he wishes to restore the empire."

"You are not Roman: What is the empire to you?"

"Very little," I admitted, smiling. "But the empire that Arthur would create is a great deal, and I am willing to wait and hope until Arthur sees that."

He sighed, a short, sharp sigh of exasperation. "So others also have said, they would rather fight for Arthur and starve than have high advancement with another, and always it is because 'he is a great emperor,' or 'he will restore the empire' or 'preserve the Light.' Very well, Gwalchmai of Orcade. Good fortune attend your waiting!" He rose and saluted me. "But should you change your mind before Arthur changes his, and should you decide that you dislike Urien, the place will still be open. You are a brave man and a fine warrior, and I have said as much to the Pendragon. Now, I believe that your Arthur is preparing to leave again, so you had best go and join him."

I bowed deeply and left, closing the door behind me.

Since Ossa could not expect a second raid so soon after the first we made a second, south of the first one, and concentrated on the newly settled border region. Ossa refused to make the same mistake twice and waited to gather his army before marching on us. In doing so he made a worse mistake, for he left his royal fortress, Catraeth (or Cataracta, as the Saxons call it) with only a light guard while he marched slowly up to where we had last been reported. But we circled around through Ebrauc as fast as we could press our horses, left the plunder from the raid there, and struck into the heart of Deira. We took Ossa's fortress, removed all the hoarded plunder, and fired as much of it as we could before retreating again to Caer Ebrauc. We were surprised at the amount of plunder; Ossa's raids had apparently been successful. Ossa had tried to follow us when he heard that we were again in Deira, but arrived in Catraeth too late, and had to disband his army for the harvest season and try to repair the damage and appease his warband, who had also lost their goods.

Urien was delighted.

"By the sun and the hosts of Heaven," he told Arthur when we were again feasting in Caer Ebrauc, "You'll have them beaten by midwinter!"

Arthur shook his head. "It will be harder from now on. They know how quickly we can move now. And we are still unable to meet their army, and they know that. They have learned, I think, not to raid too deeply into British territory, or to fear retaliation if they do. But they will guard themselves now, and probably try more short raids. Still, at this rate—perhaps by midsummer."

Urien laughed. "Midsummer? I have been fighting for

years, and have felt glad if I can manage to hold my own. Ach, well, you have fine warriors, who know how a war should be fought. Your friend Bedwyr seems capable of leading the Family on his own"—Bedwyr, near Arthur as always, smiled at the compliment but made a disclaiming gesture—"and Cei ap Cynryr is a man who could be war-leader in any other warband. And Gereint and Goronwy and Cynan and my nephew Agravain have earned their fame as well, that is plain. I cannot hope to match them with any of my own followers. And then, I must guard my coasts, or those thrice-damned Irish would burn my fortress under me." Urien paused, taking another sip of Caradoc's wine, and looked at Arthur with a gleam in his eyes. "And Gwalchmai ap Lot, though not a member of your Family, fights in such a way as to make songs for the poets."

Arthur shrugged and changed the subject.

Agravain glared at Arthur, then hacked savagely at the haunch of venison before him. Cei glared back at Agravain, then stared at Bedwyr, questioningly. Bedwyr was his friend and Arthur's, and Cei expected the Breton to take their side in the debate that had grown up about Arthur's continued refusal of my sword. Many of the warriors, who admired my fighting and my refusal to serve any other, endlessly discussed Arthur's reasons and frequently blamed him, which caused others to grow angry with them. Bedwyr alone tried to remain neutral, and Cei resented this neutrality.

"Well, but it is true, Hawk of Battle," Urien said, refusing to accept Arthur's change of subject and turning to me. "How was it in that skirmish half a day's ride southeast of the border? I missed that one."

Urien regretted it when he missed any good fight. I told him about the skirmish, and wondered when he would offer me a place in his warband. He was obviously awaiting his chance. I think that, like Caradoc, he had asked Arthur some questions in private, but did not believe the answers he had been given. Perhaps he was waiting for me to tire and leave Arthur before he made his offer. He had given me gifts, a cloak of embroidered silk, imported from Italy, and a very fine shield with an enameled boss, far too fine to be used. He was a generous man, openhanded, courageous in battle, loyal, a lover of mead and music and women, a good man, a man to trust. But not a man I wanted to follow. He was blind to too many things. The only country he knew was his own clan, though he recognized a few vague responsibilities to the clans that owed him allegiance, and a few hazy duties to Arthur. He had nothing of Arthur's transcendent vision, his brilliance, his habit of giving himself as well as his possessions to the cause, or his gallantry and gaiety. Urien's warband, too, was not the Family. I knew the Family by then, that it truly was a family, a band of brothers. I thought that it must be like the Red Branch at the time of CuChulainn, a place where courage and honor were taken for granted, filled with glory and laughter. Even though Arthur was no closer to accepting me, I did not wish to leave.

Urien would have stayed with us longer, for he was enjoying the campaign, but while in Ebrauc he received some bad news from Rheged. His warleader, in a truly spectacular piece of idiocy, allowed himself and most of the warband to be trapped by a group of raiders whom they outnumbered three to one. They lost fifty men in escaping. Beyond this, the sea raids were increasing in frequency as the summer wore on. Urien was needed at Yrechwydd. We sent some of the plunder back with him.

Arthur was very pleased with the plunder. It would support the Family for some time, and that we had been able to give so much to Urien and Caradoc would allow us to ask them for goods in return once our supplies ran out. Besides this, Urien and Caradoc had been enough impressed to promise to raise their armies whenever Arthur should request it, and the kingdoms, hopefully, had been enough impressed to answer that call to arms. The Family was proud of itself, of its strength and reputation. But we were tired. It had been a hard summer's fighting, and winter would be welcome for the rest it brought. Our weariness made us tense, and there were arguments, almost fights, between members of the Family. Arthur could always stop them, but they disturbed everyone.

It was perhaps because of this weariness and tension that our next raid was a failure. More likely, though, we failed because we attacked Bernicia.

Bernicia actually lies closer to Rheged than Deira, but Ossa of Deira had been doing most of the raiding, and so Arthur had wished to weaken it first. Now that Ossa was rendered temporarily quiet we turned our attention to Bernicia.

We struck into the southern part of the country after riding at a fast pace along the border of Deira and Ebrauc. We had a good road across the hills, a Roman road, since we were still south of the Wall. All the land that was uncultivated was heavily forested, full of lakes, an easy country to hide in. It is rich country, too: We took over two hundred head of cattle in the two days of raiding that brought us to the Wall. We were confident, certain that Aldwulf would not dare to attack us without first raising the fyrd, and that, at harvest time, even if he was alert to the threat of invasion it would take some time to do so.

Then, on the third day of the raid, one of our scouts rode up to Arthur at a full gallop, reined in his worn horse and gasped out the news: Aldwulf was within half a day's ride to our west, and had raised the fyrd.

No matter how careful his planning or quiet his movements, we all knew that he should not have been able to do it. We had ridden from Caer Ebrauc too quickly; he could hardly have received even the news of our presence from reports more than a day before. And it still took much time to lead an army, at its slow pace, down from Gefrin in the north. To have done as he had he would have had to have discovered our plans the moment we left Caer Ebrauc and have begun to move southward at once, collecting his army along the way. No messenger can ride so fast. We did not speak of it, but we could guess how Aldwulf Fflamddwyn had found out.

We turned south, hurriedly. Aldwulf did not have all the men he could muster, but his army was still a large one, over five thousand men, and he had his warband as well. There were six hundred and twenty-three in the Family, since some were sick in Caer Ebrauc and some escorting Urien and the plunder to Rheged. We were accustomed to fight against superior numbers, but the Saxons now had the advantage of the land and of allies in the south as well. To the north stood the Wall, to the east was the sea, and to the south was Ossa. We preferred to leave. However, we had not gone far south when we discovered that Ossa was approaching with part of his army and all of his warband. Their numbers were such that we could have defeated them, but that would have left us a prey to Aldwulf, whom our scouts reported as following us southward, keeping to our west. The whole land had risen against us, and sprang ambushes at every turn of the road, so that our speed was cut down. The only way to escape, Arthur decided, was to take on the stronger enemy, and pass through the Bernician army.

We made camp by the river Wir, keeping it between ourselves and the Saxons, and Arthur called the Family together to tell us what we must do. He was silent for a while, looking at his warriors, lingeringly, and then he spoke calmly and quietly: "Tonight at midnight we will lift camp and attack the army of Fflamddwyn."

A murmur like wind in the trees swept the Family, then died down again. The prospect of death was always near us and could not make us afraid.

Arthur smiled, very gently, very brightly. "We will go through them on horseback, if at all, so we will leave the cattle and the plunder behind. Fflamddwyn is camped upon the other side of the Dubhglas River, less than four hours easy riding. He will doubtless know that we are coming, but we still will have the advantage of the dark, and, I hope, a good amount of confusion. We will ride in a spear-head formation, the best of the cavalry first, the rest about the edges, and those who normally fight on foot and doctors and such in the center. If the point of our spear goes through we will escape, Aldwulf will lose many of his men and most of his credit, while we will be largely unharmed. If not . . ." Again he looked at his warband. "I have no wish to point out that there is no other way of escape, and give you examples and arguments to prove how bad your condition will be. If our spear breaks on their shield wall, I trust you to kill before you are killed, and to make such a battle that it will be sung of by all Britain, and be a light to hold against the dark. You are my warriors, my hearts; I know that you will not surrender."

They did not even cheer; their stillness was an assent

more total than any shouting. Arthur smiled again, a light in his eyes. The evening sun fell on him, on the river and its grassy banks, the forest behind, half-bare with autumn; on the ranks of men and horses with their harness and weapons dull with use, and everything was as quiet as a forest pool in the middle of a summer day. Everything seemed to be worked in gold, apart from the world, apart from time and war, one immortal, imperishable creation, and the dream was real. Then, one of our plundered cattle lowed, a horse whickered, bitten by a fly, and the spell was broken.

"I will ride at the head of the Family," Arthur continued briskly, "and with me, Bedwyr, Gereint, Cynan, Rhuawn, Maelwys, Llenlleawg, Sinnoch ap Seithfed, Llwydeu, Trachmyr, Gwyn ab Esni, Moren ab Iaen, Morfran ap Tegid and . . ." His eyes fell on me and he paused, then continued in the same tone, "Gwalchmai ap Lot."

He went on, assigning the rest of the Family their places and giving orders for the breaking of camp and the disposal of the plunder, where to cross the river and where to meet if separated, but I did not really listen. He had given me an order to ride near him with his best men, the spear point of the warband, the position of greatest danger. He was not a man to command this unless . . .

I waited impatiently until the high king had finished, then hurried toward him. Most of the Family hung about, paying close attention. Nearly all of them had taken sides with either Agravain or Cei in the dispute about me, and everyone was interested in the outcome.

Arthur had been turning toward the fire, where we would roast some of Aldwulf's cattle for dinner, but he saw me coming and waited. His face was quite still, expressionless. I knew that look, and the beginning of my hope died again.

"Lord," I said quietly, "you commanded me to take a place beside you against the Saxons."

"I did," said Arthur coldly. There was a moment of tense silence, and one of the warriors almost spoke, but decided not to. "If you wish, you can refuse. You are not my warrior."

I shook my head. "No, Lord Pendragon, I do not care to refuse." Suddenly the bloody and exhausting summer, and all the bitterness of extinguished hopes rose in me at once, and I said, "You know that I will not refuse. You know that I will fight for you. Haven't I shown you that a dozen times over? But I wish to know why."

"I recognize necessities," answered Arthur. "If my Family is to live, we must break the shield wall. You can kill from horseback very expertly, Gwalchmai of Orcade, and yes, I know that you will fight. So I use you, to aid my Family and Britain. I wish I did not have to."

"That is not what I meant," I said, softly and quickly. "Why do you refuse my sword and use it at the same time?"

"I have said that I do not wish to use it," Arthur returned, the coldness growing sharper with anger. Agravain's party among the Family stirred, muttering. The air was thick with tension. "Why have you stayed? Any king in Britain would be overjoyed to have you. Yet, you hang about me, unasked, with your killing and your sorceries and your mother's curse and Darkness . . ."

My hand was somehow on my sword. "You know nothing of that. Why do you insist on believing that I adore her? If I could work sorcery, Arthur Pendragon, I would not hang about you, plodding on and fighting and killing for you—for despite what you believe, I have no love for killing—but I would work such a work that all Britain would demand that you accept me. I swear the oath of my people, I hate witchcraft, more than you because I know more of it. Are you entirely in Darkness?"

"In God's name, what do you want?" shouted Arthur. "What have you done since you came to me except kill and divide my Family? Indeed, you have won fame, riches, and honor for yourself—shall I make return to you for that? Do you wish me to accept these things as right, good, and noble? Do you think that I will accept this knowledge you speak of, the knowledge of Darkness?"

"What do you know of my Darkness?" I hurled at him.

"What do you know of mine?" he demanded. "Too much, perhaps." He drew himself straight, standing taller than I, and his eyes were so bitterly cold that it was

more terrifying than any anger. "Now you have divided
my Family so that I seem hardly able to heal it, and yet I
must ask you to risk your life with me, in a place where
no sorcery can help you, if the shield wall holds. There-
fore . . ."—he took a deep breath, and I saw with surprise
that the sweat came onto his face as though he struggled
with his soul within him—"if we break the shield wall and
live, I will accept your sword. That I swear, by the Light
and as I hope for salvation. Be glad, son of Morgawse.
You have won."

And he turned away and walked off, stepping with a
quick, light stride through the gathering dusk.

For a while I stood, staring after him, even when he
was gone. Agravain came up and caught my shoulder, but
I shook him off. The other warriors, nearly as stunned as
I, bewildered by the speed of the thing, hung about for a
moment, then began to go slowly off to the fires, starting
to talk.

I stood silent, one hand still on my sword, then walked
away from the camp to the river and sat by it, laying my
spear in the grass. Autumn flowers bloomed raggedly by
the stream, and the evening star was appearing, a soft
gold light which the dark water reflected. The calmness
of the world seemed to make a lie of the deadly speed of
the battles of men, and of my own inner confusion. I
rested my arms on my knees and stared at the current.

Arthur would accept me if the shield wall broke that
night. It was what I wanted, wasn't it? Again and again I
asked myself that question, and always I answered myself,
"Yes, but not like this. Not because he is honor bound to
do so." But what, then? Perhaps I would die that night,
and then I would not have to decide. But if that was not
fated, if I lived, I would have to decide. And even if I
should die, I wanted to meet my death with a clean heart.

The waters in the last dark glow of twilight showed me
my face, wavering on the current. A face like Morgawse's. Always Morgawse. I thrust my fingers in the
ground, tore up earth, and hurled it to smash that reflection. The water shivered, but stilled again, and the picture
returned.

Not only Morgawse's face now, I thought, but the face
of a warrior. I studied the past months in my mind. Yes,

beyond any question. No one would take me for a thrall, a bard or a druid again. What I had become was written on me for all to read. A warrior, but of what warband, acknowledging what lord?

It didn't really matter. A warrior is a warrior, and all war is a sport, a game. All wars but Arthur's and the Light's.

I turned my thoughts from the brooding over injury and the bitterness I had grown accustomed to, and looked at what had actually happened. And hadn't it been fine, as Arthur had said, winning fame and honor and riches, taking gold and silk and fine weapons from the hands of kings who wanted my sword, drinking sweet mead and listening to the praises of poets. Yes, and riding into a town on Ceincaled with my mail coat and weapons shining, red cloaks and gold jewelry, smiling back at the girls who waved at me. War is filled with too much splendor, too much gold and swift horses, scarlet and purple silks. It is beautiful, and one forgets what it is for. I had forgotten.

I drew my sword. It had been given me for a purpose, and I had forgotten that purpose. It had been given me by a king, and I had ignored the king to whom I had sworn fealty. I tightened my hand about the hilt, feeling the way it fit, like a part of me.

I had divided the Family, Arthur had said. I gripped the sword with my other hand and held it up, pressing the cold steel against my forehead. Yes. All the arguments, the tension and anger, the breaking of friendships which I had tried to blame on weariness—all my fault.

But it had filled a part of me that had been long empty, satisfied desires I had always had and never understood. I had wanted it. I still wanted it.

Now, wouldn't Morgawse be pleased with this, I told myself. Son of Morgawse, be glad. You have won. And now, Gwalchmai of Orcade, what will you do? Lugh warned you that you had not conquered your own Darkness, but you, thinking of it in its accustomed form, ignored him. Arthur will accept you because he is too honorable to do otherwise. Arthur. He had acted with some injustice at the first, but that was a small shadow on his brilliance. What did I know of his Darkness, of the man within the king, of the forces that drove him, of his reasons? Suddenly I saw him as human, uncertain, and I knew that before I had not fought for him but for myself, done nothing to quell his suspicions and much to justify them. And now I did wish to fight, for him, and atone.

Light, Lord, I said silently. My Lord High King to whom my sword is first pledged, command me. The sword is yours, and the life you saved; you, more even than Arthur, are the one I serve and fight for; you are the one I will obey.

I already knew the answer to the problem. I stood, slowly, and saluted the evening star with my sword, the decision made. The warm red light I had not seen for months lit again in Caledvwlch's hilt, glowed brighter and more tenderly, lighting the darkness around me. I would fight for Arthur that night, and, God willing, break the shield wall; then, if I lived, go to Urien of Rheged and request a place in his warband.

I walked back to the fires for dinner.

The meal was eaten quickly. No one was hungry, but everyone knew that he should eat; and moreover, the cattle were Aldwulf's, and those we did not eat we turned loose and he might recover. After the meal we tried to sleep: A few may have succeeded, I did not. Just before midnight we rose and broke camp, leaving the plunder. I went to the picket lines and saddled and bridled Ceincaled.

"This will be the last time," I told him in Irish, as I swung up. "After this, mo chroidh, we go with Urien, if we live."

He pricked his ears and stamped, and I felt his eagerness and bright, swift pride more sharply than I had for the past months. I laughed under my breath, running my fingers through his mane. If we died, it was a good night for dying, and it would be a good death.

I rode to the front of the band, near Arthur, and, when all the Family was ready, we left without a word spoken. We forded the river—it was not deep—and rode through the forest, northwest, spread out for easier riding. The Saxons were camped on the other side of the Dubhglas River, on land that was actually British. We rode toward

them for some three hours, then tightened our formation
and rode carefully, making little sound.

Aldwulf had watchmen posted, but had not needed
them. His camp had been awake for at least an hour
when we arrived, and was bright with torches tied to
spears thrust into the ground. We had gone quietly and
without lights so as to avoid giving any additional warning to the Saxons. Our eyes were accustomed to the dark,
and the torchlight was bright enough to aim a spear by.
Arthur drew rein briefly at the top of the slope that led
down to the river, and pointed out to the "spear point"
the route we would take, speaking in an undertone. We
all knew what would follow: We would gallop down the
slope, through the trees, into the torchlight, and cross the
river to attack the shield wall which the Saxons would
raise on the opposite bank.

Arthur dropped his hand, spurring his horse to a gallop.
We followed, in silence but for the pounding of the
horses' hooves and the jingle of harness. My head was
light with a different madness and I was at peace.

At first the Saxons did not realize what was happening.
They expected us, but it was dark and they were sleepy,
expecting some torches, some war cry or warning. They
heard the sound of hooves and started, picking up their
spears and looking about in confusion. They could not
see us for the darkness, the forest, and their torch-blinded
eyes. I drew loose a throwing spear as we approached the
bank, and flung it with all my strength. Confuse them.
Get them off-balance. Other spears fell among the Saxons,
doing little damage, but startling and frightening them.
Their chiefs began to order them to form the shield wall,
and they obeyed, but slowly. We came out of the forest
and plunged into the water, (the water splashed high and
cold about our legs), the torchlight gleaming and leaping
from us, the trees casting long shadows that wavered like
a mad dream; and across the river, hurling more spears,
some of which found their marks. The horses swam
briefly, hard, their eyes rolling and ears laid back, and the
Saxon spears were falling all about us, and the horses
were running again, coming at the shield wall. Arthur
was grinning, holding his thrusting spear leveled to strike.
The shield wall opposite us was three men deep, and

more warriors hurried to support it, shouting, wild eyed. We approached, charging in silence from nowhere against an army, and suddenly Arthur threw back his head and shouted, "For Britain, my hearts! For me!"

And we answered, "For Arthur!" with one heart and one voice, a sound more terrible than death; I hurled my thrusting spear and drew my sword, blazing with white light, as we reached the bank.

My old madness did not fill me, but I did not need it. Ceincaled reared, lashing out with his hooves, and I bent over his neck and slashed down, fighting from love and from a dream, as Arthur fought. It was a few moments, no more: Had we paused long enough for our speed to slacken, we could not have done it, but the Saxons were afraid, bewildered, and uncertain, and they broke. We killed them on all sides as we went through, tearing the torches from their posts and hurling them into the camp, setting it alight, hacking through tent ropes and charging on, leaving destruction behind us. We plunged into the safety of the woods, only a few spears falling about us now as we rode down the night.

"Well done," said Arthur, softly, then he shouted aloud with joy, "Oh, beautifully done!"

We reined in our horses to a canter, thinking of the miles yet to ride. Behind us the sky paled with the first gray of the still hour that leads to morning.

SIXTEEN

I DID NOT HAVE A CHANCE to tell Arthur that I would leave
the Family for almost a month. I had received a leg
wound in the battle, a bad one which was made worse by
my riding twenty miles with it afterward. It couldn't be
helped. We had no fear that the Saxons would follow
us—they did not have the horses, and would be far too
preoccupied with their own losses, besides being busy
trying to recover their plundered cattle—but we needed a
place to stay. With a warband the size of the Family,
such a place is not easy to find. In the end we rode north
and west until we came to a clan holding near the Wall,
headed by a man named Ogyrfan. He was a tall, black-
bearded man, of some importance in those parts because
of his wealth and some Roman title. He feared the Saxons
and longed for the restoration of the empire, and so welcomed Arthur. He gave the Family food and a place to
put the wounded. I was glad of it. I was weak from blood
loss, faint, and sick with pain. Agravain and Bedwyr carried me to the cow byre—the only building available for a
hospital—where I collapsed and stayed that way for over
a week. I had the wound fever the first few days and
remember nothing of them, and when I recovered enough
to be aware of myself again, was told that Arthur and the
Family were gone, off raiding. The warband had been
weakened by the summer, but the opportunity offered by
the present situation had proved to be irresistible.
Aldwulf's credit with the other Saxons was, as Arthur

262

had predicted, seriously weakened by our victory. They could not see how, when he had had the British high king trapped and outnumbered and had himself been fore-warned, Aldwulf could have let us escape. Ossa of Deira blamed him; his own nobles blamed him; and his subjects, who had been raided and now were short of goods and angry, blamed him bitterly and deserted his army. The harvest season was nearly over, and Ossa's men also wished to return to their farms, and Ossa himself re-turned to his stronghold after some bitter recriminations with Aldwulf. The king of Bernicia was thus left with only his warband, and that a fractious one, and he too re-treated to his fortress for the winter. The countryside was thus left unprotected, and Arthur attacked Bernicia and raided as freely as if there were no king in the land, destroying all the new farms on the border and taking away grain and cattle enough to last the Family a year, with some left over for gifts as well.

For myself, however, I stayed at Ogyrfan's holding un-til my wound had healed enough to ride with, almost a month. It was a pleasant place, and ordinarily I might have been glad to spend time there. The farm was set near the Wall which wound off across the sweep of hill and field which it formed a fence to on one side. A fresh, swift stream rushed by the houses and watered the pas-tures. To the south the land rose, forested valleys and heather-clad hills melting into the tall shadow of the mountains. Ogyrfan was a strong, intelligent man, unex-pectedly friendly to the high king's servants, and able to read. He did not even mind the increased tribute that Ar-thur had caused, saying that the Pendragon took only a few cows, while the Saxons would take them all. It was true, of course, but a truth one seldom heard from those who paid the tribute. Ogyrfan's eldest daughter, Gwynhwyfar, was also pleasant company. I had not real-ly spoken to a woman since Morgawse, half-afraid of all of them for my mother's sake. Gwynhwyfar taught me to think differently. She helped to nurse me and the others back to health, and, under her father, was manager of the holding. She was strong enough to help Gruffydd the surgeon with his work without flinching, and weak enough to be afraid of a storm, or laugh at the song of a bird. She was some four years older than I, with masses of deep red, wavy hair and smiling brown eyes. There was a warmth to her, and a grace that made her beautiful, and she too was clever, and had read even more than her father. I was not attracted to her as a man to a woman, but her warmth drew me, touching one of the places Morgawse had chilled.

But despite all this, I was impatient to leave. Caledvwlch felt heavy at my side, and I sharpened my spear until it had an edge to wound the wind. Ceincaled, lord over the other horses in Ogyrfan's fields, would race along the fence in the morning, snorting white plumes, eager to be gone, to Rheged, to the south, to the north, it did not matter: He wished only to be on the road again. And my decision had been made, and I did not wish to linger on the way.

At last there came a time in early December when my leg was healed enough to ride with, if not to walk far on, and I slung my shield across my shoulder, picked up my spear, and mounted Ceincaled. Most of the other warriors who had been wounded were gone, and Gruffydd gone with them; a few would have to wait longer. The wind was cold, blowing over the Wall from the north, whispering of snow. Not a good season for traveling. Still, perhaps I would not have to travel far. East first, to tell Arthur and my friends what I had decided, and then, west to Rheged. Or perhaps, I thought, north. There was nothing binding me. North, to Din Eidyn, where perhaps there would be ships willing to brave the Muirn Orc, and take me farther north again, to Dun Fionn. Home. A sudden, sharp pang of homesickness fell on me, and I remembered my father and my kinsmen, the screams of sea birds by the cliffs, the tall banks of Dun Fionn, and Llyn Gwalch by the gray North Sea. Lot and my clan would have heard reports of me, but could not know what to think. I should have sent a message. Morgawse would know, and she was herself another reason to return. I could not live forever half-bound to her, but must meet her again, and resolve the thing. Yes. North, past Pictland to the Isles of Fear, my home.

"Give my praises and my good wishes to the emperor,"

Ogyrfan told me. He had come to say farewell, and drew his cloak about him against the wind.

I nodded, saluting him.

"And a swift journey for you, Gwalchmai, and mind how you use that leg," added Gwynhwyfar. She paused, then, smiling, and added one of the Irish phrases I had taught her, "Slán lead," "farewell."

"Slán lead," I answered, smiling back, then turned Ceincaled's head to the road. He pranced, tossing his head against the rein, eager to be off. I called out thanks to Ogyrfan and his daughter and then gave Ceincaled his head, letting him run, off down the good road in the cold bright morning. Off to sever all the ties that held me to the Family.

And why should I be unhappy about it? I asked myself. I am young, strong, and skilled. I have Ceincaled, I have Caledvwlch, and my sworn lord is greater than any other. A place with Arthur, no, but I am free and the Light's warrior. And I am going home. Who would want more?

I leaned over Ceincaled's neck, urging him on, and the winter-dull earth rolled away under his flashing hooves.

It was not a long journey. Arthur had turned north, and was raiding the Bernician border toward the central part of that kingdom. I crossed the wall and took the old road along the hills after him. There is a Roman road running that way as well, a straighter road, but from the old road you can watch the land. I followed this most of the day, riding at a trot, uneventfully. Toward evening it began to rain. My fingers froze, and the wind seemed always to blow directly at me, no matter how the road twisted. My leg began to ache, first dully, then viciously. When I reached the crest of a hill and saw the camp below me it was a grand and welcome sight. The fires burned red-gold against the slate color of the bare hills. In the dim light I could see the picket lines, and a huddled mass of cattle by a half circle of wagons taken from the Saxons. I stopped Ceincaled and stared down at the camp. Down there were the dung fires and men singing around them, hot food and strong, sweet mead, warriors laughing and boasting of their own deeds, joking about the deeds of others. I knew that it was so. I had been a part of it. Now I was where I had begun in the Orcades, watching, from a distance.

Be still, I told myself. You will easily find another warband.

And yet, how could there be another warband like the Family, or another king like Arthur?

Well, I could have it for this last night. I touched Ceincaled's sides lightly and he began to pick his way down the hill.

We had not gone more than a few feet when a figure dashed out before us, waving its arms. Ceincaled reared, wrenching my leg, and I snatched up my spear.

"No!" cried the figure, "Chieftain . . . Arglwyd Mawr . . !"

I looked closer and saw it was not a Saxon ambushing me, but a rather ragged British woman. A poor one, if she felt that I looked like a "great lord." I lowered my spear and held Ceincaled in.

"What is it?" I demanded, impatient for the camp.

"Chieftain, forgive me. I saw you on the hill and was afraid, but when you started toward the camp I knew that you must be one of the Dragon's men, so I thought, 'I must stop him . . .'"

"What for?"

She came closer and caught my foot. She was in her mid-thirties, her hair gray and face lined. A poor farmer's wife.

"Chieftain . . ."

"What is it," I asked again. "The Pendragon does not take servants, if that is what you wish." It was unlikely that she had come for that on such a night, but there was the possibility.

"No, Chieftain. It is my man. I have heard that there are skilled doctors in the camp of the Dragon of Britain. . . ."

My heart sank. "Your husband is hurt?"

"Yes, Great Lord. Some of the Saxons whom the Dragon is driving away came to our household, asking for food. My man would give them none, and they struck him with steel and fled. Our clan cannot help him. I have heard that the Dragon has skilled healers. . . ."

"Where is your holding?"

She pointed down the steeper slope of the hill, to the east. I looked down the western one to Arthur's camp and sighed.

"When did this happen? Can your husband be moved?"

"No, Great Lord. It was today, around noon. The filthy murderers fled, after they had struck my man, and they took the horses. But he could not ride a horse, he is too sick, and we have no carts. Chieftain . . . "—she shook my foot—"my man is hurt. He will die, unless he has doctors. The doctors of the camp say that they have work, and cannot come, and that I must bring my man to them. You have a swift horse. Help me!"

"Very well. Show me the way back to your household."

She held my foot with both hands. "May the gods bless you, Great Lord! May Christ and all the gods bless you! It is that way, down the path, and on to . . ."

"You must show me the way," I repeated. Country paths are impossible for a stranger to follow. "Come." I held my hand out. "My horse can carry two."

She stared at me. "Chieftain, I have never . . ."

I sighed, dismounted, helped her up—Ceincaled disliked it, shying and snorting—and remounted behind her. She showed me the path, which was a hard one. It took nearly an hour to reach the holding, and the woman was greatly impressed by the speed of our crawling pace. Her kin were awaiting her.

"But this is not a doctor!" said one old man, apparently expressing the unease of the whole clan, for they nodded and began to mutter.

"He is a great chieftain." said the woman, sliding down from Ceincaled. "I found him on the hill, after the doctors at the camp had said they had many wounded and could not leave. He has a horse that goes like the west wind off a mountain"—Ceincaled tossed his head, shaking rain from his mane—"and he will help us to bring Gwilym to the doctors."

"Gwilym cannot be moved now," said the old man.

I shrugged. "I know a little of medicine. Let me see this kinsman of yours—and take my horse out of the rain."

As soon as I saw Gwilym I knew that it was hopeless.

The Saxon spear had gone clean through his body, slanting down through the lungs. It was a wonder that he was still alive; he would certainly not remain so.

The woman looked at me hopefully. "What will you do, Great Lord?"

I shook my head. "I do not think that I can do anything."

The old man nodded. "See now? I said, pull it out yourself, and find a new husband if he dies, but don't run about soldiers' camps like a whore."

The woman only looked at me, frowing in pain. "But you said . . ."

"I had not seen him. Men with this kind of wound ordinarily die within an hour."

"You should have asked him to bring a surgeon," said the old man. "This one is no use. He is a warrior. What can he know of healing?"

"The doctors would not come," said the woman. "Chieftain, he is my man, he cannot die! Perhaps it is not so bad as you think. You must help him. Please! He is my man."

I studied Gwilym more closely. He was unconscious, luckily for him. The wound did look fatal. Still, one cannot always tell.

"You must help him!" pleaded the woman. "Great Lord, you must at least try!"

"He can do nothing!" snapped the old man. Silently, I agreed with him, but the woman was right. I had to try.

"Very well. I will try. Bring me some hot water, close the door, and build the fire up."

I tried for an hour, fighting my exhaustion and the pain in my leg for concentration on the man. The spear shaft still imbedded in his lung was keeping him alive, but all it did was prolong his time and his pain. Still, the wound was straight and clean, and I thought that if I got the spear out, and if the other lung didn't go, he might live. I worked, got the length of wood out after a struggle, and for a while thought it would work, but then the other lung collapsed and Gwilym died. The woman, who had been helping, felt his heart stop before he coughed up his last breath in blood, and took his hair and began to beg him to live, then buried her face against his shoulder and wept. The other women in the clan began to keen, and the children howled, and the men cried. The old man only nodded and said, "I said he couldn't do it."

I could feel nothing, not even compassion, nothing except the desire to get away. I washed some of the blood off, put my tunic and mail coat back on, and limped to the door. No one said a word to me, though one or two gave me stares of hatred, since their kinsman had died under my hands. I limped off hurriedly, found Ceincaled, and threaded my way back up the hill.

By the time I reached Arthur's camp the fires had burned down to embers. My leg ached violently, I was soaked and frozen by the rain, and I wanted nothing so much as some warm, strong mead. I was stopped briefly by a sentry, who, recognizing me, welcomed me warmly and inquired about my leg. I told him that it had healed, and also how the other wounded were, and passed through. I left Ceincaled, rubbed down and munching grain, at the picket lines, then limped up to the main fire.

The welcome the warriors gave me was everything I could wish for. They jumped up, crowded around me, welcoming me and asking about my leg and why I came in so late. Agravain gave me one of his bear hugs saying, "Indeed, so you finally decided to come back and earn your mead. Welcome! A hundred thousand welcomes home."

I answered the questions and was given a place next to the fire, some mead, and some food. I settled down gratefully, worn out. Only then did I notice Arthur sitting across the fire from me, unreal in the heat shimmer and watching all of it coldly. I saluted him with the mead horn and took a deep swallow.

Arthur nodded. "So. You have come back to claim my promise."

I did not feel like stating my decision and having the inevitable argument, but it seemed that I had to. I saw Agravain and several of his party stiffen, saw the rest watch them tensely. Yes, it was definitely right that I leave.

"No, Lord," I answered quietly. "I have come back only to say farewell. Tomorrow I will ride north, to see if I can return to the Orcades this winter."

Agravain drew in his breath with a hiss. "Gwalchmai, what do you . . ."

"What are you saying?" demanded Arthur.

"What do you think you are doing?" asked Cei angrily.

"But the lord Arthur has said that he will accept you," said Agravain. "You have earned it; you have won."

"Arthur will accept me because he has no other choice, in honor." I looked at the high king steadily.

He nodded. "I do not deny it. I used your sword because I had to, and you were wounded in my service. What do you hope to gain by this talk?"

"Nothing. Not now." I wished that I could tell them in the morning.

"You have earned acceptance a thousand times over," said Agravain. "What are you saying, you're going north?"

"I do not wish to be accepted because Arthur is bound in honor to accept me," I answered. "Call me too proud for it, if you wish."

"This I do not understand," said Cei loudly, his voice high with indignation. "All summer you hung around, waiting for an offer from Arthur and turning down half the kings in Britain, and now that you have it, you will not accept it, like a falcon that goes to great trouble to catch a bird it will not eat. By the hounds of Yffern, the Family is not to be turned aside so lightly!"

"Do you wish me to join, then? If so, you are like that same falcon, trying all summer to make me leave, and then, when . . ."

Cei glared. "You insult us all, and me most of all. I have a fair mind to . . ."

"What would that solve?" I asked wearily. "If we fought on foot, you would win; if we fought on horseback, I would win. Everyone knows that, so it would prove nothing. And I have never intended to insult you. You are a noble and courageous man, and I'd be a fool to try."

Cei blinked as though I had struck him. "You are mad."

I shrugged. "In battle, yes. —No man could think that I want to leave the Family to find a better warband. There are none."

"Then why will you go?" demanded Agravain.

"What else, in honor, can I do?"

"What do you hope to gain?" Arthur asked again. "Or have you gained it already? Will you return to the Orcades now, and tell your mother that the high king of Britain offered you a place, and you turned him down, like a farmer refusing bad eggs?" His voice was level, but edged with cold fury.

I remembered all of his greatness, and his anger hurt. That, coupled with my pain and weariness, made me speak more plainly than I would have. "Lord," I said slowly, "I am not the servant of the queen of Darkness. I will go because I have acted as though I were, because I have divided your Family, on which the fate of Britain rests, even as Morgawse would wish. Lord, I cannot say that I understand these things, but I will not betray them or my lord the Light. It is simpler, Lord, if I go. You have offered now, and I have refused. No one can say that you have wronged me, for it is my own will. The Family will be healed."

"But you are the best horseman in the Family!" said Agravain. "You cannot go."

"I can, and will be the best horseman somewhere else." I swallowed some more mead and rubbed my face with my free hand. "I will go, and that is all. Let us speak of something else."

Everyone sat silently for a long, long minute, staring at me. I began to eat, trying not to look back at them.

Then the sound of a harp broke the silence. I looked up, and Taliesin smiled at me, then bent his head to his work, bringing the same pure, high notes like a silver thread across the air. It was CuChulainn's song, I realized, and it was also the song in Lugh's hall, the strong, clear song of renunciation rising about the strains of battle. The rain fell down out of the night and hissed in the embers of the fire. I listened to the music, and, for the first time, understood it.

The song gave me a strength which sustained me the next day when I saddled Ceincaled to ride on. The Family clustered about me, urging me not to go, wishing me a good journey, and giving me gifts. Arthur watched, his face unreadable. I had a pack horse which I loaded with supplies and the gifts, wrapped in a blanket. It hurt to look at the warriors, and there was a tightness in my throat as I knotted the pack onto the bay pack mare and straightened, holding the lead rope.

At this point, Gruffydd the surgeon came through the crowd, followed, to my surprise, by the woman of the previous night.

"Doctors receive no farewells, is it?" he asked, "or is it that you are afraid I will look at your leg and tell you to stay down for another week?"

I smiled, dropped the lead rein, came over and took his hand. "Even if you told me to stay down, I would go."

"And your leg will give you trouble all the way to the Ynysoedd Erch," he said, nodding. "Well, go berserk and you will not feel it." He paused and added in a low tone, "Why are you going?"

"Because I must."

The woman, who had been staring about her, said, "Great Lord, I did not understand. Had I known who you were, I would not have stopped you."

I looked at her curiously, hoping that she did not have a wounded son.

She drew herself up. "My clan is poor, Chieftain, but we have honor. We do not let those who do us kindnesses leave thankless and without reward." She flushed. "Payment I . . . you would not need. But you have my thanks, Gwalchmai of the Ynysoedd Erch, and the thanks of my clan."

"But I could not help your man," I said, much moved.

She shrugged, pushed the heels of her hands against her eyes a moment before replying. "You came, and you tried. It is much."

Gruffydd looked from her to me. "She came in just now asking for a dark warrior with a limp, who wore a red cloak and had a white stallion. I think I remember her from last night—isn't her husband . . ."

"He is dead now," I said.

"Spear through the lungs, she said. I remember now. And you tried to help? That was foolish. Even I could do no good with such a case as that."

"She didn't tell me that; and there was a chance." I turned to the woman. "You honor me overmuch with your thanks, good woman. I did nothing, and your husband is dead."

She shrugged again, blinking very quickly. "You came," she repeated quietly. "A blessing on your road, Chieftain." she curtseyed awkwardly and turned, still blinking at the tears, and walked through the warriors without looking at them, beginning the long walk home.

"What was all that?" asked Agravain.

"You heard it."

"Just that? A beggarly farmer's woman, and a farmer himself who was surely dead?"

"She is an honorable woman," Arthur said sharply, "to come miles into an armed camp to return thanks for an attempt at healing; a noble and brave woman!"

Agravain stared at him in surprise. "My Lord?" Then he put the woman from his mind altogether. "Gwalchmai, I do not understand it, but . . . by the sun . . ." He looked away. "Take care, my brother. Slán lead."

"God go with you," said Bedwyr softly.

"A blessing on your road," said Gruffydd.

I nodded to all of them, turned to Ceincaled. He bowed his proud head, blew at me softly, nibbled at my hair. It made me smile. I stroked his neck and caught up the reins.

"No," said Arthur suddenly, in a strained voice. "Wait."

I dropped the reins, turned back. The high king stood behind the others, his face pale. "Wait," he repeated. I wondered if he would wish me a good journey as well.

He shook his head violently as if to clear it. "Gwalchmai. I wish to speak to you a moment first. Alone."

I paused, staring at him, then handed Ceincaled's reins to Agravain. Arthur had already set off for his own tent, and I followed, again in complete confusion. I did not see what there could be to talk about. Perhaps he still felt that he was in honor bound to do something for me. Yes, that was likely.

In the tent he caught up a jug of wine, slowly poured two glasses and offered me one. After a moment of hesitation I took it and stood with it in my hand, staring at him.

"Be seated," he said, waving to a chair at one side of

273

the tent. I sat, and he himself sank onto his cot. He took a swallow of his wine, then met my eyes.

"I am sorry." he said, flatly and quietly.

I stared at him in bewilderment. "Lord, there is no need to think that your honor binds you . . ."

"Forget that," he said sharply. "Ach, Yffern . . ." He stood, paced a few steps toward the door, stopped, and turned to me again. "I have misjudged you. Badly. And if it can be that you still desire a place in my Family, it is yours."

I felt as though the sky were caving in. "I do not understand," I said at last.

"On the banks of the Wir, you asked me whether I was altogether in Darkness," he replied quietly, "and I was. An old Darkness and one which I cannot shake off, try as I will." He turned and began to pace the floor of the tent, looking at nothing with a wide gray stare. "From the beginning, I fought with myself about you. I had heard of you, your reputation, and saw no surprising new reason to trust you, but that was not the thing that decided me against you. No: I knew you had been close to my sister, deep in her secret counsels, and, by Heaven, you look like her. That was all that was needed. Everything you did after that I twisted to fit in with my own ideas, twisted to keep you in the Darkness with my sister, and kept myself in the Darkness instead. For which now I say that I am sorry. And yet all of it, the killing, the way you are in battle, the division you caused, the horse which I thought you had captured by spells—all of it was secondary and mattered less to me than the single thought, 'He knows.' It was that that angered me, and filled me with such horror that I could not . . ."

"But know what, Lord?"

"Know about your brother, of course."

"Agravain? I don't see. Why . . ."

"Not Agravain; of course not. The other one. Medraut."

Our eyes met again, his hard and tortured, mine confused, and he stood suddenly still as the hardness ebbed out of his and they widened, a straight, gray stare of realization. Medraut's stare.

Arthur sank down on the cot again and began to laugh,

horrible choking noises almost like sobs, then pressed his head into his hands. "You do not know. You never did. She never told you."

I felt coldness in the pit of my stomach, and a sudden black terror. Morgawse, Arthur's sister, and Medraut who looked like Arthur (why hadn't I seen it before?)—and then, laden with horror, the words of Morgawse's curse returning to me, "May the earth swallow me, may the sky fall on me, may the sea overwhelm me if you do not die by your son's hand!"

"Oh, by the Light . . ." I said.

Arthur straightened and stilled. "And now you do know."

I jumped to my feet. My Lord, how? I thought she must have touched you, somehow, but this . . ."

"I consented to it," he said in a harsh voice. Again we stared at each other for a long moment, and then he said, "I did not know, then, who my father was. I swear it by all that's holy, I did not know she was my sister. She . . . she . . ." he stopped again. "She came to me, outside the feast hall, when first I won fame in the warband of her father Uther. She was staying in Camlann while her husband, Lot, campaigned in the north of Britain. She had singled me out, before then, but then . . . I was drunk, and happy, and she was more beautiful than a goddess; I consented only to adultery, but I consented to it. And later, Uther asked me about my parentage. I had not talked about it; one doesn't. But I told him, and he remembered my mother, and was pleased that I was his son. When he had gone to tell the others, I remembered her, rushed to warn her—and she"—he stood again, not looking at me, looking back in remembered agony and horror on the moment when he discovered that he had been seduced into incest—"she had known, all along she had known, and greeted me as Arthur ab Uther, and called me brother, and laughed, saying that she bore my child. And ever since I have not been able to so much as think of her without remembering that moment; and the thought that another knew, her son, and perhaps had planned with her—I could not endure it, and felt that I must rid myself of you at any cost."

"My Lord," I said, still staring in horror and pity. "My Lord . . ."

"Oh, indeed. Only you were innocent, and did not even know." He took another deep drink of the wine, and set the cup down. The gray eyes focused on me again. "You never knew, until I told you."

I went down on one knee to him. "My Lord, I . . . I could not have guessed such a thing. I do not understand why you did not send me away forcibly; especially after I had divided the Family, and killed, and made your victories bitter for you. Forgive me, I . . ."

"Forgive you? It is I who need forgiveness. Stand up. In God's name, stand. Now."—he too stood again—"I should have seen months ago that you were not what I thought you to be. You endured everything that the war and I together could throw at you and did not complain. And you worked as a surgeon. I knew nothing about that until Gruffydd told me, and shouted at me for being unjust to you. He thinks very highly of you." I stared at the king, startled. Of course. He was always busy the day after a battle, but saw the wounded in the night, when I was sleeping off the madness. "I should have seen enough, over the months you followed me, to make me realize; and I should have trusted Bedwyr's judgment, since I knew myself to be bound by the Darkness. But I persisted in wronging you. And then, last night, you said that you left so as not to divide the Family, and spoke as though you meant it. I told myself you did it only for pride, but I could not convince myself. I knew, definitely knew then, that I was wrong; and yet I could not bring myself to admit it to myself. I could have argued myself out of it, but then, that woman . . ."

"What?"

"The woman with the husband who died. A noble, honorable woman, but low born, not rich or powerful. No one who obeyed the Darkness would have looked at her twice, but you went out of your way on a cold night with a wound which must have been troubling you, to help a man whom you did not know and who could not be helped."

"I did not know he was so badly wounded when I went."

"Yet when you did know, you still tried to help. There would be no advantage from it for you, nothing to gain. It was pointless, but honorable and compassionate. There could be no doubt, after that. You were what you had claimed to be all along, and I had played the part of a fool and a tyrant."

He walked over to me and laid one hand on my shoulder. "I have said that I am sorry for it, and say it now again. Perhaps you no longer desire a place in my service. Yet I think, now that you have offered to go, there would be no further division when I asked you to remain. And you have disarmed Cei very thoroughly." He grinned suddenly, if rather shakily, something of the light coming back into his face. "Insults he can cope with, but not being told that he is noble and courageous. I think he hopes that no one will find that out, if he is quarrelsome enough." He became serious again. "Thus, if you should still desire to stay"—he sought for the word—"there is work enough and more than enough, and I would be very glad of you."

I was silent a moment, and Arthur watched me steadily, half-challenging, half-hoping, his hand still on my shoulder, almost testing.

"My Lord," I said at last, "if someone should offer you Britain, with the empire restored, and all Erin and Caledon and Less Britain besides, and the roads open to Rome—would you accept it?"

He grinned slowly, then embraced me, clumsily, still almost testing, but I realized that it was not me he was testing now but himself. I returned the embrace, then knelt and kissed his hand, the signet ring he wore on his finger.

"My Lord," I said, "I have desired to fight for you, for long and long, since I knew that you fight for the Light, and it would be better to die fighting against the Darkness than to live long winning victories to no purpose. How could I wish for more than this? From now on it will be victories only."

"God willing, even so, though I think we have had victories of a sort already. Come." He helped me to my feet, embraced me again, then walked rapidly from the tent.

The others were still waiting by Ceincaled and the laden pack mare, discussing something which they re-

frained from abruptly when they saw Arthur and me
coming. Arthur stopped, surveyed the horses, then announced calmly, "You can see that they are unloaded
again. Gwalchmai ap Lot has agreed to stay, and to swear
the oath to me, at my urging."

Agravain looked at Cei, then at Bedwyr, then at me. I
nodded. He gave a whoop of delight. *"Laus Deo,* by the
sun!" He embraced me, pounding me on the back. "I understand nothing of all this—you change your mind, Arthur changes his, you change yours—but I like it this way,
so long as you do not begin it again," he said, in Irish.
"And now, indeed, we have won," he added, in British,
letting me go and glaring at Cei.

Cei shrugged, eyeing me; then, suddenly he smiled. "It
is good news. You are a very devil of a fighter, cousin."

Bedwyr looked from me to Arthur, then, when Arthur
also nodded, he smiled slowly. "I am glad."

"Very good," said Arthur dryly. "I am glad my decision meets with your approval. You three can be
witnesses. Call the rest, and we will swear the oaths now."

It was still cold, and the wind sent the clouds scudding
across the dark sky, and whispered in the bare branches
of the trees. The Family was a splash of color and light
on the barren landscape, gathered about in a circle to
watch and bear witness. Arthur stood before his tent, tall
and straight, the wind tugging at his purple cloak.
Bedwyr stood on his right, Cei on his left with Agravain
beside him. I stared at the picture, wishing to hold it forever, then dropped to one knee, drawing Caledvwlch.

"I, Gwalchmai, son of Lot of Orcade, do now swear to
follow the lord Arthur, emperor of the Britains, dragon
of the island; to fight at his will against all his enemies, to
hold with him and obey him at all times and places. My
sword is his sword until death. This I swear in the name
of Father, Son, and Spirit, and if I fail of my oath may
the earth open and swallow me, the sky break and fall on
me, the sea rise and drown me. So be it."

Arthur reached out his hand for the sword, and I suddenly remembered.

"My Lord," I began, "the sword cannot . . ."

He ignored me and caught the hilt from my hand, lifting the weapon. The lightning did not spring from it

278

against him as it had against Cei. Instead the radiance lit it, growing greater and whiter until it seemed that Arthur held a star. And he said, "And I, Arthur, emperor of the Britains, do now swear to support Gwalchmai son of Lot, in arms and in goods, faithfully in honor, in all times and places until death. This I swear in the name of Father, Son, and Spirit, and if I fail of my oath, may the earth open and swallow me, the sky break and fall on me, the sea rise and drown me. And I swear to use this sword, of Light, in Light, to work Light upon this realm, so help me God."

The radiance faded from the sword as he returned it to me. I stood, sheathing it.

"Witnessed?" asked my lord Arthur.

"Witnessed," said Cei, Bedwyr, and Agravain. And then Agravain stepped forward with a wide grin, shouting in Irish, "And now it is truly done, and you have won! Och, my brother, I swear the oath of my people I am glad!"

The rest of the Family was not far behind.

ABOUT THE AUTHOR

GILLIAN BRADSHAW was born in Falls Church, Virginia, and graduated in 1977 from the University of Michigan, where she won the Hopwood Award for *Hawk of May*. She is now studying classics at Cambridge University, England; Ms. Bradshaw has recently completed her second novel, *The Kingdom of Summer*, and is at work on the third of this series of Arthurian fantasies.